A Long Way to Go

A Long Way to Go

BOOK THREE

Nancy Dane

Tate Publishing & *Enterprises*

Published by Tate Publishing & Enterprises, LLC
127 E. Trade Center Terrace | Mustang, Oklahoma 73064 USA
1.888.361.9473 | www.tatepublishing.com

Tate Publishing is committed to excellence in the publishing industry. The company reflects the philosophy established by the founders, based on Psalm 68:11,
"The Lord gave the word and great was the company of those who published it."

Cover design by Kristen Verser
Interior design by Kristen Verser

Published in the United States of America

ISBN: 978-1-61663-545-9
1. Fiction, Historical
2. Fiction, Romance, Historical
10.05.13

Books by Nancy Dane

Tattered Glory
Where the Road Begins
A Difference of Opinion
A Long Way to Go

Dedication

To my delightful dozen
You light up my life!

Acknowledgments

With deep gratitude, thank you to all who read, edited, and made insightful suggestions. I greatly appreciate the endorsements of Mark Christ, Andrea Romo, and James Durney. Once again, thank you Chris Kennedy of Russellville for the great cover shot.

To Les Howard, Sheree Niece, and Nancy Cook for all the hard work of editing, a great big thank you! To Jackie Guccione heartfelt thanks for all you did.

And to my family for their love, support, critique, and for cheering me on every step of the way, all my love and appreciation. To my wonderful husband—my chief editor—you make me a better writer.

LITTLE ROCK, ARK., April 16, 1864.
Colonel WAUGH,
Clarksville, Ark.:

COLONEL: I telegraphed you this morning. I want those guerrillas captured, killed, or dispersed, and the telegraph line kept in order. Where do 300 or 400 guerrillas come from? If they are indifferently armed, take them. You have done well in capturing 24. You will do better by killing or capturing the rest. I have ordered Colonel Fuller to send you some force from Dardanelle; 100 resolute, energetic officers and men on the side of right ought to kill and capture all the scoundrels around you. I hope you will do it. I have no force here to re-enforce you. Seize and impress horses belonging to rebels and their sympathizers, and drive every disloyal man out of the country. Hang or shoot every devil who robs and murders citizens or destroys the telegraph. Take good care of the loyal and the women and children. Don't burn any houses nor destroy other property. Destroy the scoundrels, and the property will hurt no one.

NATHAN KIMBALL,
Brigadier-General, Commanding.

Official Records of the War of the Rebellion SERIES I VOL 34 PART 3 PG 180

Chapter 1

October 1863

Elijah's eyes traced the rugged autumn-cloaked ridges and then dropped to see white caps on Little Piney Creek where it surged over gray boulders lining the bank. A smile softened his mouth. He figured he was the luckiest man on earth. He had come through two years of war, pretty much still in one piece. He rubbed his freshly shaved chin. There had been the scourging when he ran off after getting conscripted. He would carry those marks to the grave—as well as the scars from being stabbed once and, not too long ago, getting shot in the leg. But that had almost healed.

Those were minor happenings now. Cindy was all that really mattered. His heart beat fast just thinking about tomorrow.

Then he puckered to whistle "The Homespun Dress." He had first heard the song played by General Hindman's military band. That seemed an age ago! Now he moved his rifle to the other shoulder and wondered about his old comrades. He wished Levi could attend the wedding. The old warrior almost seemed like kin. Elijah owed him. On more than one occasion, Levi's sound advice had saved his life.

The smile faded. Most of all, he wished Pa were here. Pa would have loved having Cindy for a daughter-in-law. And what a grandpa he would have made! Elijah shook his head. He sorely missed Pa.

As quickly as a swinging pendulum, he smiled again. His wedding day was too near to stay glum. He breathed deeply of air fresh with the pleasant scent of fall as he began walking again with long-limbed, easy strides. Most favored a June wedding; but, to his mind, nothing could outdo fall in the mountains. The heavy rains of the night before had passed on, leaving the sky clear and vibrant blue. The woods were a bright bouquet, the hickory trees as shiny as a new gold wedding band and the sugar maples blazing coral. The sassafras, sumacs, and dogwoods were just about every shade of red and pink imaginable. Yes, an outdoor wedding suited him fine—better than the fanciest church he'd seen in Little Rock.

A squirrel in the oak ahead made noises that Pa had always called squawking. Elijah looked at the dozen already threaded on a dogwood stick and left the rifle resting on his shoulder. Since Cindy's ma was feeling poorly, he doubted she would do much cooking for the wedding dinner. But with Ma's squirrel and cornmeal dumplings and Granny's fried fish and cornpone, he thought there would be enough. Ma bemoaned the lack of chicken and dumplings, but there was no flour to be had at any price. And between the bushwhackers and the foraging army patrols, all the chickens had disappeared long ago. Elijah was thankful to have anything to serve the guests. There had been too many times in the last two years when his belly had been completely empty.

He stopped for a moment on the hill overlooking the Matthers' place. Nearby came the buzzing of a late wild bee, and then Elijah smelled the wonderful perfume of muscadines and looked up into the trees. A leafy vine dangling from a nearby branch hid a few small purple grapes dotted with rust colored splotches.

He picked one and dropped it into his mouth. Although the hull was tough and the pulp scant, the flavor was still delicious. In good years he had seen the wild grapes grow almost as large as a pullet egg, but this summer's drought had shriveled every living thing. For a moment his mind went to his own failed crops, the yellowed spindly corn stalks yet standing in the parched fields. He spit out the hulls and seeds and looked at the farm below.

Funny, he still expected to see dinner smoke penciling from the chimney and the gang of red-haired boys lolling about. Instead the rambling cabin had a vacant, deserted look. Like so many farms these days, sassafras and persimmon sprouts choked the wide flat fields that bordered the creek. Almost every able-bodied male between sixteen and sixty was away in the army—or hiding to keep out of it. Although the Matthers brothers had fled conscription, Elijah was mighty thankful that Dillon and Shawn had stuck around long enough to save his bacon. If they hadn't intervened a short while back, his neck would have been stretched by a Yankee noose, and he'd be buried in a shallow grave alongside his baby twin brothers on the hill behind Ma's cabin. He could still feel the rope tightening. Just thinking about it set his flesh quivering like a horse fighting flies.

He started on again, but when crows cawed and rose from the far side of the Matthers' weedy cornfield, he stopped abruptly and hurried for cover as horses approached. There were several. These days that usually signified trouble.

His mouth thinned as he hunkered on the hillside and watched them pass, streaks of tattered gray riding through trees, sun, and shadow. They rode on unaware that a pair of hard brown eyes watched. Regardless of uniform, Elijah considered every soldier the enemy now. He had no intention of giving in gracefully if they had come foraging or conscripting again.

These were regular Confederate—even if the uniforms were irregular. No one had a decent uniform anymore, at least no one in these parts. These were Brooks' cavalry; he recognized some of them. Ordinarily they guarded the Arkansas River. He wondered what they were doing in the mountains.

They rode on down the creek without stopping.

Deep in thought he chewed his jaw. Even though Michael Lane had come home to recover from a leg wound, he kept abreast of military news. The week before he had related to Elijah that General John McNeil and almost a thousand Yankee troops had just left Clarksville. They had chased Joe Shelby out of Missouri. When Shelby had given them the slip by crossing the river, McNeil's troops had all gone to Fort Smith—or so Michael thought. Elijah wondered if some had stayed behind and driven Brooks from the river. He decided to make a quick trip to Michael's to glean any news. But first he would dress the squirrels and give them to Ma.

His lips quirked into a grin. If he didn't think Cindy's ma would run him off, he would stop by for a visit and maybe steal a kiss. But he had been given strict orders not to show up at the Mason's cabin until tomorrow at eleven o'clock. Today Cindy and her ma were fixing the wedding dress. He had no idea how Cindy could wear a dress that had once fit Polly. Polly was short and small-boned. Cindy was tall, long-legged, and curvy. No matter what she wore, she'd be beautiful.

His own clothes wouldn't be fancy. About the only thing he had that wasn't threadbare was the shiny pair of boots he pulled off Bo Morrison's dead body. Elijah's eyes suddenly narrowed. That sonofabitch wouldn't need them anymore. Bo had taken his last evil step. Poor Granny would always hobble on crippled feet from his torture. Elijah wondered if folks in hell felt the least bit sorry for the wrongs they'd done. He'd ask Simon about that sometime. In spite of being a Union sympathizer, Cindy's pa was a fine man and a good preacher. He knew more Bible than anyone in the hills…except for maybe Granny. But sometimes Granny interpreted scripture with more than a hint of prejudice. In the gospel according to Granny some things got a mite skewed.

He started forward, keeping a sharp eye out for any of Brooks' men who might be lagging behind. It would be impossible to hear them over the rushing tumble of the overflowing creek. As he drew near the stream, he breathed in the clean smell of damp earth. The only thing stirring was a yearling fawn that flashed its white tail and bounded away.

Elijah stopped on the bank to skin the squirrels. He lifted one from the stick and cut off its tail. Then he split the hide across the back and pulled the skin both ways until the hide was stripped down to the feet. As he worked, his eyes constantly roamed. Everything appeared peaceful and still, but army life had made him vigilant.

He found a sapling with a fork just the right height and wedged the squirrel's head into it. Before cutting off the feet, he broke the bones just above the ankles and then turned the squirrel over, split it open, and removed the entrails. Although some folks considered the head and brains a delicacy, Elijah never used to save them. Now after cutting off the head, he threaded it along with the dressed meat onto another stick. But he threw the brains away. Food was scarce but he wasn't that desperate yet. When all the squirrels were dressed, he rinsed the meat free of blood and hair. Then he washed his knife and hands and dried them on a ragged handkerchief.

He crossed the bare pasture and the cornfield where a few shriveled stalks remained of the crop blighted by drought. His jaw tensed as he wondered for the thousandth time how they would manage through the winter without corn. There was barely enough in the crib to last until Christmas.

Just beyond stood the cabin bathed in warm morning sun. The logs had weathered to a soft, homey gray; but Elijah kept them well chinked and he kept the tall chimney, porch, and rock foundation in good repair.

Deborah sat on the front porch braiding thick, honey-blonde hair. She jumped up when he motioned and came running.

"Take these to Ma. I'm going over to Michael's for a bit, but I'll be right back."

"Oh, Elijah, may I go, too?" Her brown eyes brightened.

He hesitated. He hated to disappoint her. The child had so little pleasure in her life. But Michael might be hesitant to share information if she were listening.

"Honey, I think you better stay here and help Ma. She has a lot to do before tomorrow."

Her shoulders drooped and her eyes dimmed but she took the disappointment gracefully. "Tell Michael I said hello."

"I will," he said and handed over the naked squirrels.

"You won't forget?" she added.

Surprised, he stared. "I won't."

She smiled and turned away.

He watched her for a moment. Deborah was growing up. She was still twiggy thin, and like the fawn at the creek, mostly legs and huge eyes. But there was the hint of real beauty under the awkwardness. He suspected she was sweet on Michael. Most nine-year-old boys considered girls a nuisance, but he reckoned girls were different. He was glad she was still too young for such a thing to be serious. He liked Michael fine—almost considered him a brother—but he would be poor husband material. Michael was the footloose, rambling sort. Thankfully, by the time Deborah grew up he would more than likely be long-gone. He was here now only because of the leg wound, and Michael had barely limped the last time he saw him.

Elijah rubbed the side of his own leg. It was no longer very sore. He was fortunate the shot had only been a flesh wound.

Elijah stopped for a moment before crossing the clearing. The Lane farm had hardly changed since Michael's pa and ma died. The log smokehouse, barn, and one-roomed cabin with a lean-to tacked onto the back looked as worn and rundown as old boots. Yellowed grass and tall hogweed filled the dooryard, and sassafras and locust had encroached onto pastures and fields. Of course Michael had not been home much lately. He preferred army life. Not that Elijah blamed him…the hardscrabble farm held lots of bad memories.

"Hey, Mike," he hailed from the yard.

"Come on in," Michael's deep voice greeted.

After stepping inside, Elijah blinked, adjusting to the dimness. The tiny window holes kept the room dark no matter how bright the sun. The smoke covered walls were as bare as the scarred floors. The only furniture was a sagging bed, a rickety chair, and the pine table and benches. As his glance traced the room, he felt pity for his friend. Michael's childhood had been cheerless.

Michael glanced up with a wide smile. "Lige, I figured you'd be over at Cindy's. Glad you stopped by. I was heading over to yer place later to say goodbye." While he talked he stuffed odds and ends into a pack lying on the rough pine table.

"You leaving before the wedding?"

Michael looked sheepish. "Aw, Lige, you and Cindy will have so many stars in yer eyes tomorrow; you won't know who's there and who ain't. I was planning to come, but Hal Taylor just stopped by with news. Marmaduke is on the move again, and if I don't ride now, I'll miss out."

"Yeah, I just saw a bunch of Brooks' men heading down the creek. That's what I came over to ask you about. They didn't appear to be foraging."

Michael shook his head. "Naw. But they are conscripting, so keep yer head down. I aim to join up with Brooks, myself. They're heading out. Union patrols too thick around here just now." He stopped for a wistful look. "I wish you was coming with me."

Elijah snorted. "I never did take to the army. I can't for the life of me see why you're raring to go get shot again."

Michael gave a jaunty grin. "I plan on dodging this time."

Elijah's brows rose. "I figure you planned that last time. Trouble with war is a man's plans don't count for much."

Michael laughed. "Too true, too true. But there's a thrill to it—sort of gets in a feller's blood and makes him feel alive." Then his face sobered as he glanced through the miniscule window hole toward the rocky fields beyond. "I didn't in no wise respect Pa—but I reckon I'm more like him than I care to admit. A farm don't hold no pleasure for me." He closed the pack and faced Elijah. "And you're like yer pa. You'll make his place bigger and better than ever." He grinned. "Likely you and Cindy will have a dozen younguns who'll one day own all the land on Little Piney."

"Sounds like a good plan to me." Elijah quirked a brow. "Reckon tomorrow night I'll get right to work on it."

Michael threw back his head and laughed. He slapped Elijah's back. "You always was a lucky cuss. That cousin of mine is the prettiest gal around. Be good to her, Lige. Aw, hell, I know you will. Like I said you're like yer pa. No man was ever better to his wife and younguns than yer pa." The shine in his eyes momentarily dimmed. "I always envied you." Then he shouldered the pack. "I reckon I better go tell Uncle Simon and Aunt Polly I'm leaving. Cindy's bound to give me a tongue lashing, but I want to see little Johnny and Mattie." He shook his head. "I'll swear have you seen how that brother and sister of mine have shot up…I'll have to stop calling him *little* Johnny. Pretty soon I'll be looking up at him. Amazing how fast younguns grow up."

Elijah nodded. "By the way, Deborah said to say hello. I think she's kind of sweet on you. She'll hate that you're leaving."

"She's a sweet kid. Tell her I said goodbye." He winked at Elijah. "In about ten years, I might come courting. She's going to be a beauty like yer ma."

"In about ten years, I'll have my shotgun loaded."

Michael laughed and shouldered the pack. He stuck out his hand, and Elijah gripped it. "Take care of yourself, Michael."

"You, too." He started for the door and then stopped and turned back. "Lige, I reckon you and Cindy will be living with yer ma?"

Elijah chewed his jaw and nodded. He hated them not having a place of their own—especially right at first.

Michael looked around. "Well, this ain't exactly a palace, but it's yores if you want it—and for as long as you want. The land is poor. But you two can live here and you'd still be close enough to work yer pa's farm."

Elijah looked around with a frown. The cabin was a dark, dingy mess…but it could be fixed up. And they would be alone. Cindy had already expressed a dread of having to live with Ma. A slow smile began.

"You mean it, Michael?"

"Of course I do. Cindy might clot us both for even suggesting it."

"I don't intend telling her. I'll just tell her I've got a surprise."

"Fine, but if I was you I'd sweep up a bit first." Michael reached into his pocket and drew out a wad of money. He grinned upon seeing

Elijah's eyebrows rise. "Won it at poker. Like I said, I'm a lot like Pa. Except I win, and he most usually didn't." He thrust out several dollars. "Here—no take it. It's a wedding present. Buy Cindy something nice."

Elijah reluctantly accepted the gift. "I'll do that. Thanks." He followed Michael outside and waited as he climbed into the saddle of a tall buckskin mare. "Come back safe and sound," he urged.

"I'll sure try. I might just make it if yer Granny and Cindy keep on praying for me." Michael held the reins loosely and leaned forward in the saddle. He tried looking serious, but his eyes twinkled. "Lige, I better warn ya—that bed ain't none too sturdy."

Elijah cocked an eyebrow. "You let me worry about that bed."

As Michael laughed and pulled rein, Elijah called and waved a hand. "Take care now."

Michael's dust had not settled before he was hunting a broom. For the next three hours, he swept and dusted and then hauled water from the well and scrubbed the table and benches and finally the floor.

While he worked he planned improvements. Maybe there was window glass in Clarksville. Anyway, he could make the window holes bigger and cover them with thin cheesecloth to let in light and still keep out bugs. Cindy would want curtains. She still grieved over the hope chest that marauders had stolen, but Elijah figured Ma and Granny would have some doodads to brighten things up.

He found the rope adjuster under the bed, attached it to the sagging ropes that held the corn shuck mattress, and pulled them as tight as possible. The chore made him smile. He tested the results by pushing on the mattress. It was much firmer, he noted with satisfaction.

It was too dark to see inside the dim room. It would do—at least until they could do better. They'd make out fine. Then he looked back in the fading light and felt a twinge of doubt. The decrepit cabin looked mighty sorry.

The bouquet in Cindy's hands shook. She pressed her lips together and tried to stop trembling. She was not afraid, not really. The call of a cardinal drifted from the woods to where she stood in the front yard under the giant pecan tree. A soft breeze lifted golden-brown curls on her forehead made so carefully that morning with Ma's curling iron heated in the lamp.

Her glance stole to Elijah. His brown hair also stirred in the breeze. He stood straight and proud beside her, the firm chin and jaw clean-shaven and in perfect proportion with full lips and rounded nose and brow. He was not trembling. He felt her glance and turned to smile. His warm brown eyes caressed her. Yes, she was a blessed woman.

"Cindy, will you take this man fer your lawful wedded husband, to love and honor and obey, till death parts ya?"

She nodded at her tall, rail-thin father with his weather-beaten face and added a soft, "I do."

Poor Pa looks like he's about to bust out crying, she thought, and tender love for him filled her breast. He probably thought he was losing her. He had lost so much that was precious to him—first little Sally Ann, the sister she had never known, and then Pete. She could hardly think of Pete yet without crying. Every bushwhacker on earth should burn in hell!

What thoughts to be having on yer wedding day! She scolded herself silently and drew her mind back to the ceremony.

Simon stopped to clear his throat. His black frock coat was shiny with age but neatly pressed, as were his frayed pants and white shirt. The Bible in his long, tapering hands shook just a bit. For a second, he looked at his wife and she nodded encouragement, but her own eyes were red-rimmed.

Cindy could see no one else, but she knew they were there, standing in the yard behind her—friends; neighbors; and her kin along with Elijah's folks; his pretty, blue-eyed, fair-haired ma; his young sister, Deborah; and nearby was his tiny granny with her gray bun neatly pulled tight and her burned, tortured feet yet swathed in rags.

Alongside her would be her son, Caleb Tanner—short, stocky, bow-legged, and as bald as an egg on top. Elijah's soft-spoken cousin Jenny, with her mannish shoulders and gentle face, stood near Mattie and little Johnny. Big-boned, silent, and dark-skinned from half-Indian blood, Jenny drew children the way flowers drew hummingbirds. It was a crying shame that she had never married and raised some of her own.

Oh, well—Cindy smiled to herself—*I figure on having enough babies to make Jenny happy.*

"Elijah Loring." Simon stopped, and for a long moment, pinned him with solemn eyes. "Do you promise to love and care fer Cindy, and forsake all others—cleave only to her?" Just as Elijah started to answer, Simon added more. "And do ya promise to love her as Christ loves the church—to care fer her as much as you care fer yer own flesh?"

Elijah waited a bit to make certain Simon was finished. Then he spoke up loud and bold.

"I do."

Simon swallowed. "Then I pronounce ya man and wife." Before he had finished speaking, Elijah had kissed her soundly amid laughter and clapping that suddenly filled the balmy air.

As well wishers gathered round to slap Elijah's back and to kiss Cindy, her cheeks grew rosy. Already today she had endured countless crude remarks. Now that they were wed, the teasing worsened. It was all in good fun. But she was modest to the extreme. Even without the coarse jests, the thought of what lay ahead made her palms sweaty. If not for her deep love for Elijah, she would run off right this minute.

She looked at him. *How strong and handsome he was!* And he had never looked happier. The dark shadows were finally gone from his eyes. She prayed they were gone forever. When he had first come home from the army, wrapped in the cloak of gloom, he was a stranger. How she had misjudged him then. She quelled to think how close she had come to losing him. Thankfully, a long talk with Michael had set her straight. She wished Michael were here. He was the closest thing she had to a brother now that Pete was dead.

She dodged away from fat Tom Sorrells. He had already kissed her soundly, and judging by his foul breath, he had indulged in a jug hidden in someone's wagon. Most of the men Cindy knew took an occasional nip without getting out of line, but Tom had never been overly sensible and drink made him worse. She noticed May heading for him with a sharp look in her eyes.

It must be a trial being married to a silly man, thought Cindy as she hurried to join Ma at the tables under the spreading oak trees in the side yard. She was glad Elijah, as a rule, was not a drinking man.

She frowned and took a large kettle from Polly's small, work-worn hands and began forking sweet potatoes onto a platter. "Here, Ma, let me do that. You look tired."

Polly sighed. "I am plum tuckered out. Seems as if I won't never feel like my old self ..." Her words trailed away, and she bit her lip as tears sprang into her sad eyes. She swiped at them with the back of her hand. "I'm sorry. I want this to be a happy day fer you, and here I am digging up bad memories."

Cindy gave a trembling smile. "Don't fret, Ma. It is a happy day. But I can't help but think of Pete, either. He'd be so proud to have Elijah for a brother."

Just then someone caught her around the waist and placed a kiss on the back of her neck. She tried stepping away while murmuring, "Law, Elijah, stop that." When he nuzzled her neck she caught a faint whiff of whiskey. Someone, she thought, was passing around a jug mighty early today. It was not yet noon.

He hugged tighter. "Don't you like hugging and kissing me?"

As Cindy's cheeks grew fiery, Polly snickered and walked away.

Cindy gave him a playful shove. "'Course I do, but yo're embarrassing me."

He chuckled. "All right. I'll let you alone—for now," he said with an impish grin. "No need to turn so red. No one's paying any mind to us just now."

He was right, she noticed with relief. Everyone was looking at Pa.

As Simon took off a black slouch hat and bowed his head, everyone stilled for saying grace. In the lull, a saddle horse tied to the fence nearby snorted and stamped its feet to discourage a pestering fly. Before bowing her head Cindy looked around. There were less than a dozen families here today. She was not surprised. Folks were afraid to stray far from home these days because of bushwhackers and roving army patrols. A body never knew what might happen along the way…or what might be waiting at home.

When the blessing was over—as Simon cordially bid—everyone began loading plates. Cindy ran a critical eye over the table. The fare was certainly skimpy compared to former weddings in the hills. Before war and drought, the tables would have held mountains of food: tall fluffy biscuits; hot, yellow cornbread; loaves of yeast bread; and every variety of vegetable imaginable; crispy fried chicken from pullets still young and tender; juicy ham fried until the edges of fat had crisped to golden brown; and there would have been baked ham surrounded by mounds of golden sweet potatoes with tender flesh oozing melted butter.

Now the few bowls held field peas, mashed turnips, and cooked cabbage. Stewed squirrel swam in dark gravy alongside cornmeal dumpling that had almost melted away. It was not her mother-in-law's fault that cornmeal dumplings would not stick together as good as flour dumplings did. However, since Becky was a good cook, Cindy knew they would taste good. And so would the platters of fried fish with tails crispy brown and curling.

The biggest lack was dessert. Cornmeal pudding thick with wild plums was a poor substitute for rows of pies, cakes, cookies, and custards.

But Pa was right. They should count their blessings. Their stomachs were not empty as many in the South were. And it was mighty nice, she thought, of Elijah's ma to do most of the cooking. Ma had been poorly ever since the bushwhacker's attack and little Pete's murder.

Cindy caught her lip in her teeth. Elijah's ma was nice…and yet Cindy suspected she was secretly displeased with the match. Although

Becky had always been polite, Cindy felt countrified and awkward in her presence. Whenever they talked, she could sense Becky's inward cringe. Cindy had made herself a promise to learn to speak with better grammar, the way Becky did. Maybe then Becky would like her better. Now, while watching her ladle squirrel gravy onto plates, Cindy placed a hand on her stomach and tried to still the butterflies swirling at the thought of living with her. She had tried explaining her fear to Elijah. He dismissed it with a wave of the hand and the assurance that they would soon be good friends. Cindy was not so sure. She would much prefer living with Pa and Ma. But that was out of the question. She and Elijah could not share the loft bedroom with little Johnny and Mattie as she and Pete had done. At the Loring cabin they would at least have the loft to themselves, for Deborah would now share her ma's room.

Elijah's granny interrupted her musing. "Cindy, yo're as pretty a bride as I ever seed. And I've seed a heap of brides in my day." The tiny old woman leaned on a cane to favor feet swathed in bandages. "Them gores you and Polly put in her dress look right stylish—like they was there a' purpose."

"If you hadn't give us this lace, it never would've worked. That scrap of old satin ma had was too yellowed to match the rest until we added the lace over the top."

The long-sleeved, high-neck tailored gown of white satin, mellowed by age to a soft cream, had served four generations of Murray ancestors, but Cindy was more full-busted and taller. To accommodate her figure, the gown had required a wide insert in front and a six-inch flounce of satin and lace to cover her ankles.

"Pleasured to he'p," avowed Granny. "Good thing them bushwhacking varmints never found the trunk in the attic, or no doubt, they'd have rid off with that lace draped across the saddle." Granny grimaced, and then she smiled. "I never figured any girl to be good enough fer Elijah"—her black eyes sought and found him and softened with a tender light—"but I'm bound to admit I reckon he did hisself proud today."

"Thank you, Granny." Cindy's eyes strayed to her mother-in-law. "That makes me feel better."

Granny's bright eyes sharpened. "Becky ain't said something hurtful, has she?"

Cindy quickly shook her head. "Oh, no. She's been extra nice. It's just … well, I sort of get the feeling she's sad or disappointed …"

"'Course she's sad today. A wedding is bound to make her miss Ned. They loved each other something fierce." Her own eyes began to tear. "Can't wrap my mind around the fact that he's gone." She sniffed. "A wedding makes a body want kin around to be in on the celebrating. And Becky took hit real hard when she found out that sister of hers and her man was both took last winter. And now she don't even know where her niece went off to. Becky ain't got much other kin left."

"Maybe that's it." Cindy hunted for words before finally saying, "Or maybe she's disappointed in me …" Her voice trailed away.

Granny snorted. Then she conceded, "Oh, she might a' wanted a educated city gal fer Elijah. Becky can put on airs, all right. But she don't mean to. Look how she and Jenny hit it off. There ain't no one more down-to-earth than Jenny. And remember Becky married Ned instead of any of them city men buzzing around her."

Cindy nodded but she was not mollified. "I'll keep that in mind. Let me get you a plate. The squirrel dumplings smell good."

"Thank you, child. I think I will get off my poor ol' feet. They're still mighty tender." She pointed the cane toward a chair. "I'll sit up yonder with Polly on the front porch."

Granny had barely hobbled away when a group of horsemen galloped up, scattering dust over the crowd. Cindy shot an anxious look toward her pa. *Of all days, why had Pa's men chosen today to come by?*

"Howdy, Simon." Jared Rawlings took off a forage cap and held it in wide-palmed hands. He was a big man with thick, wavy hair and eyes as gray as a cloudy sky and just as brooding. He rode at the head of a group of local men with Union sympathies. He spoke to Simon, but his eyes never left Cindy.

"Appears we're interrupting your party."

"Cindy's wedding," explained Simon, and then he hesitated.

It was a dilemma. Good hospitality demanded an invitation; however, angry mutterings already swept the crowd. Some had come today, overlooking Simon's Union leanings because he was a good neighbor.

Jared gave Elijah a snide look. "I see she married a Reb."

From his seat on the porch, Tom Sorrells, an avid Confederate, wrinkled his big nose. "Smells mighty bad around here, Simon. You got polecats roaming around? Somebody ought to shoot 'em and clear the air."

Jared stiffened and laid a hand on the pistol butt protruding from his holster. The dozen men with him followed suit as they raked the crowd with suspicious eyes.

Simon raised a hand. "Now there's no cause for trouble. Jared, you and the men just ride on. We'll talk later."

Jared's cold eyes pierced Elijah once more before he pulled rein and turned his large roan around.

Cindy expelled a relieved breath as he rode away with his men following. Until they were out of sight, Elijah remained taut, his jaws hard and his eyes narrow. She quelled at the look on his face. She laid a hand on his arm and was taken aback to see, inside his coat, his hand rested on a pistol tucked into his waistband.

"No harm done," she ventured softly.

He ignored her. She shivered and drew away. He had worn a gun, even to their wedding. A few months ago she would have been angry. Her perspective had changed. These days violence was the rule and not the exception. She supposed Elijah was wise to be prepared, but when he went peculiar and cold like this, he was a stranger.

She turned worried eyes down the trail and prayed there would be no more trouble. There was a sinking in her stomach. Although Jared was almost as old as her father, he had tried to court her. He had not taken her rebuff kindly.

Simon stepped near. "I'm sorry about that, Elijah. I'll have a talk with 'em—tell 'em to leave you alone."

Elijah removed his hand from the gun. "I appreciate that, Simon. Even though we're kin now, your men don't feel kindly toward me." His eyes suddenly glinted. "If I'm threatened, I'll have to do something." He faced Cindy. "I'll be back in just a bit."

Cindy watched with distressed eyes as he turned and walked away. As he disappeared among the trees along the creek bank, she started to follow. Simon stopped her with a hand on her arm.

"No, daughter, stay here."

"But, Pa—"

He shook his head. "He ain't wanting you to follow."

She wanted to run into the house, hide in the loft, and have a good cry. Instead, ignoring whispers and sideways glances, she looked at the plate in her hand. Granny was waiting for her meal. She pressed her lips together and, looking through tears, dipped the food and took it to the old woman. Then she filled another plate and sat down alone to stare at the untouched food. It was not how she had imagined her wedding day.

Elijah hurried through the trees and then doubled back to the barn lot. He untied his mule from the fence and rode away without being seen. He doubted Cindy would understand. No woman wanted to be left alone on her wedding day. But he had to trail the men—to make sure they had not planned an ambush. Army life had taught him the rules of guerilla warfare: strike fast and when least expected. Jared Rawlings would not blink an eye at shooting the groom in the back on his wedding day, especially since he coveted the bride.

He rode fast but carefully watched the trail. In less than a mile, through the trees, he saw them ahead, stopped to parley. He left the road and headed through the woods. Quickly dismounting, he tied the mule and ran softly through deep leaves and decaying loam. He managed to slip near and crouch down behind a high bank.

Jared talked louder than the rest. "I aim to kill that Reb bastard. Can't you get it through your thick skulls? He's the enemy!"

"Lige ain't a soldier no more, Jared," argued one. "Besides, he got conscripted."

Elijah recognized the voice. It was Matt Carol, a coon-hunting friend of Pa's.

Matt went on, "And Simon won't like it."

Several voiced agreement before Jared snarled, "Simon be damned! Loring's a rebel. And so was his pa. And don't forget, as soon as we sign on at Fort Smith, we'll be a regular Union company, bound by oath to put down this rebellion."

"And don't you forget, Jared," came Matt's terse reply, "we aim to be army and not some lousy gang of bushwhackers who'll help you settle a grudge."

Elijah's eyes were flint. The rest would leave him alone. But not Jared. Sooner or later, he'd have to kill him. But now was not the time. He was too outnumbered. If he shot Jared, they would feel duty bound to shoot back. With that in mind he quietly slipped away and headed back for Simon's.

He kept a close watch on Simon's cabin, circling through the woods often to check the perimeter and waiting purposefully until late in the day to step into the yard. The sun sank low in the clear October sky as the last guests drove away. Cindy was not in sight. He waited in the yard.

"Johnny, run inside and ask Cindy to come out."

"All right. But I reckon she's mad at you. She might not come." Johnny scurried away.

Elijah sat on the steps and dropped his head into his hands. He hated spoiling her day. Then, with a bitter taste in his mouth, he thought how Jared had spoiled the day for both of them. He raised his head when she stepped onto the porch. Her head was high and her back stiff. She had changed into a pretty blue calico that fit her top snuggly and flared into a full skirt that hid her shoes.

"Did you have a nice walk?" She avoided looking at him and, instead, gazed across the pasture with her arms crossed tightly over her chest. When he remained silent, she finally spoke. "I don't reckon you thought how embarrassing it was to have you just walk off like that." Her eyes snapped.

He stood. "I didn't relish leaving."

"Then why did you?"

His voice grew testy. "I did what needed doing. And I don't have to ask your permission."

"*Permission!*" Her eyes blazed. "I don't expect you to ask permission, Elijah Loring." Then she drew a quick breath. "You followed them, didn't you?"

"I'd rather not talk about this. You'll just have to trust me."

She drew back. "Don't you reckon a man ought to trust his wife too? I ain't a baby to keep things from. If you keep on shutting me out, we ain't truly married."

He relented. "I followed them, but I didn't harm them." He started to say more but changed his mind. She deserved some joy today. There would be time enough for dire warnings later.

Her spine remained stiff. He stepped near and used a soft tone. "I love you more than life. You know that." He smoothed her hair.

She calmed a bit. "I'm glad no one came to harm. Most of those men are Pa's friends. I've known them all my life. Even though Jared Rawlings is awful, I'd hate to think…" Her words died.

"Let's go home," he whispered into her hair. It smelled of soap and a hint of perfume.

"I'm ready except for gettin' my satchel. Caleb already took my trunk when he drove your ma and Deborah home."

In a few minutes, clutching the satchel and wearing a wide-brimmed bonnet, she joined him. He took the satchel, tilted her chin, and kissed her. When he smiled, she smiled back, but it soon disappeared. He wondered if she was still angry. But the way her mouth trembled, he figured she was just nervous. He mounted the large, red mule and then took her hand to hoist her up onto the saddle behind. When she was seated, he kicked the mule and started down the lane in the dusk where under the trees blue twilight deepened into darkness.

Upon reaching the crossroads, he turned right.

Cindy's brows rose. "I reckon you know we're going the wrong way. You didn't forget your way home, did ya?" she asked while hugging his waist.

"Nope," he said. "I am going home." Her brows rose higher, but she kept quiet.

Chapter 2

Cindy watched the sky glow yellow, and then gold, purple, and crimson as the sun slipped below the hollow where long blue shadows smudged the trail. Then her eyes traced Elijah's lean muscled shoulders and straight back. The last trace of anger melted. *He was hers—her husband—hers to love and to cherish forever.* It was a beautiful thought. As she snuggled close and breathed in his good scent, a joyful shiver touched the arms hugging his waist.

When the mule stopped, she sat up, and in puzzlement, looked all around. A breeze drew up from the hollow to quiver tall dead grass in the yard.

"Michael's already gone. Why did ya come here?"

He turned slightly, his voice hesitant. "He gave us the place…if you want it." When she made no reply, his shoulders sagged, and he slowly let out a deep breath. "Looks pretty sorry, doesn't it? I reckon it was a stupid idea."

"Oh, no!" she exclaimed, her voice joyful. "You really mean we can live here and not have to move in with your ma?"

He turned all the way around to view her glowing face. "I never knew you were so worried about that."

She cringed. She had not meant to sound so relieved. But the truth was—living with Becky had been the only blight in her garden of dreams. Now her joy was complete. She slid from the mule, took off the bonnet, and stood gazing at the tumbledown gray cabin as if it were a mansion.

"You can fix the porch, put new shakes on the roof…I'll pull up those weeds and plant flowers all along the front there, and—"

Elijah's laugh rang out. "Whoa!" He drew her close. "Not tonight, you won't." As her cheeks grew red, he grinned and placed a kiss on the end of her nose. "Come on, Mrs. Loring," he said, taking her hand and leading her forward. "Let's go inside." Upon opening the door he frowned. "Maybe I ought not light the candle. I'm afraid you'll change your mind and run off."

She drew his face into her hands and kissed him. The hint of stubble from his chin was rough on her face. But she was glad he had shaved his beard. She thought he was more handsome without it.

"Don't talk such nonsense. We'll fix it up. In a little while you won't even recognize the place."

When he struck a match and held it close to the wick of a stubby candle stuck to a saucer, her eyes widened.

"Why! There's my trunk."

"I had Uncle Caleb deliver it here instead of sending it to Ma's."

"Then folks know where we are," she said with a hint of regret. "I was sort of hoping to avoid the shivaree—at least for a while."

"I asked Uncle Caleb to hold off on it for a bit."

"Reckon he will?" she asked doubtfully.

Elijah shrugged. "He grinned like a possum, but I figure he will."

"I hope so," she said and then looked around. She had been here countless times to visit, but now she looked with calculation. The cabin was small, much smaller than Pa's. The tiny room was crowded with table and benches and an old bed in the corner. Hooks on the wall still held some ragged clothing. The kitchen shelf sagged and the steps on the wall leading to the loft needed repair.

"This room is some cleaner than the last time I was here. But tomorrow I aim to give everything a good scrub—"

Thoughts of cleaning promptly left her mind as Elijah drew her into his arms. He chuckled as she leaned to blow out the candle.

In the quiet dawn, Elijah whistled as he let the bucket down into the well. Never had he felt happier. All the misery of the last years seemed to evaporate like the morning mists disappearing now from the hollow into the first rays of a pearly sunrise. While the pulley creaked, his gaze drifted. The place itself might look sorry, he thought, but the view was worth a king's ransom. The front yard sloped away before dropping abruptly into the cupped hollow, rimmed by folds of blue hills. The pine-covered ridges ran onward for miles. From here he could not see the creek that flowed at the bottom. But he knew it was there, swift and cold, bubbling over rocks and boulders, swirling into deep pools filled with perch and brownie and even an occasional eel.

The thought made him want to get his pole and amble down the path at the edge of the yard winding between pine and crimsoned hardwood before disappearing over the lip of the hollow. With all the work awaiting, there would be no time for fishing. He glanced around at fences with half the rails missing. Both barn and smokehouse were decrepit, and the chicken coop roof had fallen in—but with enough sweat, a few new logs, and some shakes, he figured they would soon be useable. As soon as that was done, he would begin clearing more ground. Johnny Lane had not been an ambitious farmer. Nor had his son. Michael had not even kept up the scant acreage cleared by his pa. Persimmon, sassafras, and locust sprouts dotted the pasture, and sumac and briars sprinkled the cornfield. Elijah knew it would take a lot of work, but this morning, he felt equal to any task.

When the bucket splashed, he abruptly pulled the rope that set the pulley turning. Then he lifted the dripping bucket and poured up the contents. After another quick look around at the crisp morning, he kept whistling and started for the house. Cindy would need the water. Even before he left the house, she was up and dressed and had come into the kitchen while pinning up her hair. He grinned now remembering the roses in her cheeks as their eyes met. From the way hers had sparkled, he figured she was just as happy as he was.

He stepped through the door and stopped in surprise. The unmistakable succulence of frying pork tickled his nostrils. Cindy, with face beaming, turned from the fireplace and laughed aloud.

"You never thought you'd be having ham for breakfast, did ya?"

"Where—"

"Pa shot a tiny-little wild hog day before yesterdee. It's not smoked, and it ain't as good as cured meat, but I didn't figure you'd mind too much." For a moment she grew shamefaced. "He was aiming to have Ma cook it for the wedding dinner, but I told him, since it was such a little thing, it would hardly make a mouthful for all those folks. And I knowed...knew," she corrected, "how much you love pork. You was just saying the other day how you hoped to get a wild one as soon as the weather got cold. Of course, the meat won't keep long in this weather, but Pa salted it heavy." Then she sighed. "I wish there was flour for biscuits...but thank the good Lord, we still have a dab of cornmeal. I made cornbread and some red-eye gravy to go over it."

Elijah set the bucket down and momentarily kept his back to Cindy. He knew he should be joyous over the unexpected feast. Instead he was suddenly filled with anger—an impotent rage over having to settle for so little when they should have had so much. Before the war, the farms along Little Piney had—like the Promised Land—flowed with milk and honey. He should be taking Cindy to a new log house with a bulging cellar. But after two years of raiding bushwhackers and foraging armies, almost every tame animal and half the wild ones had disappeared. They would be doing well not to starve.

While washing up at the basin, he drew a deep breath and willed himself calm. It had always been difficult to keep his anger in check, but he was learning. He dried on the piece of toweling and then, to keep from dashing her pleasure, he pasted on a smile and turned around. He tilted his head and sniffed the air.

"I can't remember when I've smelled anything as good. Mrs. Loring, I'm mighty glad you're a good cook."

"You haven't even tasted it yet," she protested.

He reached for a piece of meat from the platter in her hand, the edges of golden fat still sizzling, and popped it into his mouth.

"Ummm. That'll eat," he complimented and was rewarded by her huge smile. However, when he reached for another piece, she rapped his hand with the meat fork.

"Before you gobble any more like a heathen, you need to ask the blessing."

He grinned at her bossy tone. "Yes, ma'am." After hanging his hat on the back of the chair, he sat down and said grace. He silently hoped the Lord would forgive his murmuring. They were blessed to have anything to eat.

The food was good, cooked to perfection, the meat fried crisp but not dried-out, the cornbread baked to a crusted golden-brown. There was even a dab of butter melting on each steaming piece. He wondered how Cindy had managed that miracle. There was hardly a milk cow left in the mountains.

"Where in the world did you get butter?"

Awaiting his reaction, she had leaned forward with anxious eyes. Now, she relaxed back into the cane-bottomed chair.

"That's the best surprise yet." Her hazel eyes danced. "*We have a cow!*" She looked down and smoothed an imaginary wrinkle in the long blue apron enveloping her dress. "At least Pa has one, and he'll share the milk. He's had her for a while…kept her hid out in the woods. She belonged to old man Peters. When he took sick last month, he sent for Pa. And Pa was sitting up with him when he died. Since he lived so far back off the road, I reckon even the bushwhackers didn't find him. And he had no family—no one to claim his stuff—so Pa brought it home. There wasn't much except the cow and a few bushels of corn. I would have told you, but Pa said not to…" Her words died away.

"He's right. The fewer knows your business these days, the better. I don't fault him one mite. We shouldn't accept milk. Simon still has four mouths to feed, and I'll wager little Johnny is hard to fill up, growing like he is."

She nodded. "He eats like a wolf. I reckon he's hungry all the time. But he's a good boy and don't complain a'tall." She sighed. "I was looking forward to having a little milk to cook with. Water gravy ain't much good and cornbread is so much better made with milk. I'm affeared you'll think I can't cook. But you're right. With winter coming on, that cow won't be giving enough for all of us."

He chewed and swallowed before answering. "This is as good as Ma's cooking or even Granny's."

She glowed from the praise. "I'll learn to manage with what we have. But you could do with a little fattening up."

His eyes twinkled. "From the way you kept dodging Tom Sorrells yesterday, I never figured you preferred fat men."

She waved her hand in dismissal of his foolishness and stood to her feet. "My dishwater is about to boil away. Give me that dirty plate, and then unless you want to get roped into housework, you better make yerself scarce. I'm gonna scrub every inch of this cabin."

Instead he grabbed her hand and pulled her into his lap. She giggled and nestled close as he kissed her ear.

"You sure you want me to make myself scarce?"

She took his face between her hands and kissed his smiling mouth. Then she stood. "Uh-huh. I am. I got to get this house in shape. Folks will probably be coming before long for that shivaree."

Elijah frowned. He could well do without that mountain tradition. But if a body was well liked, it naturally followed there would be a shivaree. Because Ma had never approved the custom, she always stayed home. Tagging alongside Pa, he had been to a few. They were usually harmless. Sometimes, however, things got out of hand. He had once seen a groom ridden on a rail until the poor fellow could hardly stand. Even now he grimaced at the memory and hoped folks would just stay home. He wasn't about to submit to any such tomfoolery, and if necessary he would crack heads to avoid it. Of course, since most men were off in the army, he doubted there would be much roughhousing. The revelers were apt to be old men, women, and children.

"I suppose you're right. They may let us alone for a day or two, but sooner or later, they'll come banging on pots and pans and ringing cowbells. I don't recollect Granny or Uncle Caleb ever missing a shivaree. And I figure, there'll be a few more, like Tom Sorrells, who'll want in on the fun." He laughed at the sudden wrinkling of her nose. "I better start outside. The weeds in the yard are knee-deep."

She had already dumped the bucket of water into a pot heating over the coals in the fireplace. He took the empty bucket.

"I'll fetch some more water. I know you'll be using plenty." In the morning light coming through the small windows, he could see, in spite of his previous efforts at scouring, just how much dirt still clung to the rough floorboards. "Just as soon as I can, I'll get you a cook-stove like Ma's and Polly's."

Her face softened with a tender smile. "That's thoughtful of you. But don't fret yourself. I never even used a stove until a couple of years ago. I'm fine with having such a nice big fireplace." She gave a crooked grin. "Uncle Johnny must not have built this one—it's too well made and the chimney's too straight."

"I'd almost forgotten"—he opened the door and paused in the shaft of bright sunlight—"when I was just a shirttail kid, the old one caved in. I remember watching Pa and Johnny lay up the rock on this one."

Cindy quirked an eyebrow. "Knowing Uncle Johnny, he did more watching than working. Don't reckon I ought to speak ill of the dead, but he sure wasn't work brittle. Pa used to scold him some about his lax ways, but as far as I can tell, it never made a dent. Poor Aunt Maggie tried, but she was just too sick—especially there at the last."

"I know Johnny had his faults," Elijah interjected, "but couldn't he make you laugh!"

“For a fact,” she agreed with a quick laugh. “No one could tell a story better. And little Johnny is going to be just like him—except for the laziness. Pa won’t tolerate that. Sometimes I think Pa’s almost too hard on him. The few times Michael’s come by, I think he thinks so, too.”

“He’s never said a critical word,” said Elijah. “I know he’s mighty grateful to your pa and ma for raising the children. Not everybody would have done it, especially since your pa is Union and Johnny died fighting Confederate.”

“Why, Pa never gave that a second thought. Those younguns needed a home, and I’m glad they were with us, especially after losing Pete.”

Elijah hated the shadow that suddenly crossed her face. If he had his way, she would never have another sorrowful moment. That was, of course, out of his control. Even on the day of the bushwhacker’s raid, he had arrived too late to save Pete. “Gracious, Elijah, why you scowling so?” asked Cindy.

He didn’t answer. Picking up the water bucket, he stepped outside.

Cindy frowned while watching him leave with the water bucket in hand. It was maddening the way Elijah sometimes went off like that. He suddenly shut her out as mystically and surely as if he, like the biblical Elijah, had climbed into a fiery chariot and been swept away. He never used to be like that. Pa said war changed men. No doubt it did. Gone forever was the lighthearted boy she had fallen in love with. Of course she loved him more than ever. She cringed thinking of the scars on his back. *How he must have suffered.* The angry whip marks had faded to bluish-white now, but the beating had left deep grooves. Last night, as her fingers traced them, she had wanted to cry. She reckoned she’d just have to be patient until he could put those times behind him.

She puzzled over the viciousness in folks these days. Pa often quoted from the first chapter of Romans—how in the last days folks would be without natural affection. This must be the last days. At least it certainly appeared to be.

She sighed and poured scalding water into a basin and then picked up a knife and a gray bar of lye soap and began shaving slivers into the steaming water. The knife stilled and for a long moment she stared into space.

Abruptly the furrow between her brows deepened. Maybe *she* was without natural affection. She had killed a man. And she had never regretted it. Of course it wasn't murder. He had been about to shoot Elijah, so she had shot him. Nonetheless, she wondered if she was becoming hard-hearted. In the past she had been tenderhearted to the extreme. That had often caused trouble—some had mistaken her intentions. Because she was kind, even half-witted Vernon Millsap had thought she was smitten. Now, however, she felt no compassion for the evil men who had harmed her ma and killed her brother and were probably now roasting in hell. If she could, she'd throw a few more logs on their fire! Perhaps she ought to talk to Pa about the condition of her own soul.

"Here you go." Elijah set the dripping bucket onto the table. "As soon as I get some lumber from Uncle Caleb, I'll build you some shelves and a better table. This one is about to fall apart." Chewing on his jaw, he looked around. "This room is awful dark. I want to make those window holes bigger—let in more light. I doubt there's any window glass left to buy, but I might be able to get some panes somewhere."

"Oh, that would be wonderful," she said, leaving the dishrag idle for a moment. She wiped her hand on the apron before pushing back a loose strand of hair. "I admire how your ma's cabin is so colorful and cheerful and has more windows than any cabin hereabouts. I aim to braid some rugs like your ma has, and Granny said she'd help me weave another pretty coverlet—since the bushwhackers stole the one we made before."

"Granny will like that. She'd rather weave than eat," he said with a grin.

Cindy smiled. "She is about the best weaver there ever was. She's been teaching me. I still ain't real good but I aim to learn. After the next shearing, she's gonna show me how to make dye."

Elijah nodded. "Yeah, Ma's excited about that. Granny promised to teach her, too."

"Your ma didn't always get along with Granny, did she?"

He shook his head. "Nope. They were as fractious as two old setting hens. Granny was always possessive of Pa. Ma never tried too hard to understand Granny—and vice versa. Lately they've been getting along real well. I'm glad. I love them both, but I was getting almighty tired of trying to keep the peace between them. I reckon they're finally beginning to understand each other."

Cindy looked down at the dishpan. "Did your ma ever speak against us getting married?" she finally asked.

"Not a word," he said. He did not add that a keen look of regret had crossed her face when he made the announcement.

Cindy looked up. "I hope she likes me. I want to learn to talk proper the way your ma—"

He gathered her into his arms and nuzzled her neck where little sprigs of sweat-dampened curls had escaped the knot of hair.

"Lige! I'm dripping dishwater all over ya," she protested.

He tipped up her chin and looked into her gold-flecked brown eyes. "Ma likes you fine. Even if she didn't, I do. Isn't that what really counts?"

She nodded and returned his kiss with equal ardor. As his hand slowly traced her back, she drew in a shivery breath.

"If you don't get on with yer work," she mildly scolded, "I'll never get these dishes washed and folks will think you've married the sorriest woman in the hills."

"I don't care what folks think," he said.

At that moment she had to agree. Sun, slanting in the open door, lay across his wide shoulders and reflected in his warm brown eyes. She had loved him for years. It was still almost too good to be true that they were man and wife and free to share their love. Her heart raced. She made no protest as he drew her away from the dishpan.

Cindy suddenly held the scrub brush still and rocked back on her heels. The sun was low in the west, and she hadn't given supper a thought! There was enough meat and cold cornbread for another meal, but she had intended to boil some dried beans. It was too late now.

Her mind went to the meal she wished to cook. Chicken fried crisp but juicy inside; fluffy buttermilk biscuits for sopping tasty milk gravy made from pan dripping; purple hull peas flavored with a piece of fat pork; sliced tomatoes, ripe and red from the garden alongside slices of white sweet onion.

With a tired hand to her back, she gave a deep sigh. "Oh well," she said softly. "When the war's over, we'll have such vittles again."

She eyed the lone empty shelf that was the pantry and frowned. It was a relief that folks always brought their own refreshments to a shivaree. Of course, sometimes that was not a good thing. Two years ago, at the last shivaree she had attended, the Matthers' corn liquor had turned Lavenny Sorrell and Tod Dugan's party into a brawl. Although all the Matthers boys were gone now, she still hoped Caleb and Tom Sorrells left their jugs at home. She suddenly wondered where the Matthers had gone. She had not seen Dillon since the day he had proposed to her. She shook her head, thinking how badly she had felt as he walked away, head bowed and giant shoulders drooped. No doubt Dillon was rowdy, but even Pa said he had the makings of a fine man. She hoped he found a girl who would love him as fiercely as she loved Elijah.

She looked from the wet spot where she knelt near the door to the far corners. The room already looked heaps better—as well it should. She had wiped the walls and scrubbed the floor twice and emptied a dozen buckets of muddy water. The few things from her trunk helped brighten the room. The round metal candleholder Ma had given her, filled with six fat tallow candles of her own making, sat on the table near a white pitcher she intended to fill with flowers. Two dainty blue cups sat alongside a matching plate propped on the doodad shelf that Pa had carved. Elijah had hung it for her that morning. The rosewood clock on the mantle—which had traveled from Ireland on a ship and then from South Carolina in her grandma's wagon—had a crack in the glass but still kept perfect time. She considered it a miracle the bushwhackers had overlooked it packed away in Grandma's old hump-backed trunk in the attic. They had taken all the other valuables.

Cindy was worn out but content. It had been a good day. They were making progress. Elijah had scythed the front yard and raked the weeds and long grass into piles and burned them. He had straightened the front fence and, until more rails could be cut, had borrowed from the tumbled down garden fence to replace those that were missing.

Just then a shrill whistle pierced the air. "Hey, Lige!"

Cindy looked out the door. Little Johnny stood at the far side of the cornfield, hands cupped around his mouth. "Aunt Polly said to tell ya'll that you'll have some visitors along after dark," he yelled.

Elijah waved a hand in acknowledgement and shouted, "Thanks, Johnny."

As the boy melted back into the woods, Cindy jumped up, picked up the dishpan, and threw the dirty mop water outside with a high arch that landed far from the door. Then she grabbed the empty water bucket. The house looked much better, but she was a fright. It would take several buckets of water to fill the battered tub hanging on the outside wall of the Lane cabin. On her way out the door, heading for the well, she critically eyed the blue calico hanging on a hook. She was glad she had remembered to take the dress from her trunk. It was still a little wrinkled, but in lamplight it would look fine. The revelers would come after dark, hoping to catch them in bed. But now that Johnny had brought the warning, they would stay up.

Elijah met her and took the bucket. "I'll draw the water. You look frazzled."

She smiled her thanks and sat down on the corner of the rough rock wall surrounding the well. The crisp breeze soughing through the pines felt wonderful on her hot face and body. She breathed deeply of the strong, sharp scent of pine. No matter how often she saw the view from Uncle Johnny's front yard—the sheer bluffs falling sharply away into a deep shaded ravine rimmed by timber-covered hills—she felt awed and reverent. As Pa said, it was a testament to a mighty creator.

Elijah took hold of the bucket attached to the windlass. "Cindy, there's no need to kill yourself. Like Granny says—what doesn't get done today will be waitin' tomorrow."

She sighed. "I am tired to the bone. But I'm glad things look a mite better before folks get here." Her eyes traced the yard. "Hit…it," she quickly corrected herself, "looks a sight better without the tall grass and weeds."

He held the rope idle. "There's so much to do, I hardly know where to start. But I suppose, with winter coming on, I'd better start by skidding in more firewood. I already cut a bunch for Ma and even some for Granny. But I need to get more since Uncle Caleb's back keeps acting up. He can hardly get around. As soon as that's done, I can think about fixing up this house and clearing a bigger corn patch." He suddenly grinned and reached into his pocket and pulled out a handkerchief. "Mrs. Loring, your face is dirty."

As he set down the bucket and wiped her face, she held up her chin for his ministrations. "I'll be needing several buckets full," she said, "for a good bath. I hope that old tub don't leak. I want to soak for an hour."

"I'll draw as much as you want," he said. His dark eyes twinkled. "And, if you'd like, I'll even wash your back."

"No thank you. I can manage my own bath." She stood and walked away, but called back over her shoulder. "By the way, yer face is dirty, too."

"So's my back. Want to wash it?" he called.

She pretended to ignore him and went into the cabin. But her cheeks had pinked. His teasing would take some getting used to…but she didn't think she was a prude as Lizzy Tate had accused when Tom Sorrell's crude remarks made her face burn. *Of course, there's nothing modest about Lizzy*, she thought with a curled lip. *That hussy wouldn't blush at being caught bare naked!*

As the sun sank beyond the dark ridge, Cindy lit a candle. When folks arrived she would light more, but for now, that would be extravagant. She looked with longing at an empty lamp in the center of the table. No one had coal oil these days.

Supper was a quick meal without conversation. She was almost too weary to eat. However, after a few bites of cold pork and cornbread, she felt better and did not dread the coming ordeal as much as before. If Caleb brought his fiddle, it would be fun. She loved to dance. And with Elijah rushing off as he had, there had been no dancing after the wedding.

While she hurriedly washed the dishes, Elijah filled the tub now sitting in the small lean-to.

"I'll go feed the horse. Holler when you're ready for me to come back inside."

With an inward smile, she nodded and whisked off the damp apron. *How thoughtful of him to understand.* Instead of the long soak she wanted, she would hurry.

And it was fortunate she did. She was still sitting by the fireplace brushing damp hair when a loud bugle call rent the night.

"Here they come!" she called as the pandemonium grew louder.

Elijah's voice came muffled through the blanket hanging over the lean-to doorway. "Be right there. I'm almost dressed." While buttoning his shirt, he pulled the blanket aside. Moisture glistened in his straight dark hair.

"Here," she said and handed him the hairbrush. While he gave his tousled hair a quick brush, she lit the other five candles in the holder.

"Reckon there's many of them?" she asked looking quickly out the dark window.

"Sounds like it. They're louder than Hindman's brass band."

Cowbells jangled amid the clamor of banging pots and pans and shrieks and whistles and, loudest of all, the blaring bugle.

"It'll spoil their fun that we're up and dressed," said Elijah. "I won't let them in for a while—make 'em bang on the door. They'll like that better."

And bang they did, after they had circled the house several rounds. Cindy feared they would tear the door from the hinges before Elijah took a candle from the holder and lifted the latch. A draft of chill air entered the cabin and stirred to life embers smoldering in the fireplace.

"Thought I heard a noise," he said. "But Cindy figured it was just a stray cat yowling," he apologized with a straight face. "Come in out of the night air. Y'all lose your way home in the dark?"

With a hand under Granny's arm, Caleb stepped inside. "Well, we'd have called out—but we was affeared you might be busy. And we didn't want to disturb ya none." He glanced at the bed. "Was ya'll busy?"

Granny cackled as Cindy hung her head and her ears burned. Although she knew the teasing was in good fun, to her it was torment.

One by one, a score of neighbors entered until the small room grew crowded. Elijah's cousin Jenny had come along with her deaf pa, Pappy Campbell, who, like an ancient poplar, was tall but bent by the wind. Because of crippling rheumatism, he hardly went anywhere. However, Cindy was not surprised he had come. The old fellow loved Elijah, and he was kin, a brother to Elijah's granny. But she noted with concern that her mother-in-law was not in the crowd. Of course, neither were her own parents. They had sent word by Caleb that her ma was worn out from the wedding and needed her pa's help with the evening's work.

Elijah held the door wider to admit Tom Sorrell's huge girth. Skinny May came behind.

Then Elijah stepped back and exclaimed in surprise. "Good gosh!"

Cindy raised her eyes to see him embracing a broad shouldered man in a gray coat. Just then the man looked up. As the piercing gray eyes above a short but heavy brown beard met hers, she realized it was Elijah's cousin, Billy Tanner. She smiled and nodded. He had been away in the Confederate Army for two years, most recently in Tennessee recuperating from wounds and pneumonia. Although before the war he had lived nearby, she had not known him well. He was ten years older than Elijah and nothing like him. Neither was Billy like his jolly pa, Caleb. Although he wasn't exactly dour like his prune-faced mother, Viola, he was standoffish and hard to decipher.

Caleb's laugh rang out as he pounded Elijah's back. "Him and Viola got back last night, but I never told a soul. Hit's a grand surprise, ain't it?"

"It surely is!" Elijah grinned ear to ear. "Billy, last time I saw you, you left in such a hurry, I never got to say thanks for trying to keep me from getting conscripted."

Billy's eyes finally left Cindy. "Pa told me you made out all right."

"Yeah, I made it home pretty much in one piece. How about yourself? How's the wound?"

"I'm fine."

Granny snorted. "You ain't no such thang. Just look at them holl'er cheeks—must a' lost thirty pound. Need fattenin' up." She pointed her cane at Cindy. "Need a good woman like Elijah's—one that can cook."

Billy's glance followed the cane. He stared for a long moment before quietly saying, "No doubt."

Tall, gaunt Viola came through the doorway carrying a platter covered by a snowy white dishtowel. "Caleb, I was waiting fer a hand with the vittles. Don't reckon you'd have missed me if I'd stayed in the wagon all night," she quarreled, adding a quick, offended sniff.

"I'll go right now and get the rest of the stuff," he said, before hurrying outside.

Elijah placed a quick peck on his aunt's upturned cheek, but there was no warmth in the greeting. Cindy could not blame him. Viola

Tanner inspired about as much affection as a contrary setting hen that was forever pecking a body's hand.

"This here is Billy's favorite," said Viola with a possessive smile at her son. She lifted the dishtowel, "My cornpone fresh from the skillet."

"And I brung a bowl of my good honey to dip 'em in," said Granny. "I recollect that's how he likes 'em."

Viola's petulant mouth was a down-turned bow. "He likes 'em fine—with or without yer honey."

Cindy hid a smile. In spite of Viola having been gone for months caring for Billy, she and Granny had picked right up with their feud.

Granny's mouth opened. Tom Sorrels' shrill nasal tone interrupted her retort as he reached a thick hand to snatch a cornpone.

"Bread"—he smacked fleshy lips— "the staff of life."

Granny eyed his protruding belly. "And you been leanin' on hit way too often. I'll swan, Tom, I don't know how you've stayed so fat when most folks is starvin.'"

He ignored the remark. "Can't no one make cornpone like you, Viola. May has tried and tried but hers just crumbles apart or gets soggy in the grease. I wish you'd show her how."

"Ain't nothing to it," she said with false modesty. "Hit's two parts meal to one part boiling water and a dab of salt throwed in. Then ya pat each big spoonful into a cake and mash hit flat. Most important—ya got to make sure the water is a rolling boil. Otherwise hit won't do right a'tall. And there's a bit of a trick to getting the grease right, hot but not smoking. Fer some reason, hog lard works better than bacon grease."

When Lizzy Tate sauntered inside, Cindy hid a frown. She would just as soon the bold thing had stayed home.

Lizzy's cornflower blue dress matched her eyes and complimented her curvy figure. In candlelight her fair hair was almost silver. With hand on hip, her big eyes swept the room and then registered disappointment. "I was hopin' Michael would be here," she said. Then she brightened. In an aside to Cindy, she said, "Upon my word, there's Billy Tanner over in the corner. Ain't he just as handsome as ever! I heared he got all shot up—and he is a mite thin—but don't he look fine." She shot Cindy a sly look and winked. "Reckon I'll sashay over and keep him company."

Just then Caleb arrived carrying a basket of roasted sweet potatoes that was far from full. Even so, Cindy was sure the offerings had greatly depleted the Tanner pantry. These days no one had any food to spare. Most folks had grown tight-fisted. Hiding and hoarding had replaced the custom of casually borrowing and then repaying when it was handy. Here, where no one used to lock door or cellar, thievery had become commonplace.

Caleb's old, cracked leather fiddle case protruded from the top of the basket. He took it out tenderly and laid it on the table.

"I figured a little fiddlin' would go good this evening."

Cindy smiled. "I love your fiddling more than anyone else's."

Lizzy Tate spoke up. "Oh, Allen Matthers kin fiddle bet—." Her voice stilled.

Cindy figured even thoughtless Lizzie realized she had blundered.

Elijah quickly spoke up, "Allen's a good fiddler because Uncle Caleb taught him."

Caleb grinned. "No doubt about it, Allen is a heap better fiddler; but he ain't here, so yer all stuck with me." He pulled rosin across the bow and began tuning up.

Soon a lively tune filled the room. He winked at Elijah. "Better grab yer gal before someone else does."

Cindy laughed as Elijah's hands quickly circled her waist. He pulled her into the small empty space near the fireplace. "You need to move the table. There's not room in here fer dancin'!" she protested. Nonetheless they managed a few turns before bumping into the table. She pulled back rosy cheeked and happy. When she looked around and caught Billy staring, he quickly looked away. A body never knew what he was thinking, but Cindy sensed his thoughts were deep and often discontented.

Caleb ended the song with a flourish. He nodded with appreciation at the applause.

Amid a sudden buzz of conversation, May Sorrells called out a request, "Flow Gently Sweet Afton."

Tom shot her a look of pure disgust. "That ain't no party tune, May more like a funeral. Besides hit's a banjer tune anyway."

"I heared Caleb play it a'fore and hit was real purty," she argued.

"Caleb, put that noisy thing away fer now," said Viola. "The food's ready."

Caleb frowned but laid the fiddle back into the case.

Tom licked his lips and reached a thick hand for a round, golden cornpone and dipped it into a bowl of clear yellow honey. As he bit into it a spot of honey glistened on his chin.

"Ummm! That there is top-notch pone, Viola," he said while still chewing. And then as if for fear of offending a good cook like Granny, he added, "Granny, this may be the best honey yer bees ever made. What kind is hit?"

"Mostly yeller clover, I reckon. Maybe a dab of—"

A knock interrupted. Every eye turned toward the door. Elijah opened it. The caller had obviously not come for the shivaree. He was hatless, coatless, and had blood on his shirt. It was Randy Tyler. He had the same hooknose, narrow chin, and lanky height of all the Tylers who lived in the next hollow. As Elijah stepped outside and shut the door, a hush fell. Every ear was cocked toward the door. Without a doubt Randy Tyler did not bring good news.

In a few minutes Elijah stepped inside, and without a word, gathered a handful of cornpone and a piece of roast pork left from their supper. He wrapped them in Viola's dishtowel and then stepped back outside. Hoof beats soon drummed the darkness.

When he came back inside, his jaw was tight. His eyes sought Billy. "Yankee troops had a skirmish with Brooks' men south of Kingston. Chased them all the way to Frog Bayou Mountain and on down to the river. Killed a couple of his men. Wounded a few more and took six or eight of them prisoner. Randy got hit, but it's just a scratch." He looked at Cindy, hesitated, and then added, "Both Randy and Michael got captured." When she gasped, he hurried on. "Randy got away and he thinks Michael may have, too. Brooks made things hot for the Yankees for a while—before his own men had to scatter or get blown to bits by a Yankee howitzer. Some of them headed for Clarksville. Randy was hoping Michael had made his way here."

Cindy dropped into a chair. This favorite cousin had had so many troubles that she sometimes wondered if he was cursed. When she had voiced that fear to Pa, he had assured that the blood of Jesus could wash away any curse. Trouble was, she wasn't sure Michael had been washed in the blood. He was not exactly heavenly minded. As a matter of fact, sometimes she feared he was downright carnal—like two weeks ago when she had come for a visit just as Lizzy Tate was leaving. From the looks of Lizzy's wrinkled dress and mussed hair, they had not been praying.

"Reckon them Federal troops will chase Brooks here?" Caleb asked with concern. "Sure don't need any more foraging armies—not from neither side."

Cindy looked around the room. For the first time, she noticed that all the guests tonight had Confederate sympathies. She had no strong feelings either way. Pa was Union because the Bible commanded obedience to the government. According to his lights that meant the powers in Washington City. But Elijah's people were Confederate, and Granny knew her Bible as well as Pa did.

In quick revelation Cindy realized, now that she was Elijah's wife, she should side with him in everything. That was her understanding of scripture. A wife should honor her husband—submit to him. Knowing her own strong nature, she wasn't sure how good she'd be at the submitting part. Ma accused her of being more strong-willed than old Dan, Pa's white mule. But she intended to try. With all her heart she wanted to make Elijah happy.

Elijah was not surprised when folks decided to quickly take their leave. The thought of foraging armies was not to be taken lightly. Although folks had learned the hard way to take precaution, there were still things to be tucked away in caves and hollow tree trunks and other such hiding places, and livestock to be hidden far back in the woods.

"Lige, sorry fer such a grim party," apologized Caleb as he stepped into the night, holding a lantern with a candle inside in one hand and with the other taking a firm grip on Granny's arm. "Never even got to fiddle but one. Watch yer step there, Ma."

"I'm a'watchin,'" she said. "Hit's too bad folks can't leave home fer ten minutes without fear of bein' robbed or burned out," she complained. Then her black eyes twinkled. "'Course I reckon Cindy is right glad to see us go early without the usual leave-taking. No bride likes getting tucked into bed by the women whilst her man gets tucked in by the gents. To this day, I remember how mortified I was." She chuckled low.

"We're coming, Viola," Caleb called toward the disgruntled voice in the darkness.

"Reckon she expects me to run on my crippled feet," complained Granny.

Elijah waved goodbye as horses and wagons pulled away. Then he turned toward Billy who stood nearby, barely visible in soft light coming through the open door.

"You heard any war news?"

Billy shook his head. "Last big battle I heard of was a month or so back in Tennessee—place called Chickamauga Creek. I reckon General Bragg lived up to his name. We won. But lots of casualties—over thirty thousand last I heard."

Elijah expelled a deep breath. "Well, there ain't been much to brag about around here. In the last few months we've lost Fort Smith, Little Rock, Helena—the whole river valley. Caleb said there's talk of the

Union making a garrison at Dardanelle and maybe even Clarksville. I'm not sure there's any of our men left this side of the river, except for some hard-riding cavalry like Brooks. You plan to join up again?" he asked.

Billy took his foot from resting on the log wall and spit out a sassafras twig he was chewing. He shrugged straight shoulders. "Not likely—at least not anytime soon. I doubt I could last half a day on a forced march. But I might when I get my strength back. How about you?"

Elijah snorted. "I stuck it out for two years. Back last winter when we marched through Clarksville—hightailing it to Little Rock after the Yankees attacked Fort Smith—I decided to call it quits and came home. I don't consider it deserting since I got conscripted. If I never see another army camp, it'll be too soon for me."

Billy's even teeth flashed white. "Didn't care much for camp life, huh?"

"Didn't care for anything about the army…except for some of the men. I miss them."

"Yeah, me too. I got to say, I like the life."

Elijah's brows rose. "You sound just like Michael Lane. He took to it like a good hound to a hot trail. I sure hope he got away. No, sir, I aim to stay right here."

"Well, some of us ain't lucky like you, Lige. We don't have a pretty woman waiting at home."

Elijah glanced inside. A slow smile spread his face. "I am lucky."

"Damn lucky."

Elijah was surprised at the bitter tone. When he turned back, Billy was walking away. With a puzzled frown, he shrugged and then stepped back inside.

One lone candle now burned in the holder, and the air was tinged with smoke from extinguished wicks. Firelight cast Cindy's long shadow on the wall where she stood wiping crumbs from the table. She looked up, held the rag still, and bit her lip. "It wasn't much of a party. Not that I'm sorry," she quickly added. "I'm glad they've all gone." She began cleaning the table again. "Lige, what's to be done about Michael?"

"Nothing." He stepped to the mantle and wound the clock with slow, methodical turns. When the pendulum began swinging again, he turned and saw her frown.

Her eyes were puzzled. "You don't sound much concerned."

"It's the life he chose, and he knew the risks when he joined up."

Her mouth drew further down. "I reckon you'd be a bit more anxious if he was your kin," she sputtered and turned away.

Granny had warned him that a bride was apt to be high-strung and sensitive. He went to her and gently turned her around. He pushed a loose lock of hair from her cheek.

"Of course I care what happens to him. And I'd help him if I could. But there's nothing I can do. Besides, he's a clever fellow, and I figure he got away."

"You really think so?" When he nodded, she buried her face against his chest. "I'm sorry," she whispered. "Reckon you already knew I had a temper."

He tilted her face and kissed the end of her nose. "Uh-huh. Other than that I'd say you're perfect."

"Oh, no. I got faults a'plenty…just ask Ma. I'm strong-willed and stubborn as a mule. But you're stuck with me, Elijah Loring. Like Ma says—you made yer bed, now you got to lay in it."

His eyes danced. "Sounds like a fine idea to me."

She laughed and her eyes sparkled as he took her hand and pulled her forward.

Chapter 3

Cindy felt like a little girl playing house. With as much pleasure as when she wore pigtails, she arranged and rearranged her new possessions on the trunk Granny had just given her. Now the placement exactly suited—her Bible in the middle, a little cherrywood chest from Ma on one end, and her comb and brush on the other.

Granny had also given her enough gingham to make short curtains. The tiny red flowers on yellow background was not what Cindy would have chosen from the store. However, the colorful fabric would brighten the dim room. She sewed every spare minute, glancing often at the clock on the mantle, the pendulum swaying with each muted tick, to make certain Elijah's meals were ready and waiting.

When the curtains were finally hung, she stepped back and surveyed her handiwork with satisfaction. They did brighten and improve the room, especially by hiding the ugly oilcloth used as substitute glass.

Then her mind turned to Christmas. In the following weeks, she often walked down the trail to Granny's and surreptitiously carded and spun soft wool for Elijah's presents. When he was away from home or busy outdoors, she began knitting a warm scarf and vest.

Now she rubbed her neck, laid down the knitting, and opened the front door. With the exception of one frost, November had been mild and sunny. Earlier that morning, mists had risen from the hollow and hidden the far blue ridges. Now they evaporated into sunny skies on crisp air wafting the pungent scent of autumn. Suddenly the cabin walls seemed to close in around her. With a guilty backward glance at the sewing, she pulled the door shut and scurried down the steps. Then she chuckled. Ma was not there to scold and call her back. Of course it was foolish to go traipsing off in the middle of the morning and leaving work undone…but as Ma herself was fond of saying, work never gets done. Cindy had always loved being outdoors, especially in the fall. Gathering nuts and wild grapes had always seemed a delight rather than a chore.

Abruptly, she halted and hurried back to the cabin and got a bucket. The nuts and fruit were shriveled and tiny this year, but even a little change would add to their boring diet. When Elijah retuned that evening from cutting his ma's firewood, she hoped to have a surprise for him.

She was thankful for the early frost that had wilted the underbrush making the woods open and spacious. Even more important, it had put a stop to both ticks and chiggers. She could meander at will without needing to smear on smelly coal oil, which they had been out of for ages. In a slow stroll, she took the rutted trail along the lip of the ridge. Never had she tired of the view. Elijah once told her about fancy churches with tall steeples and colored glass windows—places where folks went to praise God. She reckoned that was fine. But she didn't see how a body could feel half as worshipful there as she did gazing out over the deep hollow, where fingers of mists curled up from the creek through colored leaves painted by God's own hand.

After one more long, appreciative look, she let out a deep breath and then angled off into the woods. She noticed a few purple flowers atop tall sprigs of late blooming boneset, and a little farther on, the white fuzzy flowers—mostly brown now—of snakeroot. She used to walk right past such things without taking notice until Granny began teaching her about herbs and roots and plants to use for medicine.

She paused for a moment and pulled off some prickly beggar lice clinging to the hem of her skirt. Up ahead a squirrel scrambled out of her path and up the side of a hickory. He jumped into a nearby tree where, with tail arched high, he sat bright-eyed and curious on a limb while Cindy raked through leaves on the ground, and after breaking off the dark outer hull, she dropped small tan nuts into the bucket. There weren't many. She glanced at the squirrel.

"Beat me to 'em, didn't ya?" She chuckled as he scampered away. "Good thing Elijah ain't here," she muttered, "or you'd be stewing in a pot with dumplings."

She ambled on through the trees, stopping often to scour the ground for hickory nuts and chinquapins. The loam was deep with pads of moss and decaying leaves. Even a careful search yielded few nuts. She wandered on and came to a spindly persimmon tree. She picked a persimmon and dropped it into her mouth. It had sweetened with early frost but the shriveled fruit was mostly long narrow seeds.

The year before she had gathered fat orange persimmons from a tree overhanging the spring. Being near the water, perhaps it had good fruit this year. Her steps quickened as she approached the shady hillside with rocky outcropping where water bubbled from the ground.

"Oh, they're most as big as ever!" she breathed with delight.

In a few minutes, the bucket was almost half full. With a wide smile, she turned toward home. Even without flour she figured to concoct a dessert with nuts, persimmons, and honey. Neither the army nor the bushwhackers had tackled Granny's hives and there was enough honey for both families to have sweetening…at least for a while.

Suddenly her smile faded and she sucked in a startled breath. Billy stood a few yards away. With a shoulder leaned against a tree, he held a shotgun in the crook of his arm.

"I didn't mean to scare you," he said, straightening.

She was flustered. "You ought to of spoke up."

"Don't take offense," he apologized. "I was thinking how…how happy you looked. I've not seen many happy things in a long while." He pushed away from the tree. "But you ought to carry a gun," he said. "What if I'd been a bushwhacker?"

She dropped her eyes. He was right. She had been careless.

An awkward silence settled—at least she felt awkward. She had no idea what he was thinking.

They both looked up as a V-shaped line of honking geese flew over. The birds were low. She could make out each individual bird, wings sweeping the sky and keeping perfect formation, just as Elijah had described trained soldiers on parade.

"Appears winter's on the way," Billy said.

"I wish the pretty days could last," she said wistfully. "I love walkin' in the woods."

"Just remember what I said about carrying a gun."

"I will," she said and turned away. She glanced back once. He still stood in the trail looking after her.

In the warm autumn weather, Elijah sweated as he mended the sagging steps, dabbed fresh chinking between the logs, and replaced faulty roof shakes. While eyeing the slow progress, he groaned in frustration. He wanted better for Cindy. Someday he would build her a tall white house like Uncle Phillip's. Before the war it had been one of the best in Clarksville. For now he chaffed over having no lumber or window glass. But he never stayed disgruntled, for as soon as Cindy stepped onto the porch and shaded her eyes looking for him, his face brightened. She often interrupted her busy day to bring him a drink or a bite of food or simply to stand nearby watching him work and offering to lend a hand. He relished those moments, and more often than not, took time out to steal a kiss.

In spite of the tranquil season, he kept shotgun and rifle near and maintained vigilant watch. In the past, he had seen calamity fall as swiftly as the blow of an ax.

Late in November, slow and steady, the rains began. For days the downpour hampered Elijah's work, but he took the opportunity to go hunting. Game was scarce, and what little there was, was scrawny, but it would prove a welcome change to their tiresome diet.

Before dawn he quietly slipped out of bed and left Cindy sleeping. He could hear her breathing, deep and even. Without a light, he dressed by feel and gathered the rifle, a short slicker, and a leather pouch filled with paper cartridges and caps. He had not seen a deer in weeks, but he hoped to find a wild hog or even a bear before it denned.

When he stepped onto the porch, he cocked his head. The rain had stopped for the moment, but the roaring creek filled the hollow with thunder. He crossed the bare field and entered the woods. As his boots sank deep into wet moss, fog dripped from trees and rolled down the slicker. Through the wetness rose the musty smell of decaying leaves.

He stopped for a moment. It had been months since he had thought of Belle. He reckoned going hunting brought back the memory. The little hound had loved trailing at his heels on such a day. He never figured to love an animal again as he had loved the long-eared pup. He missed her yet, but he had no desire for another hound. It might be childish but he never wanted to feel that loss again. He started on, but some of the joy had faded from the morning.

Circling a knob, he worked his way downward toward a swag penciled at the bottom by a natural game crossing. The trail had been made mostly by deer and hogs but back in the spring, he had seen a sow bear with two cubs nearby and figured it's den was somewhere in the jutting rocky bluffs above.

As he drew near the place, he slipped along, stopping often to study the ground. In a low spot, across a small creek, he saw the first bear sign—padded five-toed tracks half-filled with water in the soft mud. It was not the track of a large animal, more than likely one of the grown cubs from the year before. He stepped carefully across the creek on slick rocks and on the far bank followed the curve of water for a ways until the tracks turned away. Although he no longer saw tracks, Elijah continued on toward the dripping ledges towering ahead and almost obscured in fog. He traveled the base of the bluffs for a long distance without seeing fresh sign, and had almost decided to cut back toward the creek, when he saw a black shape off to the right near a white-barked sycamore. Although the animal faced him, it had not seen or smelled him and continued to paw at a rotten log, digging out grubs and rooting them with its narrow cinnamon brown nose. It was, just as Elijah thought, a young black bear, not fully grown. He was not disappointed. There would be less meat, but it would be tender and good.

With care, he brought the gun out from under the slicker and to his shoulder and waited for a good chest shot. Long ago he had learned not to take a frontal head shot at a bear. More often than not, the slanted skull would deflect the bullet. He wanted a chest shot or a side one behind the shoulder or just below the ear.

Just then the bear threw up his head, exposing its chest. He stared toward Elijah. It was the perfect shot. Elijah pulled the trigger. The bear fell without a twitch. While reloading, he kept a close eye on the beast. It paid to be cautious.

But the bear was dead. Elijah drew his knife and short-gutted it. Even before he split the hide, the strong unpleasant odor of bear arose. It was a good thing the knife was sharp, he thought. The hide was tough. He would drag the bear behind a nearby log, cover it with a pile of leaves, and come back later with the mule. Until then, hopefully, any passing varmint would be satisfied with the entrails.

It took considerable effort to drag the animal, but finally it lay buried beneath a mound of wet leaves. Elijah started home, going a beeline to save miles.

He had traveled less than a mile when he heard a dog barking. He glanced at the knob rising high on his left and realized that the Millsap cabin was around the bend and a ways off in a secluded hollow. He hadn't seen any of them since he'd returned from the army and learned that Vernon, his seatmate at school, had died. Although he'd never cared much for Vernon, he supposed he ought to look in on the family and give his long overdue condolences. He would go see them as soon as the meat was dressed.

It was, however, two days later before Elijah found time to go visiting. This time he carried a fair-sized piece of raw bear meat. At a distance the rotted cabin looked deserted. If any smoke rose from the chimney, it was lost against gray sky. A wormy, thin-ribbed hound bayed as he drew near and then leaped high, snapping at the sack of meat slung across his shoulder.

"Git down, ya sorry hound!" Cora Millsap hollered from the doorway.

The hound paid no heed. Elijah kicked at the dog and came on.

"Howdy, ma'am. How are you?" he asked. The answer was obvious. Rail-thin and shivering, Cora appeared ready to keel over. The baby she held and the small boy hanging on to her long skirt looked equally starved and hollow-eyed. As though embarrassed, she drew bare feet back inside the doorway and pushed at the loose-knotted, black hair that hung limp and stringy on the back of her thin neck.

"Elijah Loring, ain't it?" As the baby reached for her dress, she pushed away its tiny hand from her flat breast and pulled together the ragged tatters of her worn dress. "Ain't seen you in a long while," she mumbled.

As the dog whined and sniffed hungrily, circling his legs, Cora eyed the meat protruding from a cloth sack and involuntarily licked her lips. Elijah's eyes slid over the ramshackle place. The Millsaps had never been prosperous, but Andy and his grown married son had farmed enough to feed and clothe them.

"Andy or Quinton about?" he asked.

She shook her head. But her eyes, hypnotic, stayed on the meat. "Reckon you never heared—Quinton got took by the army a few months back and died fighting at Helena. Way before that Vernon got shot and killed by a conscript man. Pa died a few weeks ago. He'd been ailing ever since losing the boys. I reckon that's what finally killed him."

"Ma told me about Vernon, but I didn't know about the rest. I'm sure sorry for all your troubles." He frowned. "You living here alone now?"

She hung her head. "I got nowhere else to go."

"Ma," the child whined and pulled on her skirt. "I'm hongry. Ya said you'd chop wood and boil some turnips."

"Hesh up," she scolded. "Can't ya see we got company?"

The boy's lip jutted, and he looked down.

Elijah saw an ax sunk into a stump but no woodpile.

"You out of wood, Miss Cora?"

She swallowed. "Reckon I am. A neighbor comes by sometimes and gives me a hand with hit." She flushed guiltily. "But he ain't been by lately."

He handed the meat to her. "Put this inside where the hound can't get it. If you ain't too busy, I'm hungry myself. Maybe you could slice some steaks to fry while I get a tad of wood."

Her eyes lighted. "I don't mind a'tall. Meat will go real good with them turnips."

Elijah took the ax and headed for the woods behind the cabin. He had noticed a lightning-struck dead tree on top of the knoll that would make a quick hot fire. Near the back of the cabin was a fresh mound of dirt that he assumed was old Andy's grave. He wondered how the frail woman had managed to dig the hole. She didn't look able to heft a shovel. That neighbor must have helped her.

It took an hour before he had chopped enough dead and then green wood to last her a few days. He figured to get Billy and Caleb to help get her a good-sized stack before freezing weather. Food for her and the young ones was a bigger problem. He and Cindy had little to share. Perhaps between them all they could keep her from starving.

The boy stood in the doorway and watched as Elijah stacked wood on the porch. Rather than entering the cabin, he called through the door. "Miss Cora, I better hurry along home. My wife will be worried about me. I'll just take a piece of fried meat if it's done yet and nibble on it along the way. I'll leave that other for you."

She handed him a piece of charred meat. "I didn't have no lard to fry hit," she apologized, "so I roasted hit over the fire."

"It'll be fine—"

He turned to look as a horse came up the narrow trail. Elijah let the meat fall as his hands tightened on the shotgun. Jared Rawlings, with rifle drawn, stopped the horse and raked him with angry eyes.

"Loring, yo're pretty new-married to go tom-catting."

Elijah's eyes smoldered. "Don't measure me with your yardstick." He held the gun ready.

The door opened, and Cora stepped onto the porch. "Now, Jared, honey," she wheedled, "you got no call to say such. He never even come in the house, just cut me a jag of wood and give me some bear meat. He was leavin' just as you rode up." She looked nervously at the two bristled men. "Come on in out of the wet. Hit's starting to rain again."

Elijah watched Jared's eyes. They flickered with temptation and then hesitated. Elijah kept a thumb on the hammers, but he would not shoot unless he had to with the boy and woman looking on. He stepped back slowly, all the while keeping Jared in view. The big man shot him a surly look, dismounted, took a pack of foodstuff from the back of the saddle, and entered the cabin.

"Reckon I won't have to feed her after all," muttered Elijah. It galled him to picture Jared Rawlings feasting on fresh bear meat. He glowered at the bony hound gobbling the piece he had dropped. Keeping a sharp lookout he backed from the yard. He wouldn't put it past Jared to shoot through the window.

The first two weeks of December were pleasant, but there was a promise of worse to come in the low-lying clouds and geese hurrying south. Elijah took time out to go hunting again. The bear meat had not gone far—not after he had shared it with Ma, Granny, Cousin Jenny, and Cindy's folks. The geese flew too high, but he killed a skinny doe. It was evident that the animals had also suffered from the drought.

As Christmas drew near, wind blew over the north hills bringing cold rain along. Thanks to Elijah's diligence, the cabin was warm and dry.

He blew on his hands and held them toward the fireplace. After giving his shoulder a loving pat, Cindy stepped around him on her way to stir a kettle hanging over the blaze. He studied her face. She had grown lovelier in the past month. As with him, marriage seemed to agree with her completely. And he had not married a lazy woman. She rarely sat down and even then she put her hands to some kind of needlework—such as whatever it was she knitted on the sly and hid each time he entered the room. A Christmas present for him, no doubt.

As her face grew red from the heat, she lifted her apron and wiped her brow. "Supper will be ready soon," she said. "The beans are tender and the meat's 'most done."

"That deer wasn't fat, but it makes good-smelling meat," he commented.

"Skinny or not, I'm glad you got it. We'll have plenty of meat for a while."

He snorted. "That and a few dried beans, few bushels of grubby potatoes, and that hill of cabbage won't last long."

"We'll make do," she said. "The good Lord will provide."

"I reckon so," he said and then changed the subject. "Cindy, I've got my work pretty well caught up. I've been thinking I ought to go to town."

Her eyes widened. "In this weather? Why in the world? There's nothing we need—nothing that is still on the shelves anyway—and no money to buy it with if there was. With the roads being so bad lately, I doubt there's much chance of news."

"Probably not," he agreed. "I have another reason." He paused a minute. "Remember, a couple of months back, when we found Bessie Hadley's broach in that pouch Lew Willis wore around his neck?

She frowned at the odd turn of conversation. "I've tried putting that awful day out of mind. That insane Lew almost killed us both—and would have if you hadn't killed him instead."

Elijah stared into the fire. "I keep thinking about how all those years ago Dub got hung for Bessie's murder. He testified at the trial that the broach was missing. He said she always wore it and the killer must have stolen it. Since it wasn't valuable, the sheriff didn't think it had anything to do with the crime. The day of the murder I saw Lew in the woods all covered with blood. I was just a kid, so no one took me seriously when I said he did it. Even Pa laughed. He thought it was deer blood because Lew had just killed a deer. But when I saw the broach in his pouch, I knew he was the murderer."

Cindy shuddered. "He always was a odd one—spellbound by shiny stuff the way a coon is. I reckon he just couldn't resist taking it."

"I figure the same thing." Elijah nodded. He looked up to meet her absorbed gaze. "Old man Hadley needs to know his son was no murderer—"

"And that poor little boy!" she interrupted. "He thinks his pa killed his ma. Yes, Elijah, you should go."

He stood. "I'll leave tomorrow, first light. If there's no trouble I'll just be gone a couple of days. Likely I'll spend the night with Aunt Opal. I'd like to check on her anyway, see how she and the children are making out. And if you see Ma, tell her I'll check to see if there's any word about Cousin Nelda."

"I will. Be sure you wear plenty of warm clothes," she added. "And I'll pack you a bite of food to take along." Her mind was already worrying on that. She should have cooked more venison. There was hardly enough to pack.

The next morning when Elijah stepped from the house his breath was a white cloud in the frosty dawn. Although the sky had yellowed in the east, the ridges and hollows were blue shadows. The crisp ground crunched beneath his boots. It would be a cold ride. He was grateful for the heavy coat Granny had given him, snug and sturdy, made from the wool of her sheep.

The broad-backed red mule came trotting when he opened the barnyard gate. A small handful of corn held him docile while Elijah forced in the bit and pulled ears through the bridle. As he threw on blanket and saddle, a sharp odor rose, but the mule's smell was not unpleasant to him.

Before mounting, he stopped by the house. Cindy stood on the porch. His heart squeezed seeing her there. Face gentle with sleep and golden-brown hair loose and flowing, she was prettier than a morning glory flower turned toward the sun.

She held out a parcel. "Here's some meat and cornbread—enough for a couple of days." She bit her lip. "You'll be careful?"

"Of course. I'll be back in no time."

Worry still darkened her eyes. "I wish you'd get Billy or even Caleb to ride along. Hit's not safe going anywhere alone."

Elijah smoothed back her hair. "I'll be fine. I have the rifle and plenty of shot and powder." He patted the shot pouch hanging from his belt. "I left the shotgun for you. Keep it close."

She nodded and said no more. But after a long kiss, she hung onto his lapels for a moment longer.

He climbed into the saddle and turned the mule. Where the trail dropped below the ridge he looked back. She still stood on the porch with her hand raised. He waved back. Already feeling anxious to return, he gave an inward smile imagining her surprise upon seeing—if he was successful in finding any—glass for the front windows. He intended to borrow the wagon from Caleb and a blanket from Granny to cushion the panes. Even though Christmas was just a few days away, it would be hard keeping the secret.

An hour later, with the mule now hitched to Caleb's wagon, he was finally underway. Granny had insisted he drink a cup of parched corn coffee while she warmed rocks and then wrapped them in gunnysacks to keep his feet warm. He had to admit the heat was welcome. As he forded Little Piney Creek, the sun shone through naked hardwoods and glistened the lazy water, but it lent no warmth.

He leaned forward, elbows propped on knees with the reins held loosely in calloused hands, while he ruminated on Caleb's news. He knew Aunt Opal was struggling to feed her brood of younguns since Uncle Jim got killed. But he was surprised to learn she had packed up and headed for Louisiana to join her kin. It was a long trip anytime of year but especially in frigid weather. Hopefully, she would have no misfortune along the way. She had had enough of that to last a lifetime.

Just then he passed the turnoff leading to the Lucas hovel, empty now and falling in since the occupants had returned to Georgia. He scowled thinking of Cousin Ruby, who had married into that sorry clan. It was no surprise when Harley Lucas deserted her and the baby. He wondered if she had gone to Georgia with Harley's folks or to Louisiana with her ma. Personally, Elijah was glad to be shed of all the Lucas clan, but he reckoned Ruby was heartbroken.

He shook his head. Marrying the wrong person would be hell on earth. *Couldn't ask for better than Cindy,* he thought as his blood rushed with longing to be home again. He slapped the reins against the mule and grumbled good-naturedly, "Get up there! You keep lollygagging, we won't be back for Christmas."

Cindy watched the mule's broad rump pass from sight. The air was cold, but it was a shiver of dread that traced her spine. She pursed her lips. "Cindy, yo're being a goose!" she scolded. "He lasted two years of war. Likely he'll survive a trip to Clarksville!" But she knew she'd not breathe easy until he returned.

With the idea of staying busy, she frowned and looked back inside. Most of the laundry was done. She had already patched Elijah's work coat. The floor could use a good scrubbing, and there was a basket of socks that needed darning.

Reckon I'll—

Suddenly she gripped the doorframe and groaned. Sweat popped out on her brow. In two quick steps she reached the end of the porch just in time to retch. Recurring waves of nausea made her knees weak. When her stomach was finally empty, she leaned against the wall, shaken and spent.

"Must have eat something bad," she muttered. "Sure hope Elijah ain't—"

Then a slow smile replaced the worry creases around her mouth. *It's mighty soon,* she thought. *But it could be.* She recalled she had felt queasy the last two mornings. Both times it had worsened when she smelled meat frying. Her smile broadened, then abruptly faded. She thought Elijah would be happy, but it would mean more hardship, another mouth to feed when food was already scarce. She bit her lip while gazing toward the far wooded ridge. Abruptly, she pulled her shawl tight, got the shotgun, and headed for Granny's. Although the old woman was Elijah's granny, she found it easier talking to her than to Ma. Granny would comfort. Ma would worry.

With each step in the frosty air, she felt better. The gray hardwoods were bare now except for the few leaves still clinging stubbornly to the oaks. The ridges were dotted with tall pines and cedars that pushed into the sky, bold and proud. Her spirits lifted just seeing them.

Taking a shortcut, she left the trail and cut through the woods. The exercise warmed her, and she let the shawl fall low off her shoulders. A few feet away a buck bolted, running low to the ground and disappearing in a flash. As she passed near a pool formed by a trickle of water running downhill over craggy rocks, she stopped and looked back. Absentmindedly, she broke a limb of spicebush growing at the water's edge and, one after another, began plucking the elongated red berries from the limb.

What if she was mistaken? What if it was just a touch of stomach trouble? Then she'd feel foolish, having rushed to Granny's. She had half a mind to turn back.

Straight ahead a long curl of smoke trailed upward from Granny's chimney. She walked on. It would be a shame to get this close and not say howdy.

The neat gray cabin sat at the edge of a cornfield dotted with spindly, waist-high stalks robbed by drought. Neatly stacked firewood testified of recent hard labor. Several wooly white sheep with black muzzles grazed in the small pasture near the cellar.

Cindy had almost reached the porch when a solitary figure stepped through the front door and into the sunlight. Chagrined, she stopped dead in her tracks. She had forgotten that Billy would be here! When he nodded, she raised the shawl onto her shoulders and gathered it tighter. "I come…came" she stammered, "to see Granny."

"Glad to see you got a gun," he said. "Granny's inside. Reckon after listening to Ma's whining all morning, she'll be glad for some pleasant company." Then he stepped past and continued on his way. With puckered brow, she watched him cross the cornfield in long, determined strides. She turned back as the door opened.

"Well, howdy, Miss Cindy," said Caleb merrily as he exited the cabin. "Ain't you a sight for sore eyes! Not a prettier gal in the country. Iffen I was forty years younger and unattached, I'd a give Lige a run fer his money."

She smiled and glanced inside. "Granny busy?" she asked.

"Ma is always busy. But she'll be glad fer company. Viola ain't well this morning. She's still abed. But Ma is at the loom weaving. Go on inside."

She was not surprised to hear Viola was ailing. Viola's ill health—punctuated with timely recoveries just before a party or a trip to town—was legendary.

Cindy turned her head when a sheep bleated. "The sheep look to be doing good," she observed. "It's a puzzle to me how they never got took right along with all the hogs and cattle."

Caleb chuckled. "Ma says hit was her prayers, but I figure more likely them foragers never cottoned to dressin' out the critters. They're a plague to dress unless they're fresh sheered."

Cindy called out and then stepped inside. A large spinning wheel and homemade loom shared the cramped but neat quarters with table, chairs, benches, and a large bed with woven blue coverlet at the far end of the room.

A small blaze glowed in the cavernous rock fireplace, and the smell of breakfast's fried pork hung in the air. This time the odor did not make her queasy.

Granny sat in a chair drawn near the loom in a pool of sunlight coming through the window. The sturdy homemade loom held alternating rows of rose and buff yarn. Her face crinkled into a smile.

"Welcome! You look right pert this morning. There's hot water on the fire and some mint in that tin yonder." She pointed to a tin on a shelf near the fireplace. "Fix us both a cup of tea while I finish this here row, and then we'll have a good visit."

As Cindy crossed the floor, Granny's sharp eyes studied her. Then she lowered them to the weaving and gave a knowing smile.

"Yer pa was over here yesterdee. Whittled these-here buttons fer me." She nodded toward a small heap of glossy wooden buttons in a dish. "I shore was glad to get 'em. Caleb said there weren't a button left in the mercantile, ner a sewing needle neither. May Sorrels borrowed my needle, and she ain't brung it back yet. I only got one left. I ain't loaning hit to no one. I asked Simon could he whittle needles. He allowed as how he could. But he said they'd be too big fer fine sewing."

Cindy poured water over the fragrant mint. She paused to watch as the old woman tamped the rose-colored thread firmly in place. She itched to sit at the loom. Granny was teaching her, and she was catching on fast. She loved the rhythm of the treadles and making the shuttle pass back and forth designing something beautiful.

"There now. Ain't this a purty color? Ain't nothing like red oak bark and sumac fer making a good fast dye." Granny stood and hobbled to the table, the rags on her feet muffling her steps. She groaned and dropped into a chair. "Weather's gonna change. My joints is aching."

Cindy gave a frowning glance out the window. The sun stood in cloudless blue, but Granny's joints were reliable prophets. "I hope Elijah makes it home first. This time of the year it's apt to sleet or snow." Then she added, "Likely he'll make it back tomorrow by dark. That's a fast-gaited mule he's riding."

Granny stayed mute about the wagon the mule was pulling. Elijah wanted to surprise Cindy with some window glass, and she was not about to spoil his fun. Besides, she figured, he likely would make it home by dark.

"How you been feelin'?" she asked.

Cindy blinked. "Just fine."

Granny took a sip of tea. She sat the heavy mug down. "Even in the mornings?" When Cindy's cheeks grew rosy, she cackled. "I knowed it!"

"But, Granny," she protested, "it's too soon to tell—"

Granny shook her head. "Not for old eyes like mine. I've seed a heap of women in the family way. Most usual I can guess after a month. A body's face just glows, and there's the slightest little hitch to the step."

Cindy beamed. "I've never been so happy." Then she paused. "Do you think Elijah will be? I mean with times so hard and all?"

Granny snorted. "He'll be proud as a strutting rooster."

Cindy's apprehension melted. "Oh, I'm glad you think so! Now I can't wait to tell him." She briefly laid a hand on her stomach. "I hope it's a boy. Elijah would like a son."

"Every man wants a son," agreed Granny. "But a daughter is a great comfort to a woman."

Cindy reached across the table and patted the bony arm. She knew Granny still grieved over a long-dead daughter. "Then I just might have a girl for you to spoil."

Granny gave a quivery smile. "I'd like that. Yes, I would. I better get some soft yarn ready. We need to do some knittin.'"

"Reckon I could make a little coverlet on the loom?"

Granny's face softened. "I reckon so. That'll give me a good excuse to see more of ya."

Cindy stood and hugged her. Although she had never known her own grandmothers, she doubted she would have loved them more. Even though Granny could be vexing and at times outspoken and brash, her heart was solid gold.

"My work is waiting. I best get back."

Granny patted her arm, and her eyes shone. "Come ever chance you can. I'll hurry this piece of cloth so's you can start on that coverlet right away."

"Don't rush yourself." Cindy chuckled. "We got about eight months to go."

Her step was light on the trail home. With happy thoughts awhirl, she didn't notice low clouds gathering in the west.

As Elijah crossed the bridge over Spadra Creek, the sun lay low in the west, washing the sky scarlet. With the exception of an old man napping in a straight-backed chair in front of the mercantile, the small town looked deserted. He bypassed the brick and clapboard buildings toeing Main and headed directly for a small shack, just a short ways away and huddled near the creek. In the still air, smoke rose straight up from the chimney into the rosy sky above. A bony hound lay on the porch, not stirring. Elijah started to climb the two rickety steps and then stopped dead in his tracks just as the door opened.

"You need something, mister?"

The dark eyes were young, unfriendly, and suspicious in a handsome face looking too old for its years.

Elijah pointed to the dog. "Isn't that old Sirius, the Hortons' hound?" As the boy's eyes narrowed more, Elijah quickly added. "The Hortons are my kin."

The harsh expression softened but slightly. "Yeah, I'm keeping him for Miz Nelda while she's away on business."

"I see." He wanted to ask where and on what business. The young chin had jutted again, so he refrained.

"What you want?"

"Is your grandpa home? I have business with him."

Not taking his eyes from Elijah, the boy called over his shoulder. "*Hey, Grandpa!*" When there was no answer, he shouted louder until finally a quivery voice answered and a thin, stooped old man, with piercing eyes and a white beard worthy of a prophet, hobbled to the door.

"Can I he'p ya?" he asked, sounding not as belligerent as the youth but equally suspicious.

Elijah was not surprised—considering the bushwhacking and looting that had recently taken place in Johnson County. He swept off the wide-brimmed brown hat.

"Mr. Hadley, I'm Elijah Loring, from over on Little Piney Creek."

Recognition altered the rigid face. "Land sakes alive! Why didn't ya say so! Come in, come in." He stepped aside. "David, get this fellow a ch'ir and set hit here near the fire." He glanced back at Elijah. "Ya must be froze."

"A fire will feel good," he admitted and stepped inside. Only then did he see the decrepit musket in David's hands, held out of sight behind the door.

The boy propped the gun in the corner, got a chair, and placed it near the fireplace.

Mr. Hadley used the poker to stir up the small blaze. "Boy, throw on another log 'er two," he ordered. Then he turned to Elijah. "Plum stingy with wood—that boy is. 'Course, I don't much fault him. I can't help with the cutting now that I'm so stove up with the rheumatis." He sat down in a cane-bottom rocking chair nearby. "How's yer Uncle Caleb?"

"Fine, sir. He says howdy."

The old man nodded. "Always liked Caleb Tanner."

Elijah hunched over and held his hands to the fire. "I have some news for you—good news." Then he straightened and glanced over. "It's about your son."

The rocker stopped mid-squeak. The old man's face was a still mask, but the blue-veined hands gripping the chair arms grew white knuckled.

"He didn't kill his wife. I know who did. It was Lew Willis, a crazy man who lived in the mountains." Elijah hurried on with an abbreviated version and ended with how, in self-defense, he had killed Lew.

Enos Hadley swallowed. Then his face melted like hot wax. As he hung his head, his shoulders shook. "I knowed he never done it," he whispered huskily. "I told 'em he was innocent. No one would listen. I stood by while they hung him…hung my boy. And knowing all along, he never done it."

Elijah looked up at David. He stood statue still behind the old man's chair, his face stoic, but tears rimmed his eyes. Feeling Elijah's eyes, he turned quickly away and passed a ragged sleeve across his face.

Elijah stood. He worried the hat in his hands. "Well, I'll be going. I just figured you ought to know." He stepped forward. Then he hesitated. "I was wondering about my cousin Nelda. Before the war we were pretty close. I've not heard from her in a long while."

The old man raised his tear-streaked face. "You knowed yer aunt and uncle both died?"

Elijah nodded. "Yeah. Uncle Caleb brought the word a while back. Ma took it hard." Then he asked, "Did Nelda say where she was going?"

"Naw," David said, suddenly inclined to be helpful, "and I never asked. She went downriver on a boat with that darkie gal of hers. Never said where or how long she'd be gone. Just asked me to look after her horse and dog."

"Thank you," said Elijah as he clamped on the hat and headed for the door.

"No, hit's us should be thanking you," called Enos. "And I shore do thank ye."

"Glad to help set things straight," said Elijah. He paused. "Just wish I'd been older and wiser way back yonder. I might have stopped the hanging."

Enos shook his head. "I doubt it. In this-here country, a man's supposed to be innocent until proved guilty. Most usual, tis t'other way around. Feller has to prove he *ain't* guilty. And Dub's fiery temper went strong a'gin him. I warned him time and again…" His voice died, and he rubbed a hand over his mouth. Then he added in a choked voice, "I never faulted the jury. They done the best they knowed."

Elijah recalled that Bessie often had bruises. Folks thought ill of a wife-beater. That had gone against Dub at the trial.

The old man cocked his head. "With all your kin gone away, you got a place to pass the night?"

"I figured to make camp in the wagon yard."

The old man waved a hand in protest. "Too cold fer that!"

Elijah chuckled. "I've slept on frozen ground without a blanket. General Van Dorn seemed to think that toughened a fellow up."

Enos snorted. "Yer tough enough. You'll pass tonight here with us. David, put his wagon in the shed and turn the mule loose in the lot. I'll fetch ye a quilt to throw here next to the fire.

"Thank you, sir, but I brought quilts with me."

Elijah took the hat off and sat back down. He had no objections to the arrangement. He had dreaded camping in the cold. But when the small blaze in the fireplace was finally banked with ashes and Elijah bedded down on quilts from the wagon, cold air seeped through broad cracks in the floor and between the logs where the chinking had fallen out. He grunted and wrapped the quilts tighter around his shoulders.

Old Mr. Hadley, who was usually loquacious, had been mostly silent and gone to bed early. David had slipped out a few minutes shortly thereafter with worn boots tucked under his arm. Elijah wondered where the boy had gone. He was too young to have a girl…thirteen at the most. Perhaps he had taken old Sirius chasing coons. On second thought, he concluded, Sirius probably wouldn't leave the porch. The hound looked old as Methuselah.

Elijah's mind wandered, jumping from topic to topic, as it did when he lay down—unless he had marched or plowed all day and was too bone-weary to crawl. He had always envied Pa his ability to sleep if his head barely touched a pillow. Not him. He had to crack open the day again like a hard-shelled walnut and pry out each kernel to re-taste the bitter and the sweet.

Now he wondered where his cousin Nelda had gone. Probably north. She and Uncle Phillip had made no secret of their Union loyalties. In spite of that, they had always been two of Elijah's favorites. He felt no malice for his kin who favored the Union. Pa had died fighting

Confederate, but both Uncle Jim and Phillip, for Union. It was the way of men—to differ and if the difference grew heated enough, to fight. Elijah saw no cause for hate. The house burning and persecution of Union families in Clarksville went against his grain.

He muttered one of Granny's oft-quoted scriptures, "*Man is born into trouble as the sparks fly upward.*" Personally, he could never figure out why creation had seemed a good idea to God in the first place—not that he wasn't glad to be alive. He was. But there was an almighty lot of suffering to dwarf the good. He had seen more than his share on the battlefields at Pea Ridge and Prairie Grove and the other places his feet had tramped while first in Van Dorn's and then in Hindman's army. Sometimes yet he woke covered in clammy sweat and shaking from reliving the carnage.

He rolled over with a sigh. It was the first night he and Cindy had spent apart. He missed her soft flesh curved next to him, her silky hair spread out on the pillow. He punched up the pillow that Enos had provided, but it was still too thin to soften the hard floor.

Breakfast consisted of a thin bowl of cornmeal mush without any sweetening. There were steaming cups of Confederate coffee—corn parched and then boiled.

"Poor fare," conceded Enos, "but hit fills a holler spot better than nothin.'"

"It does," Elijah agreed and meant it. All too well he knew the pain of an empty stomach. "Any news around town?" he asked the boy who had returned home around midnight, on tiptoe and carrying the boots.

David glanced up from slurping a spoonful of thin mush. "Ask Grandpa. He spends most days sitting at the mercantile.

Enos belched. "None to speak of. A few Fed patrols comes and goes, but none stays. Captain Hill—a relation to John Hill, yer pappy's colonel—rid in with some men he gathered up to form a new company. I knowed a few— Mills and Cravens and Hardwick. Not sure where the rest come from. Ain't much but women and kids left in town. Men who ain't already in the army is as scarce as hen's teeth, and they stick close to home. Nothing left in these dang stores to buy no-how."

Elijah swallowed the bitter coffee. "I was hoping to buy some panes of window glass. Know of any?"

Enos rubbed his chin. "Well, now…" He dragged the words slowly. "Emmitt used to keep some in the back storeroom. Might have some left. Doubt they's much call fer winderglass since this-here conflabberation started."

Elijah took the outlandish word in stride. Enos invented words as he went.

He stood. "I sure do thank you for the hospitality." He shook Enos' bony hand. "Ever out my way, stop in." He put on his hat. "I'll go see if Emmitt has a few panes of glass left."

Enos raised a parting hand. He swallowed before speaking. His voice roughened with emotion. "You tell 'em down at the store that Dub never done it."

"I'll do that, sir. I surely will."

Elijah stepped outside to see a ragged V of geese flying high and fast. Clouds obscured the sun and the air was as sharp as a knife. He buttoned the coat and pulled the hat brim lower. The mule came willingly, hoping for a bite of grain. When none was forthcoming, he stood placid while Elijah hitched up.

After turning onto Main, he ruminated how Clarksville was a far cry from the bustling, prosperous town of two years ago—stores now vacant, windows busted and boarded, and the few women he passed, gaunt, big-eyed, and nervous. As he drove slowly past the newspaper office, his stomach tightened. When he was a kid, he and Pa never came to town without stopping in to jaw with Uncle Phillip over a cup of coffee. Those times were gone forever. Oh, the stores might reopen someday, and some other enterprising newspaperman might take Uncle Phillip's place, dust off the press, and put out another edition; but Pa and Uncle Phillip would not be here to see it. He thought of all the men he had seen fall on the battlefields across Arkansas.

"And this damned war not over yet," he muttered.

A trip to town had once been his biggest pleasure. Now he couldn't wait to leave.

The owner of the mercantile, Emmitt Gossett, leaned with beefy arms braced on the counter, big belly overlapping. He straightened as Elijah walked through the door and set the bell tinkling.

"Howdy, Emmitt."

Emmitt stared hard.

"Didn't reckon I'd changed that much," Elijah said with a quick laugh.

"Why! Ned Loring's boy, Lige." He eyed him up and down. "Course, you're no boy now. And from the look of you, lean and ornery as a razorback hog." He grinned and stuck out his hand. "Haven't seen you in a coon's age. How are things in your neck of the woods?"

Elijah shook his hand. "Pretty fair, Emmitt. Yourself?"

He snorted and waved a hand to indicate the bare room. "No customers, nothing to sell…things couldn't be better," he replied snidely. "And I hear there'll likely be new customers soon—a Yankee garrison planned for right here in Clarksville. Can you believe it?" Emmitt's breath retained the musty tang of liquor.

Elijah's brows rose in agreement. "You aim to stick around?"

He shrugged. "This is home. I got no place else to go. No family. Truth is, Elijah, I keep the doors open so my friends will drop by. Trouble is too many of them are dead and gone."

When Emmitt's eyes filled and his chin began to wobble, Elijah glanced away. He had no desire to see Emmitt shame himself because he had taken a nip too early in the morning.

He hurriedly said, "You might have what I'm shopping for. Any window glass in that back room of yours? I need enough panes for four windows."

"Naw. I sold all I had to Seth Brown for that two-story he was building at the edge of town." Emmitt rubbed his chin. "Come to think of it—he never finished it. Got killed at Wilson's Creek and his widow still lives in the little house. If some riff-raff hasn't broken out the windows, she might sell you the glass. Especially if you've got hard cash." Emmitt looked curious.

Elijah wanted no false rumors started about Elijah Loring having a bag full of money. "Not much," he said. "Just a couple of dollars. Maybe it'll be enough. Where is the widow's house?"

Emmitt stepped outside and pointed. "See that peaked roof yonder? Her house is the little clapboard just behind."

Elijah stuck out his hand again. Before climbing into the wagon he remembered to add, "By the way, Emmitt, reckon you heard about that run-in I had with Lew Willis?"

Emmitt nodded.

"Remember that buckskin bag he wore around his neck? Well, it had Bessie Hadley's broach inside—the one Dub said the killer must have stolen. Appears he was right."

Emmitt paled. Only then did Elijah remember that Emmitt had sat on the jury.

"Mr. Hadley wants folks to know."

Emmitt nodded, still looking dumbfounded. "I'll get the word out. This will go hard on us folks who sat on the jury."

"Maybe it should," said Elijah before slapping the reins on the mule's rump.

He knocked and found the widow and her six young children, one of whom peeped behind his mother's threadbare skirt when she answered the door. The careworn woman quickly agreed to sell the windowpanes. Although he had planned an early start home, he spent a long while at the painstaking task of removing the panes from the unfinished skeleton. The children, as shy as woodland creatures, crept near to watch his progress. Finally the glass lay securely wrapped in the wagon bed, padded in Granny's thick quilts. He hoped it survived the jostling trip over rutted trails.

Suddenly he had a thought and hurried away to speak to the widow.

She answered the first rap on the door.

"Ma'am, I was wondering if you'd be interested in selling some of that lumber."

Her eyes darted to the unfinished house and abruptly filled with pain. Her lips pressed together. Then she took a deep breath. "May as well sell it," she said sadly, "before some marauder burns it down. Yes. I'll sell it all if you want to tear it down. I already sold what wasn't nailed up."

"How much would you want for it?" he asked.

When she named a reasonable price, he nodded. "I don't have that much yet…but if it's all right with you, I'll pay for a few boards along as I can afford them."

"That'll be fine."

He held out three more bills of his quickly dwindling sum. "I can only haul a few now. It may be a while before I get back to town. You have a hammer I can borrow for a few minutes?"

She took the money and then returned shortly with a hammer.

"It would have been a fine house…" She left the sentence hanging and shut the door.

Elijah hated tearing her dream apart. But he figured the cash would help keep her family alive.

He unloaded the glass, put the boards into the bottom of the wagon, and reloaded the glass. The sun had passed its zenith by the time he turned back onto Main. He was surprised to see a large group of horsemen. He recognized Hardwick and Mills and his jaw hardened. He pulled the rifle closer. If they tried conscripting either him or his wagon, they'd have a fight on their hands.

Mills espied him and rode over. "Howdy, Loring." His eyes were bright with excitement. "You're just in the nick of time to give us a hand. Big group of Yankees—over a hundred of 'em— rode into town a bit ago and then headed out again. We're on their trail. We'll need every man and rifle we can scrape together."

"Wish you luck, but I'm not coming." Elijah gathered the reins. "I put in my time. Came through alive, and I'm not tempting fate again. I'm heading home."

Mills's lip curled. "To my way of thinking, the job's not finished until the last Yankee is dead!"

"Like I said—I wish you boys luck." He slapped the reins against the mule but kept a hand on the rifle.

With a sour look, Mills watched him go and then called, "Don't ever expect any help from us!"

All day a grin hovered. And when Cindy thought about sharing the news with Elijah, it became a full-blown smile. Down on her knees, she dipped the scrub brush into the bucket of soapy water and inhaled the clean soapy scent. For a moment she held the brush idle. In her mind's eye, a cradle was drawn near the fire and two chubby fists waved in firelight while she and Elijah hovered near, crooning to a darling boy who looked just like his pa.

The dream quickly faded as she looked around and grew pensive. In spite of the addition of colorful quilts and rugs, the cabin was still dark and small and not well situated for an infant. It was too bad they could not make improvements before the baby came. She did so love light and sunshine. From the first day here she had prayed for larger windows with real glass panes rather than the thin oilcloth stretched over the small holes now. Of course it was a selfish prayer. There were troubles aplenty in the world and much else to pray about, but she figured God didn't mind what a body asked for, just so long as you gracefully took no for an answer if need be.

By noon the tiny room was spotless. Cindy threw the last bucket of dirty water outside. She gave a worried look at the cold, gray sky and hoped falling weather would hold off until Elijah made it home.

She was tired and ravenous. Although most of the breakfast leftovers had gone into Elijah's knapsack, there was a bit of cold pork left. She wolfed it down along with some cornbread.

"Hunger is the best sauce," she muttered her ma's old saying and thought how true it must be, for even the cold cornbread was delicious.

Just then she threw up her head. Through the closed door came the sound of approaching horses. Again she wished for glass windows. It was bothersome not being able to see. Before the riders had reached the yard, she had opened the door with shotgun in hand. Without stepping onto the porch, she peered from the front door. As the group rode into sight, she relaxed the tight grip on the gun. It was only Pa's former company out patrolling. Jared Rawlings was in the lead. She had heard he was captain now that Pa had resigned. As his eyes went over her, she became aware of her mussed hair and wet, soiled dress.

He looked past her into the cabin. "Your man not home?" The tone was insulting, as he had meant it to be.

She drew up tall. She replied in clipped words, "You need something?"

"Where is he?"

"Minding his own business."

While most of the others appeared uncomfortable, Jared's eyes glittered. "Any rebel's whereabouts is our business," he snapped. "He'd better watch himself. I intend keeping a close eye on him."

Red spots appeared in Cindy's cheeks. She moved the gun slightly and scowled at him. "You best watch yerself, Jared Rawlings. Elijah ain't no one to rile. Ask those men riding with you. They know. You ain't careful you'll bite off more than you can chew."

Jared's face purpled. "Just tell him what I said." He kicked his mount and galloped away.

With deference, several men nodded to her, and Miles Carol doffed his hat.

"Sorry to bother you, ma'am."

She acknowledged his apology with a dip of her head, and then as the hoof beats pounded away, she leaned against the door jam. Still shaking with anger, she looked after them. Jared was trouble. Months ago he had been insulted when she refused his marriage proposal. But he had never loved her. She doubted he knew the meaning of the word.

Then her anger drained away and an apprehensive shiver gave her arms goose flesh. In a face-to-face clash no doubt Elijah could handle Jared. But Jared was like a skulking dog. He'd wait until Elijah's back was turned and then he'd pounce.

A shadow fell. As her head jerked up, she gasped. Rifle in hand, Billy had stepped around the edge of the cabin.

He stopped near the porch.

"You all right?"

"Yes," she answered through white lips.

"I told Lige I'd keep an eye on things." He looked down the trail and then he studied her face. "You handled that real good."

Cindy set down the gun and briefly put a hand over her pounding heart. *That Billy moved as quiet as an Indian.* It was unsettling to know a body could get that close without discovery.

"Won't ya sit a spell," she invited.

"Thanks, but I'll keep an eye out around here for a while. You best get on back inside by the fire."

She thanked him, went inside, and shut the door. As an afterthought, she drew in the latchstring. She wouldn't put it past Jared to sneak back.

All afternoon she sat in the rocking chair, straining her eyes in the dimness of the cloudy day, to darn and to mend. The task comforted, bringing normalcy to the nerve-racking day. Elijah's worn socks, shirts, and trousers seemed tangible proof that he would soon return. With stern determination, she rejected any thought to the contrary. In spite of that, as persistent as gnats, the worries hovered. Breathing a prayer, she gathered a shirt close and hugged and kissed it.

"If someone saw me, they'd think I was tetched," she muttered. Then, with a sigh, she thought, *a dragging day like this was enough to make a body crazy*.

Daylight faded early in December, even high atop the ridge. Today, due to clouds, it faded even faster. She stepped onto the porch and frowned. Rising wind stung her cheeks and filled her nostrils with sharp clean air. Although she knew it was useless, her gaze searched the road for Elijah. Of course he could not possibly arrive before the next afternoon, but she hoped he would hurry. Then she sucked in a worried breath and prayed he would not meet Jared on the trail.

Inside, the room was dark. She could barely make out the outline of table, chairs, bench, and tall bedposts. Without wasting candles, she banked the coals in the fireplace deep with ash, and then she retired early, only to stare at dark rafters and listen to wind plucking at shingles and oilcloth-covered windows. As the oilcloth sucked in and out with each sharp gust, she prayed for Elijah, for all her loved ones, and placing a hand on her middle, she prayed for the little one.

Her bed had never felt so cold. It was not, she knew, the chilled cabin, but Elijah's empty place alongside her. For weeks they had slept spooned together. Not even a pile of Granny's wool coverlets could fill that void. She fluffed the pillow, rolled over, and willed morning to hurry. Wind clawing at the cabin made a poor lullaby.

In semi-darkness, she awakened to frost on the rough floorboards. With gritted teeth, she jumped from the bed and hastened into petticoats, dress, socks, shoes, and shawl. With fingers stiff and clumsy on the poker, she finally stirred the buried coals to life. An hour later her breath still made a white cloud. Ever so slowly, the blaze chased winter from the room.

She ate a tasteless breakfast of mush but soon hurried outside to lose it all. Tall pines swayed in the wind while dim sun remained wrapped in a dismal quilt of gray. In the biting cold she hung onto the porch post and fought waves of nausea. The chill felt good on her hot face. When something stung her cheek, she groaned. It was beginning to sleet.

Before queasiness had completely abated, the wind drove her inside. Soon snowy ice pellets peppered the log walls and occasionally found their way down the chimney to sizzle in the fire. Her stomach began to feel normal, but her nerves remained taut.

The mending was done. The cabin was spotless. There was not much laundry, for she had done it three days before. Now she drew out the thin needles sticking from a ball of yarn. She ran the soft thread through her hand. It would make a fine, tiny blanket.

Mid-afternoon, she peered through the door at the shadowy trail. Both land and trees were covered in white. Heavy flakes swirled in the snowy dusk.

Some little thing delayed him. Nothing serious. At least that is what she told herself. Her stomach was a tight knot. She paced the dim room. No matter how much wood she piled on, cold crept in like a thief. Finally she banked the fire, went to bed, and lay shivering under the quilts. It was small comfort to have cabin walls holding the storm at bay when Elijah might be caught in the fury. If he were not home by morning, she would walk to Granny's and tell Billy. Her eyes widened at the irony. The silent, stern man made her ill at ease, and yet somehow she knew he would be a rock to lean on.

Chapter 4

Elijah, frowning, watched the cloudbank darken in the west. It was going to snow. He hunkered deeper in the coat and slapped the reins against the mule's sides. The animal sped up, but barely. The mule knew it was foolhardy to leave shelter on such a day. Elijah knew it, too, but he faced the north wind and slapped the reins again. He had marched toward Pea Ridge in worse. Besides it would take more than wind and ice to keep him from Cindy.

Sleet soon coated the roadbed. By nightfall the sleet had become blowing snow, but he was still a long way from home. Tall, dead grass growing alongside the trail bent lower under the onslaught. The sure-footed mule plodded through swirling darkness. Occasionally, Elijah climbed down to stamp numb feet. The heavy coat Granny had woven was a bulwark from lashing wind, but in spite of woolen socks, his feet were lumps of misery. Twice he lost the trail and had to depend on the mule to find it. Like a compass, the big, red creature pointed the way.

Even when the reins slackened, the mule went doggedly forward. As a wagon wheel jolted into a hole in the creek bed, Elijah jerked awake. He gathered the reins and then chuckled.

"May as well let you have your head, old boy. Appears as if you did just fine without me. We're almost home."

He took a roundabout route and left the wagon hidden in Caleb's barn. Then he hurried the mule homeward.

The mule's pace quickened. Elijah breathed a relieved sigh when the dim outline of the cabin came into view. All too often, he'd seen ruined cabins with blackened chimneys. It was guilt, he supposed, that made him skittish, for in the army he had been ordered to torch too many houses.

The clock on the mantle was striking three when he tried the door. The latchstring was inside. He raised a fist to knock when the door flew open. Then with feet bare and hair flying, Cindy was in his arms, sobbing.

"I was so scared something had happened to ya!" In the cold darkness, she clung to him.

He shushed her softly and pulled her inside.

"What happened? Are you all right?"

"I'm fine," he assured as her hands went over his face, "except for being half frozen. Light a candle while I poke up the fire." He stirred the coals and handed her a blazing taper.

As she held it close to the wick, her hands shook. "What took ya so long? Was there trouble?"

"None to speak of." He threw on split pine kindling and then knelt to blow on the coals. As the pine caught fire and crackled, he glanced up. "I'm glad I went. Old man Hadley was pretty solemn, but I could tell he was joyful at the news." He stood and threw sticks onto the infant blaze. "The boy, too. He's a strapping young man, now—fine looking too. Has Bessie's good looks."

"I remember she was a handsome woman," agreed Cindy. "Too bad she wasn't a good one, too. If she'd stayed true to her husband, she might be alive today."

He held his hands to the blaze. "Don't judge. I heard Bessie had a hard life."

"You sound like Pa," she said with a half-smile.

"Or my pa," he said. "Pa always looked for the best in folks."

"Well, yo're right," she admitted. "I ought not judge. I don't know the facts, just gossip."

He put his arms around her waist and nuzzled the side of her neck. "I know for a fact that I missed you. Did you miss me?"

"Not a bit," she quipped. "Hardly noticed you was gone."

"That so," he said, seeking her lips.

She laughed and melted against him. "Elijah," she whispered, "I got some good news." Then she drew back and stared at his face in the flickering firelight. "At least I think it's good..."

He saw her flushed cheeks. "Cindy, are you—?"

"Yes," she said, eyes shining.

His broad smile said more than words. He held her tight and stroked her hair.

"Best news I've ever had," he whispered near her ear, "except for when you said you'd marry me."

She snuggled against him like a happy pup. "I just know hit'll be a boy."

"Boy or girl—either is fine with me."

"I reckon you'll have to build a cradle," she said. "Ma said the bush-whackers stole the one she used with us."

"Reckon I can make a fair to middlin' one."

She squeezed his arm. "Make it strong. I aim to give you at least a dozen sons...and a few daughters for good measure."

Cindy bent over the bed to tickle Elijah's nose with the end of her long braid. "Wake up, sleepy head. It's Christmas!" As he rubbed the itch and rolled out of reach, she laughed. She stood and began wrapping the long, single braid around her head. She pinned it into place with four wooden pins. "The sun's been up for an hour. Saint Nicholas left a few minutes ago." She turned so he could admire her new hairpins. "See what he brought me? My hairpins were gettin' right scarce. Good thing Pa's good at whittling or I'd soon have to do like May Sorrels and Zora Pelts and use locust thorns to hold my bun. Ain't these pretty?"

"Yep, but not as pretty as the hair they're holding." He pulled her close for a kiss.

She snuggled next to him. "Pa shook his head at finding you still abed, but I told him you usual' weren't so lazy."

Elijah stretched and groaned. "What do I care what he thinks?"

"If Pa heared you say that, I doubt he'd have left you that present yonder."

Elijah sat up. In the dim light coming through the oilcloth windows, she smiled as he opened one eye and squinted where she pointed.

Both eyes opened. "What is it?"

"A bootjack. Pa made it. You hook the heel of yer boot in that notch in the board and then it pulls off real easy." She gave a huge smile. "Ma sent presents, too. But ya can't have 'em unless you get out of bed, lazy bones."

"Mrs. Loring," he said with mock sternness, "I'll have you know that I was up until the wee hours of the morning finishing your present. Since you insist on calling me ugly names, I'm a good mind not to give it to you."

She sat on the edge of the bed, eyes shining. Pulling her knees up to her chest, she hugged them and tucked the long white gown over bare feet. "What kind of present? Give me a hint."

He tweaked her nose. "Wouldn't you rather see it?"

Her face screwed up in contemplation. "No…I'd rather guess first. That's the most fun."

He laughed. "I believe there's still a lot of little girl in that woman's body."

"I never wanted to know beforehand what I was gettin' for Christmas. Pete would sneak around and try to find out." For a moment her eyes dimmed. "Sometimes he found out. Then all the excitement of wondering would be over." She swallowed. "Christmas is hard on Ma and Pa now—full of memories. I allow that's why Pa was here at the crack of dawn. Ma wants us to come for dinner. I told him Granny had invited us and he looked so sad…" She looked questioning at Elijah. "Well, I told him we might come anyway. Do you think we could?"

He thought for a moment. "I figure we ought to. Ma and Deborah will be at Granny's. We'll stop by there and say howdy, then go on to Polly's. Seeing as how you're the only child they have left, your folks need you at Christmas. Granny will understand. But do you think Simon and Polly have enough food to spare?"

She nodded happily. "Pa even said Ma had a surprise for dinner."

"Oh, yeah, speaking of surprises—I'm supposed to give you some hints." He grinned. "You're wiggling like a pup wanting a bowl of milk."

"Hurry up," she urged. "Give me some hints."

He scratched the stubble of a day's growth of beard. "Let's see…it's useful—"

"That's good," she interrupted. "What else?"

"It moves."

She puckered her brow. "Hit…it moves?"

"Yep."

"How fast?"

"How ever fast you make it."

"Do you hitch it behind a mule?" she asked, imagining a sled. Or maybe Elijah had built some sort of buggy from parts off the old one in Caleb's barn.

"Well, I reckon you could…but it would look pretty foolish."

"How big is it?"

"Oh, about yea big." He held out his hands.

"What color?"

"Cherry wood brown."

"You built something out of that cherry tree Pa cut down last year."

"Yep."

A slow smile spread her face. "You built a cradle for the baby!"

His broad smile was her answer. "Your pa helped. He laid out the pattern and then did the final touches."

"Oh, hurry quick, and bring it in! I want to see it."

He reached for her. "Your feet are frozen. Why don't you come back to bed and let me get them warm?"

She pulled back. "Elijah Loring!" She hit him with a pillow. "Get up from there and go bring in that cradle!"

He chuckled and swung his legs over the edge of the bed. "Woman, this floor's cold. Get your shoes on before you catch cold," he ordered as he pulled pants over long flannel underwear.

While she dressed, he poked up the fire, sending sparks dancing up the chimney. Then he threw on more wood from the small stack near the rock hearth. After pulling on coat and hat, he opened the door and then called, "Come look."

She went to the door and looked out over his shoulder. Large wet flakes sifted down like flour from a sieve, falling straight down without a hint of breeze to stir them. She could barely make out the shape of the barn through the snowy curtain that coated trees and grass and porch. In the blurry whiteness the rail fence zigzagged out of sight, iced on top, she thought, like Ma's egg-white cake frosting.

"Oh, what big flakes! That's the kind that usual' comes in late fall or real early in the spring. Never saw 'em big like that this time of year."

"Pretty, isn't it," he said. "It's not real cold out, but it's damp, so dress warm. Looks like we'll have a white Christmas after all."

She stood a moment and watched until Elijah had disappeared into the old log barn. Then she closed the door and scurried to get the wool scarf from hiding. It was thick and warm. Today, she thought, would be a good day for it.

When he came back inside her eyes lit. "Oh, Elijah!" She reached to touch cherry wood as smooth as satin. "There never was a prettier cradle in the world," she whispered in awe.

"Well, I wouldn't go that far," he said, but his eyes shone with pleasure.

"Just look at all them fancy curlicues on the headboard!" She looked at him with admiration.

He set it on the floor. "Simon did those," he admitted. "I mostly just put it together and sanded and polished it. It is built strong, if I do say so. Ought to last our children and their children."

"Longer than that," she said as her hand ran over it again and then set it rocking in a smooth gentle motion. "It's as well built as Ma's rosewood clock on the mantle and hit's…it's going on six generation." Her eyes grew soft. "Wonder what folks will sleep in this, maybe even a president of the—." She clasped a hand over her mouth and then laughed. "I almost said of the *United States!* Recollect how Mr. Saddler used to tell us at school that one of you boys might become president of the United States. Everybody knowed he was talking about you." She gave him a near worshipful look.

He grunted. "Not much chance of that now, is there? Anyway, that's about the last thing on earth I'd want." He drew her close. "I'd much rather stay right here and help fill up this cradle with big, strong sons and a few beautiful daughters who look just like their ma."

She snuggled against his chest. He still smelled of cold and snow. "We have such a good life, Elijah. We're so blessed."

He smoothed her hair and chuckled. "I could argue with you—this rickety cabin and barely enough food to keep us from starving—but I have to agree. I'm a happy man." He tilted her chin up. "And I'm about to make you a happy woman—." He put a finger to her lips to still the protest. "A happier woman," he corrected himself. "There'll soon be glass in these sorry windows."

She covered her mouth in joyous wonder. "Glass! Where did you get window glass!"

"It's sort of a wedding present from Michael. He gave me some money, and I bought some glass in town."

She clapped her hands like a happy child. "Oh, I prayed that someday…but I never thought—"

"Oh ye of little faith," he teased. "And," he added with twinkling eyes, "there might even be a few more surprises—like some shelves for the kitchen. I'll get busy right after Christmas."

She gave an impish grin and a fake sigh. "I reckon we have to go to Christmas dinner first."

Elijah laid the hammer on the porch rail and looked down the trail. He wiped his hands on a handkerchief and then stuffed it back into a hip pocket. "Step down and come in," he called as tall, lanky Simon dismounted from a mule. "I'm fixing this rickety porch," he said as Simon climbed the steps. "Cindy wants a rail. I told her it'd be a couple of years before a young'un would be old enough—"

Frowning he stopped. His gut tightened at sight of Simon's drawn face.

"What's wrong?"

Simon glanced toward the window where Cindy, with polish cloth in hand, waved through the shining glass. He raised his hand. But his smile was tight and brief. "Let's step out into the yard."

Elijah hurried off the porch and stopped at the edge of the yard.

Simon studied the ground near his worn boots and then raised troubled eyes. "I just had a visit." Then he abruptly changed the subject. "Did you know about that skirmish out near Dick's Branch a while back?"

Elijah's puzzled brows drew together. "Yeah, I heard there were a couple of Federal soldiers killed."

Simon's eyes probed him. "That all you know about it?"

Elijah shrugged. "I was in town the day it happened and heard some Yankees had just left town. Some fellers I know went after them." Then his eyes lightened with understanding. "No, Simon, I didn't join 'em. They invited but I declined."

Simon expelled a deep breath. "Glad to hear it. But there's some saying otherwise. Trouble's brewing. You best keep a sharp lookout."

Elijah's face hardened. "Who's saying what?"

Simon looked him in the eye. "Hit's Jared Rawlings. He's trying to stir the men up agin' you. Matt Carol come by and warned me. He said him and most of the others ain't siding with Jared in this, so maybe won't nothing come of it."

Elijah looked back at the house where Cindy had just stepped outside onto the porch. She was still slender, but there was a slight swelling of abdomen under the blue cotton dress. She shaded her eyes against the January sun lacing gold into her thick, brown hair.

"Elijah, you and Pa, come inside," she called. "I just cooked some sweet potatoes."

"We'll be in directly," he answered. When she smiled and returned inside, he faced Simon.

Simon rubbed his stubbly jaw. "I figure it's likely just talk." He thought for a moment and then slowly added, "But keep yer eyes peeled."

"I will." Elijah's eyes swept the winter landscape. Thick trees crowded too close to the cabin for good defense. He wished Michael and his pa had cleared more land. Even naked trees would shield attackers.

"Cindy will wonder what's keeping us," he said.

His eyes never left the horizon. And when he went inside, he immediately took down the shotgun hanging over the door and leaned it against the table. The he got the leather pouch, took out a pistol cylinder, and began loading it.

Cindy watched him as she sat plates holding steaming orange potatoes onto the table. She dropped into a chair and cut anxious eyes from husband to father. "Well, which one of you is gonna tell me?"

Simon cleared his throat. "Daughter, there's nothin' to be upset—"

She interrupted. "Elijah, what's goin' on? And don't sugarcoat it none."

"Someone warned Simon there might be trouble brewing."

"What kind of trouble?" she asked with a hand unconsciously dropping to cover her middle.

"I've been accused of being with the army at that skirmish the other day and somebody doesn't like it."

"I'll bet it's some of your old company, Pa."

"Hit's Jared," he admitted with shoulders slumping, "and maybe some more."

"O' course he'd be the ringleader," she muttered. She looked up. "We'll stand guard. I'll keep watch while you sleep."

"Simon and I have been talking. Maybe you should stay with Ma for a while," Elijah suggested, "or with your folks."

"Yes, daughter. You'd be wel—"

She shook her head vigorously. "I won't leave. This is our home, and Jared Rawlings is not running me off with his stupid threats!"

Elijah's hands stilled from turning the gun's cylinder. For a long moment, he studied the problem. Then he said, "I won't make you leave. But I think you should know the threat might be real."

"Well, if they come, I'll be here to help you." Then she answered Simon's quick protests. "No, Pa, I'm not leaving. I can help if they come.

"I know you can shoot," he admitted. "I taught ya. But yo're the only young'un I got left." His eyes began to fill. "I reckon it would just about kill me and yer ma if anything was to happen to you."

She patted his arm. "The Lord is watching over me." But the sentence fell flat as she recalled Pete. The Lord had been watching over him, too. And yet he had been cut down, murdered at seven years old by a bloodthirsty bushwhacker. She expelled a deep breath. Pete's death remained a puzzle and one that likely would not be solved until eternity.

Elijah looked up. "When I'm outside, I'll keep the rifle with me and leave the shotgun here with you. I'll keep it loaded with fresh powder and ready to fire. I figure it's best if we both stick close to home for a while."

Cindy nodded.

Simon stood. "I'll keep my ears open. If I hear 'ery other word, I'll let you know. I shore hope and pray they leave you be." His steps lagged as he went toward the door. "Love yer neighbor..." He wagged his head. "Seems as if few folks are heedin' that commandment."

When the door closed, the room fell silent. Elijah pulled a chair near the new glass window and began cleaning the pistol. The rifle propped in the corner was close at hand. Hard-eyed, efficient, and methodical, he stared outside as his hands automatically did the task. If need be, he could clean and load a weapon in the dark. The army had not been to his liking, but he had acquired some valuable skills.

His jaw a grim, hard line, he deliberated. His first instinct to hunt down the culprits and put a quick end to this might just be the cravings of a fiery temper. Temper had always been his worst enemy, but one he had learned at least in some measure to control. He had finally listened to Pa about the wisdom of caution and thinking things through. He wanted no trouble. He'd had enough of that. His eyes roved over the cozy room. In spite of the hard times, he and Cindy had a good life here. He would not fly off the handle and jeopardize that. Perhaps it was just talk after all.

Cindy started to speak and then closed her mouth. She wanted to pull the thing apart and, in a woman's way, discuss every aspect. With Elijah's face turned to stone, as it was now, speaking did no good. She looked at the new cradle sitting in the corner, and her fists clenched. Perhaps later she would be afraid. Now she was angry.

A week crept by. Sometimes she awakened deep in the night to find the place beside her empty. She knew Elijah now woke at the slightest noise. Her own sleep was restless, and in the mornings there were bulges under her eyes.

Elijah said little and ate less. The monotonous diet of mush and potatoes was not tempting, but Cindy forced herself to eat, and most days managed to keep it down. Now she nibbled on a piece of potato and walked from window to window to gaze at the dreary landscape. Nothing stirred in the dead grass and bare trees. She almost wished something would happen. Days and nights of waiting were torment. Each day she cleaned and cooked and sewed, but joy had faded from the doing.

Elijah jerked awake. The sound was faint. Near the west wall there was a muffled scraping. In one smooth motion, he slid from the bed and unsheathed the pistol hanging from the bedpost. A floorboard creaked beneath his weight. Cindy's breathing remained deep and regular. He quickly pulled on pants and shirt, but left off socks as he hurriedly tugged on boots.

The cabin was pitch dark. He cautiously glided from window to window, staying shielded by gingham curtains. A sickle moon surrounded by low clouds cast a faint glow on the yard. He saw nothing unusual. He regretted there was no window in the back wall. Finally, with stealth, he opened the door and stepped into the cold night. The porch was almost as dark as the cabin's interior. He peered cat-eyed at the fence crawling like a black snake toward the dark lump of barn. A stiffening wind rattled loose shakes on the barn roof and swayed pines near the edge of the yard. Pistol ready, he rounded the cabin. Soon the clouds blew over the moon and all became dark shadows. Abruptly, the sound came again. He held his breath and cocked the gun.

As the thud repeated just a few feet ahead, he breathed out and his tense muscles relaxed. He lowered the hammer. It was wind blowing an elm branch against the back wall. For a few minutes he stared at the cold sky, and as he'd often done as a child, wondered how far away heaven was. He chuckled at the fanciful thought. Soon his own child would pester him with such questions the same as he had pestered Pa.

Wind biting through the thin shirt reminded him of the warm bed inside and the warm body snuggled in it. With another smile he turned back to reenter the cabin.

Taking care not to waken Cindy, he struck a match and peered at the clock. Daylight was two hours away. Gingerly, he crawled into bed, relishing the warmth still emanating from his spot on the mattress. After the chill melted from his skin, he snuggled against Cindy's back, breathing in her clean sweetness. She stirred in his arms and mumbled something unintelligible. Soon his deep breathing matched her own.

"Elijah!"

Acrid smoke filled his nostrils at the same instant Cindy's cry pierced his sleep-fogged brain. He sprang up. No blaze was visible, but light flickered through cracks and there was a dire crackling in the loft. For a moment he stood blinking, even so his sleep-clogged mind sensed a threat other than the fire.

"Put on your shoes and robe," he ordered as he jerked on clothes. He grabbed the holster and shot pouch, all the while staring toward the windows.

Her terror-filled voice came from near the foot of the bed. "We got to get out! The whole roof's on fire! It's gonna cave!"

"Wait!" he ordered. "Stay back from the windows and the door. Cover your nose and get down near the floor!"

He could see her outline now.

She spoke through her hand-covered mouth. "But—"

"Do as I say," he barked while at the same time he smashed a window with the butt of the pistol. He ducked as a shot busted the sill near his head. In desperation he looked around the room. Flames lit every window, highlighting any attempt to escape. He glanced overhead at cracks in the loft floor dancing with light. Now he could plainly see Cindy on the floor, her gown a white blotch. Racking coughs shook her body.

"I'm going to draw their fire," he said. "When I do, you head for Granny's and tell Billy." He grabbed the shotgun and the rifle and thrust the rifle into her hands.

Cindy's ashen face raised, blinking watery eyes.

When her mouth opened in protest, he grew harsh. "Just do it!"

She nodded.

Elijah sheathed the pistol and threw a chair through the window. He cocked one shotgun hammer. An instant later, he flung open the door, drew the pistol, and hurled forward at a crouching run. In two leaps he crossed the porch and fired the shotgun at a dark shape near the well. The man dropped his pistol and collapsed like a felled tree. Elijah cocked the second hammer. From the corner of his eye, he saw Cindy bolt from the doorway and down the steps. In spite of the long heavy rifle, she was running fast and gaining ground.

Just then a rider exited the woods, his face a pale triangle in the dimness. His wide shoulders hunched forward, and his heels dug into the running horse. His pistol shot zinged past, nicking Elijah's right ear. Elijah leaped from the porch and crouched near a post. He pointed the shotgun, but it wavered. He dared not fire. Cindy was too near the plunging horse. She had almost reached the well when she stopped and raised the rifle. The rider jerked the reins and veered toward her. She cried out as the horse's broad chest knocked her sprawling onto the dirt.

Almost blinded by rage, Elijah aimed the barrel and fired. The rider jerked. He swayed in the saddle but held on while the horse surged forward. Elijah raised the pistol and fired. The man bent double over the saddle horn. His pistol dropped and he fell to the ground.

Dirt splayed at Elijah's feet. The shot had come from behind. He whirled and fired. The shooter near the garden fence melted back into the trees.

Cindy held her stomach. As she struggled to her knees and then stood, Elijah sprinted forward, but a volley of shots forced him into a zigzag pattern. He dove for cover behind the low rock wall surrounding the well. With relief he saw Cindy enter the dark woods in a stumbling run. Soon she was hidden from view. He crouched low. Shot peppered the ground. With hands steady and familiar with battle, he reloaded, but his thoughts were chaotic, tormented by visions of Cindy being hurled to the ground. His teeth gritted as he wondered if she or the baby were harmed.

Just then heat burst a window. Flames and glass spewed outward. Elijah avoided looking at the tongues of fire licking away at the house. He needed to see into the darkness. Although daylight was near, the field and pasture were yet black. He waited, taut and listening. Minutes passed. Low groans from the wounded man mingled with the crackling of flames.

Sporadic gunfire kept him penned. Silhouetted by the fire, his position was too precarious to risk a move. He held his fire and waited. Ever mindful of strategy learned from old Levi, he probed all directions. More than likely, at least one attacker was sneaking around behind. The frozen ground was hard beneath him. He shifted a little to ease a pain in his hip. A shot splintered rock near his left ear. He drew up smaller.

Cold seeped through his sweaty shirt, and he began to shiver. Dragging minutes seemed like hours. He pictured Cindy running through the dark. His jaw tightened. She must be cold. Her cloak was in the inferno—as was everything they owned.

A faint gray line grew broader in the east. Soon he would be able to see. For now, his eyes, straining in dimness, saw no one.

Shifting wind blew smoke and cinders toward him. Acrid air burned eyes and nostrils. There was a kerchief in his hip pocket. With care he eased it out, swiped watery eyes, and tied it around his nose.

As flames leaped high, Elijah spied a man with a rifle gliding from tree to tree. He pointed the shotgun and fired. Apparently unharmed, the attacker halted. Then he disappeared. Soon a horse pounded away. Elijah cocked his ear as another rider sped off right behind.

There had been four men. Two were on the ground. Two had ridden away. Or so he thought. He would not risk standing just yet.

A portion of the roof caved in, sending sparks and embers flying. The man lying near the porch writhed and screamed and batted at flames licking his useless legs.

"Oh, God! Help me! I'm on fire!" He managed to drag himself a few feet before collapsing to lie moaning and panting on the ground.

Elijah pulled the kerchief from his face, tied it around a rock, and gingerly moved it forward with the toe of his boot. There was no shot. He drew it back and tossed it a few feet away. Still no shots.

He crouched, held the shotgun ready, drew a deep breath, and sprinted forward. He reached the broad oak tree near the fence. The attackers had fled.

The man writhing near the fire saw him and cried out.

"Mister, please! My back's broken, and this damned fire is roasting me."

Ignoring him, Elijah paced toward the other man who lay sprawled with arms out-flung. A gash in the man's shirt ran red with blood but one hand twitched. Elijah drew a knife from his boot and jerked up the head by the hair. But the eyes were glazed. He was dead.

"My gawd, mister!" gasped the wounded man as Elijah bore down on him. He made a vain attempt to drag himself away.

Elijah stepped in his way and rolled him over. "Who was with you?"

Like a snarling cat, the man's lip curled back from bared teeth. He was about thirty, had a thick chest and a clean-shaven face. Elijah's cold eyes narrowed.

"You're one of those Rawlings from Hagarville—one of Jared's kin. I recognized your cousin over there on the ground."

"Go to hell!" The man left off holding his stomach and struggled up onto his elbows.

Elijah stepped on his chest. "You're gut shot. You're gonna die. It's up to you how. It can be quick and easy…or slow and painful. Now, I'm asking you one more time—besides Jared, who else was with you?"

The man's eyes widened and fixed on the knife blade gleaming in firelight.

"Talk or I'll drag you into that fire." Elijah knelt on one knee. "But I'll drag you out every little bit so you won't go too quick."

Sweat beaded and ran down the man's sooty face. He panted. "Jared said no harm would come to the woman…said you'd send her out and he'd let her go. Then when you came out, we'd shoot you. But hell, mister, it's war!" His eyes were pleading.

Elijah scoffed. "This has nothing to do with war. That sonofabitch just wants us dead. Now, who was the other man?"

The man's teeth clenched.

"You have a brother, don't you?"

For a second the man's eyes filled with self-less anguish.

Elijah kept his gaze locked on the prone man. "So, it was your brother."

"Damn you to hell!" cried Rawlings. Then he spit in Elijah's face.

Elijah wiped his face with a sleeve. "Rawlings, you're gritty." There was no malice in his voice. "I'll end it quick for you."

Rawlings's eyes distended with shock as Elijah grasped his hair and slit his throat. Suddenly Rawlings went limp.

Cindy stumbled through the dark. Briars caught the sleeves and skirt of her nightgown. She jerked free and struggled ahead. The heavy gun tugged at her shoulders. She was half a mind to leave it behind. A spasm of pain bent her double. To keep from moaning, she bit her lip hard. As far as she could tell no one gave chase, but they might be out there just waiting to grab her. She must hurry. She wouldn't think just now about what might be happening inside her bruised body. Elijah was in danger. Even now she winced at gunfire echoing in the hollow. As she tugged free of brambles, she envisioned shot spattering around him.

At first the sliver of moon made no inroads in the dense thicket. As she fought her way forward, a thread of silvery light near the lip of the ridge highlighted the trail. She staggered toward it. Abruptly her foot hung on a root. With a jolt, she landed hard on palms and knees on frozen ground. Pain throbbed in her scraped knees and lacerated palms, but this time her stomach had been spared the blow. Hardly slowing, she rose, picked up the gun, and pushed ahead, her breath coming in ragged pants. Sweat dried quickly in the frosty air. In spite of the exertion, soon her teeth chattered.

Here the trail shouldered a hill. Keening wind swayed the pines on the hill above but did not reach her. She hesitated at the turnoff leading toward her old home. But Elijah had said to get Billy. Besides it was a bit closer to Granny's than to Pa's. She had gone only a few feet when she looked back.

Hoof beats came fast up the cutoff. She drew back under cover of dark trees. Then her breath exhaled in relief. It was Pa galloping his mule. Even before she called out, he spied her and sawed on the reins.

"What happened?" he shouted. "Who's firing them shots?"

"Hurry, Pa!" She pointed a shaking hand and breathlessly blurted out, "They set the cabin afire, and now they're shooting. Elijah sent me after Billy and Caleb."

Although Simon wore a pistol, she handed him the rifle. "Here, take this, too. Ya might need hit." Her anguished, upturned face was white in moonlight. When he spurred the mule and hurried away, she began to run until pain stabbed her abdomen. She stopped, bent double, and groaned. The second it lessened, she hurried on.

The trees thinned and visibility improved as she drew near the spring. For a moment she stopped to catch her breath, sucking in deep draughts that made her lungs burn. Her hand rested on icicles dangling from the ledge of silver rock. She shivered, longing for a coat. Something stirred in the brushy growth near the spring, and she began to run again.

The cabin was dark. She pounded the door. Soon a dim light shone through the cracks and the door opened. Caleb, dressed only in long underwear, held a shotgun. Behind him, stood Billy, gun in one hand, as he pulled dangling suspenders up over his long underwear. Granny stood in the center of the room in a long white nightgown, holding a candle high. Nearby, Viola's thin frame made a long narrow shadow. Her gray hair usually slicked back into a tight bun fell thin and stringy onto her shoulders.

Cindy held the doorframe and croaked through parched lips. "Go help Elijah! Jared Rawlings and some more fired the cabin, and now they're shootin' at him."

Billy whirled and began strapping on a holster.

Viola paid no heed to Caleb as he grabbed a shot pouch and started for the door. "No!" she cried, grabbing Billy's arm. "No, son! You can't!"

He shook the hand free and glared.

"Viola Tanner!" Granny was aghast. "A man goes when his kin needs help."

Viola's pinched face worked with anguish. She stepped to the door as if to block Billy's way.

His jaws hardened. "Get out of the way, Ma."

"No, Billy," she pleaded. And yet her shoulders sagged in defeat with the knowing—there was not the least doubt he was going.

Cindy crumpled into a heap. Although her eyes were closed, she knew it was Billy who lifted her. His arms were steel. Another spasm gripped her. She writhed from the pain. His arms tightened.

"Put her yonder on my bed." Granny barked the orders. "Viola, fetch my yarb satchel!"

Viola stayed rooted to the spot, staring into the flames as Granny stirred up the coals in the fireplace and threw on a pine knot.

Billy bent and laid her gently on the soft, feather mattress. When Granny pushed against his shoulder, he straightened but not before he touched Cindy's cheek. "What's wrong with her?" he asked. "She smells like smoke, but I don't see any burns."

"I'll tend to her," Granny snapped. "You get on and he'p Elijah!"

Cindy opened her eyes to meet Billy's concerned gaze. Another cramp gripped, and she moaned.

He winced. Abruptly he strode to the door and followed Caleb into the night. Viola watched his tall frame disappear. Then she clamped a hand to her mouth, rushed to her bedroom, and shut the door.

Cindy clutched Granny's arm. "What's happenin' to me?" she groaned. "Is it the baby?" Her face was deadly white. "Oh, Granny, don't let me lose it!"

Granny patted her shoulder. "I'll do my best, child," she soothed.

Simon yelled from the trail. "Lige! You all right? I just seen Cindy back on the trail."

He whoaed the mule and jumped down. With a horrified look of disbelief he crouched beside the dead man.

"Gerald Rawlings," he muttered. "I knowed him well." He turned accusing eyes on Elijah. "You slit his throat like he was no more than a fattenin' hog."

"I did him a favor. He was gut shot and bound to die slow and painful. I'd have shot him, but I don't have shot and powder to waste. There's precious little left in my pouch." Elijah bent and rubbed blood from the knife onto the grass and sheathed it into the pouch inside his boot. Levi had taken the knife off the body of a dead Indian at Pea Ridge. Likely it had been used to scalp Yankees. Ever since the day Levi had given it to him, he had never been without it.

Elijah stood. "They were all Rawlings—Jared and his kin. Jared and one more rode off." He gave Simon a hard stare. "Before you get too worked up about what I did, take a look at the cabin. We could be dead right now. I'm going after them. Look after Cindy. Tell her to stay with you or Granny and tell her I'll be back as soon as I can."

Simon rubbed a hand over his face. His mouth worked a minute, then he said, "I know the poison that eats at a man when something like this happens"—he waved a hand toward the smoldering cabin—"but vengeance is mine sayeth the Lord—"

Elijah interrupted. "There's no sheriff now to handle this. I can't just let Jared go. He damn near killed us this time. And now I've killed his kin. You know as well as I do, Jared won't let this drop. And neither can I."

Simon wilted. "Then take my mule. He's done saddled and ready."

In cloudy gray dawn, wind whipped, cold and cutting into Elijah's face, and rattled the bare tree limbs alongside the trail. The shot pouch bounced against the side of the coat that he had borrowed from Simon. As he hunched forward and urged the mule across the creek, water splashed onto his boots. He slowed to keep from getting his pants soaked. The mule responded willingly. Simon had fed the animal well. It was in good shape, better than most around. With head bent, Elijah watched the trail, and yet he rode with care, expecting the Rawlings to circle back to aid their kin. After a few miles it became evident they had left the mountains.

"They figure both men died in the shootout; otherwise they'd have stayed to fight," he muttered. The Rawlingses were well known to be clannish.

As the mule trotted over frozen, rutted ground he contemplated where they had gone. They would be looking for him—but not soon. More than likely they'd expect him to spend some time licking his wounds. He carefully weighed the idea of waiting for Billy. But Billy would follow. And surprise was now his best ally. With a grim face, he headed the mule off the mountain and straight for Jared's farm.

As miles disappeared under the fast-gaited mule, his thoughts turned to Cindy. He wanted to see her, to hold her close and reassure her everything would be all right, but that would come later…if he survived. A ripple of fear traced his spine. It surprised him. He'd faced battle without flinching. Then he knew. It was not fear for himself, but dread for Cindy and the baby if anything should happen to him. He'd watched Ma wither away like a flower without water since Pa died. He wanted to raise his child in a happy home, the way Ma and Pa had raised him. To that end, he said a short but fervent prayer. Then with respect for the Almighty, he hoped what he had set out to do today would not call down God's wrath upon him.

In the stinging wind, his face grew numb and his hands half-frozen. Turning up his collar, he pressed on, only stopping occasionally to let the mule blow, while he put first one hand inside his coat and then the other. The country opened into rolling hills rimmed on one side by a line of steep, jagged crests aptly named the Seven Devils. Near the trail and below a bluff, Little Piney cut a gash in the earth, fast flowing past high cliffs of gray rock.

There had once been farms in the fertile creek bottoms. War had raped the valley. What foraging armies had not destroyed, the bushwhackers had. When Elijah passed a blackened ruin he slowed and stared. One tall chimney was the lone remains of a raid last spring. His face tightened with anger as he recalled the smoldering heap of his own cabin. Everything gone. All of his and Cindy's hard work for nothing.

Before last night the specter of war had quieted in his memory—the sight and sound and smell of death, of men in anguish. Days had become peaceful and filled with hope. He had envisioned his happy children laughing and wading and fishing in Little Piney. As in his childhood, the creek flowed through fields ripe with tall corn, pastures grazed by fat, slick, cattle, and flocks of plump red chickens scratching in the dirt. For no good reason, Jared had ripped their lives apart. No matter what happened today, it was not over. Jared wouldn't stop until he was dead. If Elijah was killed, Billy and his own kin would take up the fight. And if he survived, the Rawlings would want revenge.

He pressed down the rage coursing his veins. Anger could blind a man. He'd need keen wits for what lay ahead. He kicked the mule and rode on.

Pale sun was directly overhead as he neared the settlement. Here the land flattened into wide fields. To his left a tree line marked the course of Little Piney as it meandered across the flats on its way to join Big Piney. Just ahead, chimney smoke from a small cluster of houses blended into the gray sky. He bypassed Hagarville. A mile further, he slowed and grew cautious as he neared Minnow Creek and Jared's land. Near the road's edge, the ring of an ax halted him. He turned toward the sound. It was a scrawny boy of about thirteen hacking away at a fallen hickory.

The boy eyed him warily as he rode up and halted. Elijah spoke first.

"Howdy. Cold day to be cutting wood." He tried to appear casual as he leaned on the saddle horn and held the reins slack.

"Cold day to be travelin,'" the youth shot back and Elijah smiled.

"So it is," he acknowledged. "I've not seen anyone else on the road." He blew on his hands and looked down the road. "In this wind, I reckon most folks are staying in by the fire."

"Reckon so," the boy agreed. "I've been here all morning chopping at this lam-blasted hickory and not seen a soul."

Elijah sat up straight. "None of the Rawlings rode by?"

"Nope."

Elijah tugged on the reins and kicked the mule's flanks. To make certain, he trotted across the field until he spotted Jared's chimney. The lack of smoke meant he was not home.

Elijah's eyes darted back toward the mountains. His insides twisted as he relived Cindy hitting the ground and then running toward the dark woods with terror in her eyes.

For a moment he sat indecisive. Jared might have circled back. But his gut said otherwise. With one swift motion, he wheeled the mule and headed for Clarksville. If the mule kept up a good pace, he could reach town by mid-afternoon.

He had no idea where to look. Jared, a heavy drinker, frequented saloons. When the Confederate troops pulled out, the grog shops in Clarksville had closed. Elijah decided to ride straight to the Hadley's and ask the boy to do some spying. The Hadley boy seemed canny. Elijah thought he could be trusted to discretely find out where Jared and his cousin might be.

Daylight was fading as he neared town. The wind lay, and yet damp cold seeped through his coat and made his arms wooden. He would have to warm before they would be of use. Rather than crossing the long covered bridge over Spadra, he crossed the mule upstream and out of sight before angling across rough ground toward the decrepit shack.

Before he knocked, the door opened.

"It's that Loring fellow," David called loudly over his shoulder in answer to the old man's question.

Enos leaned forward in his chair and pulled together a worn quilt draped across his thin shoulders. "Well, don't keep him standing there. And shut the door quick. Hit's cold as a well-digger's butt out thar.'"

Elijah stepped inside where a shock of heat engulfed him. He stumbled on his way toward the blazing fireplace.

The old man, chuckled. "Yer lips is blue as a fishhook. What in tarnation you doing traveling in this weather without a hat and gloves?"

"I rode off in a hurry."

The old eyes sharpened. "Had trouble did ya?"

"Yes."

"David, don't stand there gawking. Pour him a cup of that Confederit' coffee. Tastes awful, but it warms a body up."

Elijah gratefully took the chipped mug. The parched corn water tasted worse than a dose of Granny's sulphur and molasses, but it sent immediate warmth flooding though his belly. When he had drained the cup, Enos eyed him expectantly.

"I'm looking for a couple of men. I think they rode in not long ago."

David looked up from refilling his cup. "I saw the Rawlings ride in."

Elijah's eyes glittered. Somehow he had missed the trail where Jared and his cousin had cut straight for town, but he'd lay odds that Billy would find it. Billy was the best tracker he'd ever seen—except for maybe the half-breed named Hawk who had scouted for Hindman. Billy should arrive anytime, unless there had been more trouble.

He looked at David. "Do you know where they went?"

"The mercantile. Since the saloons closed down, it's the only place in town to buy a drink."

"Would you go see if they're still there?"

When the boy nodded, Elijah said, "I'll wait in the alley behind the store. Come and tell me. But don't let anyone see you." As an afterthought he added, "Don't say a word to anyone." He turned to the old man. As he talked—in case the powder had gotten damp—he reloaded his guns. "They burned me out and tried to shoot me. I killed a couple of their kin."

David, big eyed, jerked on a coat and cap and bolted out the door.

Enos tugged his beard. "Watch yerself. Them Rawlings is rattlesnake mean. They's a provost marshal in town now—Gill Harris. No worry he'll interfere. He'd hide under the bed at the first hint o' trouble."

Elijah left the shack behind. Circling behind the buildings, he hitched the mule to a post near the edge of the wagon yard and slipped into the alley between the mercantile and Uncle Phillip's old newspaper office. The shadows were deep with the coming night. In the stillness he fancied he could hear his own heart beat. A whiff of hickory smoke drifted downward from the store's chimney. He drew a deep breath and waited.

In the west, streaks of crimson and amber shot through thinning clouds. It was a sight that made a man want to live. His thoughts abruptly jumped to Cindy. He pictured her in firelight, her hair a flowing river down her back, her dark eyes shining. He drew a ragged breath and hoped that he would live to see her again.

Something rubbed against his leg, and he jerked. It was a skinny tomcat he'd seen in the store. He shoved it away with his boot.

Did the man with Jared have a handgun? This morning he'd used a rifle...

Once again, he cocked his ear to listen. A door slammed. It was a few minutes before steps scurried toward the alley. David rounded the corner, still looking back over his shoulder.

"They're in there," he panted, "leaned up against the counter drinking." Excitement made his voice break and then squeak.

Elijah gave a half-smile. He remembered the humiliation of a changing voice. "What about Emmitt? Where is he?"

"Way over by the stove. He don't like the Rawlings none since they turned Yankee."

Abruptly Elijah's lips thinned and he raised the shotgun.

"Thank you, boy. Now go home and stay there." He watched David slowly back from the alley. With a stern look he added, "I mean it, boy. No matter what, don't come back here tonight."

Elijah stepped to the edge of the building and waited until the boy started toward the wagon yard. Then he braced himself and strode quickly forward. Rounding the corner, he pulled back both hammers on the shotgun.

Jared glanced up when the bell above the door jingled. Shock washed his face, and he grabbed for the pistol on his hip. The bell's tinkle melded with a roar of angry flame. Jared slammed against the counter. The man standing alongside him jerked then crumpled to the floor. Elijah took two quick steps and pulled the other trigger. The impact spun Jared. He clutched the counter. As his grip loosened, his hands left a bloody smear. His riddled body fell near the stocky man already lying on the floor in a pool of blood and gore.

Emmitt Gossett started to rise but sank back into his chair. His eyes swung from the men on the floor back to Elijah. He gripped the arms of the chair and his face went sickly gray.

Elijah stood in the acrid, swirling powder smoke and waited. With pistol drawn, he watched the bodies twitch and flop like dying chickens. He'd seen men shot at close range on the battlefield and in skirmishes along the White River. These two wouldn't live long. He glanced up when Emmitt made a guttural sound in his throat and swallowed back a gag. Elijah had long since steeled himself from that tendency. But he'd never become calloused to the gruesome sight of faces blown apart and bowels spilling onto the ground.

Jared's chest and jaw were blown away. His wide-open eyes registered stunned disbelief. Strangled words were lost in a gurgle of bloody froth.

Elijah swung his gaze to the other man as he jerked once and then lay still. His features were unrecognizable pulp. Then Elijah looked back at Jared's sightless eyes, sheathed the pistol, and began reloading the shotgun.

He glanced at Emmitt. "Before daylight they set fire to my place and then tried to kill my wife and me when we ran out. I killed two of them and then followed these two here."

"There'll be a dozen Rawlings on your trail," said Emmitt. Then as an afterthought he muttered, "I hope they don't think I had anything to do with this."

"Who does the burying in town?" Elijah asked.

"Whitey Lawrence. He's no real undertaker, but he nails up a coffin of sorts and lays out the dead pretty respectable."

"Hope he can clean them up before their kin sees them. The last I knew, Jared's ma was still alive."

Emmitt nodded. "If I were you, I'd hightail it home and have eyes in the back of my head."

Elijah turned and saw David staring from the doorway, his face ghastly green. The stricken face pained Elijah. He had hoped to spare the boy such memories. Elijah knew the gut-wrenching horror. All too well he remembered his first such gruesome sight on the frozen fields at Pea Ridge. He had gazed, sickened, at Price's men, hundreds of them, lying in frosty moonlight on cornfields as lifeless as the brown-riddled stalks studding the ground. He could yet see them — men with upturned faces and uniforms ghostly white — their limbs blown away and lying every which way with gaping jaws and glassy stares.

"Go home, boy." Elijah strode past him and mounted the mule. Night was falling fast. But he had traveled in the dark before.

Chapter 5

Granny's eyes were filled with sympathy as she held a damp cloth to Cindy's forehead. Cindy pressed her lips together and turned away. The quilt was warm, but she had never felt so cold. She stared out the window at a leafless catalpa tree swayed by the wind. The mournful sighing at the eaves echoed her anguish. Tears stole from the corners of her eyes and lay cold and wet against her cheeks as they slipped onto the pillow.

Her baby was dead. Her mind rebelled, but she must accept it. She had never even held it. Granny had wrapped the tiny form that was flesh of her flesh and given it to Caleb to bury on the hillside behind Elijah's ma's cabin. There had been no mention of a funeral. There wasn't any way of knowing this soon if it had been a girl or a boy. Cindy doubted the child seemed real to anyone but her and Elijah. And this minute Elijah might be dead. She writhed at the thought.

"You hurting?" Granny leaned and touched her forehead with blue-veined hands that were dry and bony and yet gentle in the caress. "You ain't hot. But I want you to get this last bit of willer bark tea down. Hit staves off childbed fever."

Dutifully, Cindy drank the bitter draught and sank back onto the pillow exhausted.

"Granny, do you think Elijah is all right? I've tried to pray, but…"

"Yer faith is weak just now, 'cause you feel like the Lord has let you down. You don't feel so now—but hit'll come to you in time—these is the kinds of things that makes us strong. I've lost my own unborn babes and buried many another loved one. There's been other hurts that don't make no sense to me." She looked at her misshapen feet swathed in rags. "Hit ain't easy. But I reckon this here life is one big trial to see if a body will turn towards the good Lord er away from him. His comfort ain't never failed me."

Cindy pressed her lips together and tears flowed down her face. "Pray for Elijah."

"Child, I been prayin' for the both of ya since you first banged on the door. In my bones, I know Elijah is fine." She patted Cindy's arm. "Now get some sleep. Them yarbs I give ya will help ya rest. "

Cindy doubted even the herbs could make her sleep. "Wake me—"

"I'll wake you the very second we hear a thang."

Cindy nodded, then curled onto her side and glanced at Granny's clock. Her heart twisted. Until now she had given their possessions no thought, but everything was gone! *Ma's rosewood clock!* The clock that had survived five generations and tossing seas and jolting wagons could not survive those angry leaping flames.

She drew a ragged breath. None of that would matter if only Elijah came home.

For an hour she lay in a semiconscious doze, jerking at every sound. Then she heard voices out on the porch and propped up on her elbows and stared at the door as Granny opened it, stepped outside, and hurriedly closed it.

It was Pa and Caleb, and they would have news of Elijah!

Amazed at how weak she felt, Cindy sank back down, her breathing ragged. The slight exertion had her arms trembling. She bit her lip and waited impatiently until the door opened again.

Simon stepped inside and swept off a black slouch hat. Viola opened the bedroom door. But rather than entering the main room, she clung to the doorframe, her face pasty white.

"Pa!" Cindy swallowed before she could utter the question. "Elijah?"

"Last I seen him, he was fine," he reassured.

When he stared at the floor, she grew anxious. "But where is he?" she asked, dreading the answer.

His narrow brown face was sober—far too sober—and when he looked up he had difficulty meeting her eyes. "I ain't right shore—"

"Tell me!" she ordered. Her voice was sharper than she had intended.

"He's trailing them who got away."

Cindy's hand went to her throat. "How many?"

He shook his head in uncertainty. "Two of 'em is dead already."

Viola gasped and sank to the floor with a whimper. Simon hurried to help her stand.

Granny scowled and then hollered for Caleb. "I'll swan," she muttered, "you'd think Billy was still in swaddling clothes the way that woman takes on about him."

Simon and Caleb helped Viola into bed. But even with assurance from both of them that Billy was fine, she grimaced and turned her face to the wall.

Worry and sorrow deeply etched Simon's haggard face as he walked slowly to Cindy's bed and patted her hand. Tears rimmed his tired eyes and his Adam's apple bobbed as he swallowed. He avoided mentioning the baby.

"I'll go home and get yer ma. She'll want to be here."

"Oh! Pa!" She grabbed his arm and sobbed great, racking sobs.

"There, there," he shushed her.

Granny interrupted. "No, Simon, that's what she needs—to cry hit all out." But under her breath she quoted, "'Lamentation and mourning—Rachel weepin' fer her children and not comforted, because they are no more.' Oh, Lord," she whispered, "how many times..."

"I'll go along home and get yer ma," said Simon. "Try and get some rest. Elijah will be home before you know it."

When Cindy's eyes opened, it was her mother-in-law who sat by her bed. Becky's golden hair was pulled back into loose waves that ended in a bun on the nape of her neck. A slat bonnet lay in the lap of a blue cotton dress that was faded but neatly pressed.

Becky leaned forward. "Your mother wasn't well this morning. I told her to stay in bed—that I'd come check on you." Upon seeing the pained look, she squeezed Cindy's arm.

Cindy dropped her eyes and swallowed. She could think of no one she wanted less just now than this stiff, starched woman! She wanted no proper reassurances, no promises that soon she would have other children, no sugarcoated comfort. And yet, to be fair, there was real sympathy in the woman's sad eyes.

Becky bit her lip. She opened and then abruptly closed her mouth, searching for the right words. Finally she spoke. "When Elijah was ten, I buried two babies, twin boys, who lived only a few hours. I still grieve for them," she said.

Cindy appreciated the honest words. It was the first personal conversation she had ever had with Elijah's ma. They usually talked about the weather or the drought-stricken gardens or some such general topic. This was a side of Becky she had never seen. Perhaps she had misjudged Becky—perhaps even misjudged Becky's opinion of her.

"Has any word come from Elijah?" Cindy asked.

Becky's face was drawn. "No. But I'm sure he's fine…" Her words, however, trailed away on a doubtful note.

Cindy felt the need to comfort the bleak-faced woman. "He's got a level head on his shoulders, and he'll go careful."

Becky gave a wan smile. "I'm sure he will." She smoothed the quilt of colorful blocks and intricate circles. "Can I get you anything? Something to eat—a cup of tea? Granny said you ate no breakfast or dinner, and it's getting on toward the middle of the afternoon."

She was not hungry, but she consented to a cup of tea since Becky seemed anxious to do something for her.

The clouds broke and drifted away. A few feathery wisps covered the slender moon. On the long ride home, bitter cold penetrated Elijah's bones and his mind. Jared's mangled face rode before him in moonlight. He had no regret for killing Jared. But he detested the necessity of it.

If only Jared had not…

Finally, with determination, he pushed the thought from him. He and Cindy would have to start over. They would live with Ma, and he would work Pa's land. Before the baby came he would build another room onto the cabin. Later he would build a nice house—a wooden frame house—far nicer than the shamble of a cabin Michael had given them. And even nicer than Pa's cabin.

The sky was rose-tinted in the east when Caleb's hounds began to bark. Elijah whoaed the mule. Bone weary, he slumped in the saddle, but his spirits lifted as he smelled the smoke from Granny's breakfast fire. He actually gave a weak smile as the door opened and the tiny woman raised her hands joyfully.

"Yo're home!"

Then her smile faded much too quickly, and he frowned and dismounted.

"Is Cindy all right?" Not waiting for an answer, he strode fast across the yard. "Where is she?"

At the door Granny halted him with a hand on his arm. She lowered her voice.

"She's fine, but…but she lost the youngun."

Elijah blinked, for a moment unable to absorb the news. "Lost the…"

"But Cindy's gonna be fine."

He felt as if he'd been kicked in the belly. With a groan he dropped to sit on a step on the porch. A second later he sprang up. "Where is she?"

Granny nodded inside and he pushed past her, blinking in the dimness. Then he saw her on the bed, at the far side of the room, propped up on pillows. His heart squeezed. She looked dead. He crossed the room in four long strides, and her eyes flew open.

"Elijah!" She reached for him, and he bent and grabbed her. He kissed her forehead and held her as she cried.

She trembled all over. "I was so afraid!"

He shushed her and drew back. "I'm fine. But I'm worried about you. Are you all right?"

"Oh! Elijah!"

He shushed her again as a fresh wave of weeping swept her. His scared eyes sought Granny.

"She's pale on account of losing so much blood—but that's slowed down," assured Granny. "I figure a week in bed, and she'll be up and around again."

Cindy clung to his hand. "I'm so sorry," she whispered. "I reckon I just wasn't strong enough."

His brows drew together. "You're plenty strong. This wasn't your fault. It's a wonder you're still alive." He gently pushed her hair back from her forehead. "For a second there when that horse was coming at you…" He gave his head a half shake and left the sentence hanging, but his hand tightened its grip on hers.

Caleb, his arms loaded with wood, came in the back door. His eyes lighted at sight of Elijah.

"So yo're back safe." His eyes jumped to the door. "Ain't Billy with ya?"

Eliajh frowned. "I never saw him. I guess we crossed paths somewhere without knowing it."

Viola's door opened. Like a thin wraith in long white gown, she stared hollow-eyed from the doorway. "Where's Billy?"

"I don't know. But don't worry. The trouble is over."

Like a woman possessed, she flew at Elijah and pummeled him with her fists.

"You killed him!" she shrieked. "You killed him, didn't you?"

Caleb's mouth fell open. "Wife!"

Elijah caught her flailing hands. "Calm down, Aunt Viola. Billy will be back any minute."

Her mouth twisted into a snarl. She raked both Elijah and Caleb with hate-filled eyes.

"Viola, come sit down," said Caleb as he drew out a chair. But she pulled back and fled to the bedroom. Caleb flinched when the door slammed with a loud bang. "I don't know what's come over her."

"Her mind has snapped," avowed Granny. "Fear for Billy has drove her crazy."

Caleb wiped a hand over his face and said nothing else.

Granny set a plate on the table. "Unless I miss my guess, Elijah, you ain't et in a long while. When yo're ready, here's a bite of breakfast." She looked at Cindy. "And you didn't eat a bite yesterdee. You both need something hot and nourishing."

As Granny handed Cindy a bowl, Elijah walked to the table, but he hardly tasted the hot grits. Viola had always been a sour, unhappy woman, prone to faultfinding and complaints—but not to violent outbursts. He'd never figured her to go insane. He hoped Billy arrived soon. Otherwise poor Viola might snap for good.

He darted worried eyes at Cindy. Granny was usually right about sickness, but Cindy looked as white as the pillow under her head.

He looked up as his ma and Deborah came through the door. Their eyes gladdened at sight of him, and Becky gathered him into a hug and kissed him. When Deborah laid a timid hand on his arm, he reached and pulled her braid as he had done years ago. It brought a tiny smile to her face.

"Sit yerself down, Becky," Granny invited. "Deborah, I reckon you'll be wanting that seat yonder at the loom."

"Ma said you wouldn't have time for a lesson today."

Granny shrugged. "Don't reckon I have much else to do just now, and weaving takes my mind off of troubles."

It was afternoon before Billy rode into the yard. The muffled sound of Caleb's glad voice came from the porch. Then the door opened with a blast of frigid air, and both men stepped inside. Blowing on his hands, Billy went to the fireplace and bent to warm them just as the clock on the mantle struck four.

"Those brown beans smell powerful good," he noted. "I could eat a horse."

"They ain't tender yet," apologized Granny, "but I'll fix you a bite of something else."

He nodded to Elijah where he sat by Cindy's bed. "Figured you'd got back all right," said Billy. "I got to town just after you left. I stayed around to see what would come off. Just like I figured, some of the Rawlings rode in. They were square jawed. Some of 'em are in that Yankee home guard—near about eight or ten, best I could tell."

Elijah nodded. He had mentally come up with that tally himself.

Billy continued, "Lige, you better head out. And I mean right soon. Jared has five brothers—let alone all his cousins and nephews. Some of them are bound to come after you."

Elijah stiffened. He had purposely ignored the obvious, wanting only to return to Cindy and their life together, but it had been chewing away at the edges of his mind. Their idyllic time together had ended—at least for now.

Billy went on, "They may not face you man to man. They might just hide in the brush and back-shoot you."

Caleb's shoulders drooped, and he swallowed. "I hate to name it, son, but I figure he's right. You ought to leave—give this a chance to blow over. Let folks forget about hit fer a bit."

Cindy rose off the plump pillows and clutched his arm. Her terrified eyes were dark caverns in a bloodless face.

Becky's eyes darted from Billy to Caleb. Then she looked at Elijah and gripped her hands together in her lap to still the trembling.

Granny looked up from bending over a kettle on the fire. Her black eyes were piercing. "You got to. Ain't no buts about it. I knowed the Rawlings back in Tennessee. Some of 'em is good folks, but most is rattlesnake mean and vengeful. They'll not rest till yo're dead and in yer grave."

Billy, usually slow to speak out, now added, "I've been studying on it all the way home. If I was you, I'd join up again." When Elijah opened his mouth in protest, he hurried on. "I know you got no liking for the army. But the way I see it, it's yer best chance to stay alive. Even the Rawlings will go slow about wading into a Confederate camp.

Everything in Elijah rebelled at the suggestion. Oh, he had been a good soldier—good at staying alive, good at killing. He had done his duty. Even in a firing squad with his rifle pointed at the breast of a good man, he had not wavered. But now he gave an inward groan recalling faces of men he'd killed. The reality of battle was worse than any nightmare. Only lately had he begun to forget the horror, the screams, the stench, the heaps of severed arms and legs, some still encased in boots or sleeves.

His jaw hardened and he looked at Cindy. "I'm not leaving."

Billy persisted, "If you stay there'll be more killing."

Elijah's shoulders drooped. Billy was right. By staying, he would endanger them all. Defeated, he said, "I'll leave as soon as I know she's all right."

"Oh, son!" Becky gave an almost imperceptible moan. Then she pressed her lips tightly together and gripped Deborah's arm as if this child too might flee.

Cindy's chin trembled but her look did not waver. "No, Elijah," she whispered. "You go, right now. I'll be fine. But I won't be if anything happens to you."

Although he did not want to admit it, he knew they were right. He reached a hand and stroked Cindy's hair, hating the anguish in her eyes. All of his good intentions to protect and provide for her had disappeared in a cloud of black-powder smoke.

Slowly, he faced the inevitable. He did not want to go. He wanted to stay and if necessary face them all. But he had to leave. By staying, he would jeopardize the rest of them.

He turned to Simon. "Can she live—"

Becky interrupted, "She should stay with me. Polly isn't up to nursing just now, and Granny has her hands full with Viola."

Elijah looked askance at Cindy, and to his surprise, she slowly nodded.

Granny stood. "I'll pack you some vittles. Billy, you got some extra clothes fer him?" As he nodded she went on, "Becky, since Billy is three…four inches taller, you hem the pants whilst I fix a pack. I'll send a wool blanket. He kin take yer wool coat, Caleb. I'll make you another." Granny was all business, but when no one was looking, she swiped tears from the corners of her eyes with the long gingham apron.

Elijah half turned and leaned a hand on the pack tied across the back of the saddle. The cabin was a small black splotch on the bleak landscape. Once before he had left here against his will, bound and gagged, conscripted into the Confederate army. He had endured an eternity of hell before returning. He wondered how long it would be before he returned this time.

Cindy's kiss was warm on his lips. He wished they had been alone for their parting. But all the family had stood nearby as if loath to let him from their sight. All except Viola. She had refused to leave her room even when Caleb had wheedled that Elijah might be gone for months. Caleb had shut the bedroom door and shook his head again at the strange twist of her mind.

The image of Cindy's white face haunted Elijah. His insides twisted recalling how many neighbor women he'd known who died in childbirth. He wasn't sure if it was better or worse to lose one early on as she had done, but fear gripped him. There was hardly a family in the hills who hadn't lost a woman or a baby at one time or another. He mourned the loss of the child, but it was nothing compared to the thought of losing her.

He hunkered deep into the wool coat. The blood red sun hanging low in the sky seemed prophetic. He kicked the gelding's flanks and headed south. The horse was a sleek-limbed bay with a broad chest. It had once belonged to a bushwhacker who now lay buried near a big elm at the edge of Simon's field.

Simon had insisted he take the horse. It was, Simon avowed, doing him no good hidden away in the woods. Elijah figured he'd have a fight on his hands to keep the animal. Every thief and soldier in the country would covet it. The bay was well fed and in good shape, a rare thing these days.

The horse stepped out brisk and willing. As Elijah carefully hid his trail, he discarded plan after plan. He wanted to hunt the Rawlings down one by one and put an end to this. But Billy was right. They were a big clan. It was best to leave. Perhaps, given time, their hot blood would cool.

Cindy had begged him to ride to Indian Territory and hole up. For hours he struggled with the decision. The territory was not far away, just across the river from Fort Smith. But he was loath to go there and den up like an animal along with almost every crook in the country.

He pointed the bay off the mountain onto a little used rocky trail that disappeared between black folds in the hills. On through the shadows and into the night he rode, hunched forward, with only a dome of cold stars to light the steep, rugged decline. Near the bottom he heard the creek. At first it was a soft murmur in the dark, and then as he drew close, it grew bold and loud. He stopped for a moment and watched it tumble into brief falls, silver water spilling over rocks in the starlight to churn and whirl before once again speeding on its way.

The bay dipped his head and nosed the water but barely drank. He blew and water dripped from his wet muzzle onto tufts of frozen dead grass on the creek bank.

Billy had said that some of Brooks' men were camped south of the river. Elijah decided to ride on though the night. He would camp near the Spadra Crossing and try to join them tomorrow.

He patted the horse's neck and then took off his gloves, cupped his hands, and blew on numb fingers.

"You got the feel of a good horse," he said, trying to recall what Simon had named the bay. "Reckon I'll just call you Bay." Then his eyebrows quirked. "Doubt I'll keep you long enough to call you anything," he muttered, remembering how the army confiscated mounts—especially good ones. He figured the first officer who saw the bay would relieve him of both horse and saddle. His only chance of keeping them was finding and joining Brooks. Since Brooks was cavalry, he would require a horse.

He kicked the gelding's flanks and pulled the reins back toward the trail. "Come on, fellow. We've still got a far piece to go tonight."

Cindy gasped as the window shattered. The shot had gone high in the pane, an obvious warning. The sheep grazing in the yard bleated and ran. The bell on the largest ewe clanged madly.

"Loring!" a loud voice boomed. "Come on out, and no one else will get hurt."

Then in the stillness the clock's ticking sounded loud. Cindy rose up from the pillow as Granny started to the door.

"No, Granny—"

"They'll not shoot a old woman."

She opened the door and hobbled into the cold morning on rag-wrapped feet.

Cindy stood and held to the bedpost. Black spots danced in her vision, and she feared she would faint. Her knees almost buckled as she picked up the rifle leaning against the wall. She steeled herself and, holding to the wall with one hand, weakly made her way across the floor, leaning on the gun like a cane. The wood was cold on her bare feet, and she shivered. Staying well back from view, she sank into a chair and propped the gun on the table. Through the shattered window, she saw a drizzling mist had wet the porch, leaving an icy glaze. Almost obscured by thick fog, several horses stood in the trees.

Granny pulled her shawl tight and squinted toward the woods.

"Calvin Rawlings, come out and talk. Ya know I'm a Christian and I give you my word, no harm will come to you. There ain't a man in this cabin."

After a while a big man on a scrubby sorrel left the trees and rode slowly forward. His wary eyes darted all around as he rode into the yard and stopped.

Granny drew herself up and looked him squarely in the eye. "I know you come to kill Elijah...and I know why. But I reckon you might not know the whole story. Jared provoked this here whole thang. He set on Elijah in the middle of the night—set the cabin afire with him and his woman both inside and then shot at 'em as they run outside. He's been full 'o spite ever since Cindy turned him down to marry Elijah."

She went on, "Yer kin run over Cindy with a horse and hurt her. She lost the youngun she was carrying."

For the first time a flicker of emotion crossed the face of the silent man before her.

"Elijah has left the country. They ain't no need to try trailing him. He's gone to join up with the army ag'in. They's been enough killing, Calvin. Tell yer family to go home and bury their dead, and we'll do the same."

Without a word, he turned the horse and rode back into the fog-shrouded trees.

"Do you think he listened?" asked Cindy as the old woman stepped inside and shut the door.

Granny stiffened. "Cindy, sakes alive! Get back in the bed 'fore you catch yer death!" she ordered and then hurried to assist.

Cindy, white and shaken, lay back on the pillow. Her breath came in pants as she repeated, "Do you think he listened?"

"I reckon so. Calvin and Jared was twins—but as different as Cain and Able. Calvin is one of the few good ones in that bunch. I seen

Lester and Frank out there in the edge of the woods. Them two is a different story." She glanced at Cindy. "But don't you worry. Lige is a fur piece from here by now."

Caleb entered the back door. He propped a shotgun in the corner. "They rode off. But Billy is trailing them to make sure they leave the mountains. Calvin is no fool. I figure he knowed we had guns on him the whole time. They might circle back." He warmed red-knuckled hands at the fireplace and then poured a cup of cornbran coffee and stepped to examine the broken window. "Ma, you'll have to stuff rags in this hole." He took a sip. Without turning, he asked, "Viola still in the bed?" His voice was bitter.

Granny sat down at the loom. "I've not heared a peep out of her." She cut her eyes sideways and gave Caleb a pitying look.

He stepped away from the window and approached Cindy. His smile was warm. "You up to a little trip in the wagon? Becky is a' faunchin' to have you over to her place."

Granny's hands stilled on the shuttle. She turned and frowned. "That fog is thick as pea soup. Besides I ain't sure she ought to be moved just yet. It ain't good to even walk fer nine days—"

"I'll be fine," Cindy protested. She did not add that she intended being out of bed as soon as her legs were steady. Nine days in bed would drive her mad. She could barely lie still now, tormented by visions of Elijah possibly lying dead in the road. "Besides," she added, "Becky's lonesome and scared about Elijah. It might be a comfort having me to wait on."

"I'll fix her a pallet in the wagon, and you can cover her with lots of quilts," Caleb suggested.

Granny gave over slowly. "I reckon so...but at least wait fer Billy to lift her. She ought not be walking, and yer back is in no shape to tote her."

Just before noon, Billy stepped through the door. He gave Caleb a quick nod and then said, "They've left, Pa, heading down the creek. They ain't trailing Elijah. I saw where he dropped off into Bear Creek Holler. Calvin never even tried to cut his trail. I reckon Granny's words hit the mark."

"Thank tha Lord," breathed Granny.

Cindy sagged with relief. *Elijah was safe!* At least for now…

To her mind the army was not a good idea. She and Elijah had almost quarreled before he left. She did not want him in more battles. She did not want him reliving the dark brooding that had once gripped him when he had come home a hard, cold stranger. He had not decided if he would join up again, but he had promised to send word as soon as possible. At least she could look forward to that. She thought of happy days they had spent together. Like the cabin that she had taken so much pleasure in fixing up, those times were gone now. She hoped they were not gone forever.

"I seen the wagon outside. You going somewhere?" asked Billy.

"Yep, I'm taking Miss Cindy over to Becky's. I need you to do the lifting. I used to be stout as a mule," he grumbled, hating to admit that he could not carry her, "but my poor ol' back ain't what hit used to be."

Billy glanced at Cindy and shook his head. "I don't know, Pa. She's not quite as big as Tom Sorrells, but she's tall. I might not be able to heft her."

Cindy's eyes batted in surprise. It was the first time she had ever heard Billy joke, and there was a twinkle in the serious eyes. When he smiled, his face changed completely. She gave a wavering smile in return. Not for the first time it struck her how little he resembled short, bald Caleb, or for that matter, any of Caleb's family. Billy's dark brown hair and beard were thick and heavy. Although well muscled, he was tall and slender and—with the exception of a haunting sadness in the gray eyes now fixed on her—a handsome man.

"Hit's a crazy fool notion to move her on such a day. But since yo're bound and determined"—Granny bustled over to the bed—"let's get her wrapped up good. The rain has stopped and hit's as warm as it's gonna get today…which ain't none too warm."

Cindy rose weakly off the pillow and pulled on the cloak Granny held out. Billy lifted her and started for the door.

As he stepped onto the porch, cold damp wind blew into her face. His arms felt strong, but she recalled that he had been wounded, shot in the side.

She suddenly asked, "Am I too heavy?"

"No."

"I ain't quite as big as Tom," she said with a light note, "but I'm tall—and not tiny-boned like my ma. Reckon I get my height from Pa's side."

"You're just the right size, I'd say." There was a shadow of pain in his smoky eyes staring into her upturned face.

He laid her gently into the wagon onto deep layers of quilts and then covered her with more. "Likely you'll suffer more from heat than cold," he said with raised brows as Granny hobbled out with more quilts tucked under her arm.

"Caleb, you leave plenty of these quilts with Becky. She's short of covers since them danged bushwhackers stole hers." She thrust a pungent-smelling cloth bag into his hand. "Here's some yarbs—burdock and comfrey and yeller dock—best things I know of fer strengthening the blood. Be sure and tell her to come get more if she needs hit. Cindy ought to drink at least three cups of tea a day. And—"

"And," Caleb interrupted, "if ya don't stop jawing, we won't never get her in out of this damp."

"Oh, off with ya then," she conceded.

Billy climbed onto the seat alongside Caleb. The mule bobbed his head. As the wagon wheels began turning, Granny gave Cindy a worried parting look.

"Tell Becky to send fer me day er night if ya have any trouble," she called.

Cindy pulled one hand from beneath the quilts to wave and then let it fall back to her side. She was surprised at how feeble she felt. And it was all she could do to keep tears from flowing. She longed to be alone. Although she had greatly appreciated Granny's care, there had not been a moment of privacy.

Tucked into a hillside, the rambling cabin surrounded by stately pines was cloaked in swirling fog that froze into crusted ice on dead grass and tall green boughs. Chimney smoke smelling of hickory lay low to the ground. Before the mule had stopped, the door opened and Becky stepped outside holding a gray shawl over her head. Deborah stood in the doorway, a pleased smile on her lips. Behind her blazed a roaring fire in the wide rock fireplace.

"Stay there," called Caleb. "Ya might fall on them slick rock steps. Billy will tote her in."

"I have the bed all turned back and ready," called Becky. "Careful," she cautioned as Billy approached the ice-glazed steps carrying the quilt-swathed Cindy.

Cindy ran her eyes over the warm inviting room. As usual it was meticulously clean and pretty. Only the year before bushwhackers had stolen almost everything but the bare walls. Somehow Becky had managed to make the room homey again with colorful rag rugs and a quilted pillow perched in a new rocking chair made by Caleb. The front room was spacious, free of the usual front room bed. Ned Loring had been a good carpenter and had added onto the cabin's main room that was first built by his great grandpa.

As Becky directed Billy to a side bedroom, Caleb stepped inside and removed his hat. He tweaked Deborah's nose. "What you cooking? Smells powerful good in here."

"Ma made a squirrel stew." The large eyes in her thin face grew excited. "And she's boiling peanuts! Elijah thought there weren't any, but Ma and I dug through the dirt in that sandy patch we planted down by the creek, and we found some!" She beamed. "They taste wonderful. We fixed these for Cindy but you can have some."

He laughed. "Naw, but thank you. Yer granny had dinner cooking when I left, and she'd be mad as a wet hen if I was to eat here."

As pale sun peeped over the horizon, the bay's feet left no tracks on the frozen ground. Elijah doubted anyone—except maybe Billy—could track him. Even Billy would have difficultly over the ground he had traveled this night. Bleary-eyed, he pulled the bay to a halt and looked at distant columns of chimney smoke rising over Clarksville. He involuntarily flinched as his eyes passed over the roof of the mercantile. With arms stiffened by weariness and cold, he reined the bay off the hill and toward the river. He dreaded the crossing. The water would be ice. Upon reaching the other shore, he would build a fire and dry his clothes. But first he must cross the telegraph road and make his way to the river. He wanted to give the bay a rest before the long swim. The sun, fighting through thin clouds, had not topped the far pine-covered ridge. Now would be the best time to go without attracting attention, while the river was cloaked in mists and before folks began stirring.

As he let the bay pick a descent off the rocky incline, its ears perked forward. Elijah pulled the reins and strained to listen. The road lay directly ahead. Horses were coming. Quickly he guided the bay back into the trees, dismounted, and held the reins under the bay's chin close to the bit. He put a hand over the gelding's nose to block the white cloud of breath. He wanted no whinny giving away his position.

The mounted troop of about three hundred men wore uniforms, faded but distinctly blue. Bleary-eyed and slumped-shouldered, they appeared exhausted. Two mule-drawn wagons covered with tattered canvas rattled by. Elijah frowned. This might be the much-dreaded Union contingent heading to set up a post in Clarksville. It was bound to happen, but folks would take it hard. Then he gave a grim smile picturing Hindman's provost marshal. Gill Harris would choke this army with heel dust as he ran away. Enos was right about the man. Hindman could not have appointed a bigger coward.

The sound of wheels crunching on frozen ground faded. After listening a while longer, Elijah released the bay's nostrils. The horse snorted and shook his head. The saddle creaked as Elijah mounted. Watchful, he crossed the narrow road between new yellow poles with wire stretched taut. The newly constructed telegraph line marched down the road like a sentinel. Just then a rooster crowed. It was the full-throated crow of a mature bird. Elijah wondered how the bird had survived the stew pot. He had figured every chicken in the country was dead.

"Old fellow," he muttered, "it's a good thing those Yankees didn't hear you, or you'd be floating in gravy by dinner time."

He entered the trees again and headed directly for the river, avoiding a scattering of houses, and then he skirted a large river-bottom field that had once held cotton and rode on through skeletal hardwoods and scrubby cedar. Finally, just ahead the river glistened, cold and uninviting in the wintry morning light.

It was secluded here, and not a normal crossing. But the bay was in excellent shape and should do fine. Elijah stopped in a brushy thicket near the bank and fed the horse a few nubbins of corn from the pack slung across the saddle. While it chomped hungrily on the grain, Elijah looked north, toward home. The mountains were not visible from here. His breath caught in his chest with an ache. In his worry for Cindy, he had given the child little thought. Now the disappointment pressed in deep and raw. He would have no son to work alongside him in the fields, no tow-headed boy to take fishing. He stared at the ground and his jaw tightened bitterly. When he had pressed Granny for information, Cindy did not hear the worried whisper that there might never be another child. It was often the case, Granny admitted, when a woman had been injured.

Simon was right. An eye for an eye was Old Testament, rather than New. Even so, to Elijah's mind, Jared had stolen more than his death had repaid.

Taking matches from his pant's pocket, he put them into his shirt. Then he took off socks, boots, and pants and put them into a gunnysack along with his pistol and extra cylinders. After remounting, he drew the rifle from the saddle scabbard and walked the bay toward the river. He took the reins into his teeth, and while holding sack and rifle high, he kneed the horse forward, down off the bank and into the icy water just below where the river gurgled over a lip of shoals. The bay walked boldly forward and then began to swim.

As frigid water lapped his thighs, Elijah kept his eyes peeled, darting back and forth along both banks. A hawk swooped low over the river, and then with a mighty flapping of wings, flew away. Nothing else moved except the muddy flowing water.

Without incident he reached the far bank and slid shivering from the saddle. He dried as best he could on his extra shirt and dressed with clumsy haste. He mounted again and rode on until he found a secluded spot out sight of the river. Drawing far back into the trees he tied the bay and then quickly gathered twigs and sticks and the dry pulp from a rotted pine log. His numb fingers fumbled striking the match. It broke. He tried again and this time the tip blazed with yellow fire and set the tiny pile ablaze. Soon there was enough fire to add the deadfall he had chopped with the hatchet from his pack. Purposefully keeping the fire small, he added a bit more wood and then hunkered near and ate from the sack of vittles Granny had prepared. As the fire settled into glowing coals, he unsaddled the bay, took a long pull of fresh water from his canteen, and then spread his bedroll on the ground. Although he intended to be wary, he fell into a deep exhausted sleep.

He awakened, stiff and cold. His first thought was that Cindy had let him oversleep and the fire had gone out. Then with awful knowing, he remembered and groaned. He lay for a moment wishing sleep would return and blot out reality. Anger and frustration jerked him fully awake. He stood.

The fire had burned to ash, and through a gap in the pines, the setting sun washed the sky crimson. With awkward movements, he rebuilt a blaze and then sat brooding and staring into it while he finished off the lunch Granny had packed. The cornpone was cold and tasteless but he ate to keep up his strength.

Traveling at night was risky and apt to be counterproductive. He might cross Brooks' trail without seeing it. There was fresh water here from a stream that flowed into the river and there were deadfalls aplenty for firewood and browse for the horse. He would camp here until the morrow. In spite of the day's sleep he soon rolled into a blanket and slept again.

Long before dawn he was awake and ready to travel. Restlessness pressed heavy on him as he waited for daylight, anxious to get on with whatever lay ahead. The air was still and laced with cold, the sort of morning that made a man long for a hot cup of coffee. Swirling the pale corn-bran brew in a tin cup, he took a swallow and then spit it out. He couldn't remember the last time he'd had coffee or when he had craved it more.

The bay snorted, and Elijah turned his head. "Sounds like you're as ready as me." He stood, threw the rest of the corn-bran water into the fire, and put the cup back into the saddlebag. When the sun laid the first yellow glow on the river, he climbed up and headed the bay mostly south and a little east. Likely Brooks' men had forded the river at Spadra Crossing. This route would cut their trail.

He rode slow and watchful, always checking the ground for signs. For more than an hour there were only animal tracks. Then he came to a clearing that had been used as a camp not long ago. He studied the signs and determined it was army, probably Brooks' men, about twenty of them. He scouted ahead and found another camp a short ways away and bordering the same small stream. It was normal army protocol to spread out in the search of browse and water and join up later on the march. If he rode hard, he should catch them before long. He kneed the bay and started ahead at a canter.

As the morning waned and the air grew mild, Elijah removed the heavy coat and lashed it across the back of the saddle. He glanced up at a pale sun just overhead and then started forward again. Abruptly he halted.

“Stop right there!” a man called from the brush. “Put your hands up slow and careful. Now, don’t you even twitch an eyelash, and I might not shoot you.”

A lanky man stepped onto the trail. The left side of his face was a jagged scar running from forehead to chin, the sightless marled eye unpatched and grotesque.

“Yankee saber?” asked Elijah.

The man grinned. “You’re a right calm pilgrim, ain’t ya?”

“Sometimes.”

“Why you trailing us?”

“If you’re part of Brooks’ regiment, I want to join up.”

The man cocked his head sideways. The good eye grew suspicious. “Sort of late in the game to just now be joining.”

“I’ve served before. Pea Ridge, White River, Prairie Grove.”

“Where you been lately?”

“At home farming and getting married.”

A slow smile warmed the harsh face. “That a fact? Is she pretty?”

“Prettiest you ever saw.”

He chuckled. “Ride on in,” he said, “but first take that gun out of the scabbard real slow and toss it on the ground and that handgun too.”

Elijah complied with extreme caution. Instinctively he knew here was a gritty man who would shoot without hesitation.

Never taking his eyes from Elijah, the man gathered the weapons and then nodded ahead. “Major Kirby is just up ahead. You can tell him your story.”

Elijah rode on until he saw horses hitched to trees and bushes. When a sentry stopped him, the one-eyed man called out.

“Let us through, Perry. He wants to see the major.”

The man stepped from the road and let him pass.

“That’s the major yonder—sittin’ on the end of that log.”

The group of about fifty tattered men—few in full uniform—lounged about, sitting on logs and rocks. They left off eating and drinking to eye Elijah as he rode slowly forward and then dismounted.

"Major Kirby?"

The arrow-straight, slim man nodded and lowered the tin cup he drank from.

"My name is Elijah Loring."

Elijah quickly related his military history, not leaving out the fact that he had been conscripted and had then deserted. The major studied him with keen gray eyes. Elijah finished with the information that Michael Lane was his neighbor and could vouch for him.

"Lane was captured a few weeks back," drawled the major. He stroked a neatly trimmed beard and went on in a soft Virginia accent, "You might already know that. There's lots of Yankee trash around here now, putting up telegraph lines, and you just might be one of their spies. I'm sure they'd like to know where and when we aim to tear the wire down again."

The one-eyed man spoke up. "John, if I recollect right, wasn't that fellow that Lane told us about—that friend of his who was so good at boxing—named Loring?"

"You know, Hankins, I believe you're right."

Hankins grinned and the good eye glittered. "I know a good way to prove if this is him. With your permission, sir."

When the men guffawed, Elijah surmised they were a loose-knit group, not overly concerned with protocol and regulation.

The major's eyes swept Elijah for a moment like a man appraising livestock. He stood and sloshed the remainder of his drink onto the ground. "I suppose we should check his story."

"Hey, Sampson!" Hankins called toward the back of the crowd.

A mountain of a man with massive shoulders stepped forward. His beard was long and ragged, and his overlong black hair hung loosely about a wide, craggy face. He stepped in front of Elijah and began taking off a threadbare coat. No sooner had his arm slipped from the jacket than he hurled a swift right with a ham-like fist.

The unexpected blow rocked Elijah back on his heels. Had it not been for the boxing lessons he had received from Dixon back in his army days, he would have been whipped before the fight started. Sampson lived up to his name. The blow was formidable. Elijah staggered back and shook his head to clear the ringing in his ears. He swiped at blood flowing from his nose.

Men gathered around and instantly began placing bets, few on him. Even Kirby bet, double or nothing, on Sampson.

Sampson circled, looking confident. Then Elijah, regaining equilibrium, stepped forward, dancing his feet and feigning a punch with his right. Instead he landed a hard upper cut to Sampson's chin. The giant's head hardly moved, but his eyes suddenly narrowed. Both cheers and taunts rose from the men urging them on.

Sampson jabbed, but Elijah was never in the same place for two seconds. He ducked and weaved just as Dixon had taught him. With little difficulty he avoided Sampson's menacing fists. However he dared not dance in too close to the long arms and dangerous fists, so his own lightning quick jabs did little damage to the big man.

Sampson, strong but cumbersome, quickly grew vexed. With the back of one clenched fist, he wiped a glistening drop from the end of his nose. "Bastard won't stand still and fight like a man," he grumbled, shooting a glance at the major.

Elijah had been waiting for just that opportunity. He hurled all his strength behind a smashing right that connected with Sampson's midriff and a second later landed a chopping slash to his windpipe. The big man bent double wheezing and fighting for breath.

Hankins turned his good eye on the major. "Damned if I don't think it's really him, John."

Major Kirby, chuckling, stepped forward. He clasped Sampson's shoulder.

"Sampson, we'll call it a draw. It's plain to see, if he'd stand still you'd best him. But the way he dances around we might be here all day." He glanced at the men. "For now all bets are off. Perhaps they'll have another go around later, but for now we need to ride." He faced Elijah. "Welcome. We can always use another good man."

Elijah ran a shirtsleeve across his bloodied nose and nodded. He extended his hand to Sampson. "That right of yours could easily kill a man," he said. "Hope I never feel it again."

At first the big man thrust out a belligerent chin. Then slowly he took the hand while his stiff face relaxed. "Well, I never seen your like in a fight. You ain't much big, but you dance around faster than Sadie at the Last Chance Saloon." His voice was surprisingly high-pitched for a big man. But when he turned his head away for a moment, he sneezed with a force that jarred like thunder. After pulling a red bandanna from a back pocket, he blew the bulbous nose and then sniffed. "Damn nose runs all the time," he complained, "winter and summer."

Hankins mounted up nearby. As he put a foot in the stirrup, he chuckled. "And when Sampson sneezes, stand clear—trees topple right over."

Elijah wiped his own smarting nose. It was still dripping blood. "Maybe so, but I reckon it's his fists bears standing clear of."

Sampson's lips parted in a wide smile. "Want the loan of my bandanna?"

"Thanks, but I have one." Elijah mounted the bay and then pulled out his own handkerchief and wet it from the canteen. Gingerly he wiped his nose and then tipped back his head and held the wet rag tightly to staunch the bleeding. As he joined the long file of riders, Sampson came alongside.

"Fine animal you got there." He sniffed and rubbed his running nose with the back of a big hand.

With his head still tilted back, Elijah glanced over. His eyes widened seeing the scrubby short-legged black horse overlapped by the giant's wide hips.

"Aw, this ain't my horse." Sampson unhappily nodded ahead toward Hankins. "See that big ol' rawboned pie-bald? Hankins won him off me last week in a poker game. Then the captain said it was this-here bag of bones for me or a mule. I don't hold with mules. They don't like me—and I don't like them. I'm aiming to win back old Baldy. But I got to wait till Hankins has a snoot full. He ain't no hand at cards when he's drinkin.' But don't you never bet agin' him if he's sober. Ain't no better card player on earth then." His mouth drew down. "I never would've bet old Baldy if I hadn't been drunk myself." Suddenly his eyes lit as he ran an appreciative eye over the bay. "You a card-playing man?"

"Nope. Never cottoned to cards."

When Sampson's face fell, Elijah hid a smile. A poker face was definitely not Sampson's strong suit.

Chapter 6

Cindy tiredly leaned her head back on the rocking chair. The crackling blaze in the fireplace warmed her feet, but she still felt chilled. As a hard gust rattled the windowpanes, she pulled the shawl close around her shoulders and closed her eyes. She thought, with a shiver, that February had lasted forever.

Becky glanced over and then left off peeling a potato and wiped her hands. In a moment Cindy felt the added weight of a soft quilt. As Becky tucked the quilt around her, she opened eyes that instantly grew tear-filled.

"You been mighty good to me," she said. "For weeks you've waited on me hand and foot."

Becky squeezed her shoulder. "It's been my pleasure. Since you came, I haven't been as...as lonely." She swallowed. "Sometimes I feel I can't bear that Ned won't ever walk through that door again—but you being here has helped a lot."

Cindy sat up straighter and stared at the door with troubled eyes. "If anything happens to Elijah, I reckon I'll die."

Becky shook her head. "No. You won't. You'll think you're going to...but you won't."

She glanced at Becky's face, gentle in the firelight. The flickering blaze added more gold to her fair hair. "You know something? I used to be afraid of you." As Becky's eyes widened, she hastened to add, "I thought ya didn't like me—or maybe ya wanted someone else for Elijah."

Becky's eyes dropped and her face flushed. "I confess, at one time, part of that was true. Oh, it was nothing personal—I've always thought you were a sweet girl. But you see, I had grand plans for Elijah. I wanted him to leave here and pursue a formal education and a profession." She shook her head. "That means nothing to me now. And now that I really know you, I could ask for no one better to share his life. If you and Elijah can be as happy as I was here in this cabin with Ned, I'll be more than satisfied."

Cindy put a hand on her arm. "I'm sorry you've known so much hurt."

Becky patted the hand. She quickly turned away and lifted her apron to her eyes. "If I don't get those potatoes on to boil, we'll have no dinner."

"I hope I'll soon be strong enough to he'p. I can't believe I still feel sa weak."

"You're getting better. You hardly lay down yesterday. It takes a while when you've been through so much. You'll feel like your old self again before you know it." Then Becky glanced out the window. "Here comes Billy. Law, I don't know how we'll manage without him. He's been so much help. I was dreading the spring work, but he says he'll get the plowing done before he leaves."

Cindy turned. "He's leavin'?"

Becky nodded. "He's going back to the army. He said with the Federals at Clarksville now, he's not safe here. And with spring coming on, unless he hides out, the Rebels will just conscript him anyway. Besides, I think he's feeling better lately—at least he seems brighter somehow. I've often wondered about him…he's always seemed so distant."

"I felt that too," commented Cindy. "He sure ain't nothing like his pa. Of course, he ain't nothing like Viola, either."

With a quick lift of eyebrows, Becky agreed. "No, he's not. Something in his eyes tells me he's been hurt—and I don't mean in the war."

"Reckon he ever had a sweetheart?"

Becky bit her lip in thought. "Not that I ever knew of," she said slowly, "but he was gone for a couple of years. Before the war he went to Texas to work cattle for Viola's uncle—"

A rap on the door halted their speculation. Billy stepped inside. "Morning." As he removed his hat, he nodded to Becky, but his eyes darted to Cindy. "Good to see you sitting up," he said. He turned quickly back to Becky. "I'll start by plowing your garden plot before doing the cornfield. Too early to plant much except potatoes. You have enough for seed?"

She nodded and wiped her hands on a dishtowel. "I think I hoarded enough."

"Better get them cut up tonight and ready to plant tomorrow. Granny says the crows are cawing for rain."

"Dinner's almost ready. Won't you join us?" invited Becky.

"Thanks, but I'm not hungry." He turned away. "I need to sharpen your plow a bit before I hitch my mule."

The wind caught the door and banged it against the wall as he opened it. Before stepping outside, he turned for a last glance at Cindy.

"Don't let the wind blow you away," she teased.

For just an instant a smile softened his reserved face.

A month later Cindy awakened one morning and lay listening. Wind no longer moaned around the cabin rattling the windowpanes. A wren called from the persimmon tree right outside the window. Still groggy from sleep, she swung her feet over the edge of the bed. Then it struck her: she felt good—almost like her old self. In the last weeks, she had gained strength, and this morning it was as if a heavy weight had lifted from her heart. The smile broadened as she came awake. Quickly she lay back down and snuggled near the warm body beside her. She watched the covers rise and fall with each breath Elijah drew. He had surprised her by slipping into bed in the middle of the night. In the whispered conversation, she learned he could only stay a day. Of course she was disappointed, but she would savor each minute.

As if he felt her eyes lovingly trace his face, his own eyes opened. He put an arm under her neck and drew her close.

"Morning, Miz Loring. You sure look pretty this spring morning."

She smoothed his ragged beard. "You look pretty good, yerself, but ya could use a trim on that beard."

"Ain't had much time for grooming anything but horses lately."

She sobered and propped up on an elbow. "What have you mostly been doing? Fighting?" she asked with a worried pucker between her arched eyebrows.

With a thumb he smoothed at the pucker. "Nope. Riding and riding and riding some more—so don't you go worrying and spoil our day together. Besides, I haven't so much as fired my rifle since I left. Mostly we've been tearing down telegraph wire as fast as the Yankees put it up." He stretched and yawned and then pulled her back into his arms. "Keep your voice down or Ma and Deborah will wake—"

Her kiss silenced him.

It was an hour before there was a small rap on the door. "Cindy, would you like a cup of sassafras tea? I'll bring you a cup if you don't feel like getting up yet."

"No. I'm fine. I'll be right out," she called. She giggled softly and slipped on a shoe. "Yer ma is going to be so happy to see you," she whispered.

Suddenly Elijah's mouth drew down.

Cindy left off lacing the shoe and held the buttonhook still. "What's wrong?"

He drew a deep breath. "I was just remembering how one morning Deborah and I woke up and found Pa had come home from the army. He had slipped in during the night without us knowing it. Sure was a happy day."

Cindy glanced at the closed bedroom door. "Yer poor ma." Then she grasped his arm. "Oh, Elijah, I couldn't live if anything was to happen to you." She buried her head on his shoulder.

He tilted her chin. "Hush now. Nothing is going to happen to me." He stood and quickly drew on shirt and pants. Carrying his shoes, he walked to the door. Waiting until Cindy joined him, he put an arm around her waist and opened the door.

"I set your tea on the—." Becky turned. As her mouth fell open, her eyes sparkled. In two strides she flew across the floor and gathered him into a fierce hug. "When I heard birds singing this morning, I just knew it was going to be a good day." She laughed while wiping away happy tears.

While Elijah sat at the table and made them laugh with tales of his new army comrades, Becky and Cindy cooked a feast from the supplies he had brought along. Granny and Caleb were coming for dinner so Becky stirred extra batter for cornbread. No one was surprised when Viola declared she was too poorly to come and asked Billy to stay home with her.

"Where in the world did you get tins of meat?" asked Becky as Elijah cut slits in a can of beef and peeled back the top.

"Like I told you—Captain Hankins is as resourceful as he is ugly. He made a sashay into a Union camp the other night and came back with a gunnysack slap-dab full of the stuff."

"The Union army must be eating pretty well, then," observed Becky.

Elijah shook his head. "Nope, not any better than us. But there's a few officers who have special supply lines going and coming," he said with a frown. "When they forage, it's not just for food. Hankins says they're bushwhackers in uniform. They take anything that ain't nailed down and freight it up to Kansas in wagons. He says he's seen wagons piled high with furniture and household truck—and no telling how many tons of cotton. I reckon along with getting lots of money, they get personal supplies when the wagons come back. Hankins identified a couple of 'em, and he delights in tormenting them."

Deborah's eyes grew round. "He went right into their camp?"

Elijah grinned. "Yep. He said none of the soldiers even stirred."

"Laws a'mercy!" Cindy exclaimed. "Just like David in the Bible when he slipped into King Saul's camp. The Lord must have been watchin' over him. Is Mr. Hankins a godly man?"

Elijah threw back his head and roared with laughter. But when he wiped his twinkling eyes with the back of his hand, he merely said, "Not so you'd notice."

Then he turned to Deborah perched close alongside him on the bench. "I have a surprise out in the barn. Come help me bring it inside."

Her eyes shown with anticipation as she followed him out the door into the sweet-smelling air filled with sunshine. They were gone only a few minutes. Elijah returned carrying a blanket-covered basket, and Deborah held something hidden inside of cupped hands.

The women gasped when tiny cheeps rose from the basket. Elijah folded back the blanket to reveal a black speckled hen. No chicks were in sight but tiny peeps rose from under the outspread protective wings of the frantic clucking mother.

Deborah opened her fists. Her eyes danced. "Look, Ma! A baby chick! And there's nine more under the hen!"

"She's just a banty hen," said Elijah, "but she'll give you a start on another flock, Ma."

"Oh my," breathed Becky as she reached a hand and stroked the ball of black fluff in Deborah's hand. "I've missed my chickens more than anything else the army foraged. And Bantams make the best mothers. They're wily. Foxes and hawks have a hard time catching them. Where did you get her? Between the bushwhackers and the army, I didn't know there was a chicken left in the country."

"Another gift from Hankins. When he found out I was coming home, he sent the hen along. Said he found her roosting in an old deserted barn back in the woods. I had quite a time hauling her and that basket hanging from my saddle."

"I've never allowed any kind of fowl or animal in the house," said Becky, "but I'll swan, until the chicks are a few days older, I'm keeping them inside."

The day passed much too swiftly. And in spite of Cindy's vow to be cheerful, as the shadows lengthened in the afternoon and Granny and Caleb went home, she grew morose.

"Let's take a walk," said Elijah and reached for her hand.

Becky quickly shook her head as Deborah jumped up intending to go along. With a disappointed face, she sank back onto the floor near the basket of chickens and contented herself with staring at the babies who had ventured out from under the hen to peck at the bottom of the basket.

The sun was warm on Cindy's face but in shady spots, the air grew chill. Elijah chose a path in slanting sun that led past the cornfields. The clean smell of freshly plowed earth rose from the straight furrows where the sun-warmed ground sent forth the first hint of spring.

"Billy's done a heap of work," he observed. "I want to stop by Granny's and thank him.

"He's been here almost every day. He plows Caleb's fields in the mornin' and then plows here all afternoon. It's a good thing you brought that seed corn. I don't think we had enough left to plant both fields." She was quiet for a while. "I reckon you have to stay in the army," she finished lamely.

"It's best this way for now. Someday I'll come home and we'll start over. I spend most nights staring into the campfire and planning the kind of farm we'll have and the cabin I'll build."

"Your ma has been extra kind to me, and I'm mighty grateful—but I might-nigh ache for our old cabin. Seems as if I can't stand being apart from you for one more second." Her lips trembled and she buried her face in her hands.

He held her close and smoothed a hand over her long, taffy-colored hair. "I'm glad you left your hair loose," he said. "I like it best that way."

"I know," she whispered against his shoulder. "That's why—"

Just then a sound startled them. Billy, leading a harnessed mule, stood near the trees at the edge of the creek. The mule blew again. As they quickly drew apart, Billy dropped his head. In an instant he looked up, stone-faced and emotionless, and Cindy wondered if she had imagined the pained expression a few seconds earlier.

"Howdy, cousin," called Elijah as he strode forward. He clasped Billy's hand and affectionately slapped his back. "You saved me a trip. I was fixing to stop by and thank you for all the work you've done here. It makes my mind easier knowing Ma and Cindy have so much help. I was afraid with Caleb down in his back they'd try to wrestle that mule and plow." He glanced over at Cindy and smiled. "Of course I figure Cindy could do it."

Billy's eyes swept her. "Yes, she's a right capable woman." He fiddled with the mule's harness. "There's a bit of daylight left so I figure to get that last little bit of the upper field plowed. It'll be a while yet before corn planting time, but I aim to get it done before I leave."

"Caleb said you were going back to the army."

"Yeah. Might as well before they come for me."

Elijah's brows rose in understanding. "Where will you go?"

"No real plan yet—I'll just start riding south."

"You ought to come with me. Kirby is a good officer—easygoing—and a good fellow to ride with."

"I'll think on it. It'll be about a week before I have all the work caught up. Well, I'll get on with the plowing," he said. "Lige, take care of yourself."

"You too, Billy. Hope we run into each other."

Billy paused for a moment and lowered his voice, but Cindy still heard when he asked, "Don't guess you've had any more trouble with the Rawlings clan?"

"No. I've not seen a one of them. You?"

Billy shook his head.

"We'll just hope it stays that way." Elijah raised a hand in farewell and then walked back to Cindy. "Now where were we before we got interrupted? I seem to remember you were about to kiss me again."

Like a precious jewel hidden in a pocket, Cindy carried the day in her mind and brought it out secretly to enjoy the beauty of Elijah's visit. And as her strength returned, hard work gave her less time to brood. She and Becky planted the early garden with potatoes, peas, and cabbage. In the house feathery tomato plants grew in buckets to await planting after the last danger of frost.

When the baby chicks lost their pinfeathers, Becky let the hen outside, but gave Deborah strict orders to be on the lookout for hawks and coyotes. One morning as the women started to the corncrib to shell seed corn, Cindy looked at the girl and the chickens and smiled.

"I don't think the banties know which is their ma, Deborah or the hen."

Becky opened the gate and nodded. "I hope nothing happens to any of them. She'd be heart-broken. I know the child is lonely for someone her own age to play with, but—." She gave a pained cry as she stepped forward. A jagged piece of metal protruded from the sole of her thin shoe. "Oh!" she moaned and leaned against the fence.

"Are you bad hurt?"

Becky, gritting her teeth, raised her foot and pulled out the metal. She took off the shoe, and gingerly probed the broken skin. "I'm afraid it stuck into my foot pretty deeply." She grimaced. "I've been meaning to pry that stake out of the ground. Ned used to tie the gate to it. I knew it was dangerous when it rusted and broke in two, but I kept forgetting."

Cindy frowned and looked at the drops of blood clinging to the rusted metal that Becky had tossed aside. "Granny says rusted metal is just the worst thang. You best go right into the house and soak hit…it." Cindy quickly corrected herself. As Becky limped away, she called after her, "Don't you worry about the corn. I'll get it shelled."

Although Becky soaked the foot, dabbed on turpentine, and doctored it with a generous dollop of Granny's goldenseal salve, it grew red-streaked and angry. Finally on the third day—after tossing and turning all night in pain—she sent Cindy after Granny.

Granny pulled off her bonnet and stared at the swollen foot. Sunlight streaming through the kitchen window revealed the sparseness of the gray hair pulled tightly back into a bun. She squinted at the foot and then reached into her pocket and took out a snuff tin and took a dip before she spoke. With her tongue, she tamped the snuff firmly between gum and lip.

"I've seed worse," she finally said, "but hit ain't good. We got to get right after this, so's ya don't lose that foot." She turned to Caleb. "Hand me my satchel." She turned back to Becky. "Ya got to soak hit real often in Epsom salts—can't buy none since the war commenced"—she pulled open the satchel and rummaged inside—"so I made my own. Boiled down some salt, leeched hit and scraped the leavings." She drew forth a small pouch with satisfaction. "Here 'tis. After ya soak hit, I want ya to tie that foot up with some mullen leaves to draw the poison." She looked Becky straight in the eye. "Then with plenty o' prayer we just might save yer foot."

Becky held her bottom lip in her teeth and stared at the red streaks running up her ankle. "Pray hard, Granny."

Granny patted her arm. "I will, child, I will."

Cindy began praying that very moment.

Hidden in dusty-blue shadows, Elijah sat beneath a fragrant pine, watching a doe drink at the river's lapping edge. Fat-bellied with unborn fawn, she gazed warily around in the twilight and then dipped her muzzle into the water. He stared at the sunset and thought how much Cindy would enjoy the beauty of the sky awash with coral reflected on the rippling water. Already, he ached for her. Going home for only a day had been painful—almost more painful than not going at all. In the routine of camp life, he had grown a little numb to the loneliness; but, like worrying a bad tooth, the short visit had made their separation a fresh, throbbing misery.

When his horse blew, the doe threw up her head. Water dripped from her chin as she glanced his way, gathered her legs, whirled, and fled. Elijah himself gazed warily about and especially fixed his penetrating gaze on the far bank. There had been no travelers on the rough route he had taken out of the mountains. And, so far, although he had seen an elderly couple out working in a garden patch, he had seen no sign of riders in this remote valley. And yet he turned often to watch his back trail. Bitter experience had taught him that there were those who could take a body by surprise. He did not intend to be taken by surprise, not ever again.

Finally he kneed the bay and rode quickly toward the exposed riverbank. Without hesitation the bay entered the water and soon swam with flared nose pointed toward the opposite shore. Elijah, in order to be a less prominent target, lay low on the outstretched neck. The far bank was steeper, and the horse struggled a bit before pulling up the rocky incline. Elijah did not draw an easy breath until they had once again gained the wood's cloaking shadows.

Brooks' regiment never stayed long in one place; however, Elijah knew the general direction of their intended travel, so he pointed the bay south. He rode cautiously, pausing often to listen. He heard only land echoing springtime—singing insects, fast-rushing creeks, and night creatures scurrying away through the brush. Evening air grew chill against his wet clothes. He paused long enough to draw out a slicker and put it on. Full dark was upon him by the time he smelled campfire smoke tickling the night breeze.

The bay's ears pointed forward. Elijah gave a soft whistle. Upon hearing two notes of reply, he rode into camp.

Dozens of men lolled around small campfires where steam rose from boiling pots and the smell of roasted meat drifted from a forked stick spit holding a skinny rabbit. A few men nodded as Elijah rode past. Sampson looked up from a fist full of cards held close to his wide chest. His face worked with both exhilaration and agitation.

"Hey, Elijah, loan me a dollar. I got a doozy of a hand here, and Hankins has just raised the bet."

Elijah climbed stiffly off the bay. He stripped off the saddle and called over his shoulder. "I haven't even seen a dollar in a coon's age. Besides that, Hankins looks stone-cold sober to me."

As Sampson quickly studied his opponent his eyes narrowed. With instant disgust he threw the cards onto the ground. "Why! You ain't drunk! You was play-acting. That was a low-down scummy trick."

Hankins' good eye cocked toward him sparkled with humor. "But I enjoy fleecing you. I've been missing our card games." He picked up Samson's discarded cards and the grin widened into wicked delight. He fanned them out and then fanned his own. "Lookie here, your full house beats my pair of queens. If you hadn't folded, you'd have cleaned me good and won back old Baldy."

Sampson's eyes bulged and his jaw worked.

"Aw, hell, you ain't gonna cry, are ya!" Hankins slapped his knee and haw-hawed. As Sampson stomped away, Hankins raked in the pile of loot—a half-empty tobacco sack, a ragged pair of socks, and a shiny silver dollar.

Elijah drew near the fire and poured a cup of steaming brew. "Hankins, surely you could find some real coffee in a Union camp. This parched corn water gives me the bellyache."

Hankins paused from stuffing the coin into his side pocket. "Now that is a right fine idea. I just might be able to sniff some out. The other day I ran into an acquaintance name of Callaway—Tyler Callaway. He swears some gal in Clarksville still has a heap of real coffee beans. At least she brewed him a cup a while back. Made me drool just listenin' to him." He pushed the coin deeper into his pocket and stood. "Think I'll go this very night. You wanna ride along?"

Elijah slopped brown water from the tin cup into the fire. Through the hiss of rising steam, he faced Hankins.

"I'll not rob a woman."

"Aw, I ain't going after the gal's coffee. But I'll just bet those Feds at Clarksville has some Lincoln coffee—I'll bet the officers have some stashed."

Just then the major walked into the flickering light of the campfire. "Hankins, you are going to Clarksville, but not after coffee," he said. "I've been running a plan through my head ever since I got word there's to be a concerted effort to retake the whole river valley this spring. There are already Texas troops—and some from Missouri—heading here for that very purpose. Your idea to sneak into town fits right in with what I've been thinking. We know there are howitzers at the garrison. When we charge down Main Street, I'd just as soon not run slap-dab into them."

"You want me to disable them."

The major nodded. "And while you're at it, find their powder magazine and blow it up."

Hankins drew a pipe and pouch of tobacco from his pocket and pulled it open. Nonchalantly, he packed the pipe and struck a match. After puffing the blaze to life, he drew deeply and then sent out a wreath of strong-smelling smoke.

"When do you want me to go?"

"The sooner the better." The major chewed his lip a moment and studied Elijah. "Loring, you go along with him."

Elijah tensed. "With all due respect, sir, I've got reasons for staying out of Clarksville."

The major's easy-going attitude vanished. "Reasons be damned. You know the town. You're smart and quick on your feet. Hankins will need you."

Elijah curtly tipped his head in acknowledgment of the order.

The major's terse stance softened a bit. "Besides, you're already wet."

Elijah quirked an eyebrow. The major was right about that. He was wet—wet, cold, and tired. There was no remedy for that now. He would be soaked again and colder and wearier before this night was over.

While Hankins saddled the piebald, Major Kirby gave Elijah a fresh horse. It was a skittish black gilding with long legs and a wide chest. Sampson arrived with a bowl of hot, watery soup and a piece of corn cake that was more bran than corn.

"Troy," he said and looked at Hankins as he handed the food to Elijah, "don't you go getting old Baldy shot out from under you…or confiscated by no Yankee."

Hankins turned his head until the good eye rested on Sampson. "Well, sugar dumpling, I'm touched by your concern for my hide."

Sampson glanced worriedly around. "Aw, Troy, you promised…"

Hankins grinned. "No one heard me. Besides sugar dumpling isn't such a bad name. Just shows your mama was right fond of you."

Sampson shot him a murderous look. He rubbed Baldy's face and then stalked away. Hankins watched him go and chuckled.

"I take it you two go back a ways," commented Elijah.

"A long ways," said Hankins. "We grew up neighbors at Danville, right across the field from each other. I'm a couple of years older so he's sort of like a kid brother to me." He looked after the big man. "He's got a wife and seven children back there. I was gonna let him win Baldy back tonight, but maybe it's a good thing—I might need a fast horse and ol' Baldy is greased lightning."

Elijah eyed the black. "This one looks like a runner, too."

"He is," agreed Hankins. "He belongs to the major."

They mounted up and soon were swallowed in darkness. They headed straight for the river, a black ribbon under the velvet, star studded sky. Without a hint of moon they rode slowly, carefully, almost blind, waiting for eyes to adjust to the night. They followed the dark gurgling flow until the high bank gave way to a well-worn path leading into the water at a crossing.

Elijah frowned. "I'd rather cross someplace less conspicuous," he said in quiet tones, "but it's pretty late for travelers. Maybe no one will see us."

Abruptly they both whirled. At the rustling in the brush both men reached for rifles.

"Don't shoot." The voice was high-pitched and breathless. "It's me." With a grunt and a curse, Sampson, crashing through the brush, hove into sight overlapping the undersized horse.

"Whathahell you think you're doing?" snapped Hankins.

"I'm coming with ya, Troy."

"No, you're not!"

Sampson squirmed, creaking the saddle. "Now, don't go sending me back. Three heads is better than two. An if nothing else, while you two sneak around blowing up stuff, I can hold the horses."

Hankins seemed to consider. Then he relented. "All right, but you better do just what I say—and nothing more. You hear?"

As if fearing Hankins would change his mind, Sampson immediately headed the small horse into the water.

"Wait!" ordered Hankins. "Damn it, trade horses with me before you drown that poor little thing."

Sampson's teeth gleamed white in starlight. "Thanks, Troy."

As if greeting his old rider Baldy bobbed his head and blew. As soon as both men had remounted, they rode forward.

As cold water from the Arkansas crept to his waist, Elijah stiffened and came fully awake. As the frigid water crept higher, he gritted his teeth to keep them from chattering. The night air was mild, but the river was only a few shades warmer than winter.

They rode single file down the narrow trail. Without incident, after a ride of two hours, they drew near town. Elijah pulled the gelding to a halt.

In low tones he said, "We'll circle around north of town and come in along Spadra Creek. I know an old fellow who can give us the lowdown on how many and where the troops are. I doubt there's much he doesn't know. He's a good old fellow, but nosey as a woman."

"But can you trust him?" asked Hankins with a keen glance from his eye.

"Yes."

"All right then. We'll follow you." As an afterthought, he asked, "He wouldn't happen to have a good horse, would he?"

"Naw. Just an old hound and a flea-bitten mule."

"I sure hope we don't have to make a run for it," he mumbled.

The shack was dark. Peepers, loud along the creek, masked the sound of the horses as they rode carefully forward. Elijah climbed down and handed the reins to Sampson.

"I'll be back quick as I can," he whispered. "I figure it's along about midnight."

Hankins dipped his head. "We'll be waiting. I sure would like a smoke," he muttered.

The old hound stood stiff legged and growled low in his throat when Elijah approached the porch.

"It's only me, Sirius."

The dog sank back down with a near human sigh. Elijah gave a pat to the flat grizzled head as he stepped past and knocked softly on the door. He gave a wry smile when he heard a shotgun cock.

"It's me, David," he said low. "Elijah Loring."

The door creaked opened. David's outline was barely visible in the dark room. He stepped aside to let Elijah enter.

"Howdy, son. Sorry to bother you, but I need some information from your grandpa."

David turned his head and looked behind where raspy wheezing emanated from one corner. "Grandpa is awful sick. I doubt he can tell you anything."

A frown creased Elijah's forehead.

"Can I he'p?"

"You just might…David, do you know how many troops are in town and where they're camped?

"I ain't sure of the exact number—but they's not too terrible many. Right about two hundred, I'd guess. Not much more for sure. But I heared 'um say they're expectin' reinforcements in a couple o' weeks.

They camp on yon side of Main Street, spread out up and down the creek in tents. Except fer the officers, and they stay in folk's houses."

"Where's their headquarters?"

"Ya know that big ol' two-story red brick house cattycornered to the courthouse and a ways to the north? That's it. They're using the Methodist church to store their food and stuff."

"What about ammunition and gunpowder?"

David's white teeth flashed in a grin. "I know that, too. Hit's in a little hut back of the church. Time to time, I help myself to a bit fer squirrel hunting when I run low. There's a loose board in the back wall."

"That what you do on your night rambles," asked Elijah, "help yourself to stuff?"

He thought the boy hung his head a bit before it rose high and defiant. "I don't take from no person—just from whichever army is in town. And sometimes from one of them sheds where they keep stuff they call contraband. Them Yankees ain't nothing but thieves."

Elijah glanced to the back of the room. "I'm sorry about your grandpa. I sure hope he gets well." He stuck out his hand and shook David's. "Thanks. You've been a big help." He turned and then quickly turned back. "What about the cannons—where are they?"

"Usual they're up on East Hill. But they headed out with 'em lickety-split somewhere's the other day, and when they brought them back, the last I seen they was right alongside the church."

"Thanks."

Before the door softly closed, Elijah had melted into the darkness. As he made his way back to the horses, his steps were muted by soft ground and patchy dead grass not yet pushed aside by new growth. After a hurried confab, he remounted and the three men cautiously passed behind the buildings hugging Main Street. A short way out of town Elijah crossed the dirt road and led them back toward town and the bell tower of the Methodist church. It rose stark and unfinished, dark against the sky, awaiting the bell that had not been hung. Well away from the building, he stopped in the deep shadows of a black walnut grove and peered toward a small log shed with padlock gleaming in the light of a small campfire. Near the door a tall, loose-limbed sentry paced back and forth. After a bit he sat down on a knapsack and leaned his head back against the rough log wall. He held a rifle between his knees. A few yards beyond the shed, near a white picket fence, loomed two short-barreled cannons attached to high-wheeled limbers. After a bit the sentry yawned loudly and shook his head to clear away drowsiness and then stood and began another slow ramble back and forth, holding the gun propped negligently against one shoulder.

Hankins swore softly. "How we gonna keep him from squealing like a stuck pig?"

"Give me your pistol," whispered Elijah as he drew a knife from his boot and stuck it into his belt. "Sampson, hold the horses quiet." He nodded at Hankins. "You be ready to come running." Quickly and silently he slipped through the trees and across the short grass behind the shed. He inched his way along the wall and waited for the sentry's return trip. Just as the soldier passed the edge of the building, Elijah pointed the pistol. The sentry froze as the grating cock of the pistol echoed loud in the silence.

"Toss the rifle away and don't make a sound."

The man hesitated.

"A little gunpowder ain't worth dying for," prodded Elijah.

The man's shoulders slumped just a bit. When the gun hit the ground, Hankins ran forward and scooped up the rifle while clutching his own.

"Tie him up and stuff a handkerchief in his mouth. Then leave him with Sampson." Elijah was busy prying at the lock. It held fast. But the hasp was old and rusty. A sharp blow with the rifle butt separated it from the door and left the lock dangling useless.

Inside the shed was pitch black. He struck a match just long enough to see the position of boxes and barrels. Kegs of gunpowder were near the door. He had just hoisted one onto his shoulder when he heard steps. He frowned. Hankins should be halfway to the horses. He froze and his mouth went dry.

"Richard," a man called. "Richard, where are…What the—"

Before Elijah could move, a gun blast split the night calm followed by the shouted warning, "*Trouble at the powder magazine!*"

"Mister, back here!" The hiss had come from inside the hut. "There's loose boards here where you kin slip out."

Elijah made a dash for the sound of David's voice. "Right here. There you go."

Elijah scraped through the too small opening and then held the boards apart for David. To his surprise David refused to follow. "Naw, you go on," he said low and urgent. Before Elijah could protest, David disappeared back inside.

In seconds, as he crouched and ran through the dew-wet grass, he heard the boyish voice near the front of the hut. "Mister, stop yer bellering. You don't need the whole dang regiment to take me."

Elijah paused behind a tree long enough to watch as the sentry held a lantern high with David's skinny frame highlighted in its pool of yellow light.

"Where's Richard—the guard?"

"My grandpa has a good jug of shine fer sale and sent me to fetch anybody stirring. I told that guard feller I'd stay here till he come back. Then I just leaned on that old door and the latch popped loose. I never meant no harm—I jest wanted to see what was inside. Then you 'most scared the pants off me—a shootin' and bellerin' like that."

"I'll wring that damn Richard's neck," the soldier muttered.

More soldiers, with tousled hair, came running, armed, wide-eyed, and suspenders dangling. The soldier quickly shut the door and hid the broken latch with his body. "False alarm, fellows," he called. "Just a snot-nose kid nosing around. Go back to sleep."

Elijah let out a long-held deep breath, shook his head, and made for the horses. *That David is a shrewd one*, he thought. *I owe him.* He almost bumped into the bound and gagged sentry who was tied to a lead rope.

Sampson and Hankins were mounted. Even in the dim light Elijah saw beads of sweat on Sampson's broad white face. Hankins held the prisoner's rope, and yet the black's reins were still tied to a sapling. He held a cocked gun on the guard. "Hurry up," he snapped. "We were just about to leave you."

Abruptly they all stiffened. In a flash, Hankins pressed the gun to the guard's temple. Two soldiers, one carrying a lantern, cut through the trees, just yards from their position. One of them yawned loudly.

"I was sleeping good until that dang fool waked me," he complained.

Elijah's eyes darted toward Sampson who gave a muffled snort. His face was screwed up, his nostrils flared, and his mouth opened. Hankins glared and then quickly reached up and pinched Sampson's nose.

The steps passed on. Hankins eyes and voice were murderous. "Until we're out of town, if you sneeze, I swear I'll shoot you!"

Sampson, stricken, slowly nodded and swallowed, making his Adam's apple bob nervously.

With keen, watchful eyes, they prodded the guard along and inched their way through the trees and past darkened houses. Each careful step echoed like a drum roll in Elijah's straining ears. A short distance from town, they finally halted.

"I don't suppose we need a hostage now," Hankins said. "We're still too close to town. A shot might bring them running. Loring, you got that knife handy?"

The soldier's horrified eyes widened.

"We'll leave him here," said Elijah. "We'll be long-gone before he makes it back all trussed up like that."

Hankins rubbed his chin in deliberation. "It sort of galls me to just let a Yankee go."

"No need to stir the pot just yet," said Elijah. He eased around a bit in the saddle and faced Hankins. "Besides, I admire how his friend tried to cover for him back there. Means a lot—just like you leaving me the black when you'd have had a better chance riding him."

Hankins curled his bottom lip and rolled the good eye disdainfully, but he capitulated. "Aw, all right. Let him go."

"Take his gag out. I need my handkerchief," said Sampson. "It's the only one I got and my nose is a pourin.'"

"No," said Hankins, "use your shirtsleeve. I'm taking no chances on him bellowing out and someone hearing."

Sampson sniffed loudly as if to emphasize his great need. "All right, but my poor sleeve is shore gonna get snotty."

They rode on, walking the horses quickly over uneven rocky ground. When at last they entered the road, they spurred the animals into a trot. They paused occasionally to listen, but all was quiet to the rear. At the river's edge they stopped. Elijah stifled a shudder. Sight of the swift, black water gave him gooseflesh. He had not been warm since sundown.

"John won't be pleased with this night's work," grumbled Hankins, his lips down-turned. "We didn't accomplish a thing."

"Maybe we did," Elijah said slowly. "We found out their numbers are really low just now—less than three hundred. And they're expecting reinforcements soon." He gave a slight grin. "I figure the major will appreciate knowing that."

Chapter 7

Cindy leaned on the hoe for a moment as she glanced back at the long, straight furrow, now neatly covered with clean-smelling earth. A soft smile curled her lips when she noticed Deborah had gone immediately to the next row and begun dropping kernels of field corn seed meticulously sixteen inches apart. The girl was a hard, diligent worker.

Deborah paused with one hand inside the bucket and looked toward the far edge of the field where the trail crossed Little Piney Creek. "There's a rider coming," she said and leaned the bucket of seed against her hipbone.

Cindy turned, shading her eyes against the morning sun. Worry lines puckered her brow when the horse and rider left the road and headed for the cabin. It was a lone rider—definitely not a gang of bushwhackers—and yet her mouth went dry with visions of Pete's bloody head hanging off the porch.

Her heart skipped a beat and then thundered in her chest. Quickly she dropped the hoe and gathered her skirts. "Deborah, go fetch Caleb and Granny," she ordered.

Deborah squinted her eyes. "It's only Mr. Emmitt, the storekeep from town."

"Do as yer told," snapped Cindy. Emmitt Gossett riding all the way from town could only mean bad news.

Deborah's blue eyes shadowed. Without another word she whirled and fled. Long legs and bare feet flashed from under the calico skirt that was at least five inches too short. She paused at the edge of the creek and looked back once before crossing on the steppingstones.

Emmitt was already in the house as Cindy ran across the yard. Out of breath, she stopped on the porch and braced herself. Then she opened the door.

Her mouth went dry. Becky leaned forward in the chair with her face in her hands. Cindy clung to the doorframe for support. The words almost hung in her dry throat.

"*Is it Elijah?*"

Becky raised a tear-streaked face, but her eyes blazed with joy. "Ned! Ned is alive!" She looked heavenward. "Oh, dear God, thank you!" she whispered. Then she laughed aloud. "Oh, Cindy. He's alive!"

"He sure is!" Emmitt stood with arms crossed on his chest and broad face beaming.

Becky's words gushed out. "He's been in a prison camp in Mississippi, but there was an exchange. Michael saw the roster when he was exchanged, and he sent word to—"

Cindy's face brightened even more. "Michael—he was exchanged?"

"Yes!" Becky nodded vigorously. "He wasn't in the same prison camp, but there was a long list posted of exchanged prisoners and he saw Ned's name on it! Michael got word to Clarksville and Mr. Gossett came to tell us." Her laughter bubbled over, sounding almost hysterical.

"Then he's all right?" Cindy questioned.

For a moment Becky's face grew grave. "Michael said Ned was sent to a Confederate hospital near Shreveport, Louisiana. As far as he knows, Ned is still there. That was weeks ago," her voice grew distressed. Her shoulders straightened. "No. I won't despair. The Lord isn't cruel. He wouldn't let me rejoice so only to have Ned snatched from me again." She stared at the bandaged foot. "But I must go to him! Those hospitals are death traps. More men die there than on the battlefields."

Cindy also stared at the foot. Becky was not able to travel.

Just then the front door flew open. Caleb carried a shotgun resting in his arms. His face was tight. His eyes sought Emmitt.

"Deborah said she seen you ridin' in. What's the news?"

Just then Granny hobbled inside.

"What—?"

"Ned is alive!" Becky laughed through tears as she talked. "He's been in a prison camp, and he's ill now and in a hospital in Louisiana, but he's alive."

The old woman's knees gave way. But for Caleb's arms, she would have fallen. Then she quickly righted herself. "I knowed he was alive. I just knowed it. The Lord heared my prayers." She sank into a chair. "Hit's a miracle, Becky, I tell ya, a honest to goodness miracle!"

Becky cried, "Yes, yes, it is!"

Caleb's face was a wreath of smiles. He hugged Granny hard with his short, powerful arm. Then as though they had not yet heard the news, he repeated, "Ned's alive. He's coming home!"

"Oh, I wish Elijah knew," said Cindy.

Deborah stood in the doorway. She glanced at Cindy. "Granny told me to stay in the wagon, but I—"

Becky held out her arms. "Come here, honey. No, it's wonderful news." She took the child's hands. "Your pa is alive. He'll soon be home…at least I pray it will be soon." As Deborah drew in a sharp joyful breath, Becky turned to Caleb. "We'll have to go fetch him. You know they get poor care in those military hospitals. We need to leave right away."

Granny's mouth drew down. "Becky, you ain't goin' nowhere. That foot of yers, is still festering. You ain't mighty careful, you could still lose hit."

"Caleb can't go alone," Becky protested. "Ned will need nursing on the trip home."

Granny looked at her own crippled feet. "Yo're right. I'm half a mind to try—"

"Now, Ma," Caleb put in, "you ain't in no shape to go neither."

"I'll go," said Cindy. All eyes turned to her. When Becky started to protest, she added, "I'm the perfect one to go. I'm well now. And Granny already taught me a lot about nursing."

Granny, with face serious, nodded slowly. She turned to Becky. "You can't go—neither kin I. Viola's most a idiot these days—just sits in her rocker staring at the wall. She'd be no help a'tall." She nodded again. "Yep, Cindy would be a good hand. I'll send lots of yarbs along and tell her how to use 'em. I wish we knowed Ned's trouble."

"Hit's settled then," said Caleb. "I got a good bit of gettin' ready to do 'fore we go. I'll ask Simon to watch out fer you women," he commented to Becky. Then as he urged Granny toward the door, he called back over his shoulder, "Cindy, get yer things all ready. We'll leave here day after tomorrer."

"I'll be ready," she said.

Deborah tugged on Becky's sleeve. "Can I go too, Ma? Please?"

Becky gathered her into her arms. "If you went who would take care of me?" she asked gently. "I know the waiting will be torture but I need you."

Cindy poured water into the basin and began washing her hands. Her mind was in a whirl thinking what to take. She had little to pack for herself, but Ned would need every comfort they could arrange. How she wished Elijah could go with her! So far as she knew, Brooks' men were nowhere near. Maybe they could get word to him somehow.

Cindy slept little that night. She had no illusions. The trip would be long and hard—and dangerous. On the way to Louisiana, they would pass through both Union and Confederate territory. She hoped Caleb could get a pass that would let them through without delays.

The next day flew by, filled with washing and ironing and packing. Simon stopped by with a tub filled with offerings donated by neighbors who rejoiced at the news. Although they had little enough to share, Ned was well loved, and folks, as Simon said, just wanted to help. Out of hidden stashes had come jerked beef, potatoes that were shriveled but edible, dried apples, dried beans, cornmeal, and even a small keg of molasses.

Simon held up a used but serviceable black frock coat. "I figure he might get chilly of a night. And Polly throwed in two pairs of socks she was knitting."

"That is so kind of both of you—of everyone." Becky wiped tears from her cheeks. "Seems I can't stop crying," she said and drew a white handkerchief from her apron pocket and blew her nose. "Please tell everyone how grateful I am." Her blue eyes shone with tenderness. "When Ned gets home, we'll have a party and invite everyone."

Before climbing onto the wagon seat, Simon faced Cindy.

"Daughter, I shore don't cotton to the idea of you going. I'd go, but Caleb's right—one of us men ought to stay behind. And I reckon I ought not leave yer ma. She has more bad days than good." With the frown his narrow face became deeper seamed with wrinkles. "But hit's awful dangerous fer a woman to be travelin.'"

She patted his arm. "Don't fret, Pa. Caleb will look out for me. I'll be back before you know it."

He gathered her into a hug. As he swallowed, his prominent Adam's apple bobbed. "The Lord bless and keep ya."

After the short benediction and a quick kiss on her forehead, he climbed onto the seat and flipped the reins on the mule's back.

Cindy's throat tightened watching him go. She dreaded the trip. But it was the right thing to do.

They left before daylight. The trees along the creek were shrouded in darkness but the sky had lightened to a faint gray. The two mules hitched to the wagon stepped lively, frisky in the mild spring air and satisfied with the light load.

Caleb was unusually quiet, and Cindy, also, stared ahead lost in thought. Except for jingling harness, brisk mule hooves, and newly awakened birds, they rode in silence. She daydreamed of crossing paths with Elijah. And he would then go with them. She knew it was unlikely, but it read in her mind, over and over, like a well-loved storybook. As the sun popped over the lip of the ridge, she let the shawl slide from her shoulders. It looked to be a perfect day with only a smattering of white puffy clouds to soften the sky.

Caleb broke the silence. "Hope the telegraph ain't down ag'in. I aim to send word to that-there hospital—let 'em know we're a comin.' Shore hope they don't move Ned 'fore we get there."

Cindy frowned. How awful to travel all that way only to find him gone!

Caleb hunched forward, resting short but muscle-corded arms on his legs and holding the reins slack as he stared ahead and once again grew silent.

Cindy glanced over. "Wouldn't it be wonderful if we found Elijah on the way?"

He nodded. "Or Billy."

She would much prefer to find Elijah, but she kept that thought to herself.

The sun was low in the west as they crossed the long covered bridge over Spadra Creek. Nonetheless, Clarksville was astir. Cindy's eyes widened to see scores of blue-coated troops scurrying back and forth busily loading wagons with dismantled tents and supplies.

Caleb slowed the mules and studied the melee. "Appears they're pulling out. Before we make camp, I better stop by Emmitt's and find out what's afoot."

Main Street was dusty in twilight. The other buildings were dark, but a lamp burned in the mercantile as Caleb pulled the mules to a stop.

Emmitt's broad face beamed as they came through the door. "Reckon you're on your way to get Ned?" he guessed.

"Yep. What's going on? Looks like the army is pulling out."

"Some of them." Emmitt nodded and then his lip curled. "Unfortunately not all of them. Some are staying. Not sure of the particulars, but rumor is that most of them are heading for Little Rock to join up with troops there for some sort of foray down into Texas or Louisiana."

Caleb's brows drew together. "I don't like that a'tall. Wish they was headed the other direction."

Emmitt leaned on the counter. "Aw, I doubt you'll run into them. Takes a army a heap longer to travel than one lone man in a wagon." He grinned at Cindy. "Of course I forgot you're hauling a woman. Miss Cindy didn't load you down with lots of trunks, did she?"

Caleb snorted. "After that riff-raff burned her out, this child don't hardly have clothes enough to cover her back!"

Emmitt nodded. "I reckon that's too true. Miss Cindy, if there's a thing left on the shelves that you need, just help yourself." He frowned. "Of course there isn't much left that the army didn't take." He started toward the back of the store. "There is a dress or two that just might fit you. Not likely I'll sell any dresses until the war is over. You may as well get some good out of 'em before they rot."

As she protested, he shook his head. "No, I insist. It's seldom enough I do something nice. But Ned Loring is one of the best men on earth. I'd like to help out. Caleb do you see anything you need for the trip?"

Caleb blinked in surprise. Emmitt Gossett was not known for his generosity. "Why, thank you, Emmitt. But I reckon we got enough to make do."

Cindy had never owned a store-bought dress. She eyed the printed shirtwaist with pleasure. It was a pretty pattern of tiny white flowers on a deep green background in simple classic lines, free of ruffles and flounces, just the right style for travel. And there was a blue one also just her size. But it was fancy and not suited for travel. She looked at it with longing but chose the green instead.

To her surprise and pleasure, Emmitt gathered up both and folded them into a parcel. "Like I said, you may as well get some good out of them."

She accepted the gift and squeezed his hand. "Thank you so much, Mr. Gossett. The Lord bless you."

He swallowed and looked at the floor. "Never give religion much thought until lately. Life is sure uncertain these days."

"Fer a fact," Caleb hardily agreed. "A feller does hisself a service by thinkin' on such things. We shore ain't promised tomorrer. It's right comfortin' knowing a body is ready to meet his maker."

Emmitt cleared his throat and quickly changed the subject. "Staying in the wagon yard?"

"Yep. We're fixed up tolerable comfortable with a little tent fer Miss Cindy." Caleb opened the door but paused to ask, "Is the telegraph working?"

Emmitt shook his head. "Nope. As fast as the Yankees put up new lines, someone tears them down. Last week I rode out of town a ways and saw a couple of dead soldiers right by a pole. Trying to keep those lines up isn't a healthy job."

"I reckoned that was how it would be." Caleb looked toward the courthouse, and his frown deepened. "Shore hope I don't have no trouble gettin' a pass. I ain't looking forward to asking."

Emmitt joined them near the door. "For a Yankee, Colonel Waugh ain't a bad sort. At least he tries to keep his men on a tight leash. There hasn't been much trouble out of them…not like some places I've heard of where troops are taking anything not nailed down and shipping it back to Kansas in wagons. Some woman passed through here a while back and said they even took her piano!"

Caleb scowled. "I reckon some folks think war gives 'em the right to steal. But I got news fer 'em—the good Lord is watchin.' They ain't gonna get away with it."

"Maybe so," said Emmitt, "but right now it appears the Yankees have the upper hand."

Outside the tall white courthouse, Cindy sat in the wagon in spring sunshine, waiting and praying as Caleb talked with the authorities inside. She kept her chin high and her eyes forward while pretending not to hear the comments of admiring soldiers who lolled nearby. So far none had been insulting, but her cheeks burned at the compliments. She hoped her sunbonnet hid the blushes.

Soon Caleb exited the building. She leaned forward to see his face and then relaxed back against the hard seat. He did not look upset. As a matter of fact, she thought he looked downright glad as he folded a piece of paper and put it into the pocket of his worn trousers. It must be the pass!

He hurried with bow-legged stride and climbed aboard the wagon. "Waugh give me the pass. And he promised to send a telegram down to Shreveport just as soon as ever they get the lines up again."

"That's wonderful!"

As he chirruped the mules and headed out of town, she waved to Emmitt Gossett where he stood in front of the mercantile with arms crossed on his broad chest. He returned the wave with a big smile. Then she looked around at the nearly deserted town and wondered how long it would be before they saw it again. Although Pa was a Union man she could not help but hope that Elijah would be here with the Confederate troops in control when they returned.

"That colonel says there's less trouble on the other side of the river just now. And he says there's a boat at the dock that'll ferry us across so we'll cross here at Spadra."

She nodded and settled back to enjoy the fresh morning. In spite of the hardships they would surely face, today she felt a keen sense of adventure as she peered at houses, joining dooryard to dooryard where fresh grass crept up through long yellowed sprigs, the leavings of winter. Never had she set foot on a boat. She smoothed the skirt of the new green dress and was glad she had worn it. Tomorrow she would pack it away and wear her old brown dress. She would like to keep the new ones as nice as possible.

Cindy Loring, you're gettin' downright vain, she mentally scolded. Nevertheless her lips curved into a soft smile as she daydreamed of Elijah seeing her in the new dress.

Her eyes strained ahead for sight of the boat. It was not until Caleb guided the mules around a corner where a steep grade ended at the river's edge that she saw a large boat with smokestacks belching plumes of gray smoke.

"Appears they're about ready to shove off. We got here just in time," said Caleb as he hurried the mules along. "Whoa, there, Sam, Pet!" he calmed them as they shied from the shrill whistle announcing the boat's upcoming departure.

Cindy experienced a few nervous butterflies. Mostly she enjoyed the crossing. The river, blindingly bright in full sun, was wider than she had supposed. It took a good while to steam across. She shaded her eyes and watched the paddlewheel slice the water.

Once ashore Caleb led the nervous mules away from the pier. "We got purt-good level road fer a ways. I been asking about the roads on to the south." He squinted toward a distant blue line of mountains. "Those ain't so good. But we'll manage."

"I reckon we will," she agreed. "Ain't this sunshine a blessing."

"Shore is," he agreed. "Rain means high rivers, and we don't need none of those to cross."

After a few miles, they took a short cut across Pleasant Valley, a route that Caleb said would save miles. Cindy was glad for, although the wagon road was narrow and rutted, it fronted a beautiful meandering creek, the banks awash with gentle dogwoods and spring wildflowers. Through the pines and across the green water rose steep bluffs of mossy rocks in cool shadow. But she averted her eyes from a small cemetery nestled under the pines. She wanted no reminder of death just now.

As they camped near the creek that night, Caleb was solicitous of her every comfort. The little tent pitched near the campfire held not only a feather tick, but also a small chamber pot, for which she was doubly grateful; she had a dread fear of meeting a snake in the bushes.

Caleb even insisted on doing the cooking. Now in flickering fire light, he took a bite of cornpone and grimaced. "I'll swear, Miz Cindy, hit might be scandalous to name it, but I downright sympathize with them Israelites fer complainin' about manna day in and day out. Sometimes I look at a ear of corn and gag." He wiped his mouth. "Course, I am right glad my belly ain't plum empty. But wouldn't some flour bread go good?"

She laughed. "It would." Then she took a bite of the fried, soggy cornbread and chewed for a second. "Uncle Caleb"—her eyes twinkled—"since we're stuck with corn, I reckon you ought to let me do the cooking. I'm a better hand at making pone than you."

He gave a jolly chuckle. "You'll get no argument from me. Viola says standing over a hot fire ruins a woman's skin—and you got such purty skin. But since hit's a toss-up betwixt your skin or us starving, I'll let you cook."

"Tell you what, you fiddle me a tune while I cook."

"Now there's something I can do," he said with a smile.

His face fell. "I knowed I was forgettin' something. Miss Cindy, I left that blamed fiddle at home!"

The next morning Cindy stepped from the tent just in time to see a mockingbird swoop down from the elm tree shading the wagon. It dove a straight line to peck Caleb's bald head. He howled and swiped at the bird with the hat in his hand. The bold creature flapped and then flew back to alight on the elm limb.

"Gol-durn bird!" grumbled Caleb. "If I had powder and shot to waste, I'd shoot hit." He gingerly rubbed his head. Tuffs of gray hair surrounding the baldness stuck out, waving in the breeze. "That hurt like the dickens," he quarreled and slammed on his hat.

Cindy turned away and pursed her lips tight. But her middle shook.

"Aw, go ahead," said Caleb, "I know yer bustin' to laugh."

She threw back her head. Even Caleb chuckled as her laughter spilled into the golden morning and echoed off the rocky bluffs.

Caleb's information about bad roads proved correct. Steep pulls taxed the mules, and the downgrades were equally hazardous. On the steepest, Caleb felled a large hickory to use as a drag. Every mile was hard won. And each night Cindy, bone weary, could barely keep her eyes open during supper. Just as soon as the dishes were washed, she always retired to the little tent and fell into deep slumber.

As much as possible, they avoided houses and fellow travelers. Caleb kept a sharp eye out for Army patrols. Several times they left the trail to hide in the tress while horses passed.

After days of rugged country, the mountains gave way to rolling hills. Then the land suddenly flattened, making travel pleasant.

"I never seen such flat land!" exclaimed Cindy. Then she pointed at a distant white house with four massive chimneys against the cloudless sky. "Nor such big houses. I don't reckon the heavenly mansions will be much bigger."

Caleb motioned to the black bodies bent over hoes in the wide fields. "Lots of slaves hereabouts," he said. "More cotton growed here than you can shake a stick at. Lots of rich folks, too, I'd say."

"They may be mighty rich," she said with brow puckered, "but how can they stand this ugly flat land. Why, there's not a hill in sight! Reckon I'd die without a hill or a pretty holler to gaze at."

During the third week, the sky turned gray and the sun disappeared. Cindy lost track of endless dreary days as the mules plodded along muddy roads shrouded by overhanging trees. Although they had passed through beautiful country, this forest was dense, bushy, and oppressive. Constant rain had turned the flats into swampy pools. Gnarled trees blocked the sky. Even if the sun had been shining, she doubted it would penetrate the smothery, leaf mantle. For the past week both she and Caleb had worn slickers more often than not. In spite of that, their clothes stayed damp. And Caleb had developed a deep, racking cough that worried her.

Finding a dry spot to make camp was impossible. Caleb settled for ground with enough dead falls to replenish the dry wood kept in the wagon under a tarp.

Now he straightened from slumping over reins held loosely in his hands. He coughed deeply and then spit over the side of the wagon and wiped his mouth.

"Ain't shore if it was smart to take this here back trail, even though that feller said hit'd save us several mile. Shore is deserted along this here stretch. If I recollect right, he said after we cross the Little Missouri at Elkin's Ferry, we'll come to a prairie. I ain't gonna miss this here river bottom country. Gives me the miseries."

Cindy gave a shiver. "Reminds me of a scary fairy tale. Them big stumped trees in the water is the queerest things I ever seen. How soon ya reckon we'll come to the ferry?"

"I calculate about—." Halting, he threw up his head. "Horses coming." His scowl deepened as worried eyes searched about. "Wagon would sink to the hubs if we left the road here."

Cindy cast eyes in all directions. The road was indeed bordered on both sides by brown pools.

"We jist have to face 'em and hope they're friendly."

Nonetheless, he eased the shotgun onto his lap and gripped it tightly as a motley group of Union soldiers rode into view. The ragged blue trousers and holey boots were as frayed as any Cindy had seen in the Confederate ranks. While still out of earshot, they halted in the road and held a hurried confab. Quickly most of the men dismounted and scattered out as three of them cautiously approached the wagon with pistols drawn but not pointed.

The sole officer in the group of eight was young but with the stamp of hard living on his lean face. He nodded to Caleb while his eyes stayed on the shotgun. "I have to ask you to give over your gun, sir. And will you both please step down from the wagon."

Caleb's jaws tightened, as did his grip on the gun.

The officer's wary eyes narrowed. "No use resisting. There are eight of us."

"Mister, I need this wagon. Me and this woman is a hundred miles from home on our way to fetch a sick man and bring him home. By my reckoning hit's two days walk to the next settlement."

The officer shifted a bit in the saddle. "Be that as it may, I've orders to confiscate all wagons in the area. And we will take this one. If you resist, someone is sure to get hurt."

Caleb scowled. "All right," he finally said. "I'll give ya the wagon. But I ain't aiming to give up my gun. Man's life ain't worth spit in this country without a gun. And I got Cindy to think of."

"I've no more time to waste. Drop that gun and climb down before someone gets hurt." The sergeant kept his eyes on Caleb as he barked the order. "Lawrence, Williams, help the gentleman and lady down and confiscate the wagon."

As both men hesitated and then rode slowly forward, Caleb raised the shotgun. Now it pointed directly at the sergeant's chest. "Call 'em back."

Instead the sergeant dove off the far side of his horse. At the same time, he raised his pistol and fired. The mules shied just as the shotgun blast rent the air. The full force of Caleb's fire riddled one of the troopers. His horse went down with an agonized scream. A volley of shots rang out. Caleb's hat flew off. When he slammed back against the seat, Cindy stared in wide-eyed horror and gave a choking cry.

"Oh, Caleb!" she cried. But there was no answer from the slumped heap lying on the seat. Then she stared in shocked silence. His eyes were open. His wispy white hair clung limp around the baldness already glistened with rain. Color vanished from his face while over his heart seeped a pool of bright red blood.

His shotgun clattered to the ground as the mules plunged forward. She grabbed the reins and urged them faster. Horses scattered. Dismounted soldiers leaped from the road. As she lurched past, she saw guns pointed, but she heard no shots. With one hand, she grabbed for

Caleb to keep him from falling from the wagon. Then she sucked in a jerking sob and lashed the mules.

Trees flew by. The wagon careened as the frightened mules rounded a bend. Cindy, glancing back, whipped them harder. Close behind sped a handful of soldiers with the hard-faced sergeant in the lead.

She knew it was useless. They would catch her. And then…Her frozen thoughts would go no further.

Stiff, with straight spine, she uttered no word as they headed the mules and pulled them to a halt.

The sergeant dismounted. "I ought to shoot you, too," he bit out. "Get down!" he ordered.

Chin high, she gathered her skirt and climbed down. With a swift jerk, he pulled Caleb from the wagon. The body crumpled to the ground. Just then the remaining troopers joined them. Every eye looked at the body draped behind the saddle of a trooper's horse.

The sergeant's scowl deepened. "That was a damned fine soldier the old man killed. Put William's body in the wagon." He addressed a young trooper, "Stevens, you drive the team and let's go."

"Sir," worried Stevens, "there's not a cabin for miles. You aren't just going to leave the woman?"

"Damn right I am," he snapped.

Dry-eyed Cindy stared as the wagon rolled past. The young trooper looked back with concerned eyes until the road swallowed him.

Warm rain wet her hair. She pulled up the bonnet that had slipped off during the flight. Then, with dread, she knelt and touched the still shoulder. In her mind's eye she saw Pete's lifeless head hanging off the front porch, shot by murdering bushwhackers. These men had been soldiers wearing Union blue, but they were bushwhackers nonetheless. And now Caleb was dead.

A yellow jacket darted past to alight on the pool of blood wetting the ground. Cindy sat in stunned apathy and watched as it crawled for a moment and then flew away. She raised her eyes. She had no tools to dig a grave, nothing but her hands. Besides this was no fit place to bury the dead. Along both sides of the road bogged dismal swamp. Soon a score of yellow jackets arrived. She shooed them away but they persisted. She must do something. She would not leave Caleb here to be swarmed by insects. But she could not stay day and night guarding his body like brave Rizpah had guarded the bodies of King Saul's sons to keep away the birds of the air and the beasts of the field.

She must get the pass. And Caleb had a little cash money and a pocket watch. She needed the coin and Viola or Billy would want the watch.

Feeling like a vulture, she searched his pockets and then put all that he had into the pocket of her skirt. It was only four dollars, but it might buy some food. Tears flowed as she bit her lip and stared at the murky waters. Kneeling she prayed and then with mighty heaves she pushed kind, good Caleb toward them. It took several tries. Finally he slid into the wet bog with a splash.

Quickly she turned away. Holding a hand over her mouth, she began to run. If she started screaming, she feared she would never stop. She would never, never tell Granny of Caleb's watery grave. Let her suppose he lay in a proper winding sheet under the loam of some forest or the sweet smelling grass of some prairie!

A sharp pain in her side finally forced her into a walk. Her mind whirled with thoughts of Caleb, Ned, Granny, Becky, Pa, Ma, and most of all Elijah. Would she ever see Elijah again?

For miles, wet by fog and rain, she plodded along the deserted trail. The torturous day stretched into eternity. As the sun crept lower the drizzle stopped. A patch of blue showed in the west amid coral clouds. Surely she would come to a cabin soon. Her heels were blistered and mosquitoes feasted on exposed flesh. She hardly noticed. Thirst burned her throat raw and throbbing. Pa had taught her that death lurked in bad water. She was afraid to drink from the murky bog alongside the road or the muddy puddles at her feet. In a daze she plodded on until her feet did little more than drag. Itching welts rose with each onslaught of ravenous mosquitoes. In her agony, thoughts of Caleb vanished. Never had she been in such torture! Hot breath sucked between cracked, swollen lips while spots danced before her burning eyes. Finally she decided to suffer the consequences, dropped to her knees, and lapped from a muddy rut.

As mud coated her tongue, she rasped, "Lord, if you don't help me, I reckon I'll die right here on this road." She leaned against a scrubby tree. But something drove her on. After a short rest, painfully, she stood and hobbled forward. The ground was not swampy now but overgrown with brushy thickets. She rounded a bend.

Suddenly, in a stumbling run she started forward and fell on her knees and plunged her face into the flowing water of a small creek. Gulp after gulp of cool wetness slid down her parched throat. She knew it was dangerous to drink too fast, but she could not stop herself. She drank and drank and then pushed back. As spasms clenched her stomach, she retched and vomited. Slowly she drank again. With a shaking hand she wiped her mouth and stood. Shuddering, she watched a snake glide from the bank silently into the water.

She must find shelter soon. She could barely see her own hand in the shadows. There was a tall elm tree nearby with a big forked branch where she could at least be up off the ground.

"But," she whispered with her eyes looking after the snake, "snakes can climb." Then she eyed the creek. If she pressed on and crossed the creek, her feet would be wet and cold all night. Already she shivered from the cool April evening. With a prayer that the Lord would keep serpents from her bed, she climbed the tree.

Exhaustion demanded sleep but she rested little hugging the miserable perch. As weak as she was, she must keep a tight grip to keep from falling.

The night's chill made her shiver as, over and over, she saw Caleb jolted by the gun blast. Other ghosts arose to torment: Pete's murder, the stricken eyes of the bushwhacker she had killed, the cabin collapsing in flames, the cold tiny dead babe wrapped in Granny's blanket.

Would life ever be good again, safe and happy? Would she ever get home again, ever see Elijah? Tears slipped down a cheek pressed against rough bark. Although fear was rough and bitter on her tongue, she opened her mouth to quote, "I will never leave you nor forsake you."

She must have slept. Heavy eyelids lifted with a shaft of sun full on her face. Every joint and muscle screamed. And her empty stomach gnawed from hunger. Clumsily she descended and stood straight. As her stomach roiled, a spasm suddenly gripped feet and legs. Finally, as the cramping eased a bit, she hobbled painfully forward.

Removing socks and boots, she stepped into the cold water and sucked in a shocked breath. She must go on, put one foot in front of the other. She fervently prayed for something to eat, and she prayed her bed tonight would not be a tree!

Exercise and morning sun drove the chill from her limbs. Soon, however, to her regret, the sun disappeared behind a cloudbank. Midmorning, she threw up her head. In the distance came the distinct boom of large guns. Although she had never before heard cannon fire, the horrific blast was unmistakable. Somewhere off to the right was a battle. Although the sound was distant, the ground beneath her trembled.

As the morning passed, her eyes swept the thickets and small patches of piney woods that now bordered the road. Granny had taught her many edible wild plants and herbs, but it was too early in the spring for some, such as the Indian potato that grew in watery places and the pin oak acorn that was filling and hardly bitter. She was reluctant to stray from the trail but finally decided to go a short way. Even a bite of something would give her weak knees strength to press on.

She had not gone far when her gaze fell on a patch of big-stemmed plants with tops of marbled white ridges with dark brown pits. Hardly pausing to make certain the mushroom caps were directly attached to the stems—unlike the kind that Granny had so sternly cautioned against when the cap hung free like a skirt—she grabbed them and stuffed them into her mouth. The woody-flavored morsels only whetted her hunger. Resisting the temptation to wolf them all, with reluctance, she picked the last three and put them into her pocket. While she retraced her steps to the trail, a rising wind swayed the pines and large drops of rain wet her head and arms. The cannon blasts coming in intermittent volleys, now became punctuated with thunder.

Cindy groaned. There was no shelter here, no bluff or cave to protect from the coming storm. The best she could hope for was a bushy tree to shed the worst of the rain. As the downpour began in earnest, she bolted for a scrubby cedar and hunkered beneath it just as vicious hail pounded the earth. She bent over, hugging her knees, with her face low. The cedar was a poor shield. She cringed as icy marbles pelted her back. Like a beast of the field, her only choice now was to endure. Ice soon covered the ground near her muddy boots and sodden dress as the roar of storm drowned the boom of cannon. If the hail grew larger, she feared it would be fatal. Bruised and battered, she prayed for the beating to stop.

And it did as abruptly as it had begun, although the rain continued to stream down. She longed to never move again, nonetheless, she forced herself to stand and plod on. The drenching rain had at least halted the mosquitoes. Her hands and face were already a mass of huge welts.

The next two days passed in a blur of pain and suffering. At times she sat and weakly stared into the swampy woods. But some steel determination always brought her to her feet again to stumble forward. She knew she had missed the main trail at some fork and taken a wrong road or she would have come to the ferry by now. Each night she found a dry spot and lay down, almost hoping not to awake. Her stomach gnawed from hunger but the few bites of edible plants she found came right back up.

Her eyes opened to another downpour. This time she had no will to go on. She groaned, rolled to her stomach to stop rain from pouring into her face and lay still.

Just then a horse thundered around the bend and skidded to a stop.

"What in the world—"

Cindy did not bother to answer.

The man slid from atop a tall buckskin with black mane and tail.

He gently took her arm and helped her sit. "What in the world are you doing here all alone?" he asked as he peeled off his slicker and draped it over her. He was muscular, dark-haired, and young.

"Do you have any water?" she croaked.

He strode to the horse and returned with a canteen. When she had gulped several draughts, she lowered the canteen and took a bite of the corn cake he offered. Between ravenous bites, she answered his question.

"Yankee soldiers wanted our wagon. When my uncle refused, they shot him and took the wagon."

His head jerked up. "How many soldiers?"

"Eight."

"How long ago?"

"I don't know."

His mouth drew into a frown as he looked down the road. "Ma'am, I have to get this dispatch I'm carrying back to my general."

She slumped even more.

"There's a small settlement just ahead. I'll take you that far, but I have to hurry on to camp." He lifted her onto the horse and then mounted himself.

Rain poured from the wide, down-turned brim of his fawn-colored hat to puddle in her lap on the folds of the slicker. His clothes were already soaked where her arms surrounded his waist.

His voice rose over thunder and moaning pines. "Who are you?"

"Cindy Loring from Johnson County. I was traveling with Caleb Tanner. He is…was," she stammered, her weak voice almost a whisper, "my husband's uncle."

He turned in the saddle, and his eyes had widened. "I thought I'd seen you before. I know your husband," he said. "And Mr. Caleb fiddled at our last party. I'm Bud McConnell. Before the war, my father owned the drugstore in Clarksville."

Now she recalled him. Sometimes he had worked in the drugstore. The McConnell family was strongly Confederate.

"My husband," she said, "is with Colonel Brooks' regiment."

He faced forward. "What are the chances?" he muttered. Then he called back, "I'm riding dispatch for General Cabell. All hell's broke loose over yonder a ways. Joe Shelby's cavalry is pounding the Yankees while they try to cross the river. I'll try to get back and help you find a way home—"

"I can't go home yet," she argued. "I have to go to Shreveport and fetch Elijah's pa. He was a prisoner, but he's in a hospital now."

"That's great news about Mr. Ned." He twisted in the saddle again. "But, miss, you've got no wagon now."

She fell silent. Oh course he was right. But she must not disappoint Granny and Becky and Deborah. Surely the Lord would make a way…

Three dismal cabins made up the settlement, and one of them leaned so sharply that Cindy thought the storm would cave it in. Bud drew up at the porch of the largest dwelling. He threw a leg over the front of the pommel.

"You stay here while I check out who lives here."

She sat slumped and shivering but thankful to at last be rescued. Bud soon returned. A middle-aged, large boned woman stood in the cabin's open doorway, her face wreathed with kindly concern.

Bud helped Cindy dismount. "She seems to be a kindly woman," he assured, "and she says you can stay here."

He steadied her arm as she limped to the porch. "If the general won't let me come myself, I'll ask him to send someone to help you. Meantime you just stay put. It won't help Mr. Ned any if you get yourself killed…or worse," he added reluctantly. "Woman's got no business traveling the roads these days. I've seen some awful things."

So have I, she thought. *So have I.*

Chapter 8

Major Kirby knocked a pipe bowl against the large rock where he sat. Then he drew out a cloth pouch, opened the drawstring, and refilled the pipe with strong-smelling tobacco. He put the pouch back into the jacket pocket, clamped the pipe stem between strong white teeth, stuck a small stick into the blazing campfire, and held it to the leaves. While puffing vigorously, he squinted against the smoke and eyed Elijah.

"Less than two hundred you say?"

Elijah nodded. "That's what the boy said. And that appeared about the size of the encampment along the creek to me. Many more than that and they'd be camped down by the river instead of the creek."

A few feet from the campfire the night was black, but a pencil of gray edged the east. Kirby sat in silent contemplation, drawing deeply on the pipe. Finally he glanced at Hankins.

"What do you think, Troy?"

"I think we can whip the bastards and take Clarksville back. Sure, they still have the big guns, but we outnumber 'em two to one, and surprise is on our side. If we join up with those Missourians over near Roseville we'll have even better odds."

Kirby nodded. "I got a dispatch yesterday from Colonel Battle, the commander of those Texas and Missouri troops. He's been ordered to destroy the cotton the Yankees have stored at Roseville before they can ship it." He took a long draw on the pipe and exhaled a cloud of smoke. "If we join in on that job, more than likely, he'll reciprocate and help us with the attack on Clarksville. Since we're facing howitzers, I prefer better odds than we'd have going it alone." He chewed the stem for a moment. "Of course if we attack Roseville first, it's highly likely the command at Clarksville will be ready for us." He stood. "We can stack the deck a bit more by tearing down the new telegraph lines that good Yankee Colonel Waugh just put up again. I'll send a detail to tend to that and a dispatch to Colonel Battle. Let's hope he's aptly named. You boys get some sleep. You'll need it."

Elijah felt as though he had barely closed his eyes when Hankins nudged his side with the toe of a worn boot.

"Rise and shine. The major says ride."

Elijah glowered, sat up, and rubbed at burning eyes feeling gritty and sand-filled. Sampson lay a few feet away. His broad chest rose and fell with each loud snore.

Hankins smirked. "Haven't you learned by now that rest and good food are against the rules in this man's army?" Then he proceeded to nudge Sampson, but the giant snored louder. Hankins walked away and returned carrying a water bucket.

Elijah scrambled up. "Hey, wait a minute. Let me out of the way before you do that."

Hankins chuckled. "Good idea. He'll come up swinging. Always does."

"That how you lost your eye?" called an unkempt blond soldier named Brady who stood nearby hitching a team of mules to a wagon.

Hankins paused with the bucket dangling by his side. "Naw, Brady, I accidentally stabbed myself while I was carving the liver out of a no-account mule skinner who tried cheating me at cards."

Brady's grin abruptly faded as he quickly dropped his eyes and began buckling the harness.

"I thought so," muttered Hankins under his breath with a sour frown, "damned cheat." Then he hefted the bucket and let fly a gush of cold water.

Sampson, bellowing, charged up, flinging his arms and swearing. He shook his head like a dog shaking off water and wiped his face with a sleeve. Then he pierced Hankins with a hot, belligerent glare.

"I told you last time not to never do that no more, Troy. I ought to tear your arms off," he growled.

"You don't like it—get up when I call you," said Hankins unperturbed by the string of oaths Sampson heaped upon him.

Major Kirby's arrival put an end to the tirade. "Men, we ride to Roseville. We've to burn the cotton and the gins as well. That ought to put a stop to some Yankee profiteering."

Elijah picked up the saddle and swung it onto the bay. The action felt surreal, like a dream. He needed sleep, but likely, sleep would be a long time in coming. Groggily he mounted and rode behind Hankins out of the clearing and toward the river. The air was soft with morning dampness. The men, silent and solemn, rode single file in a column that snaked back through the woods and then disappeared over a rise of brushy ground near the riverbank. While a scout went forward and scouted along the river, Elijah waited with the column hidden in the trees at the river's edge. Early sun danced on the ripples, scattering diamonds on the water. Except for the low band of pink shouldering the sun, the sky was cloud-free. It would be a good day for farming, he thought. He wondered if Caleb and Billy had planted all the corn. He shivered and stifled a yawn. Hunched forward in the saddle, he dozed a bit and then straightened and started forward when the scout gave the all clear.

Roseville was little more than a few clustered houses, backed by barns and an occasional outbuilding, on a hill breasting the river. There was, however, a cotton gin at the far edge of the settlement. Near it stood a few dozen army tents alongside another long log building that appeared to be headquarters for the Union Army. Breakfast smoke rose from campfires and chimneys but in the still, rosy dawn, few people were visible in the camp.

Major Kirby, shielded by trees, sat atop the black horse and conferred with an officer in charge of Texas troops. They sized up the encampment while a scout gave a low-voiced report.

"Like I told you last night"—the scout pointed to a weathered building—"the cotton's in that barn over yonder. Near as I can tell, there's more than a hundred bales. And the gin is right over there down the river a ways." He gave a shrewd, knowing grin. "We took care of the sentries. Most of the blue bellies are still in their tents."

After consulting with the Texan, the major turned to Hankins. "Burning the cotton is our main objective. Pick four men and slip down to the barn. When you get there, we'll come in firing. Make sure things are blazing good before you leave. We'll keep them busy."

Hankins dismounted. He nodded at Elijah and three more. Sampson's face fell.

"I wanna go," he protested.

"Nope. You're too damn big to slip anywhere—let alone across that open field yonder."

Hankins instructed a tall skinny man to pass out the pitch-pine torches. Then he looked at Sampson. "Dumpling, don't get yourself shot. But just in case you do, be sure to tell the major that horse you're riding is mine." He grinned at Sampson's dour expression.

The sun inched over the hill and intermingled long shadows of sycamores with the shadow of hidden troops. Birds twittered and a horse blew softly. Elijah had the thought—as he had done in other battles—what a shame to ruin such a beautiful morning.

"We'll circle back a ways and then slip back by working our way along the riverbank," Hankins instructed the huddle of chosen men. "Tim, everything ready?"

The skinny man nodded. "All they need is a match."

"Do you all have plenty of matches?"

Each man nodded.

Hankins rose up from squatting on his heels. "All right, boys. Here we go. Move careful but fast. The major will charge when he sees our smoke."

Right on Hankins' heels, Elijah moved quickly down the hill and over the riverbank near a noisy shoal. The bank was steep here, but before reaching the barn it fell away and flattened into a natural sandy-bottomed crossing. There, Elijah figured, was the worst danger of discovery. But Hankins was right—it was safer than crossing the open fields in front of the barn.

They made their way swiftly along the river, slowing in the places where the bank plunged abruptly into the river. Here the men waded the swift water, holding to brushy limbs extending over the river's silt edge. Suddenly Hankins halted, pressed hard against the bank, and flicked a warning hand. Elijah peered over Hankins' rigid shoulder. Just ahead, where the bank slopped gently down to the river, a soldier hunkered near the water's edge with a steaming cup in his hand. The man yawned and then continued staring across the river. Elijah followed the gaze and saw a deer midstream, swimming toward a small brushy island. Abruptly his eyes and mind darted back to the man on the bank. Although the soldier's presence created peril, one part of Elijah's thoughts remained on the deer. It was far too early in the season for antlers, but the broad shoulders and head indicated a fine buck.

Hankins stayed motionless. Ankle deep in the lapping water, Elijah's feet grew numb. The minutes seemed hours before the man finally drained his cup and then stood and stretched with arms out flung. He turned and sauntered back toward the tents. Hankins let out a deep breath and began creeping forward again.

Without mishap, they darted across the open space and gained the shadow of the barn. A quick inspection revealed only one door, latched but not locked. While Elijah unlatched and pushed it open, Hankins held a rifle ready as, one by one, his men slipped inside. Feeling his way between the rows of bulky bales, Elijah made his way to the far end of the barn, tearing bales apart before stopping to strike a match. The bundle of splintered pine caught instantly and blazed. He touched it to the cotton.

Elijah had never grown cotton, but he knew the labor involved. Some farmer had poured sweat and blisters into the crop. Now it was going up in useless smoke. But war thrived on waste—waste and destruction. How he hated it.

At first the cotton merely smoldered. He tore at the bale, pulled out a bigger wad of fibers, and put the torch again to the course cotton. Soon flames leaped from the bale and acrid smoke roiled upward. As men ran from bale to bale, all across the barn the cotton burst into flames.

Outside shots ripped the calm. Shouts rang out and running feet merged with swift hoof beats.

"Come on, fellows. It's blazing good now. Let's get out before the smoke chokes us."

With alacrity, Elijah followed the order. His eyes were already burning. However, he had to duck back inside when a volley of shots peppered the barn door.

"I'll cover you." Hankins stepped to the edge of the door and returned fire as Elijah darted outside and rushed toward the steep part of the riverbank. After piling over the bank, he stopped alongside the others hunkered behind a rock and snapped off a quick shot. A blue-shirted soldier grabbed his arm and jumped behind an outbuilding. In a thunder of hooves, Major Kirby and a score of riders swept past again, keeping up a rapid fire. Hankins dove past the barn and toward the river. A shot clipped rock near his head as he plunged over the embankment.

As Elijah quickly reloaded, he grinned. His teeth gleamed white in a smoke-streaked face. "Wakes a fellow up, doesn't it?"

"Makes a fellow need a corncob," grumbled Hankins as he wiped a sharp sliver of rock from his cheek. He tore open a paper cartridge with his teeth and rammed in a minnie ball. "We lost some men. I saw at least three fall out of the saddle. Never saw Sampson—but that big sonofabitch makes a good target. I hope he didn't stop a bullet."

Hankins' face remained tense as he reloaded. Then he looked around. "We better get out of here. Those Yankees are pretty riled. They just might get their wits together enough to charge us."

Elijah nodded and then quickly followed as Hankins hunkered and ran, keeping his head well below the top level of the riverbank. The Confederate troops made one last charge while they scurried along the river and then darted toward the trees on high ground. Sampson stood holding the reins of several horses and wearing a scowl as they topped the hill.

"Troy, the way you kept stickin' your fool head out that barn door like a dumb chicken, it's a thousand wonders you didn't get it blown off!"

Hankins scoffed. "Well, I haven't figured out how to aim through a closed door. But when I do, you can bet, I'll keep my fool head inside."

After a bit, the major rode up. "What are our losses?"

A trooper with swarthy face answered. "Looks like about a dozen on the ground back there. And about an equal amount here are wounded. Some of them can't ride."

"Have a medical detail take them deeper into the woods and stay with them. We'll send wagons as soon as we can. Come on, men," ordered the major as he pulled the reins on his horse. "We'll cross upstream a ways."

Elijah looked back often, but no one pursued. After swimming the river, the major paused for a bit to let the horses blow. Elijah checked the load in his pistol. Satisfied he slipped it back into his belt and let out a slow breath.

The countryside was pretty here. Dogwoods dotted the woods like designs on a pretty dress. He plucked a large white blossom and rubbed it through his fingers. Granny allowed how the flower, blooming right at Easter time, preached the gospel. And it was the shape of a cross with the four ragged blood stained-looking edges and a center like a crown of thorn. He reckoned that was a right good picture of crucifixion. As a shiver traced his spine, he dropped the blossom. Right before another skirmish, he didn't relish such doleful fancies.

Two days later Colonel Battles lowered the telescope. Frowning, he turned to Colonel Brooks. Major Kirby stood nearby.

"Like the scout said," acknowledged Battles, "they're expecting us. The streets are barricaded and the howitzers ready for action up on that hill."

"Those guns are pointed right at us. I don't intend to charge head on. They'd rip us to shreds," Brooks commented. "I suggest that you strike from the west while I circle around to the east, and take the guns from the rear. As I pass north of town, I'll dismount some of my men to strike from that direction. With the howitzers out of action, we'll be able to storm the post. Most of the troops seem congregated right over there along that creek. Tell the men to move quiet and cautious. Those pickets your men killed bought us a little advantage. They know we're coming, but they don't know we're here."

Battles nodded. Swift but silent, the main body of troops moved out, the faint thud of hooves blending with morning bird song.

Major Kirby spoke low and fast, coordinating the attack. He clicked open a pocket watch and then spoke to Hankins. "Scout forward for pickets. Then take your men, dismount, and get in close. Hold your fire until straight up eleven." The two men compared timepieces.

After the consultation with the major, Hankins gathered his men, Elijah among them, and related the plan.

"Sampson, whathahell you doing? Did you hear a word I said?" he snapped.

Sampson stuffed a meaty pork bone into his hip pocket and quickly rubbed grease from his chin. "Just finishing off some of that hog we et last night. Been so long since we had any decent vittles, I don't aim to waste 'em. I saved a bait fer breakfast."

Upon seeing Hankins' disgust, he wheedled, "Aw, Troy, a fellow don't fight near as good on a empty stomach."

Hankins' lip curled even more. "A fellow can't grip a rifle with hog grease on his hands."

Sampson wiped his hands down his pants leg. He belched loudly.

Hankins turned his head. "Hellfire! You're worse than a dang mule, always blowing at one end or the other!"

Sampson shrugged. "What da you expect when they mostly feed us fodder."

Hankins glowered. Then abruptly he faced the men. Quickly he split the squads and issued orders. Elijah was assigned to the group of one hundred who would assault from the north.

"Loring, you know the area. You scout ahead for the pickets. We'll slip along the creek behind that old man's cabin. When the major's had time to make it around the hill, we'll commence firing." He turned in the saddle to address the men. "And not until then!" he added with emphasis.

Elijah dismounted and moved forward, silent and stealthy, as his eyes penetrated the bushes. He stopped. Far ahead a lone sentry sat against a tree, eyes closed and mouth open. A rifle rested across his chest as it rose and fell with the deep, regular breaths of sleep. Elijah pulled the knife from his boot and crept forward. It was not a job to his liking. War involved killing. But if it must be done, he much preferred to shoot a man with eyes wide open even if he was shooting back. There was at least a sense of honor in battle. This felt like murder. Of course a sentry ought not be sleeping. He should know better. That was a death sentence in any army. Elijah gritted his teeth and crept forward.

Although no one was out and about, smoke snaked from the chimney of the Hadley shack. Elijah hunkered near the creek bank to await the others. He looked at his knife and grimaced before plunging it into the creek. Red water swirled away to be swallowed by the clear.

On a nearby limb, a cardinal warbled. Elijah pictured the fields at home. Yes, it was a perfect day for plowing and planting. He sheathed the knife, stood, and dried his hands on his pants as horses approached. They came slow and single file, but the men quickly dismounted. Hankins pointed at a few soldiers and signaled them to hold the horses. Elijah was not surprised to see Sampson chosen. The others, Hankins motioned near for a hurried confab.

Elijah retrieved his rifle from leaning against a tree just as Old Sirius, the hound, padded over to sniff at his feet. He patted the dog's head. With a fight coming off, he was glad Nelda was no longer in town. Howitzers could do some ungodly damage. He hoped no harm came to the civilians still here, especially David and the old man.

"Elijah," whispered Sampson, "hold these here horses fer just a second. I got to step into the bushes. That fresh hog meat is tearing up my innards."

Elijah glanced over at Hankins and frowned. Then he nodded.

"All right, but hurry up."

Sampson gingerly hurried out of sight, holding his rifle in the crook of his arm and taking small but quick steps. Elijah grinned. While holding the reins, he stepped near to hear Hankins.

"Form a line along here." Hankins pointed from the creek toward the west. "When I give the signal step out on the double quick and—"

A gunshot smashed the silence.

Hankins whirled. "What the—"

The sound was near, in the direction of the creek, right where Sampson had gone.

In the Union camp a bugle sounded alarm. Shouts and orders rang out.

Hankins cursed. "Line out, men!" he shouted. "We can't wait now. Forward!"

The men fell into a ragged line and surged forward. Elijah, still holding the reins scowled toward the creek, wondering if Sampson had accidentally shot himself. The bushes parted and Sampson stepped out, suspenders dangling, face beet red.

"That damned hound smelled the hog meat in my back pocket and slipped around behind me. Just as I squatted, he stuck that wet cold nose..." There were tears of frustration in Sampson's eyes. "I was usin' my gun as a prop. When I jumped, hit fell over and went off." He stared at Hankins's disappearing back. "Troy's gonna kill me."

Elijah stuffed the reins into Sampson's hands and ran to catch up with the advancing line. On the double quick the men rushed forward.

Minnie balls clipped the brush near his head. He zigzagged forward. Cannons boomed. The ground shook. Although musketry rained hail, no canister came their way. The big guns on the hill had been swiveled toward Battle's cavalry attacking from the west.

In spite of their superior numbers, the rebel attack was doomed. With the loss of surprise and the lack of coordination, chaos reined. From behind high barricades, volley after volley peppered the air. They made scant progress, hunkering behind trees and buildings to return fire. Eventually, Hankins barked the order to retreat. Elijah had not even made it as far as the covered bridge.

He snapped off another shot before falling back alongside the others. Without stopping they all mounted and scattered, plunging through the brushy thickets along the creek until finally regrouping on the road west of town to await the major. Sampson, eyes downcast, slumped in the saddle, the image of self-loathing. And Elijah silently acknowledged that Sampson had a lot to be miserable about. He had single-handedly botched the assault.

When Major Kirby and some of his men arrived, he asked for the casualty assessment. Although they had been bloodied, no one had been killed.

He bit out, "What happened down there? Who fired that shot?"

Sampson wiggled uncomfortably. Hankins glanced at him suspiciously. For a long moment Sampson didn't answer. Finally, after a doleful look at Hankins, he confessed.

Kirby simply stared at the big man in silence.

"I ought to hang you," he finally said. "It's a good thing none of us got killed, or else I think I would. Colonel Battles might feel differently. He lost men and horses."

"Major," he beseeched, "I'm sorry. Mighty sorry! I'd not have done it for the world. I was tensed up, ready for the big fight—then all of a sudden—I had a terrible pain. I headed fer the bushes and had just dropped my britches when that old hound cold-nosed my bare rump! Aw, Major, can't you see how it was?"

Major Kirby leaned forward, propping his hands on the saddle horn. Lips pressed tightly together, he stared at Sampson and then shut his eyes. His lower jaw worked back and forth. Suddenly he roared with laughter.

He wiped his eyes. "Oh, Sampson, I'm trying hard *not* to picture that.

Hankins' lip curled with disgust. Eyeing Sampson, he did not join in the laughter sweeping the men.

"Accidents will happen," conceded the major. "We'll chalk this loss up to an unexpected contingency."

In spite of Hankins' scowl, Sampson smiled. "Thank you, Major. Thank you!"

Kirby pulled rein to turn the black horse. "In case they give chase, we're splitting up. Battle and his men rode toward Dardanelle. I'm taking a few squads and heading for the Mulberry. Hankins divide your men into squads and then scatter. We'll meet up day after tomorrow at our last old camp on the south bank across the river.

"And, Hankins, no more fresh pork for Sampson," he called back over his shoulder.

Water gently licked the bank where the bay stepped off into the river. Elijah would feel better when they were well across. More than likely the Feds would stay put, licking their wounds and crowing over the victory. They had won but not without getting stung. He had seen at least three men mortally wounded. Now, after gaining the far bank, he pushed those gory scenes aside to focus on the lovely morning. As after most defeats, the men were taciturn.

They traversed dense timber hugging the river's edge; predominantly oak, ash, willow, sycamore, and pine interspersed with bushy flowering dogwood. Soon the shadowy forest gave way to prime bottomland. The fields, however, were poorly tended now with grass encroaching where cotton had once flourished, royal and kingly with crowns of white. They rode far around settlements and gave Roseville a wide berth. They had ridden several miles when Elijah's eyes lifted from the fields.

He halted.

"Look at the buzzards over yonder!" exclaimed Sampson. "Never seen so many. Must be something big."

With tacit agreement the men began loping across the field. Buzzards rose only to alight a short way away when the horses halted.

Elijah stared. He had seen more than his share of horrors. But nothing had prepared him for this sight. The bodies strewn on the ground had been wearing blue uniforms, but none remained blue; all were seeped in blood and hung in shreds on contorted bodies. Arms and legs were hacked away. One man's eyes were shot out. Flies crawled over them and over the dead mules as well.

"My gawd," whispered Hankins.

Sampson leaned over the saddle and vomited.

As Hankins climbed down, Elijah pulled out a handkerchief as a shield from the stench.

"More than twenty of 'em. Wonder who butchered them like this?" Hankins picked up a medical bag lying open on the ground. Nothing was left inside. He pointed to one arm severed from the body but still encased in a bloody sleeve with an insignia. "This one was a doctor."

Elijah's eyes met Hankins' good eye. "Bet they were heading to Roseville to patch up the wounded. A thing like this will set off a powder keg. Folks will naturally blame our cavalry."

Hankins rubbed his jaw. “You’re right. Maybe we’d better find out who it was and make sure the blame gets put at the right source.” He turned to a small man with narrow shoulders. “Will, study the tracks. See if you can tell how many and where they’re headed.”

Will returned shortly. “There were a bunch of them, Captain, about two hundred, I’d say. Mighty big bunch for bushwhackers, wouldn’t you say? They took off that direction like they’re headed for Booneville.”

Elijah’s stomach twisted. His eyes passed over the horror again. No gang of bushwhackers numbered so many. This had been done by army—perhaps guerrillas, but army nonetheless.

Hankins raised a brow. “Could be we’d best let well enough alone. It’s not our affair. And some pots are best left unstirred.” With that he mounted up.

Elijah chafed at the decision. Although there had been many rebel troops in the area—some from Texas, Missouri, Oklahoma, as well as Arkansas, this area was known as Colonel Brooks’ territory. The colonel wouldn’t tolerate a thing like this. Elijah greatly doubted that any of his command had done this, at least not with the colonel’s knowledge. He wanted no such taint falling on them…on him.

Hankins turned the horse. “Well, we can’t hang around to bury them. Let’s go.” He kneed the horse and rode away. It was the army, so Elijah followed.

Chapter 9

"I don't have much food," apologized the stout woman with china-blue eyes who handed Cindy a cup of steaming broth. "My Tommy, yonder"—with a nod of head she indicated a fair-haired boy who looked to be ten or eleven—"shot a squirrel this morning so there's some heartening meat in the soup today."

"Oh, thank you!" Cindy took the cup with shaking hands and devoured the soup. She hugged tight the blanket draped around her and hitched the chair nearer the small blaze in the fireplace. "Bless you for taking me in. Yo're a real good Samaritan. I was about dead."

"I'd say you were, you poor thing," she agreed while rearranging Cindy's damp clothes hanging near the fire to dry. "I've seen drowned rats look better. Step into the pantry over there and slip on this night-gown. It'll swallow you, but the flannel will help warm you. The bed is turned back with a hot rock for your feet. You get some sleep, and then we'll talk."

Cindy gratefully took the gown and did as bidden.

It seemed only moments but was the next day when, from a fog of deep sleep, she heard voices. She knew she was dreaming because one voice was Billy's. *How odd to dream of him*, she thought and forced herself awake. Then her eyes blinked. He stood not three feet from the bed, his face a mask of worry.

"Billy?" she gasped.

"You all right?" he asked.

She sat up. "Yes…yes, except I must be out of my head. Is that really you? How—?"

"Bud McConnell. He rode into camp and looked me up because he knew we were kin. He told how he found you alongside the road."

Cindy's face blanched as she recalled this man standing before her was Caleb's son. "Did he tell you about your pa?"

For a moment Billy dropped his head. When he looked up, his eyes were pained.

"Seems I owe the Yankees more than ever."

Cindy wanted to reach out and squeeze his hand. His reserve prevented any such intimacy. "Hit was real quick. Caleb never suffered."

"That's good," he said. For a moment his jaw worked, and he swallowed. Then he went on with no evident emotion in his voice. "Bud said you were on the way to fetch Ned. Where is he?"

"At a hospital in Shreveport."

"Then I'm going to get him," he said.

When he turned away, she got up and took her clothes from the foot of the bed and hurried into the other room. Before slipping into the dry clothes, she checked the pocket. Her belongings were still there. She would give Billy the watch. She glanced into a small mirror hanging on the wall. Her face was a splotched mess of bug bites. And she had lost flesh. Her dark eyes were set deep in their sockets. With surprise, she noted a resemblance to Ma. Although she had never seen it before, she looked much like her, especially the way Ma looked now, thin and wan since Pete's death.

Voices came plainly through the thin door.

"I wish I had coffee to offer. But this soup is hot."

Billy murmured his thanks.

"You said there was a battle at the ferry?" questioned the woman. "My man is riding with Marmaduke. Were they in the fight?"

"His cavalry is out there along the river, but I ain't sure they were in this particular tussle. I wasn't there, but the boys said we got driven back. Even then we taught 'em a lesson they won't likely forget."

"I hope so," she said, eyes snapping. "Hal rode in last night and left out this morning. He warned me there was trouble coming. He told me to load the wagon and go to my folks. They live over in the next county."

"Oh," he said, "I was hoping Cindy could stay with you for a few days until I got back..."

"I suppose she can go with us," she said slowly but without conviction.

Cindy opened the door. "No, Billy, I want to go and help care for Ned. I promised Granny and Becky."

She was weak, but already feeling stronger thanks to the nourishment and sleep.

He rubbed his chin a moment. "You up to traveling?"

"Yes."

When he drew coins from his pocket, Cindy noticed he was not in uniform. His clothes were the butternut weave of Granny's loom.

"Ma'am, I sure do thank you for looking after Cindy."

The woman gently pushed his hand away.

"I'll take no pay for doing the Christian thing. I'll fix a bait of food for you to take along, a little cornbread and squirrel meat. I'll tuck in a little packet of salt if you have none?" She made it a question.

"I've not," he admitted.

"It's dirty brown—leeched from the dirt of my smoke house floor. But it's salt. It'll at least keep a body alive."

"I'm much obliged, ma'am."

Billy looked at Cindy as she drew near. "Looks like the bugs about ate you alive."

"I look a fright," she admitted. Then reaching a hand to her tousled hair, she added, "Those soldiers took everything I had, even my hair brush. I wish they'd have tossed off my trunk. It won't do them any good."

"Oh, honey," protested the woman, "your stuff is probably already on its way to Kansas. At least that's what's happened to every other valuable the Yankees lay a hand on. My sister who lives near Fort Smith says they've stolen clothes and furniture, even pianos, and put them on wagon trains headed for Kansas to sell and line their pockets. But the thing that makes me the most furious, she said they took our old family Bible where all our births and deaths for generations were written. And the scoundrels even took our family portraits. One was the only likeness we had of Papa and Mama."

She went on, "My poor old rags won't fit you, but I do have an extra hairbrush you can take along." She handed it to Cindy. "And here's a few more things. I tucked in an old cape along with a pair of knitted cotton hose."

With heartfelt gratitude, Cindy took the bundle. Around the lump in her throat she said, "I know a body has nothing to spare these days. But just like that widow in the Bible, you're givin' me out of yer little."

The woman's ample chin shook as she chuckled. Even though Billy was talking to her son, she lowered her voice "Since I don't have but one extra pair, I suppose those under-drawers are sort of the widow's mite. You know, I always wondered what happened to that good woman. I sort of figure the good Lord gave her an extra special blessing."

Cindy hugged her. "I'll be asking him to do the same for you. I'll ask him to bring your man back safe and sound."

Tears sprang to the woman's bright eyes. "Oh, please do. I pray that a thousand times a day, but it would be comforting to know that someone else is praying for him too."

"Cindy," Billy said, "we best be on our way."

The woman and her son followed them onto the porch. The sun sparkled puddles in the yard where rainbow-hued drops still clung to wisteria vine and tree. The wagon in the yard was small and drawn by only one skeletal mule. Billy took the bundle, held out a hand, and helped her climb up. She turned to wave as they rolled from the yard.

Suddenly Cindy asked, "Where are we going now?"

Billy slapped the reins against the rump of the lagging mule. "After Ned."

"Did you get leave to be gone that long?"

When he didn't answer she grew quiet.

Finally he spoke. "Tell me what happened."

She swallowed and then managed to speak past the lump in her throat as she stared at the hands clasped together in her lap. They clenched tighter. By the end of the telling, they were white.

"What about his body?"

She shot him a sideways look. Billy's jaws were as tight as her fists.

Her voice was a whisper. "I rolled hit into the water."

He grimaced.

"I couldn't just leave him," she protested. "The flies and yellow jackets had done…" Her voice faded. She sat miserable, accused by his silence but wondering what else she could have done.

"I don't see as how you had any choice," he finally said. "I'd have done the same."

"I ain't aiming to tell Granny or yer ma. It would hurt 'em so."

"My ma," he spat out, eyes flashing with a look kin to hatred, "couldn't care less."

"Why, Billy," she sputtered, "I'm sure your ma loved your pa—"

"She loved my pa all right—just not Caleb."

Cindy blinked.

Birds sang and the sun shone brightly, and yet she felt as if a bolt of lightning had struck dead center.

Billy still faced her. "That's right. Caleb wasn't my pa. You want to know who was? The man I hated almost as much as I loved Caleb." He gave a dry laugh. "Well, I'll tell you. And then you can hate me, too. Jared Rawlings. Jared Rawlings was my pa."

Cindy was struck dumb. Jared Rawlings! Surely not, surely Billy was mistaken. Caleb had worshiped Billy. Then she stared horrified. "But Elijah—"

"Killed him. And did the world a favor." Billy faced forward but went on in a colorless tone. "Ma's wasn't the only woman to have a roll in the hay with Jared. And Jared never was the marrying kind. Wish I'd never known, but she just had to tell me, like it was some big honor being that scum's son."

He leaned forward and dropped his head to stare at the floorboards at his feet. "No man was ever a finer pa than Caleb Tanner. He deserved better than my ma."

As reality flooded, Cindy felt great pity for the man beside her.

"Did Caleb know?"

He shook his head. "Nope. That's my one comfort in…" he faltered, "…in his death. He never found out. I threatened Ma. But with her mind like it is, sooner or later she'd have told."

"Granny?"

"Not that I know of." He shook his head. "But I sometimes wondered. No, so far as I know, no one else knew but Ned. I told him once when it got to pressing on me so hard I thought I'd choke." He chewed his lip before softly adding, "I'd take a bullet for Ned. I sure am glad he's alive."

Her thoughts were as interwoven as the threads on Granny's loom. No wonder Billy was so different from anyone else in the family. Now that she looked closely she saw Jared's profile, the black hair, straight nose, firm jaw, and high cheekbones. And, yes, the eyes were the same brooding gray. Because of Jared's character, she had never thought him handsome. But Billy was. So, he was no kin to Elijah. It would certainly take some getting used to…

Billy looked down the muddy lane and changed the subject. "All the bridges are flooded." He eyed the mule with discontent. "No way this pitiful critter could swim a creek—let alone a flooded river. We'll have to wait till the river goes down or cross at some ferry, but not at Elkin's. There's still fighting there. And there's skirmishes between here and Camden. I think I'll circle way around Elkin's on a back road that woman told me about. She said it comes back toward the river yon side of Elkin's. By then the bridges up that way might be passable. We'll have to go mighty careful. Too many patrols. Likely we'll have the devil's own time getting across the river without running into them. Most of the Union forces in Arkansas are on the march—heading to Texas, hoping to take it for the Union. That's why Marmaduke, Shelby, Cabell—all of us—were ordered down here."

"Oh, Billy, is Elijah's company here?"

"Don't think so. Last I heard they were still south of the river, staying close to Roseville."

She leaned back relieved. There was no fighting at Clarksville. It was good to know Elijah was close to home. If only they could get Ned and hurry home! She might see Elijah again soon. Then she frowned. With each step, sticky mud encased the mule's hooves. His slow plodding did not bode well for a quick trip. And Billy was right. The poor, bony creature looked as if he might drop any minute.

At a fork in the road, Billy headed north. Cindy chaffed at going the wrong direction. But he was right. It would do them no good to run into a patrol—Union or Confederate. She had a growing suspicion that he had left without permission. And more than likely he had stolen the wagon and mule. If they were caught he might hang.

As Cindy ruminated upon Billy's shocking revelation and the horror of the last few days, she had to admit it was a relief to have a capable man to lean on. Gooseflesh peppered her arms as she relived the vision of Caleb's body slipping into the dank waters. Never had she felt more helpless. It was nothing short of a miracle she was still alive. And it was a huge miracle that Billy was seated alongside her now. With the good Lord's help, they just might make it home again.

She tried to push all else from her mind and stared with appreciation at the sun-drenched piney woods dotted with tall spikes of purple snakeroot and delicate blossoms of wild yellow indigo. Granny had taught her well the treasures of the woodlands. Then she sighed aloud, thinking how hard Caleb's death would be on the old woman.

Billy glanced over. "You all right?"

Without elaborating, she nodded.

Abruptly Billy threw up his head. Musket fire erupted nearby. Another volley resounded just around the bend. He swore softly and began turning the mule. Then he changed his mind and headed the animal directly into the woods and toward a dip of land dissected by a small, frothing creek. Cindy gripped the edge of the seat as the wagon careened down the bank. Just then a Yankee patrol raced into sight. The blue-coated troopers paid them no heed as they too raced toward the incline, seeking the slight protection of the creek bank from the hail of minnie balls now riddling the trees.

Now, hopelessly tangled amidst the firing troopers, Billy halted the mule, jumped down, and turned to help Cindy. She grabbed the bundle, took his hand, and quickly climbed from the wagon. In a crouching run, she followed him toward the bank where they hunkered near the water. The mule bolted and then went down in tangle of harness, mortally wounded.

"Lay flat and keep your head down," Billy shouted to be heard above the roar of musketry and canister. He flopped down nearby and pulled the pistol from his belt.

Shells burst overhead to splatter all around. Cindy's cheek bit into the ground, and yet she could see a man with gold braid on sleeves and collar shouting orders. Suddenly he flew backwards as his skull exploded. She groaned and squeezed her eyes shut. But the grotesque image remained vivid on the dark canvas of her mind. Her eyes opened of their own accord. Billy's hand pressed down on her back. He spoke near her ear.

"Rebel cavalry's about to charge. We're gonna make a run for it down the creek. Stay still till I say and then follow me. Run as fast as you can."

She kept her eyes shut and prayed.

The ground shook. Horses stormed over the bank. Amidst the clash of sabers, Billy jerked her up by the arm. They dashed through plunging horses and splintering trees. Blood flowed from men and horses as steel struck steel and flesh and bone. Cindy, her breaths ragged gasps, held her skirts above her racing feet and tried to keep from tripping as Billy zigzagged through the warring men. He held the pistol in one hand and yanked her along with the other. Miraculously, they seemed invisible.

No one struck out at them. No one even glanced as they darted through the melee. Cindy recoiled in horror from a young soldier sprawled on the damp ground. His handsome face was contorted and his side blown away. In the exposed cavity, his heart beat, squirting blood like a fountain. A pistol had dropped from his out-flung hand. Billy scooped it up, stuck it into the waistband of his pants, and kept running.

He led the way toward a bushy thicket. They crouched there to catch their breath as the battle raged on. She tried to avoid looking at the mangled bodies. Nonetheless her stomach churned.

"We made it through that without a scratch!" she whispered in awe. "We ought to be dead!"

"Well, lookie here," he suddenly interjected. A sorrel mare with empty saddle had bolted a short ways from the skirmish and now stood white-eyed and quivering.

Billy stepped from hiding to gently coax the mare with soft words. She came willingly. "There, now, girl. You're all right." He ran a hand over her side. There was a welt on one hip just below the US army brand, but the wound appeared superficial.

"Come on, Cindy." Even as he spoke he swung into the saddle.

She hastened forward, took his hand, held back her skirts, and swung up behind him. He kicked the mare's flanks. Bushes tore at her clothing as trees flew by. On and on they raced. Finally, when the sound of firing grew muffled and distant, he slowed the mare to a walk.

Cindy looked back. There was nothing but wilderness. Then she noticed the army brand on the horse's rump. "Reckon they'll hang us as horse thieves?" she asked.

She was surprised at the hint of humor in his tone as he said, "At least that'd sound better than being hung as a mule thief."

He took off the broad-brimmed hat and wiped his forehead. "We'll make faster time on the mare, even riding double. We'll worry about a wagon after we get to Shreveport."

"How long you reckon that'll take?" she asked.

"If we're lucky and don't run into any more patrols, I'd say, riding as the crow flies, about two days. Of course we'll have rivers to cross. With all this rain, that might delay us. And we'll have to find food."

After the harrowing sights of the skirmish she was not hungry. But of course he was right. They would need food. And likely that would pose a problem. No one had extra to share, especially with strangers. She dreaded the thought of stealing, even from the army. Pa had taught her better.

"I think this horse is strong enough to swim the river—especially if I get off and hold her tail."

Cindy swallowed. She had no desire to swim a river on horseback, but she bit back a protest. It must be done. The sooner they reached Ned, the sooner she could go home and see Elijah.

To reach the best crossing, they traversed a narrow, wooded gap that widened into flats. On the rocky riverbank, she eyed the Little Missouri in flood. The roiling waters foamed white over rocks and boulders. Although Billy assured her the river was not too wide here, the far bank looked far indeed. When he climbed from the saddle and pulled off boots, she scooted into the saddle. While still hugging the bundle, she drew a ragged breath and braced for the coming ordeal.

"Let me lash that bundle onto the saddle," he said. "You'll need both hands." He studied her white face. "We'll be fine. This horse is in better shape than any I've seen in a long time. I figure she belonged to an officer. At least someone's been feeding her good."

Not especially comforted, she nodded and grabbed the saddle horn with a death grip.

Billy pointed downstream. "I figure we'll come out down there somewhere along that flat piece of shore.

Her face grew whiter when he asked, "Can you swim?"

"Some."

"Good. Hold the reins, but let her have her head."

She blinked when he asked for her bonnet. Quickly he rolled the holster tight around the pistol and then took it and the shot pouch and stuffed them into the bonnet. He tied the bonnet strings together and looped them around her shoulder. "If you can, keep the powder dry." He clicked his tongue to the mare, and they started into the rolling waters.

The mare stepped forward, walking confidently on the rocky riverbed until the waters were chest deep. Then she began to swim. Cindy wedged the pistol against her chest and held her breath. She glanced back. Like a rudder, Billy surged through the current, holding the mare's tail. She had no idea how tightly her jaws were clenched until they began to ache. Taking a deep breath, she willed them to relax.

The horse made slow but steady progress against the fast current. Finally, with a big scramble, she found solid footing and stood. They had, just as Billy predicted, come ashore on the flat portion of sandy loam just above where the river curved from sight. Cindy was as exhausted as if she had swum the swirling current.

As the mare's easy gait ate up miles of sparsely settled prairie, Cindy barely touched Billy's shirt. He had grown solemn again, answering her few comments with only a word or two, reverting to the stranger he often seemed. She hated the familiarity of being so close to the aloof, silent man. Finally drooping, she leaned heavy against his back and then quickly jerked upright again.

"Go ahead," he said, "put your arms around my waist and lean on me. Get some sleep if you can. I know you're about done in."

She hesitated only a second and then did as bidden. Never had she been so tired. Horrible pictures danced in her brain. It was not the first time she had witnessed violent death. But that had been good versus evil. This somehow had been more ghastly: perhaps good men, honest men, tearing away at each other. Surely, it would stop soon.

She had no idea how long she slept. When her eyes opened, the mare had stopped and Billy was preparing to dismount.

"If these folks are friendly," he said, "we'll stay the night."

The white house was small with a shake roof overhanging a wide front porch that bordered generous flowerbeds filled with yellow spring lilies. Lazy smoke curled from the chimney into a crimson sunset. The woman and her elderly father-in-law were, if not overly friendly, at least accommodating. Almost as much as food and bed, Cindy appreciated the soothing ointment the woman shared. The bug bites had become painfully irritated. After a comfortable night in the cozy house, they started on their way just as soon as the sun had risen.

"I figure the Cotner family back there are Union like your pa," commented Billy.

"What makes you think so?" she asked.

"Reckon you noticed that was real Lincoln coffee this morning. For the most part, genuine coffee is unheard of in these parts. Only ones I've heard about who still have any are a few Fed officers. I figure her man is in the Union army and slipped some coffee beans home."

She swallowed bile rising in her throat. "Hit tasted good, but it never set well on my stomach. I reckon, hit's been too long since I had any."

He went on, "I asked the old man about the back trails. We'll take them. Less likely to run into trouble."

She was glad Billy was less withdrawn today.

That night they camped alongside a creek. He spread the horse blanket for her while he slept on bare ground. She slept little, and, she imagined, he even less. Low misty fog curled in the morning breeze. She stood stiff and sore while rubbing her neck.

"Reckon you rested well on that feather bed?" he jested.

In answer, she merely groaned.

He moved a smoke blackened pot off glowing coals. "Too bad Miz Cotner's generosity didn't include some coffee to go with this old pan. But I'm glad to have something to boil dried corn in—otherwise it takes a mule's teeth to chew the stuff." He handed her a tin cup. "There were a few things in the Feds' saddlebags, even some money. This cup and—." He stood quickly and took her arm. "What's wrong?"

Pale and shaking she sank down to sit on the ground and lowered her head. It was a few seconds before she could speak.

"I don't know…I reckon it might be the bad water I—" She stood and hurried away to retch and throw up in the shaggy grass nearby.

"Is your stomach cramping? You got any other problem?" he asked delicately.

"No. That bran cornbread was a mite hard on my stomach. But no cramps." She looked worried. "Pa warned me about drinking bad water. I sure drank lots on this trip. I've not felt this bad since…" Suddenly she paused. Her hand dropped to her belly, and her eyes rounded. Maybe it wasn't the water after all. She had been queasy in the mornings and then it passed.

He stared at her for a moment and then dropped his head to stare at the cup he had picked up when she dropped it. He turned the cup a bit and traced the handle with a finger. "Unless I'm mistaken," he said slowly, "you were sick yesterday morning about this time."

"Yes, I was," she said.

"That what you're trying to tell me?"

Her cheeks grew rosy, but her faced beamed. "Oh, I've wanted a youngun so bad."

He refilled the cup with water from his canteen. When he faced her, his look was grim.

She wondered why Billy looked as if he'd been kicked in the middle. Of course this did complicate things a mite. But she was strong. He need not worry about her. She would be fine. Last time had been a fluke. Even Granny had said the next time it was likely she'd have no trouble.

"I wish there was some way to send you right home. I reckon I ought to turn around right now and take you."

She hurried forward and placed a hand on his arm. "No. Ned might die if we don't get to him quick. Everyone says those army hospitals are terrible dangerous. Men die like flies."

Billy studied a while. “We have no way of knowing if he’s even still alive.”

She was adamant. “Then we better hurry and find out.” Without a backwards glance, she walked toward the horse and stood waiting.

Without argument, he saddled the mare, repacked the saddlebag, climbed up, and reached to help her mount. It was not until they had crossed the small creek and started along the narrow trail before he spoke.

“We need a wagon. You ought not be riding horseback.”

“I emptied your pa’s pockets. He never had much—just a few dollars. You got enough to buy a wagon?” she asked despondent, already sure of the answer.

“Nope.”

“Then how—“

“Take one from the Yankees. I sure as hell don’t aim to take from some farmer or from my own army.”

She tensed. “That’s a good way to get yerself shot.”

“They took my pa’s wagon, so they owe us. Besides the Feds’ mules are in better shape—not much, but some.”

She knew argument was useless but her stomach knotted.

Just before dusk they entered a broad road where fresh tracks sank into muddy ruts. Columns of campfire smoke marked the distant sky.

“Big camp,” observed Billy. “Plenty of mules and wagons. And those narrow deep ruts yonder are caissons. Question is, whose?” He turned the mare out of the road and stopped under a small-leafed, tall pecan tree. “I don’t want to run slap-dab into the flank of the Union Army with you along.” He helped her down, climbed down, and then handed her the pan, a pouch of corn and jerky, and a few matches. He tied the horse securely to a tree near the mouth of a small creek where it emptied into a marshy bog. “There’s a little creek yonder. Fix us a bite to eat and be ready to ride. I’ll be back shortly.”

With a fast-pounding heart, she watched his back disappear into gathering shadows. What would she do if he got himself killed? Eyes wide open, she whispered a prayer.

Then as she began gathering sticks to make a small fire, her mind returned to the battle. Try as she might to erase the grueling scenes, they persisted. She grimaced and her hand dropped to her belly. *Had what she witnessed marked her baby?* Pa said such things were superstition. But Granny said even the Bible spoke of such things...Jacob placing stripped sticks in the water troughs. Cindy sighed. There was nothing to be done now. It was over and done. And there was no use borrowing trouble.

She was not hungry, and yet she knew she should eat. Constantly, her ear stayed cocked toward the camp. She dreaded any second to hear a fateful shot. When the fire ate the kindling and began to blaze she went to the stream. She crouched on the bank and dipped the pan.

Just then the horse snorted and pulled against the reins. Cindy drew back in horror. Not ten feet away stood a huge grayish black reptile covered with spiny bumps. She had seen teacher Saddler's book with sketches of birds and beasts; but it had not revealed the size or the hideous reality of the creature. With a dry mouth she inched backwards. She had no idea if alligators could run—or if they favored human flesh. It was certainly large enough to eat her. Suddenly, it turned on short legs and slithered from the creek bank into the water.

"Gracious!" she muttered as it disappeared beneath cattails dotting the water. "That critter must have been spawned in the pits of hell!" With a shudder she took the dripping pot and hurried away to set it on the small blaze. "Reckon I'd rather face a Yankee cannon than that critter," she said with another shudder. Once again, her eyes searched the horizon for Billy. She sank down near the tiny blaze to wait. Periodically, as she added corn and jerky to the water, she glanced toward the stream to make sure the scaly creature stayed put.

It was full dark before she heard hoof beats and creaking wagon wheels. Billy whoaed the mules and stepped down. He gratefully took the cup of soup and gulped, hardly chewing.

"We'll have to travel tonight." His eyes clouded. "I hope you're up to it."

"I'll be fine," she assured.

Hurriedly, he kicked the blaze apart and untied the horse. Then he tied it to the back of the wagon and helped Cindy climb over the wheel.

"This is a nice big wagon."

"For a fact. Complete with toolbox, ax, tar pot, water barrel, and a durn good wagon jack. There's even some canned stuff, a few sacks of corn and one of meal and a couple of sides of rancid bacon. Not sure we can eat the bacon. The meal is a bit weevily, but we can sift out the weevils." Then he gave a crooked grin. "Best of all, what do you think I found hidden between some barrels?" Without waiting for an answer he said, "Real, honest to goodness coffee beans! Not many but enough to last us for a bit."

She glanced through the canvas opening. There were dark shapes of barrels and boxes. "Someone's gonna be hoppin' mad come daylight," she commented.

His teeth flashed white in the dim light. "That's why I figure to put as much distance as I can between me and a certain Yankee mule skinner." He slapped the reins on the mules' rumps and the wheels began turning.

"How did ya do it? Get away without them hearin' you?"

"Pure-dee good luck," he said. "And a keg of whiskey someone brought into camp."

She gave a soft smile. "More likely hit was prayer," she disagreed. "I said a plenty for you."

He chuckled softly. "Could be."

The pontoon bridge spanning the wide Red River into Shreveport was crawling with soldiers. Cindy eyed the swaying passage with trepidation. Then she squared her shoulders. She had survived so far on this journey. In the last hundred miles, she and Billy had managed to hang onto the wagon by hiding from patrols in the swampy brush without getting eaten alive by alligators. She shuddered just thinking of it. She reckoned—if she closed her eyes tightly—she'd make it across the bridge without throwing up. But her stomach grew queasy at the thought.

When Billy urged the mules forward, they stepped out without hesitation. Cindy figured it was not the first time the army mules had been on such an unstable contraption. She glanced at the union brand on their broad hips and hoped no one noticed. It would raise unpleasant questions. Then her heart beat fast. They would soon see Ned! At least she prayed so. Surely he was still alive! She gripped the side of the wagon and closed her eyes, while silently counting each clip-clop of hoof.

Once across the bridge, Billy weaved through army traffic and stopped to seek directions from a knot of lounging soldiers. The hospital was at the edge of town, on a grassy knoll. Tents sprinkled the lawn around the office building. The area appeared neat, but Cindy put a hand to cover her nose as a breeze brought the unmistakable odor of sickness. She averted her eyes from the cripples lying on pallets near the brick wall in the sunshine and sitting near the open door—men with faces marled by sword, men without arms, and men without legs, propped with crutches like a rail fence of misery. Her mouth went dry with sudden fear for Elijah.

Billy stopped beneath a giant oak shading the building. "Wait here," he admonished and looped the reins fast to the wagon before climbing down.

Cindy was glad to avoid closer contact with the inevitable foul odors and sights of the infirmary. Her nerves were taut. So much happiness or sorrow hinged on what Billy was about to learn!

Just then a small black boy struggled past, toting a water bucket almost as large as he was. He dipped his head to her in respectful greeting before entering a nearby tent. He scurried out quickly carrying a covered chamber pot. Cindy looked away, stifled a gag, and quickly swallowed. These days, even a thought could make her queasy. She would be glad when the months of nausea were past.

She sat up straight as Billy exited the building accompanied by an officer. When they entered a tent, her hopes rose. Ned must be alive! But it seemed an eternity before anyone exited the canvas flaps.

"Ned!" she whispered, although she hardly recognized the man on the stretcher as Elijah's handsome pa. Gray streaked the shaggy brown hair and beard. Thin as a blade of grass, he stared with sunken eyes. But he was alive! And he had both arms and legs.

She sprang from the wagon and ran forward. His sallow face broke into a smile. The brown eyes were as kind and warm as ever.

"Well, I never seen a angel before," he said, "but I reckon I have now."

Tears ran down her face. As she squeezed his hand, her eyes narrowed with concern. His hand was hot. She followed as a soldier helped Billy carry him to the wagon.

"Kiss the gals back home fer us," called a one-armed soldier.

Billy nodded. "Take care, boys."

Wistful eyes in haggard faces followed them.

"I fixed you a pallet here in the back."

Ned shook his head. "Wish I could sit and feel the sun."

Cindy and Billy exchanged worried glances. Flushed cheeks accentuated the sickly yellow of Ned's face.

"For now, why don't you try out the pallet. With Cindy's good nursing, you'll be better in no time," assured Billy.

After Ned was situated, Cindy climbed onto the back of the wagon. After Billy turned the mules into the main road, he called back through the canvas opening. "Ned, they never told us what your trouble was. You don't appear shot up?" He made it a question.

"Lung fever—so the doctor says—mostly compliments of Yankee food and lodging at Ship Island Prison."

Billy's eyebrows rose. "I've heard about that place. Reckon you're lucky to be alive."

Ned's features hardened. "I reckon." Then he drew a shaky breath and glanced at Cindy. She sponged his face with a cloth dipped in tepid water and bent forward to better hear the weak voice.

"Well, daughter, Billy told me my Becky is fine, but tell me about everyone else."

She noted the use of the term *daughter* with a smile. "Then I reckon he told you that Elijah and I got married?"

"Best news I've heared in ages."

Her cheeks pinked with pleasure. "Elijah is back in the army now."

Ned grew puzzled. "You mean he was out for a time?"

Cindy realized there was much to tell. She hardly knew where to begin. Some she dreaded telling. She wondered if Billy had broken the news about Caleb. She'd leave that for later. For now she would only relate the good things.

As they traversed the crowded streets of Shreveport, Ned listened while she related details of the wedding and added news of Granny and Deborah and Cousin Jenny and various friends and neighbors. Then he seemed to brace himself.

"Now tell me the parts you been keepin' back."

"Oh, there'll be time enough to catch you up on all the news," she said with an unconvincing smile.

"Knowin' will be better than imagining," he insisted.

She swallowed and stared at the hands clasped together in her lap. "Some of hit is real hurtful…"

"Go on."

She stared straight ahead. "A good while back bushwhackers killed Pete."

His jaw worked.

"And a conscript man burned Granny's feet real bad. He was trying to find Elijah."

Ned groaned.

She hurried on, "But you know how tough she is—she's fine now.

Well," she quickly amended, "she hobbles a good bit, but she don't let that slow her down much." She hesitated long before adding, "On the way here, Union soldiers killed Caleb."

Ned's face crumpled. When he began to cry, she stopped the narrative. She did not have the heart to tell him that Elijah had watched as Ned's brother Jim had been hanged as a Yankee spy.

"Becky will skin us alive if we don't take good care of you. You need to rest."

Ned did not argue when Cindy climbed through the opening onto the wagon seat.

As they crossed the bridge this time, Cindy kept her eyes open.

"What makes the water red?" she asked.

"I've heard-tell it's from the red clay in the Texas country."

She noticed a large amount of debris in the water. "There's a fierce lot of stuff floating. The river's plum full of trees and logs."

Billy glanced over. "The Great Raft, they call it. Hard on river traffic, but at least it'll slow the Yankees."

She pointed to a distant hill. "That and those cannons."

Billy glanced up and raised a skeptical eyebrow. "With half the Union Army heading this way, it's too bad most of them are just Quaker guns."

"Quaker guns?"

"Blackened logs set up to look like cannons."

Her eyes widened and she took another look. "They look real from here."

"That's the idea. It's worked before in other places—even halted some advances. But I figure General Steele and his Yankees will be determined to get here, what with this being the headquarters of the whole Trans Mississippi."

"Then I'm glad we got Ned away before trouble commenced." She sat up straighter. "Oh Billy, we'll be headin' back right through the thick of all the fighting!"

"No. We'll go back another way. I doubt there's as much chance of running into either army if we head up along the western border close to the Indian Territory."

Cindy sighed. It had been a torturous, long journey coming; it would be even longer going. She hoped Billy was right about avoiding both armies. On the trail she dreaded seeing any uniform. They must keep the wagon and the supplies. Ned would perish without them. And since her perilous time in the swamp, she was keenly aware that being afoot could be deadly for anyone.

That night they camped under clear skies a few miles from the Arkansas border. Ned was quiet, but composed, lying in the wagon near the supper campfire with a gray blanket draped around thin shoulders. Propped up on another blanket for a pillow, he ate only half of the golden brown corn cake and just a few bites of canned beans.

"That was tasty." His hands shook as he handed Cindy the metal plate. "But it's been so long since my poor innards feasted, I better take it easy."

Cindy retired early beneath blankets near the fire. Although Ned insisted she take the space inside the wagon, she refused. He needed to be inside out of the dampness. Billy said he'd sleep on the floor alongside Ned in case he needed anything during the night.

The next morning, Ned was worse. Cindy's heart pounded when Billy stepped from the wagon. Morning light glinted between knotty cypress trees to dapple the trail and the worn canvas covering the wagon.

"He looks mighty bad. I guess yesterday wore him out. And he's burning up with fever."

"Would you fetch some fresh water—it'll be cooler than what's in the bucket. I want to sponge him off," she said and took Billy's hand as he helped her into the wagon.

Ned's eyes were closed. When she touched his brow, his fevered flesh almost burned her fingers. Billy returned with a pan of water. Cindy looked up. "I wish Granny was here," she whispered.

"You'll do fine," he assured.

She was not convinced. If it were wound or snakebite, she'd have a notion how to proceed. But Ned was bad and she was less certain how to treat this unseen illness. She probed her memory for Granny's words about lung fever. When frail old Pappy Campbell had almost died a few winters ago, Granny had brought him around—if she recollected right—with onion poultices on his chest and willow bark tea. Cindy had helped peel and roast the fat yellow-skinned onions. Granny insisted on the strong-smelling kind that made a body's eyes sting and weep.

There were willows growing along the creek bank. *But where would she find onions at this time of year?* She sighed. Tiny wild green shoots would have to suffice. It was all she had at hand. She'd tell Billy to keep an eye out for them alongside the trail.

That afternoon, Billy whoaed the team. He stuck his head through the opening.

"I spied clumps of wild onions in that field yonder. I think we'll camp here until Ned gets stronger."

He strode over the field pulling the short green shoots and then peeled them with his pocketknife, exposing the small teardrop bulbs. After dropping them into a pan of boiling water on the campfire, he mashed them into a pulp with a spoon.

"There was some wild garlic, too. They're bigger heads than the onions so I threw them in. Don't know if they'll help, but I figure they won't hurt him."

Over and over again, Cindy applied the rank smelling poultice on the thin, bony chest. She reckoned—while stifling a gag—if smell was any indication, the poultice ought to do the trick. Then while Billy raised Ned's head, she spooned strong willow bark tea though pale lips as his feeble chest rose and fell. Each rasping breath was a struggle. She lifted worried eyes to Billy.

"I sure wish Granny was here. I can't think of 'ery other thing to do for him. I'm prayin' ever minute..." Her concerned words trailed away.

He nodded. "I reckon that's all Granny could do."

She lowered the spoon to the cup. Her hand accidentally brushed Billy's. He flinched as though he'd been burned. When he bolted from the wagon, her puzzled eyes followed him. Billy was skittish as a new colt these days.

Ned's eyes opened. "I sure hate being such a bother," he rasped and then coughed violently.

Ned was such a kind, gentle man. She could hardly reconcile Granny's tales of his hot-tempered youth. Secretly she hoped Elijah mellowed as well as his pa. Thankfully he had mellowed some already. And yet a few times since they had wed, he had exploded worse than the gunpowder that Pa hammered on the anvil to celebrate the Fourth of July—such as the day he'd mashed his thumb with the hammer.

Cindy wiped spittle from Ned's chin. "Yo're no trouble," she lied. In truth she felt half-dead from fatigue and worry. She hoped the babe wasn't suffering from her lack of sleep.

As Ned's eyes closed tiredly, she smoothed gray-streaked hair back from his forehead.

Cindy wrestled the death angel. Ned's life hung by the merest thread. She feared closing her eyes lest it break. After three days, Billy, his own eyes red and grainy from lack of sleep, insisted she rest. She resisted until he pointed out that exhaustion endangered the young one. Even then her sleep was a stupor filled with listening for Ned's every tortured breath.

This evening, however, her smile was broad as she stepped from the wagon. In fading twilight, she sank onto a log drawn near the fire, and with a grateful smile, took the steaming cup that Billy offered.

"His fever's broke." She took a sip of coffee and let out a deep breath. "I don't usual drink coffee of a evenin,' but I don't reckon anything could keep me awake tonight."

His gray eyes rested on her face before he spoke. "You did real good nursin' Ned. In fact you saved his life. Granny could have done no better."

She flushed with pleasure. "I just hope he keeps getting better!" She took another sip. "Wasn't it a blessing that you picked this particular wagon to steal?" Then she chuckled. "Somehow that doesn't sound just right," she said with a smile. "But it has been a blessing having real coffee and plenty of cornmeal and canned beef." Her eyes twinkled. "How did you know which wagon to pick?"

He grinned. "Oh, I poked around in all of 'em. Along with what was in this one, I lightened the load on a couple more."

"I'm surprised you didn't get killed."

He paused with his cup halfway to his lips. "Would you have missed me?" His tone teased but his eyes were serious.

"What a foolish question." She sat down the cup and stood. "Since Ned is so much better, I'm going to bed early. I think he'll sleep the night through."

The next day they moved on. With each passing day, Ned grew stronger. His appetite returned and Cindy breathed a relieved sigh. Soon he was able to sit and began to show interest in the surroundings.

Billy buckled the last buckle on the hames of harness and turned to Ned, who, for the first time, sat on the wagon seat. "I'm not real familiar with the route we're taking. But I still think it's best to go this way. That colonel back at the hospital told me it's a real beehive over east, especially around Camden. General Steele and half the Yankee troops in Arkansas ended up there without enough supplies to feed his men. He sent out some troops with a bunch of forage wagons. They found forage all right—about two hundred wagons piled full of corn and about ever' valuable in the country. Before they got to Camden, though, Marmaduke relieved 'em of all of it. Killed a pile of Yankee soldiers, too. Pretty near wiped out a troop of colored infantry."

Cindy stood near the wagon, with head bent, fighting waves of nausea. Upon hearing his words, she looked up. "My cousin Michael used to ride with Marmaduke."

Billy nodded. "I know."

"I wonder if he's with him now," she ventured. "He got captured and then paroled."

Ned put in, "When a fellow gets paroled, he's not supposed to take up arms again. Of course that seldom stops him."

"Yeah. Michael's just as apt to be with Marmaduke as not," agreed Billy.

Cindy hoped Michael had not been. Although Billy had not mentioned it, she was fairly certain that Marmaduke had lost men in the skirmish, too. She would rather picture Michael fishing on Little Piney. Then she looked at Ned.

"You won't go back to the army will you? That would just about kill Becky."

He gave a dry chuckle. "If I live to get home, no one can pry me off that place again. I doubt I'll even go to town." He paused and then said. "Now, tell me the truth. Why did Becky send you instead of coming herself? I've been mulling it over. I know that woman, and wild horses couldn't stop her from coming if she was able."

Cindy told him about the foot. The news seemed to age him right before her eyes.

"Surely the good Lord wouldn't spare me and take her." He stared at the ground and swallowed. "Granny will fix her up if anyone can," he muttered and raised his head. "Billy, don't try to spare me. Let's get home as fast as we can."

Billy nodded and then helped Cindy climb onto the wagon seat. Under his breath he asked, "You all right?"

She barely nodded. If Ned could take the jolting rough ride in his pitiful condition, she was not about to let morning sickness slow them down.

As the morning wore on, she felt better. She shed the thin blanket she used as a shawl. For days now the rain had ceased. The sun shone with brilliance and the wagon wheels sent curls of dust into the still, breezeless air. Nights still bore an uncomfortable chill, soon driven away each day by the sun. And by noon she invariably wished for a cooling breeze.

Now they traversed farmland abundant with creeks and wide flat cotton fields. She grew accustomed to seeing dark bodies bent over hoes. Without fail, heads roofed with ragged straw rose as dark eyes watched them pass. Occasionally a wave and a greeting accompanied the stares. She felt dwarfed and small in the vast openness. As the sun beat down, with hardly a tree to shade the trail, she looked longingly into the distance for the blue shadow of mountains.

Two days later she saw them, faint and distant on the horizon. They were just hills and far away, but her spirits lifted. Before reaching them they would have to cross more swampy ground and a wide, swollen river. Thankfully, there was a ferry that had not been washed away by the recent flooding.

Once across the river, the mountains loomed nearer and larger, the blue peaks beckoning like familiar friends. Soon Ned began to eat with a hearty appetite. After another week he left the wagon seat for occasional short walks. Each evening before retiring, he sat by the fire for a short while. When the men thought Cindy was asleep on her pallet under the wagon, their conversation drifted to things military.

Billy laid another stick on the fire. Glowing embers sent sparks dancing into the sky. "Yeah, I know what you mean," he commented. "We hated that damned Bragg almost as much as we loved Lee. Some say he just ran a tight ship. But I think he was a mean sonofabitch who took pleasure in our misery. He had no feelings for his men, not a smidge of compassion. Marched us till our feet was blood raw and made us lay down on froze ground with no blankets. Bragg never even tried to keep us supplied. Just treated us like we was brute beast. Once we got so blamed hungry we killed a young beef and ate it raw and without salt."

Cindy suddenly broke into a sweat. She put a hand to her mouth to stifle a gag. She had never heard Billy string much more than two sentences together. Now with Ned, he was downright talkative, but the conversation made her sick. She pursed her lips together to keep from groaning as Billy went on.

"I stood duty on a firing squad in Mississippi when he ordered two smooth-faced boys shot for some little infraction. He starved us and marched us into the ground until we got so's we hated even the name Confederacy. I was almost glad to get shot at Corinth. Anything was better than serving under that devil."

Ned's voice came softly, "You're not the only one thinks so. At the prison I knew fellows who swore they'd kill him someday."

Billy gave a dry laugh. "I've thought as much myself. But I reckon that bastard lives a charmed life. I heard-tell his own men tried to kill him. Blew up his tent and yet he walked out—pretty as you please—without a scratch. I reckon old Lucifer is protecting him."

"No doubt there's devils on both sides of this war," Ned agreed.

Wide awake, Cindy stared at the bottom of the wagon bed and wondered what tortures Elijah was enduring. She had of course heard of General Lee. Everyone spoke well of him; even Pa, who was a Union man, said he was a fine Christian gentleman. She knew nothing of this General Bragg. But she prayed he stayed far away from this side of the Mississippi.

Chapter 10

At midday Hankins called a halt to eat a few bites of scant ration. They had put enough distance between themselves and a Union patrol to relax a bit. The parched corn did little—or so Elijah thought—except make a man thirsty. He wondered what Cindy and Ma were eating today. A vision of hot apple pie danced through his mind. But he knew even Ma couldn't work that miracle with no flour. He chewed and swallowed and washed it down with another swig from the canteen.

Sampson ate nothing. He still looked green. Elijah could recall a time when such a sight as they had just seen would have sickened him for days. Now he simply pushed it back to a corner of his mind and pulled a curtain.

From a nearby field came a bobwhite call. Elijah whistled an answer.

"That was pretty good," said Hankins. "Can you call a turkey?"

"Had 'em come right to me."

"Wish you'd do it again. I'm sick to death of corn—parched corn, dried corn, corn coffee, weevily meal. Bah!" He capped his canteen and stood.

Sampson groaned at the order to mount again.

Hankins chided him. "Look here, you big lump of lard, you could be marching instead of riding."

"Cap'in Hankins, we ain't in no particular hurry to get nowhere, are we?" questioned Brady. He held a hand full of cards. "Me and Tom here got a bet goin.' I win, I get his watch. He wins, he gets my mouth harp and change."

Hankins paused a moment. "All right, finish out the hand." Then he sank back onto the log to watch.

Elijah knew little of cards. Granny thought the game sinful. He hardly knew the rules. But he recognized Hankins' displeasure when Brady dealt himself another card. Shortly, with a mocking chuckle, Brady gathered the watch and the small pile of coins. "Well, Tom," he bragged, "cream rises."

Hankins stood. He looked directly at Brady. "And so does scum."

Brady's face flushed, but he let the insult go unanswered.

Just then Will returned from riding scout. "Trouble ahead," he said. "Looks to be bushwhackers—cabin still burning."

They mounted, spurred their mounts, and galloped forward. Then Elijah's blood ran cold. Surrounded by smoke, a young woman sat on a stump. Her feet were bare and her gingham dress torn. White flesh showed through numerous rents. Blood trickled down her legs and dripped onto the hard-packed ground. Dazed and speechless she stared at the smoldering ruins of a small cabin. About Cindy's age, she had probably been pretty. Now her face was a battered mess.

When Elijah sprang down, Hankins handed him a slicker. He quickly draped it around her nakedness. He thought her mind had frozen until she spoke.

Her voice was flat and emotionless. "My baby is in there." She stared through him into space. "They held me back and laughed." Then she repeated, "He just laughed and laughed and said, 'Nits make lice.'"

Rage, red-hot and murderous, flooded Elijah's breast. Blood pounded his ears.

A ragged sob caught in the woman's throat. She clutched her hair and wailed a keening screech, a sound unlike any Elijah had ever heard. His hair stood on end as the pitch rose. Then the sound died in a low moan. He caught her as she fainted. He laid her gently onto the ground and got the canteen from his saddle and wet his handkerchief.

Hankins turned in the saddle. He chose two men. "See if you can find a neighbor woman to come take care of her—or borrow a wagon and take her there. Elijah, you stay with her. We'll ride ahead a ways and see if we can catch them."

Even though he was gentle, she came awake with a groan when he wiped her face. As if she were a small child, he shushed her. Tears streamed down her face in silence while she lay motionless, staring at the sky. He wished she had remained unconscious. Her eyes were dreadful to behold as they sought the smoldering mound that had been a cabin.

Drifting smoke stung Elijah's eyes. It seemed an eternity but was only a short while before the two privates returned with a creaking wagon. An elderly man held the reins. He stayed in the wagon looking somber while the old woman climbed down. Although the woman was big-boned and fleshy, her competent, compassionate manner reminded him of Granny as she knelt to minister to the suffering girl.

"I got a pallet fixed fer her in the wagon bed," she said. "She's my niece. I'll take her along home with me and send word to her man." She looked at the ruins. "Carrie. Poor little thang. She weren't even a year old. Reckon hit'll be too hot fer a while yet…" She smoothed the young woman's hair. "Betsy, honey, when hit cools off enough we'll come back and give her a proper Christian burial."

Elijah picked the girl up. She hung limp in his arms.

After he laid her onto the pallet, the old woman tucked a quilt around her shoulders. "Me and my man kin manage now. Thank you fellers fer helpin' her."

Elijah nodded. As he walked to the horse, he checked the caps on his pistol and the load in the extra cylinder in his pocket. When he climbed into the saddle, he felt the knife stiff against his leg in the boot. Before the day was through, he might need it.

By riding hard they soon caught up with their troops, who had been going slow and studying tracks. Hankins nodded as they rode abreast.

The group had halted as Will leaned over the saddle and studied the ground. "Like I said before, not many. For sure less than a half-dozen," he said. "Looks like they're headed for Charleston. Colonel Battles said to watch out that direction. There's a Yankee force camped near there."

"How far ahead?"

"Not far."

Elijah's lips narrowed pencil-thin.

When the horse blew, Elijah gave its neck a pat. In fading twilight awash with crimson, he watched the evening star, bright and steady in the heavens. Will hunkered in the brush and scooted back from the rim of a low hill to join them.

"Four of them. Union soldiers. Look to be regular cavalry. They're making camp back a ways from the creek bank."

Hankins chewed his bottom lip. "You sure it's them? I mean could we have mixed trails back there?"

Will's mouth drew down. "No way. It's them."

"Well, then." He shifted in the saddle. "We'll leave the horses here. Go careful and surround them." He pointed to a bearded sergeant and a long-legged private. "Cross the creek upstream and then come down. Make sure they don't get across. Don't fire unless you have to." His jaw was tight. "I don't want this to be too quick and easy on them. I intend to hang them."

A whippoorwill called on the far side of the gurgling stream. Low voices drifted and a man laughed. Elijah smelled campfire smoke tainting the sweet scent of honeysuckle.

Once in place, they struck fast. In spite of that, the Yankees managed to grab pistols and rifles. Powder flashes lit the dimness. A minnie ball whizzed past Elijah's ear and clipped a branch near his head. He pulled the trigger. The gun misfired. As a man dropped to his knees and drew a pistol, Elijah piled off on top of him. Cold fury burst in his brain. Oblivious to the fight around him, again and again, Elijah used his pistol butt to smash the narrow face. Merely raising his arms against the onslaught, the man gave up trying to fight back.

Elijah avenged the woman. He avenged Cindy. He avenged Ma. He avenged himself, for the taint of such men fell on all men. The man grew still, and yet he pounded.

Finally Hankin's caught his shoulder. "Leave enough of him to hang. He's not feeling it anyhow. You beat him senseless."

Elijah blinked and lowered the raised gun. When he released his grip on the man's hair, his head lolled sideways, his face a bloody pulp. Elijah stood and recapped his gun until it was ready to fire again. Then he holstered it.

The other three stumbled forward, hands raised, flesh wounds bleeding. As they were prodded into a tight group, Hankins faced the one with a chevron of two yellow stripes.

"Corporal, we saw your leavings back along the trail."

The man snarled. "Yeah, well we saw yours too!" He spit in Hankins's face.

Will raised a rifle butt and smashed him in the mouth. When Will raised the gun again, Hankins halted him.

"No, Will, I want to hear what he has to say." Then he drew out a handkerchief and wiped the spittle. "I assume you mean the mutilated troopers?"

The man wiped blood from his busted lips. "Yeah, that's exactly what I mean." His eyes blazed with hate. "Twenty good men hacked and gutted and left to be picked apart by buzzards. And us with no shovel to bury 'em."

"We had nothing to do with it." Hankins' eyes blazed. "Neither did the woman and child."

"Her man is one of you. Rebel whores make nits. And nit's make lice." His eyes glittered. "We all had a go at her. Then we left her alive to tell the tale. Wouldn't want bushwhackers getting the blame for Union vengeance."

When Will raised the gun butt again, Hankins did not stop him. The corporal crumpled to his knees.

"Mister," put in a nervous Yankee. "Owens is lying. None of us touched her except him. And he's the one set fire to the cabin. I swear we never even knew about the baby till the woman started screaming. By then it was too late." Sweat beaded his brow. "I swear on my mother's grave."

Owens, still on his knees, spit out blood. "Hell, Tom, don't beg," he snarled.

"Get a rope," Hankins ordered. "That limb yonder looks stout. We'll hang them one at a time." He pointed at the corporal. "Him last so he can watch—"

Elijah interrupted. "If we hang them here, it'll be a while before they're found. The cabin's on the main road, and if we take them back there, it'll send a loud message to any Yankees with revenge in mind. After the word of that mutilation gets out, I doubt any Southern family around here will be safe."

Hankins thought for a moment. "You're right. We're going that direction anyway. Let that cabin be their last sight before they drop into hell. Yep, I like that idea. We'll camp here and head out first light."

Elijah slept little. Like a vise, fear for Cindy squeezed his breast. No woman was safe. He chaffed to be home protecting her and Ma and Deborah and Granny.

It was a chilly morning, unusually so for April. Even good-natured Sampson arose surly and sharp-tongued. In spite of the fact they had purloined real food and coffee beans from the Yankee knapsacks, he glared over the rim of his cup. "I got seven beautiful younguns," he said, staring at Owens. "Them and my woman don't live far from here. I'm gonna enjoy watching you swing. I hope you gag and choke for a good long while."

"You ever see a man choke to death, Sampson?" asked Hankins.

"No, I've not."

"I didn't think so," said Hankins and took a sip of coffee.

Elijah had witnessed a hanging. This one was well deserved. And he felt no compassion for these men, especially Owens. Yet, he felt no pleasure or anticipation.

The condemned men looked wan and haggard in the first rays of morning sun.

"I suppose you still intend to hang all of us," said the man named Tom, who had decried his innocence. When Hankins didn't bother to answer, he went on. "I'd like some paper and pencil to write my wife a letter."

Hankins pulled a tablet and pencil from his saddlebag. While the others ate cold hardtack and canned beef, the grim-faced man leaned the tablet on his knee and wrote. As soon as he had finished, he handed the paper to Hankins. "Please see that this gets to a Union officer."

Hankins pushed the letter into his pocket and then ordered their hands retied.

The ride was silent, quick, and uneventful. No bird sang. Nothing stirred in the brush. Nothing broke the stillness except the creak of saddle and the tread of hooves.

The heap of gray ash stood stark and smokeless amidst new spring grass. At their approach, a flock of crows flew from the yard.

"I thought I recollected a big oak in the yard," said Sampson, swinging down. "That one there should hold 'em all." After he dismounted, he drew a rope from behind his saddle. "This rope isn't long, but it should do. Anyone know how to tie a hangman's knot?"

Elijah walked toward the ruins. Carefully he moved debris. It was only a few moments until he saw the tiny charred body.

"Just make a loop, Sampson." Hankins watched Elijah as he hunkered and brushed away ashes. "Will, check the barn for a blanket—a tarp or something to wrap the baby. And see if there's more rope. I want to leave them all swinging."

When Will returned with more lengths of rope and a piece of canvas, Elijah gently eased the still form onto the rough shroud. He started to wrap it, but Hankins called out.

"No. Bring it over here. I want them to see what they've done."

He laid the tiny body on the ground near the oak in front of the condemned men. Every soldier looked in cold-eyed silence.

"Mister"—Tom swallowed—"like I told you, I swear before God, we didn't do it. Only Owens. I know you're going to hang us all, but please get that letter to my wife. I want my family to know I never did it."

"You never stopped him." Hankins eyes were granite.

Tom hung his head.

Sampson looked from the baby to the Yankee and then at Hankins. "What are we waiting for?" He kneed his horse forward, took a rope from Will, and threw it over a limb. Tom sat stoic while Sampson slipped it over his head.

Sampson hit the horse across the rump. It jumped forward, jerking the man from the saddle. Eyes distended, shock washed his face. Guttural sounds gurgled deep in his throat. Saliva dripped from the gaping mouth. Legs kicked and jerked, but finding no prop, they continued to flay. Soon his tongue protruded from a tortured purple face.

In silence Elijah watched. A tragic memory brought sweat to his brow. Uncle Jim had died the same slow, violent death.

It was a gruesome hour before they left the yard where four distorted bodies hung, limp and lifeless. Elijah faced forward; but Sampson, wiping sweat from his broad face, looked back once and muttered an oath under his breath.

They spent the next weeks staying out of sight of the Union Army. Several times patrols rode near, but other than a bit of sniping along the telegraph lines, the Confederates refrained from open combat. Word drifted in of heavy fighting in south Arkansas. One incident in particular generated conversation.

Hankins raked his spoon across the metal plate and ate the last bite of beans.

"Well, I don't hold with shooting prisoners—never did. Black or white. Killing men who've already surrendered is murder."

Brady looked over a hand full of cards and snorted. "Them darkies knew what they'd get if they put on a uniform. Jeff Davis hisself said any black caught carrying a gun for the Union would be given no quarter."

Sampson studied his cards and frowned. "Brady, I'll swear if you ain't got a black ace in yer chest instead of a heart."

Brady gave a snide yellow-toothed grin. "Don't know about that, but it'll cost you two bits to see what I've got in my hand."

"Aw, you know I got no more hard cash, but this here pocketknife is good and sharp. You can shave with it."

Brady studied the knife and shrugged. "All right. Let's see your cards." Then he perused Sampson's hand, laid down his own cards, slapped his leg, and cackled. "Sampson, you're the unluckiest fellow I ever had the pleasure of beating." He reached to rake in the pile of coins and the knife.

Abruptly, Hankins caught his arm. "Let's see that deck."

Brady stuck the cards back into his pocket. "Hell, you want to play too, just ask civil like," he blustered, his face growing red.

"No, I want to see the deck."

Brady's eyes darted back and forth.

He reminded Elijah of a trapped fox searching for a way out of a chicken coop.

Hankins' voice was ice. "I've been watching you deal off the bottom. And I suspect that deck is marked. A flush with only two playing—I'd say the chances of that are slim to none. If I'm wrong you can tell me to go to hell."

"I'm telling you to go to hell right—"

Just then a rider galloped up. "Captain," he said and slid off a lathered horse, "Major Kirby sent me. General Price ordered a cavalry advance along the river. You're to ride to Dardanelle immediately and join General Shelby in the attack. With so many of the Union forces scattered in the south, he thinks it's a prime opportunity to retake the River Valley."

"I thought Shelby was still down south. Hankins sloshed the last bit of cornbran coffee to the ground. "Let's get going, then," he ordered. Then he eyed Brady. "I'll tend to you later."

With hot, surly eyes, Brady watched him mount. Then, gathering the reins of his horse, he mounted too.

They rode fast. By the time they arrived at Dardanelle, the post was already in Confederate hands, and Shelby was preparing to advance on Clarksville.

Elijah sat the restive bay as it switched a tail at pestering flies. He wiped sweat from his brow. It was hot in the May sun near the river. Today no breeze stirred the feathery willows. Dried mud along the bank was hard and cracked. If this was any indication of the summer ahead, he dreaded it.

Billy pushed the mules. They made good progress. Thus far they had seen no army patrols and few travelers. As much as possible they avoided contact, but when they saw riders or drew near settlements or farmhouses, he suggested that Cindy remain out of sight.

"I just think it best," he advised, "the fewer that see you, the better."

Ned agreed. "I know it's irksome," he said, "but if old Abraham had kept pretty Sarah out of sight, he'd have had a heap less trouble in his travels." He softened the words with a kind smile.

Cindy did as suggested. Whenever they were likely to encounter others she climbed into the canvas-covered wagon, but she chafed to be out on the wagon seat to view the few towns they passed through. She enjoyed time on the wagon seat in open country. It was disturbing, however, to see the gaunt women and children. Dressed in rags, they watched with listless gaze from cabin doors and garden plots; the spindly plants yet too early to ease the pinched look of hunger. Often a woman or a thin-shouldered youth worked a pitiful mule in an equally pitiful corn patch. Cindy felt almost sinful driving past while the wagon held a good supply of corn. But Billy was right—they did not have enough to share with everyone. The folks at home needed corn, too.

Ned often gazed north with deep worry wrinkles between his eyes. Cindy was thankful they had few delays. Morning sickness was trouble enough. The jolting wagon seat was almost unbearable, yet the few times she had tried lying in the back of the wagon had been worse.

In a bright morning full of birdsong, she pointed toward a small wooded hill and spoke to Ned, who sat alongside her on the wagon seat. "These woods sort of look like home. I never knew there was so much country in the whole world," she said. "Of course before this trip, I'd not been farther than Dover. Still and all, I've not seen 'ery place yet as purty as home." She shuddered slightly. "I'll swan, why do you reckon folks would live in that awful, ugly, swamp country?"

Today Ned's face was relaxed. Cindy noted with pleasure that there was more color in his cheeks. *It's such a relief to see him gaining,* she thought. *I couldn't face Granny and Becky if he was to die!*

He chewed his jaw a bit before answering. "Oh, I reckon every place the good Lord made has some beauty. Even the swamps are sort of pretty with all that moss hanging from the trees. And the country is full of birds and critters."

"Well, I had all I wanted of it and the critters too. I come near stepping on an alligator. And if I never see another, hit'll be too soon."

Ned chuckled. "Got to admit—they give me the shivers. But I've heard-tell they're good eating."

Cindy gagged. "Law, I'm sorry," she apologized. "It don't take much to turn my stomach lately."

Ned eyed her closely. "I figure you know why."

She blushed and nodded.

"Elijah know?"

Billy abruptly flicked the reins urging the mules along.

"Not yet," Cindy replied softly. "I've not seen him since I found out."

"He'll be mighty glad. A man wants a family—young ones to pass along his name and his land. That's fine, Cindy, real fine." Then he sat up straighter. "Why, I'll be a grandpa and Becky a grandma." He grinned ear to ear. "She'll be happy as a coon in a corn patch!"

Cindy did not tell him about losing the first baby. Surely this time would be different!

Both men were always considerate. Billy insisted she sit in the shade while he washed the supper dishes in a nearby gurgling stream. Cindy did not argue. She ought to wash her dress again, but tonight she felt poorly. Her head throbbed. She sat on the grass and leaned back against a broad-leafed catalpa tree heavy with white bloom. From across the stream drifted a redbird's trill. The sound reminded her of Granny's claim that the vain bird was sinfully declaring itself *pretty, pretty, pretty.*

The evening breeze teased tendrils of Cindy's heavy hair. With a sigh she took out the hairpins, unwound the knot at the nape of her neck, and shook out the thick coil. She studied the hairpins that Pa had carved and then gave a deeper sigh. *What was happening at home to Pa and Ma and Becky and Granny? Most of all, what was happening to Elijah? Not knowing was torture!* After modestly drawing her skirt over knees and ankles, she pulled knees to chest and bent forward to rest her head. But as the heavy fall of hair touched the ground, she abruptly straightened. Billy stood a few feet away, statue still, holding a pail of water. She was taken aback by the stare. He quickly averted his gaze, but not before Ned glanced from Billy to her and his frown deepened.

With flaming cheeks, she stood, swept up her hair, and fastened it tightly into a coil again. *Laws-a-mercy!* She hoped the men did not think she was being immodest! As much as any good woman, she enjoyed compliments—perhaps even took vain pleasure in being thought pretty. But she had never sought or wanted the wrong sort of admiration. She despised loose morals and she despised loose women like Lizzy Tate!

That night conversation was nonexistent around the campfire. Cindy had no idea what Ned and Billy dwelt on as each sat silently staring into the fire. As for herself, she could not forget the embarrassment. It made her stiff and uncomfortable in their presence.

She walked away from the crackling fire to stare into the night sky. The pretty sight eased her nerves. It seemed every star in creation sparkled in the clear sky, and every night bug sang. And yet it was not an unpleasant sound. Tonight her heart ached for Elijah. She longed to share news of the baby with him—in spite of the niggling fear that it might be bad luck to even speak of it so soon and get his hopes up. Surely this time things would go well. Pa often said the Lord would never put more on a body than he was able to bear. Well, she didn't see how she could bear it if anything happened this time.

A scurrying in the brush sent her back to the safety of the fire. Billy glanced up and then looked back at the ground. Ned stood and stretched.

"That pallet will feel good tonight. It's been a long day. How many miles do you—"

He stopped and looked into the night when Billy raised a cautioning hand and then quickly reached for the rifle.

"Cindy, get in the wagon," Billy ordered as he reached under the wagon seat and handed Ned the pistol he had taken from the dead Yankee at the Elkins' Ferry skirmish. Then he handed Cindy the extra rifle. As she scurried into the wagon, both he and Ned stepped into the shadows.

Cindy's ears strained. At first all she heard was katydids and crickets. Then came the muffled thud of hooves. There were several horses, and they were close together. They stopped.

"Hello, the camp!"

"Ride in slow," answered Billy. "Keep your hands where I can see them."

Cindy peeped from the puckered canvas opening. There were six men, all in rough garb, two in worn Confederate uniforms.

"Hey, Tanner," said the tall man, the first in line. He was sparsely fleshed, had bushy eyebrows, and a crooked scar on one cheek. "Guy said it was you. But I never figured you for a Yankee muleskinner." He nodded toward the picketed mules wearing Union brands. "When did you change sides?" he asked with a grin.

Billy lowered the rifle and stepped into the firelight. "Riley, you damned well know I didn't," he said. "Step down and have a cup of real coffee."

"We smelled it five miles back," declared the tall man as he licked his lips and then, along with all the men, dismounted.

Billy shook hands with Riley but merely stared at another. "So, Guy, that was you nosing around down by the creek." There was malice on Billy's face. "I heard you lite out when I was fetching water." He turned back to Riley and indicated Ned with a nod. "Meet my kin, Ned Loring."

"Glad to make your acquaintance." Riley nodded and extended his hand for the steaming cup Billy had just filled.

All but the man named Guy seemed intent on the fragrant coffee. Guy's eyes, however, scoured the camp. Although Cindy was well back in the shadowy wagon, she felt his gaze probing the opening. Since he had scouted the camp earlier, of course, he had already seen her. Nonetheless she stayed discreetly out of sight.

The men hunkered around the fire and sipped the coffee. Billy occasionally glanced at Guy and then at the wagon.

"Any war news?" he asked.

"Reckon you know all about us teaching General Steele and those darkie troops of his a lesson or two at Poison Springs?"

Billy nodded.

"Marmaduke's men hardly left one of those black bastards alive. Some of 'em played dead but they shot 'em anyway. A few crawled off into the brush. And I heard some of them made it back to Camden. But that'll teach 'em what happens when they fight for the damned Yankees."

"Steele hanging around Camden?" asked Billy.

"No, he tucked tail and headed right back to Little Rock—with us nipping at his heels the whole way." Riley went on. "Things have been humming back east, too. Big battle—might nigh the same ground as Chancellorsville and just about a year to the day. Heck of a come-off. Not sure who won this time, either. Couple of thousand men killed."

He went on, "Another odd coincidence—Longstreet was shot by his own men not four miles down the road from where Stonewall Jackson was shot by his the year before."

"Kill him?" asked Billy.

"Naw, but he'll not be leading troops for a while." After savoring another sip of coffee, Riley went on, "Lee was way outnumbered. Grant was the big pum'kins for the Union this time. That rugged terrain whipped him as much as anything." Riley paused for a moment and shook his head. Then he went on, "Awful brushfire broke out during the battle." He grimaced. "Said you could hear the wounded screaming a mile away. According to the reports, I reckon most of them got roasted like a Christmas goose."

Silence greeted the last remark.

Sweat broke out on Cindy's brow. She swallowed warm bile rising in her throat.

Finally, Riley spoke, low and solemn, "I wonder if there'll be a man-jack of us alive when this war ends."

"Where is Lee now?" asked Ned.

"Still slugging it out with Grant, I guess. I've not heard any news lately." Riley spoke again. "Couldn't help but notice, mister, you look like you've seen some hard service yourself."

"A bit," Ned agreed.

Billy spoke up, "Ned was just paroled from Ship Island. I went to Shreveport to fetch him home."

Riley whistled low. "No wonder you're skin and bone. I've heard Yankee prison camps are real hell holes."

When Ned made no comment, the conversation shifted to other topics. Upon overhearing coarse remarks about a town the men had recently visited, Cindy's ears burned. It was obvious they had no idea she was listening. The voices rose and fell with talk and laughter. When the men eventually quieted, Cindy fell into a fitful doze.

She awakened from a desperate need to relieve herself. There was no way to exit the wagon without stepping on Billy. He was bedded down right behind the wagon. And the soldiers had posted a guard. She was not about to go traipsing past that group of men now dozing by the campfire. She had observed from Elijah that soldiers had a way of sleeping with one eye open. Finally, she found an empty bucket, and as quietly as possible, emptied her swollen bladder. Then she slept.

She awakened to deep voices. She sat up, and with a silent groan, glanced outside. A golden sunrise glistened on low mists swirling over the creek and the weedy fields beyond. She longed to step out and stretch the kinks from her back and legs.

Hopefully, those men will leave soon, she thought, and then lay back and strained her ears to listen. Always before coffee had smelled good to her. Now she covered her nose and swallowed.

After a hurried breakfast, the soldiers prepared to leave. Abruptly Cindy sat up. The conversation had taken an unexpected turn.

Riley's voice was hard and calculating. "Billy, we've reason to believe you've got Yankee gold in that wagon. You can hand it over peaceable or otherwise. But we aim to have it."

In the silence Cindy heard a pistol cock. Then the same sound echoed under the wagon where Ned had been folding his bedroll. She slipped from the bed and grabbed the rifle. Still keeping well out of sight, she looked out.

Riley's pistol pointed at Billy's chest. It was a moment before Billy spoke. His empty hands hung at his sides.

"There's no gold. Not even a dollar. I figure I know where you heard the lie—and why. Guy wants me dead. Me and Ned. He wants what's in the wagon, but it sure ain't gold."

"What the hell—"

"Ask Guy." Billy turned hot eyes to the man who now took a step back while eyeing him nervously.

When Guy's glance darted under the wagon, Cindy was certain Ned held the pistol ready. Her heart pounded, and her palms began to sweat. She was a good shot. Once before she had shot a human, the rabid bushwhacker in the gang who had killed Pete. Without a doubt, this time lives again hung in the balance. She prayed her aim would be true and put the sight on Riley's chest.

"I tell you he stole a Yankee payroll—"

"Ned's daughter-in-law is in the wagon." Billy let the words sink in before adding, "We can't take you all, Riley. But she's got a rifle, and Ned's a crack shot with that pistol. I reckon he'll go for you first." He raised his voice. "Cindy, stick the barrel out just a hair so Riley can see it."

She let the tip protrude. Riley sucked in a quick breath. Then he turned.

"Guy, you lying sonofabitch! There's no gold. You knew we'd not go along with you on this."

"We could use the wagon. We know they've got coffee. No telling what else they've got in there.

Billy's hand dropped to the pistol in his belt.

"Stay put!" Riley gave a warning wave of his pistol. "I can't let you shoot him. Oh, I know Guy's a maggot. He needs killing. But we've been riding together a long time, and he's done me a good turn now and again." He took a step back. "Tell your kin to let us ride out, and we'll let you be."

Billy gave a hollow laugh. "And let Guy come right back here and put a bullet in my back."

Riley lowered his pistol. "I swear I'll keep him on a tight leash till you're well out of the country. I wouldn't lie to you. You know that."

Billy slowly nodded. "All right. Get him out of here."

They quickly mounted and rode south, leaving the camp strangely quiet and empty.

Billy spoke softly, "You can come out now, Cindy."

Still gripping the rifle, she stepped into the sunlight and blinked.

Ned stood. "You trust him?"

"Riley, I do. We go way back. Rode together before he joined up with Hindman's Partisan Rangers. He wanted me to join, too. But they're guerrillas. I never could stomach that kind of warfare." He turned to Cindy. "I saved you some breakfast."

While she finished eating, Billy hitched the team. All the while his eyes roved the trail. Before pulling out, he made a quick sashay on horseback heading down the trail they had already traveled. When he returned he climbed onto the wagon seat, and they headed north on the sun-dappled trail.

"Your eyes are red as a rooster comb. You didn't sleep much, did ya?" she guessed.

"Not much," he admitted.

The uneventful weeks of good travel brought them close to journey's end. Here in rolling hills the vibrant spring foliage had matured into deep green. Trees, now thickly leafed, made inviting shade. Wild pink roses edged the trail along with masses of honeysuckle sending out fragrant perfume. Berry briars loaded with tiny white blossoms and clumps of colorful wild flowers hummed with bees. When Cindy spied the spiked red blossoms of a buckeye bush, she began to feel at home.

One morning Ned arrived from the creek. His hair and beard were damp and freshly combed. He smiled at Cindy.

"Miss Cindy, you're looking chipper this morning."

"Pot calling the kettle black," she quipped. "Just look at you! All curried and combed."

"Figured I'd do you both a favor and take a real bath. First good soak I've had in a while." Then the smile faded. His face took on a hunted look. "Being clean. In that filthy prison, I missed that most as much as good food."

Billy looked up from sifting cornmeal through his fingers into a pot of boiling water. "Prison ain't the only place. Seems to me the whole Confederate Army is over-rich with lice and dirt. Some fellows don't seem to mind so much. But I can't abide filth."

"Could be 'cause we were both raised by Granny." Ned's eyes twinkled. "I never saw a body despise dirt like Granny. I've missed that old woman. It'll be good to see her again."

Billy nodded. "She never quit hoping and praying you were alive. I sure dread her finding out about Pa, though."

Ned's eyes saddened. "Caleb was as fine a man as ever drew breath. I hate that he died tryin' to help me."

"Don't blame yerself. It was just his time."

Ned let out a deep breath and then asked, "How soon do you figure we'll get home?"

"We'll cross the Arkansas today. I aim to cross at Roseville and then take the wire road to Clarksville." He lowered his voice but Cindy overheard. "That fellow I spoke to yesterday said there was quite a fight at Clarksville a while back."

"Soldiers killed?" asked Ned.

"Some maybe."

Cindy swallowed a sudden lump of fear in her throat.

Billy looked at the bubbling gruel. He drew the pot off the fire and began ladling mush into a bowl. He handed the first steaming bowlful to her.

She sat the mush, untasted, onto a rock and gazed at a hawk sailing overhead.

If only she had wings like that hawk, she'd fly away quick to find Elijah!

Chapter 11

With Elijah's first glimpse of Joseph Shelby, he was struck by the general's resemblance to his own Uncle Jim. The general was slender, with a high forehead, dark shoulder-length hair, a heavy beard, and deep-set eyes. And just now he was in a somber mood akin to Uncle Jim's brooding personality. Elijah supposed last night's dream of Uncle Jim and his gruesome hanging made him more keenly aware of the likeness. Of all the nightmares he had experienced—and there had been many since his first battle—the dreams of Uncle Jim were the worst.

Hankins left the knot of officers conversing with the general and stopped near Elijah and Sampson. "Well, Sampson," he said, "we're having another go at Clarksville. And this time I hope you don't side with the Yankees."

"Aw, Troy, you know good and well that was a accident. It was that blamed hound—"

With a scowl, Hankins interrupted, "Just don't load your gun until the firing commences."

Now Sampson scowled.

"Well, there's good news," Hankins went on, "since Sampson wasn't around to spoil things, Shelby, Marmaduke, and the rest managed to route the Yankees down south. General Steele scurried back to Little Rock with his tail tucked between his legs."

Elijah shook his head in disbelief. Months ago he had given up any chance of a Confederate victory. Perhaps he had written them off too soon.

When Hankins walked away, Sampson cursed under his breath.

Elijah slapped his back. "Don't take it personal. Everyone messes up now and again. Besides Hankins is likely just testy right now, with a fight coming up."

"Troy is testy all the time," Sampson muttered and pushed out his lip like a spoiled child.

Soon the army moved out from the crude enclosure that housed the post of Dardanelle. Elijah's bay crossed the river with ease. With such a large force of men, several hundred of Shelby's command as well as Marmaduke's entire cavalry, Elijah had little doubt that this time capturing Clarksville would be no problem.

Soon however, Shelby and the main body of cavalry broke away and headed in the opposite direction. Elijah learned that their smaller force was thought sufficient to retake Clarksville. He rode along Cabin Creek Road with the scent of locust blossoms heavy in the still air. The smell took him back home, his mind far from the upcoming battle. Now he recognized every rock and bush. Most of the fields along the way had remained unplowed and unplanted. It was, he thought, a crying shame to let such rich bottomland grow up in weeds. The bright sun and open land made his hands itch for a plow handle. If the war ever ended and if he survived, he intended to try his hand at growing oats. He had no idea if they would thrive along the creek, but Hankins claimed they made the best fodder on earth.

All along the road, wide-eyed youngsters ran out of houses and cabins to watch them pass. Often an anxious-faced woman scanned the ranks looking for a familiar face. When they drew near Uncle Jim's deserted cabin, he wondered afresh how Aunt Opal and the young ones were doing living with her kin in Louisiana.

Abruptly his musing was interrupted. Far ahead, Kirby called a halt. Although Elijah could not hear the conversation, a newly arrived scout pointed down the road and gestured toward Clarksville. Suddenly Kirby ordered them forward at a gallop.

They had not gone far when Elijah looked up and groaned. Columns of black smoke roiled against the cloudless blue. The Yankees had torched the town!

He was not surprised. It was common practice to burn supplies before an advancing enemy. While obeying orders, he had done it himself at Fayetteville. Nonetheless, the waste of valuable supplies had always rankled him. With pulsing blood, he urged the bay forward. Perhaps they could still save some buildings! His thoughts flashed to David and old Mr. Hadley and to Emmitt and his store.

Just ahead two young boys sat on a fence rail gesturing wildly, faces shiny with excitement. The oldest—no more than eight—yelled, "Damn Yankees skedaddled, but some of 'em are still there burning things. If you hurry you can catch 'em!"

At a gallop, they raced toward the long boxed-in bridge spanning Spadra Creek. Smoke billowed from under the wooden roof, but the bridge was still intact. Elijah did not slow to help the riders who piled off to kick out the blaze. The bay's hoofs thundered on the wooden floor and then raised dust on the street beyond.

Elijah noted with relief there were no flames near the Hadley shack. Main Street was eerily vacant although flames shot from the courthouse roof. Beyond the courthouse, tongues of fire licked hungrily at the bell tower of the wooden Methodist Church. As Kirby urged them forward, Elijah saw David and even old Enos Hadley in a group frantically dragging boxes and barrels from the burning church. He recalled David saying the Union Army used the church for a commissary. The major ordered a few soldiers to aid the crowd and then divided the rest into separate groups. Elijah, along with a dozen men including Hankins and Sampson, continued along the short main street toward the far edge of town.

The mercantile was unharmed. Emmitt, wearing a large white cobbler's apron across his barrel chest, stood in the doorway with a shotgun in the crook of his arm. He nodded as they rode past. Now they proceeded with extra caution. If the boys were right, the Yankees were not far ahead. Here the buildings fanned out with wide empty spaces between. Hankins signaled them to spread out and check the side streets.

Suddenly, the hair on the back of Elijah's neck stood. As his old comrade Levi had taught, he never ignored the sensation. He reined in the bay and studied the area ahead. Just then a shot grazed his sleeve. He snapped off an answering shot as he spurred the bay forward and then piled off alongside an unfinished building. For an instant he recalled removing the window sashes from it for his own cabin, then he gave full concentration to the sniper. The shot had come from the low squat building further down the street. As a Union soldier stuck his head around the corner, Elijah aimed and fired. The man drew back.

Soon a lighted torch arched the sky and landed in the vacant building.

Then the Yankee yelled, his voice slurred from drink, "Hey, Reb! How'd you like them apples?" A raucous laugh followed the taunt.

Elijah hunkered, sent a shot in the soldier's direction, and then quickly darted across the wooden floor and threw the torch outside through a window opening. It landed harmlessly in the dirt. He particularly wanted the building saved. After the war he intended to buy the lumber.

While hurriedly reloading the pistol cylinder, he glanced up to see Hankins riding cautiously along the back street, attempting to circle the Yankee.

In a running crouch, Elijah crossed to the back of the next building. And then he sprinted again.

Just then the man in frayed, rumpled uniform stepped around the edge of the building. Along with a rifle, he clutched a whisky bottle. Elijah raised the pistol and fired. The soldier pitched forward.

Then Elijah froze. Directly across the street, Brady hunkered behind a building. His rifle was pointed directly at Hankins! Elijah raised the pistol. He abruptly halted. The tall black horse Hankins rode blocked his line of fire.

Sweat beaded Elijah's brow. With a yell and a headlong dash, he sprinted forward, pistol raised and pointed in Brady's direction. Any second he expected to see Hankins fall. Almost simultaneously two shots exploded.

Elijah dove behind a nearby shed. He looked out. Then his eyes widened. Across the street Sampson lowered his rifle and stared at Brady's inert body sprawled in the alley.

Hankins rode swiftly forward. "What the—"

"Damned sneak was trying to shoot you and lay it on the Yankee," Sampson growled.

Surprise washed Hankins' face.

"I knowed you needed lookin' after," said Sampson as he began reloading his rifle. "Ain't I told you time and again? I've had the devil's own time trying to keep you from shuffling me off to do some piddling chore every time you head for a ruckus. Let this be a lesson to you, Troy." With a disgusted look at the prone body, he reached a boot to scoot Brady's out-flung arm away from a rifle and then bent to pick up the gun.

Amusement glimmered in Hankins' good eye. "Well, dumpling, today has been a real eye-opener. Thanks for saving my hide." Then he looked at Brady and shook his head. "Come on, fellows. Let's go help those folks fight fire."

When they stopped at the mercantile to get buckets, Emmitt handed them over willingly. By the time they arrived at the church, boxes and barrels were piled across the road. The building—the caved roof a torch of dancing flames—was past saving, so they turned to the courthouse. A line of soldiers formed a bucket brigade stretching from a nearby well to the building. Elijah was first in line. As sweat ran down his face, he charged forward, again and again, to wet the blaze nearest the door. The moment he turned around another full bucket waited. At first it seemed futile. Smoke billowed and the blaze crackled as loudly as ever. Slowly but surely, they made inroads. As Elijah gained ground, he stepped farther into the building until Hankins tapped his shoulder and motioned him back.

"Let someone else take over while you get some air," he ordered.

Elijah backed away and then sank onto the ground in the shade of a giant oak and began coughing and gulping in fresh air. Gingerly he touched his blistered face. His eyebrows were gone, and he smelled his own singed hair. Although he didn't recall getting burned, he espied an angry red blotch through a new hole in one sleeve.

After a bit he stood to rejoin the brigade, this time farther down the line. When the fire was finally out, one wall and some of the ground floor were gone; but most of the second story was intact.

Exhausted men dropped onto the grass. Soon townspeople also gathered on the courthouse lawn. The women, vociferous in gratitude, were equally vocal with rants against the Yankees. David held onto his grandfather's arm and steered him toward Elijah. The old fellow looked more dead than alive.

"Howdy," greeted Elijah. He helped David lower the old man onto the grass. "You two look worse for wear," he commented.

David wiped a sleeve across a soot-covered brow. "You don't look so good, yerself," he noted.

Elijah quirked what was left of a singed eyebrow. "Appears the Yankees kept us all hopping today." Elijah frowned as Mr. Hadley's breath rattled in and out. "You all right, sir?" he asked.

"Damn Yankees," the old man wheezed.

"I tried to get him to stay home in the bed, but he's stubborn as the worst mule ever lived," David scolded, but his eyes were worried.

Elijah stood. "Let's get him home. He can ride my horse."

Mr. Hadley did not object as Elijah practically carried and then lifted him onto the sorrel. After getting the old gentleman tucked into bed, David followed Elijah outside. A decrepit-looking mule approached the leaning porch and brayed.

"Go on away, Jepner." David shooed the mule. Then his frown deepened. "This will kill Grandpa sure," he said.

"He doesn't look good," Elijah admitted. As he eyed the boy, he noticed David did not look good either. His faced was pinched and thin. Elijah suspected there was little food in the ramshackle cabin. "You got any other kin?" he asked.

David shook his head. "Nope. Grandpa is all."

Elijah chewed his jaw a bit. "Any idea what you'll do if he dies?"

"Stay here I reckon." David turned away long enough to swipe tears gathering in his black eyes. "Got nowhere's else to go."

"Well, I'll come back and check on your grandpa tonight if I can," he said.

David called after him, "Much obliged fur your help."

Elijah turned and waved. The boy in the ragged clothes and bare feet looked forlorn staring after him.

After rejoining the unit, Elijah went to the supply wagon and purloined a few supplies. He did not consider it stealing—the army had foraged the corn and pork from civilians. It seemed fitting to return a bit.

The troops were mounting as he put the supplies into his saddlebag,

"We'll push on this evening and camp at Horsehead Creek," said Hankins. "Tomorrow we'll head over and see if they need our help at Ozark. The Feds might have been more persistent there."

Elijah mounted but made a quick detour to the Hadley cabin.

David took the supplies gladly. The old man had fallen into a fitful doze.

"I'll come back every chance I get," assured Elijah. He went outside, looked back, and shook his head.

The boy has a hard row to hoe, he thought. He spurred the sorrel and caught up just as the troops left town.

A ways down the dusty road, he paused. He could see a blue line of mountains from here. For days he had been unable to shake a premonition that something was wrong at home. He turned in the saddle and waited until Hankins drew abreast.

"Captain, I sure would like to make a little sashay home and check on the folks."

Hankins smiled. "Natural for a fellow with a young wife waiting. I'll tell you what, wait a few days. I figure the Yankees will swarm right back here. More than likely, they'll know we don't have enough force to fend off a big push. But if I'm wrong and they don't come back, I'll ask the major if you can have a few days leave to go hug and kiss that pretty wife."

"All right," Elijah agreed. Of course he wanted to go this minute. But Hankins had been good to him. He didn't want to disobey a direct order. Hopefully he would see Cindy soon.

Billy eyed the river a long while before urging the team closer to shore. A freight boat, lapped by gentle waves, was held fast to the dock by ropes. Along the bank stood blackened skeletons of buildings.

"Look at them burned-out buildings," muttered Cindy.

Billy squinted into the evening sun glinting on the water. "Last time I was through here, that one over yonder was a big gin. Those others were warehouses stuffed with cotton bales. I supposed Joe Shelby dispossessed a few greedy Yankees of some cotton."

Ned put in, "Or they might have fired the buildings themselves before they pulled out."

"Could be," agreed Billy. "Either way, all that waste is a crying shame."

Ned gave a solemn nod of agreement. Then he asked, "Since this war commenced, I've sure seen a lot of black chimneys pokin' up from heaps of rubble. Any houses burned around home?"

Cindy cut her eyes at Billy and let him answer.

"Some. Jared Rawlings tried burnin' Elijah and Cindy out. Lige put a stop to that. Jared won't be doing any more mischief—not ever."

Ned looked from one to the other but kept silent.

Cindy had long admired Ned's quiet pondering ways. As one of her pa's favorite proverbs said, Ned was quick to listen and slow to speak.

"Don't worry," assured Billy. "Elijah didn't run afoul of the law. As you well know, the Rawlings weren't well thought of around these parts."

"Any trouble from the rest of his kin?"

"None to speak of."

Mid-morning they crossed the bank-full river on a creaky steamboat piloted by a captain that Billy knew. He confirmed that the area was, for the moment, again in Confederate hands. But as he removed a stained cap from thinning hair and scratched his head, he said, "But who knows for how long. These days a fellow never knows how loud to whistle Dixie."

As Roseville disappeared into gray haze hovering the water, Cindy found herself straining forward. Once across the river, home would be close. Of course, it would still take two days of hard travel—but what was that compared to how far they had come!

The plantation fronting the river lay eerie and deserted, the wide flat fields overgrown with weeds and the tall white house shut tight and shuttered. Billy said the owner, loyal Union, had fled north two years before.

Although Billy kept the mules at a brisk pace, it was dusk when they reached Clarksville. The town was ghostly quiet. Main Street lay in shadows, but Cindy perceived the tall courthouse was a mere shell, one wall completely burned away. As the wagon rattled through town she saw curtains flutter and occasionally a pale face peeked out. There was no sign of either army.

"I know it's late, but I figure to press on a ways," he said. "Less likely to run onto trouble camping outside of town than staying in the wagon yard."

Cindy was bone weary, but she did not protest, and Ned heartily agreed.

Billy added, "I know a likely spot we can reach before black dark."

The mules, however, balked upon approaching the long Spadra Creek bridge. Disgusted, Billy climbed down and after much pulling and prodding led them through the wooden tunnel. It was almost too dark to see when they finally stopped in the trees alongside a creek just a short way from town. Cindy almost fell as Billy helped her from the wagon. As his arm quickly encircled her waist, she clung to him for a moment to regain her balance. She stepped away, but not before Ned rounded the wagon.

"Gracious, I'm wobbly as new colt," she apologized and stepped farther away.

Although Cindy was exhausted and retired to the wagon shortly after supper, sleep was illusive. The warm night was alive with sound. Katydids and tree frogs competed with deep-throated bullfrogs and the plaintive call of a whippoorwill. But it was thoughts of home that kept her tossing. Overshadowing their joyful homecoming was the tragic news of Caleb's death. *That would just about kill Granny!* Abruptly she sat up and hugged her knees to her chest. More than anything she feared tragic news of Elijah. News of wounds and death were slow to reach the mountain, but whenever possible the army informed a family.

"No use borrowin' trouble," she muttered. She sighed and lay back down and shut her eyes.

The words she heard were low and not meant for her ears.

"You're right," said Billy, "I do care for her. I've fought it, but how could a man keep from it? I'll tell you one thing for sure. I'm not like my real pa. I've kept my distance."

For a while silence reigned. Then Billy spoke again, "As soon as I get you both home safe, I aim to leave and never come back."

Ned's words were indiscernible. But Billy's impassioned answer came clear.

"No, Ned, my mind's made up."

Cindy bit her lip. She had known. But hearing the words made it real. Poor Billy. He was a good man. Tears wet her cheeks and dripped onto the pallet.

Oh God, she silently cried out, *why is life so hard?*

The next morning they rode along with scant conversation. Cindy was ill at ease and avoided eye contact with both men. She could not relax after overhearing last night's conversation. They would be home soon and then things would return to normal...at least she hoped so.

They forded Minnow Creek and passed through Hagarville, ringed with hills blue in the distance. Sunbeams streamed from the clouds, bathing the sky with glory. Cindy imagined it would look just so when the last trumpet blew and Jesus returned in the clouds.

She leaned forward as if willing the mules to hurry. Every rock and tree and silvery glimpse of the creek seemed like old friends. As they topped a steep ridge, she resented even the short stop to let the mules blow.

They made good time. However dusk had settled, deep and blue, when they crossed Little Piney Creek on the trail leading to Ned's farm.

The cabin stood mellow gray, whole and solid with dim light rosy at the windows. Before Billy called whoa, Ned was on the ground. The door burst open. Becky went into his arms. She laughed and cried and touched his face. "How I've prayed for this minute. Oh, Ned, you'll never know how I've missed you and how I grieved—"

He shushed her and gathered her into his arms again. "No more tears, girl. I'm here now." Then he pushed her back and looked down. "You all right?" he asked. "Your foot?"

"It's fine," she assured. "I only limp a little. But what about you?"

"Never better in my life," he said, drawing her close again.

Becky spoke against his chest. "Oh, how I missed you!" She suddenly pushed back. "Deborah spent the night at Cousin Jenny's. She'll be so disappointed to miss—"

"Is there news from Elijah?" Cindy interrupted.

"Not a word since you left."

As Cindy's shoulders sagged with relief, Becky suddenly saw Billy and her face became a question mark.

Billy gathered the reins. "I'll head on over," he said.

"Wait. We'll come with you," said Ned. "I want to be the one to tell Granny."

Becky looked from face to face. As she guessed the problem, her hand went to her throat. "Where's Caleb?" she asked in a whisper. Then she groaned, for Cindy's quick sob was her answer.

"Poor Granny," Becky whispered. "And poor Viola," she added.

No one but Cindy noticed Billy's jaws tighten.

And poor Ned, thought Cindy. She would sooner face a firing squad than tell Granny.

The cabin was dark. Ned climbed the steps. A window opened and a shotgun barrel poked out.

"Who's there? Ya better answer quick!" Granny's harsh command overrode the shrill screech of tree frogs.

"Granny, I've survived a lot. Don't shoot me now."

In a moment the door jerked open. Dressed in a long white nightgown, the tiny woman, minus the gun, enveloped Ned in an embrace. "Ned, Ned, Ned! Oh, I knowed in my bones, I'd live to see ya again!" She hugged and kissed him and patted his bearded face. "Praise the Lord," she whispered and then drew him forward. "Come on in so's I kin strike a light and really see ya." She hobbled to the table and lit a tallow candle. "I never give up prayin' you'd come home. Hit appears you even still got all your limbs. But from the feel of yer ribs you can use some fattenin'..."

When she turned around, her beaming face stilled. She looked beyond Cindy who stood near the doorway, face white and tears streaming.

As Billy stepped inside, Granny gripped the table and sank into a chair. "Where's Caleb? Where's my boy?"

Ned took her shoulders. He swallowed. Finally the words came. "Granny, he's not coming home."

Cindy steeled herself. She clenched her jaws tight, awaiting wails and tears and loud laments. Instead Granny bowed her head. After only a moment, she looked up again and drew a ragged breath.

"The Lord giveth. And the Lord taketh away. Blessed be the name of the Lord." She slowly patted Ned's arm. "I imagine him and yer mama is having a fine reunion in heaven. Reeda May and Caleb was always close. They never fought and scrapped like most brothers and sisters. Hit about kilt him when she died." She shook her head. "I've lived too long. A body ought not outlive their younguns…and I've outlived both of mine." In the candlelight her wrinkled skin was pale as parchment, and for the first time Cindy could remember, Granny's dark eyes had no shine while she listened stoically to Ned briefly relate what had befallen Caleb.

A bedroom door opened. "Billy!" Viola cried and hastened forward.

He stood like stone while she hugged him.

"Pa is dead."

When he spoke, she drew back and stared.

Her voice was flat. "I reckon you mean Caleb." Then she muttered, "So Caleb is dead, too." Then she touched Billy's face. "But I still got you—the spit and image of yer pa."

He pushed her hand aside and stepped away. Before going outside, he made a detour to lovingly squeeze Granny's shoulder. She reached a frail hand to touch him as he passed. After one quick stifled sob, she recovered and looked at Cindy.

"Come sit down, child. You look plum wore out."

"*Oh Granny, I'm so very, very sorry.*" Cindy rushed forward and knelt in front of the chair. "I wish I could have stopped 'em. I didn't know what to do—"

"Laws-a-mercy, girl. No matter what you'd have done, hit was just Caleb's time. Life and death is in the hands o' the Lord. He knows the day of our death from the day of our birth." She softly repeated, "Hit was just Caleb's time."

Cindy laid her head in Granny's lap on the starched cotton apron. While Granny stroked her hair, she sobbed.

How she longed for Elijah's strong arms!

Viola looked out the window and then stepped to the door and opened it. The scent of Granny's roses wafted inside.

"Billy, you come on back in here."

There was no answer from the darkness.

Viola's voice was petulant. "Don't know why he left in sech a hurry. He ought to stay and take care of his ma now that Caleb's gone."

Granny abruptly stood. Her eyes blazed. "Hit never dawns on you to think about 'ery soul but yerself, Viola Tanner!" Then she paused. "No. I'll not be calling you that. *You ain't no Tanner*. Never was. You jest used Caleb's name, like you used him—fer a convenience. Oh yes. I knowed. I knowed all along. I knowed the day he brung you home and said you was married. And I knowed fer sure when Billy come. He had no look of a Tanner about him—ner even the birthmark that's marked ever babe with a drop o' Tanner blood." She looked at Ned. "Ain't hit true, Ned. You got it. Elijah's got it. But not Billy. No, not Billy."

Viola stepped back. Her hand went to her throat and her eyes widened.

Granny took two steps forward. Her voice shook. "I kept shut fer Caleb's sake. But he's gone now. And thank God you can't hurt him no more!" Ned took her arm as she turned and sat back down. The bedroom door slammed when Viola rushed from the room. Into the silence came the distant hoot of an owl.

"I'm fine, Ned," assured Granny through tight lips. "I been wantin' to do that fer many a year." Then she took Ned's face into her hands. "These old eyes has been hungry fer the sight of you. But you get on home now. You look worn to a frazzle. You and Becky can come back tomorrow. Cindy kin stay here tonight." She stood and started toward her bedroom. "I want to be alone fer a bit, and then I want to hear all about Caleb."

Each day Ned gained strength. Each day Becky scolded and fussed over him, urging him not to work so hard. Cindy noticed anytime he was within reach, Becky kept a hand on his shoulder, as if assuring herself he was, after all, alive.

"Wife, I'm fine," he assured, rising from the breakfast table and putting on a straw hat. "Plowing and hoeing is a pleasure to a fellow whose been staring at the ceiling as long as I have. Besides the corn is ready to lay by; this will be the last plowin.' You know as well as I do, we have to make this crop."

And they did. There was scarcely enough corn left to last until the crop matured. While he pushed himself to keep the young corn hoed, Cindy, Becky, and Deborah tended the flourishing vegetable garden.

Cindy stood and brushed dirt from the skirt covering her knees and then dusted off her hands. She breathed deeply of the fresh smell of turned earth and then stilled for a moment, listening to the cooing of a mourning dove in the wild plum thicket behind the barn. It was not a mournful sound. She thought it gentle and soothing. A soft smile curved her lips as she looked back down the row of thin green stems holding up small feathery leaves. They looked puny now, but in the fertile soil and warm sun they would soon become hearty stalks dotted with ripe red tomatoes. It was late for getting the plants into the ground, and they had grown tall and spindly, crowded in the buckets, but as Granny often said, better late than never.

She put a hand to her back and then arched it. The queasy stomach had lessened but the low backache had become a constant bother. Granny said a woman in the family way was more apt to have aches and pains than not. Cindy tried pushing aside the fear of losing the baby. And yet it persisted like the dull ache.

Deborah ladled a dipper of water to pour around the roots of a plant and looked up. "Why don't you go sit in the shade. I'll finish this."

"Thank you, honey." She smiled at the child.

"Cindy," Deborah abruptly asked, "have you had any word…I mean…do you have any idea where your cousin Michael is?" she finished with a stammer.

Upon seeing the blush, Cindy stared. *Upon my word,* she noted with raised brows, *Deborah is not such a child.* The girl's spindly frame was filling out with the first soft curves of womanhood.

"No, I haven't heard a thing lately—not since he got paroled. He's likely back in the cavalry. He'll come ridin' up one of these days and surprise us all," she added with a smile.

Deborah lowered her head and gave a firm pat to the damp earth hugging the slender plant. "I hope so," she said with fervor. "I reckon you miss Elijah a lot, don't you?"

"I surely do. I keep looking down the road, hopin' I'll see him."

Deborah looked down the trail where it crossed the easy flowing creek, silver with sun, and sighed. "I know what you mean."

Ned kept a rifle handy, and they all kept a vigilant eye out for bushwhackers and foraging armies. Sometimes in the evenings Ned rode to visit neighbors to inquire about war news and news in general.

"Tom Sorrels just got back from town. He says Isaac Murphy, the new Union governor, is pushing hard for a peaceful settlement of things in Arkansas. Reckon he wants us to kiss and make up," said Ned. "But that ain't fazing Shelby. He's stirrin' the pot all over the state. Tom says he's rounding up deserters and enlisting guerrillas, tryin' to organize a whole new force. He vows he'll either enlist men into the Confederate Army or drive 'em into the arms of the Union."

"Why in the world would he do that?" asked Becky perplexed.

"I reckon he just can't stand shirkers. Men who fight take a poor view of them that could but don't."

Her lips thinned. "Ned Loring, you'll never go back," she said with determination.

He chuckled. "If Joe Shelby ever comes after me, I'll just tell him that yo're a Yankee and I'm already in yer arms."

Becky, however, did not even smile.

Ned returned one evening with sad news. Jenny's pa, Pappy Campbell, had died just before dark. The next day, while neighbors stood in the shade of a tall hickory growing near the freshly dug grave, Simon preached the funeral, extolling the stouthearted pioneer who was the first white man to settle along Little Piney.

Granny stood dry-eyed as her only brother was lowered into the ground. She laid a handful of roses on the mounded earth. "Well, Horace," she said matter-of-factly, "tell Pa and Reeda May and Caleb howdy. And tell 'em I'll be seein' y'all soon."

Cindy shivered. How would they get along without Granny and her knowledge of doctoring? Cindy was counting on her to deliver the baby. Just in case, she made a silent vow to learn all she could from the old woman.

Jenny declined Becky's invitation to come home with them. She had to get used to being alone she said, but thanked Becky kindly.

Becky was silent all the way home. "I wish that brother of mine would write," she finally said.

"Still aiming to play cupid, are you?" said Ned.

Cindy recalled that Elijah thought Jenny was sweet on his ma's brother. And he thought Tap was equally smitten with the tall, quiet woman.

"Well, Jenny needs someone. And so does Tap for that matter," declared Becky. "High time he settled down to raise a family."

Ned's brows quirked. "They're a bit old for that, don't you think?"

"Not really," said Becky, a little miffed.

As spring gave place to summer, days grew hot and sultry. Cicadas rasped a constant drone. Nights cooled only slightly, the humid air loud with katydids. The corn was head high now, the long-leafed stalks topped by pollen-coated tassels pointing skyward. Silks protruding from the husks were still milky green except for a few that had begun to purple. Cindy's eyes strayed to pea and bean vines full of swelling pods and tomato plants covered with white blossoms and small green fruit. If the rains came, they would not go hungry.

Lately she did not have an appetite. It was hard to force food down, but she decided that butter-coated roasting ears might be tempting.

Today the sun stood directly overhead when she climbed the porch steps and sat down the full basket of black-eyed peas braced against her hip. After mopping sweat from her face, she took a sip of water from the bucket sitting on the rail. She grimaced. The water in the dipper was almost hot. If she weren't so listless, she would go draw a fresh bucket from the well. Instead she dropped onto a chair on the shaded porch and reached for a handful of peas to shell.

"Dinner is almost ready," Becky called from the kitchen. "Why don't you come inside and rest until it's on the table."

"I think it's cooler out here." In reality Cindy did not want to stand. Today her energy had evaporated like dew in the morning sun. Tiredly she broke one end from the pea and pulled down on the long string. As gray peas with dark eyes spilled into the pan in her lap, they made a plinking sound.

As the pan filled, the plinking ceased. Cindy worked without looking at her busy hands. Instead she eyed the road. It was habit. There had been no word from Elijah, but she constantly watched. She looked west and noticed with relief a few thunderheads forming.

"Maybe hit'll rain and cool things off," she muttered.

"Dinner's ready," called Becky.

With eyes still on the thunderheads, Cindy finished shelling the pea in her hand. Then her breath sucked in and her hands stilled.

"Elijah!" she whispered.

She jumped up, sending both pan and peas rolling. She dashed down the steps and across the yard toward the creek where a sorrel's pounding hooves sent water flying. He slid from the horse into her upraised arms.

Finally she laughed and pushed back. "Yo're about to squeeze me in two," she quipped.

"How is everyone?" he asked. Then as his eyes fell on her swollen middle, they widened.

She smiled. "There's lots of news—but I reckon you know the best already." As his hand touched her stomach, she added, "Coming in November." She took his hand. "Oh, so much has happened...but are you all right?" She looked him over now, carefully, head to foot. His clothes were rags, but his lean face was tanned and more handsome than ever.

"Reckon I'm all in one piece." He took her chin in his hands. His brow furrowed. "You're still pretty as a picture, but you're pale. You all right?"

"I'm fine," she said, snuggling close. "All this heat and worrying about you is enough to make a body peaked."

He draped an arm around her. "Then let's get you out of the sun." He took the horse's reins and started forward through sun dappling the willows near the creek. "How's Ma?"

Her smile grew even wider. "Better than she's been in a long while. She has a surprise for you inside." Her heart leaped anticipating his joy.

He squeezed her shoulder. "Can't say I ever outgrew liking a surprise—if it's a good one." He glanced at the fields of tall corn and shook his head. "For weeks I've been worried something was wrong here, but things look better than ever. Looks like Billy and Caleb are making a heck of a corn crop."

Cindy swallowed. She would not spoil his joy...not yet.

As they climbed the steps Becky came to the door, drying her hands on a dishtowel. "Cindy, didn't you hear—"

She dropped the towel and crossed the porch in two steps. "Oh, son!" She embraced him. She glanced at Cindy. "Did you tell him?"

Eyes dancing, Cindy shook her head.

Becky took his arm, tugging him forward. He stopped for a moment to hug Deborah who came running out the door.

"What did you do with my baby sister?" he teased staring at the tall slender girl. "Why, you're all grown up and a beauty to boot. Wouldn't have known you if I passed you on the street!"

She flushed with pleasure. Then she also tugged him toward the door. "Come on, Lige!"

"Why are ya'll so all-fired anxious to get me through the door? Ma must have something good cook—." He froze. His arm around Cindy's shoulder tightened as he stared at the man standing in the center of the room.

"Pa!"

The women hung back as Ned crossed the floor. Solemnly the men shook hands and then embraced. Cindy could hardly see through her tears.

Elijah was home. Ned was home.

She had never been happier. Then she felt a twinge in her middle and grimaced. She prayed the baby was all right.

Cindy tried not to remember that Elijah was only home for a short time. During the day he helped his pa with the million chores that needed doing, but she loved the evenings when they strolled hand in hand down by the creek and dreamed of all they'd do when the war was over and he was home for good. Today they sat in the shade on a big rock near the water's edge and listened to the gentle gurgle of the stream while they planned the house they would build. As Elijah broke off a sassafras twig and chewed it, a lemony scent filled the air.

"I want four bedrooms," he vowed.

"Four!" she hooted. "No one has four bedrooms, Elijah Loring—except maybe for plantation mansions. Billy and I saw one that must have had a dozen bedrooms."

"I reckon you were mighty uncomfortable on that trip," he said. "I know you always said Billy is so stiff and offish that he makes you nervous."

"Oh, I got over that in no time," she said quickly. "He was so good to me—and thoughtful. Elijah..." she started to mention Billy's infatuation, but as her cheeks grew rosy, she stopped. It was embarrassing. Besides, Elijah used to be fiery jealous. She decided to keep quiet.

Elijah suddenly frowned and his brow puckered. He toyed with her slim fingers held in his rough hand. "Well, I'm glad you're home safe and sound. Hey, I might just build us a big house with a dozen bedrooms. It doesn't hurt to dream, does it?"

She smiled. "No. I reckon dreamin' is something even we can afford." She looked across the creek toward tall sandstone bluffs deep in purple shadow. "You know, I've been thinking—if Michael would sell us the place—I'd like to build back on the same spot. It has the prettiest view in the country."

He chewed the twig again before speaking. "Yeah, the view is pretty. But the land's not fertile like land close to the creek. Besides, I figure Michael will want to keep that place for little Johnny and Mattie."

She nodded. "Yo're probably right," she agreed with a sigh. Then she went on, "Even after the war, I doubt Michael will come back here to raise his brother and sister. It shore was nice of your Cousin Jenny to take those younguns. Pa was mighty relieved. Ma is so poorly, she hardly gets out of bed. It was a handful for Pa, having to care for the young ones, cook and clean, and do all the farm chores besides. I had even thought about us taking them...if we build us a house."

"The way cousin Jenny loves children, I doubt she'll ever want to part with them. Besides we'll have a houseful of our own." He turned her palm over and kissed it.

She gave a wan smile. Then, as he kissed the back of her neck, she whispered, "I surely hope so."

Chapter 12

Elijah dried his hands and face and then straddled the bench drawn near the table.

"I'm worried about Cindy," he said. "That tonic Granny gave her doesn't seem to be helping. Her back hurts all the time, and it looks to me like she's losing weight instead of gaining."

"I been right concerned myself," admitted Ned.

Becky sat down. She put an elbow on the table and cupped her chin in one hand. For a moment her face drew into a worried frown. "She doesn't complain," she said slowly, "but I've been worried. It could just be the heat. We're all working too hard. That's enough to make a person lose weight. I had to insist that she lie down. I can tell she's exhausted, but she hardly ever rests."

"I ought to report back tomorrow," said Elijah. "I should have gone back last week. But with Cindy being poorly, I just couldn't get the notion to go. I'm planning to take her along. There's an old doctor at Dover who treated some of Jackman's troops when they got shot up a while back. I'm thinking he might take a look at her."

"That's a good idea," said Ned.

"It wouldn't hurt," quickly agreed Becky.

Elijah had suspected that Ma was more worried than she let on and now he was certain. "We'll leave early in the morning."

"Good," she said. "I have some garden truck to trade at the store. And I imagine Granny will want to send along some honey."

He nodded. "Get your stuff together and make a list. Soon as we're done eating, I'll ride over and get Granny's list and barter goods."

Elijah bowed his head as Ned blessed the food. And when he also prayed for Cindy, Elijah gave a heartfelt amen.

He reached for the bowl of early potatoes swimming amid green peas, ladled a large helping, and took a bite. He chewed slowly, savoring the taste. "This is wonderful, Ma. Sure don't get this kind of grub in the army."

Becky smiled.

"That's a fact," agreed Ned, looking up from a full plate. "No one on earth cooks better than your ma." Then he abruptly changed the subject. "Son, I don't have to tell you to keep a sharp eye out on this trip. There's more guerrillas than ever. And no conscription officer will believe you unless you've got proper papers."

"I've got papers," he said ruefully. "Of course the date on them ran out last week."

The next morning they left before sunrise. Already the air felt heavy and there was no dew coating the tall grass alongside the trail's edge. As a red sun rose and the day filled with birdsong, they left the creek bottoms and headed out of the hills toward the valley. Elijah kept a sharp eye out for patrols or travelers, but the road was free of traffic today.

As the sun climbed higher, he drove slowly and tried to avoid the worst jolts. He glanced over and noticed with concern that in spite of a golden tan Cindy looked pale. Her bonnet hung down her back by the strings, and her dress lay open at the throat where she had loosened the top buttons while she wiped face and neck with a handkerchief.

"Land sakes! It sure has turned off hot," she complained and then pulled the bonnet up to shade her face. "Even if we get soaked, I wish it'd come a big ol' rain—"

He interrupted, "If the creeks get up, we won't be able to cross."

"Oh, that's true," she said. "I'll just hope it rains as soon as we get home." She smoothed the green gingham skirt. "Wish this dress wasn't so faded," she fretted. "Jenny's old shirtwaist was plum wore out even before I cut it down. But I'm thankful to have it," she quickly added. "On the trip to get your pa, I saw women with clothes so ragged they wasn't even decent. I got threadbare myself. I only had what was on my back. I slept in my chemise—and had to wrap in a blanket to wash that."

After a while, she poked him in the side. "You sure are bein' a old sourpuss. You've not said three words the last hour."

"I got nothing much to say," he said. Then he squeezed his eyes shut and rubbed them in hopes of wiping away the image of Billy staring at Cindy draped in a blanket while her under things dried on the bushes. When his eyes opened he did not even enjoy the sight of the graceful doe crossing the trail ahead with a gangly fawn in tow. As the doe stepped quickly into the underbrush, the fawn looked back at them and then, in awkward long-legged sprints, bounded after.

On the second day, it was growing dusky when Elijah urged the mules across the wide flats near Dover. He stopped away from the main trail but handy to the creek. The water in the Illinois Bayou was low. He made camp where Cindy declared it a pretty spot, near a rocky shallows bordered by deeper pools that were shaded by overhanging sycamore, oak, elm, and willow. From a nearby tree came the raucous call of a redheaded wood hen.

Cindy sat down tiredly. Uncharacteristically, she stayed seated while he worked. As he unharnessed the mules, she sighed and shifted on the rock.

"I figured we'd stay in the wagon yard."

He shook his head. "Best to keep to ourselves as much as possible. No telling who might be around. Union and Confederate patrols come through here. And if not them, there's apt to be conscription agents. Best if I'm not seen by any of them."

"Oh, Elijah, no wonder you been so quiet," she said as her spine relaxed. "Yo're just worried. I thought maybe you was mad or somethin.'"

"I'm not mad," he said

While adding wood to the cook fire, he made an effort to sound cheerful and began whistling "The Homespun Dress," a tune he'd once heard General Hindman's band play. But he stopped abruptly when it brought to mind Cindy's ragged state. The calico was threadbare. He could see the patches as she bent to stir the pan of beans warming on the small campfire. The glow was soft on her face. His insides twisted. He didn't know what he'd do if anything happened to her.

The doctor's dwelling, located on the outskirts of Dover, was a small frame house badly in need of fresh white paint. The stooped old man answered at Elijah's first rap. He gruffly ushered them inside, all the while grumbling about the heat and his aching knees. While pointing them to ladder-back chairs in a neat but shabby parlor, he peered sharply at Cindy. There was, however, kindness in the faded blue eyes. He got right to business.

"What's your trouble?"

She began hesitantly but as the troubling symptoms grew into a list, Elijah's frown deepened.

The doctor stared at the floor covered with a faded floral carpet, pursed his lips, and made a tent of his fingers. Occasionally he nodded. When she finished he looked up.

"Young man, wait here while I examine the young lady." Then he led a wide-eyed Cindy through the door into the next room and shut the door.

Elijah paced the parlor like a caged bear. It seemed an eternity before the door opened. The doctor stepped out and shut the door.

"She'll be out shortly," he assured Elijah who sprang forward. "She's getting dressed." He indicated the chair again, and Elijah sank down as the doctor went on. "The baby seems to be developing at a normal rate. If your wife is careful and doesn't exert herself, I think she'll carry the child. However in spite of her otherwise ideal size, she has narrow hipbones. She might have difficulty with the birth."

Elijah dropped his head into his hands and groaned. He had once helped Pa pull a calf from a heifer that was too small. It had been a gruesome thing. Both cow and calf had died.

"I'd advise she have a doctor or at least a good midwife. Is there someone near where you live?"

Elijah nodded. Granny was as experienced as most doctors at birthing. He instantly decided he would not return to the army. They might try to arrest him, but he was not leaving Cindy.

She arrived looking paler than ever and headed straight for the door.

Before stepping into the sunlight, Elijah carefully surveyed the surroundings. It was a habit formed in the army, and more than once, it had served him well. This morning he saw no threat, just a dusty wagon road leading into a lazy town with tall false-fronted stores lining a broad dusty main street.

Cindy accepted his hand, climbed onto the wagon seat, and rearranged her bonnet. She pulled the strings tight. Pink momentarily tinted her pale cheeks. "I'll swan, that was just about the most embarrassin' thing ever happened to me. If I'd knowed he was going to do that, I'd have stayed home," she avowed.

Elijah climbed up, unwound the reins, and slapped them against the mules' rumps.

"He's a doctor, Cindy. That's what he does. He has to examine you before he can tell what's wrong."

She sat stiffly, eyes straight ahead. "Be that as it may, it was downright humiliating."

Elijah noticed that she was in a better humor by the time they arrived at the mercantile. But, as he took her slender hand to help her alight, he kept remembering the doctor's haunting words—*she might have trouble…*

He opened the door and waited as she entered. The store was larger than Emmitt's but equally void of merchandise. Although the shelves were almost bare, the room had retained the pungent odors of leather, dry goods, foodstuffs, and spices. It took a moment for Elijah's eyes to adjust to the dimness, but almost immediately Cindy noticed the table with two bolts of fabric.

"Oh, what pretty yellow gingham," she said fingering the cloth. "It's almost the same pattern as the dress Mr. Emmitt gave me."

When she looked down, while her fingers pleated the dress where it hugged her rounded belly, Elijah knew she wished for a new dress. It smote him.

Damned war, he thought. Someday he'd buy her a dozen new dresses! But today they needed soda and salt. And salt these days was as costly as gold.

The gray-haired buxom woman tending the store hurried forward. "Isn't it just the prettiest cloth! Richard—that's my husband—bought this fabric from a soldier a few weeks back. I told Richard he should have kept what little hard cash money we had in the till. Everyone in Dover is going ragged. No one can afford new cloth."

Elijah figured the soldier had helped himself to the stock in some Missouri store. Although most of the Confederate officers he knew were opposed to pillaging, it was still being done by both armies. He walked away to examine the shelves holding a few canned goods. He glanced around and then froze. Billy had just walked inside, and for one brief unguarded instant he stared at Cindy. As she turned from the table, he quickly masked the look and replaced it with a lazy grin as he said, "Pick yourself out a dress pattern—my treat."

"Billy!" A glad light shown on her face. She held out her hand, and he took it. As Billy's eyes lingered on her swollen middle, Elijah's gut twisted.

"Why, I never dreamed I'd see you here!" Abruptly she released his hand. "Look, Elijah! It's Billy!"

Elijah stepped from behind the shelf. In response to Billy's cheerful greeting, he curtly nodded.

"What are you two doing so far from home?" Billy asked.

"Trading for supplies," said Elijah.

He figured Cindy's problem was none of Billy's business.

"Everyone all right at home?"

"Fine," said Elijah in clipped tones. "What are you doing here?"

"My company passed through north of here. I thought I'd see if there was a pair of socks left in town. Mine are all holes." He turned to Cindy. "But, hey, I wasn't kidding about the cloth. Get yourself enough for a new dress."

Ever so slightly, Elijah's chin jutted. "No. Keep your money."

Billy said lightly, "I figure half of this Yankee coin in my pocket belongs to Cindy. She was helping out when I took it. She was a real trooper. "

Elijah shook his head. He struggled to keep his voice even.

"No, like I said, keep your money." He turned to Cindy. "Cindy, get the stuff on Ma's list. I'll go get the barter goods out of the wagon."

He wheeled and left the store. His teeth gritted as he leaned against the back of the wagon. Dust feathered from a passing wagon and blew into his face. He paid no attention. *No two ways about it—Billy was in love with Cindy*. His stomach roiled as he recalled the desire on Billy's face. He balled his fist. They itched to smash Billy's handsome face.

Even when Cindy had related that Billy was not actually his blood kin, he had felt no differently about him—until now.

Of course nothing had happened between them. Cindy was as true as could be.

And yet when he recalled her glad smile, a red-hot knife twisted in his middle. With difficulty he pulled his mind away from where it had gone galloping. After a few deep breaths, he regained control.

When he returned inside, Billy was busy shopping. Elijah walked past him and set the honey and basket of vegetables onto the counter. Cindy stood nearby alongside the small mound of supplies already stacked there.

When the transaction was completed, he stiffly shook Billy's hand and then watched as Cindy made her farewells. She looked ill at ease as she wished him well.

"Tell Granny hello for me," Billy said, conspicuously avoiding a greeting for Viola. "And tell Uncle Ned I'm mighty glad to hear he's getting along so well."

Elijah gave a brief nod. He could feel Cindy's troubled eyes boring into him.

As town fell behind, Elijah held the reins slack and stared at the trail ahead. "You and Billy were on the trail a long while alone." He glanced over. His stomach knotted. She had blushed scarlet. Her eyes dropped to stare at hands grasped together in her lap. "I hope he never got out of line," he ventured. As her head snapped up, he went on, "I mean it's like Granny says, the apple don't fall far from the tree. And now that we know Jarred Rawlings was his real pa—"

Her eyes flashed. "I'll ask you to remember that he was raised by Caleb Tanner and there ain't a finer man to take after!" She turned her head. "Billy was a pure gentleman."

"I guess that's why you keep blushing every time I mention him?"

"You always was as jealous as a broody hen!" she snapped. "That's what made me uneasy. I feared you'd get around to quarreling about him. I've not forgotten what you did to Dillon Matthers on account of me."

Elijah said no more but he was not mollified. They passed the day speaking little as the mules plodded along in the August heat.

The sun was low when they made camp near a small creek. Elijah unharnessed the mules and tied them with picket ropes. Finally he broke the long silence.

"I'm going to slip up to the top of the hill and see what I can see," he said. All afternoon he had seen signs of a large force going ahead of them. From the tracks he figured it was cavalry, but which army?

When he returned, sparks danced from the campfire into the black, starless night framing Cindy as she abruptly stood. "I'm glad yo're back," she said. "A bit ago I heared horses crossing upstream. It sounded like quite a few."

"Yeah, some troops just rode through. Confederate," he answered before she could ask. "They've gone on. Things are quiet. You'd better get some sleep. I'd like to get on the road home early.

"I'm ready for bed. I'm so tired, I don't reckon I'll ever feel rested," she said.

He lay on the quilt, listening to her even, soft breaths; but he did not sleep. Suddenly he jerked and sat up. Cindy spoke in her sleep. The single word froze the marrow of his bones. "*Billy!*"

Wretchedness shot bitterly into Elijah's very soul.

"Here's some water, Mr. Ned." Cindy could not get used to calling him Pa.

She stood near the edge of the field where he and Elijah were cutting hay. A field mouse scurried out of the grass and into the woods.

"Much obliged." He reached for the dipper and drained it in long slow swallows. "I was about to spit dust," he said with a smile. Then he replaced it into the bucket in her hand, took off a ragged straw hat, and wiped his brow and inside the hat brim with a handkerchief. From somewhere in the woods came the drumming of a woodpecker.

She drew in a deep appreciative breath. "Fresh-cut hay smells as sweet as flowers," she said.

"Have to agree with you, Miss Cindy. Not many smells I favor more. I used to love mowing. I can't hold out long these days." He looked across the wide hay field. "But Elijah takes up the slack—goes at it like he was fighting fire."

Her eyes fell on Elijah where he stooped, swinging the scythe in long, smooth sweeps that laid the tall grass low in waves. She thought how for the past two months, like the scythe, her emotions had swept back and forth between frustration and anger, confusion and sorrow. One thing was certain: his coldness had severed her from him as harshly as the grass was now severed from its roots.

She glanced hesitantly at Ned. "Does Elijah seem…well, different lately?"

Ned picked up a grass stem and began chewing. His eyes also rested on Elijah's bent back.

Cindy's eyes filled. "He seemed fine at first, but for the past two months he hardly says two words a day. And then he just sort of growls 'em."

Ned slowly nodded. "Reckon I know what you mean."

Her free hand rested on her swollen middle. "I thought he'd be happy about the baby. But now I'm not so sure. Anytime I start talking about it—wonderin' if it's a boy or a girl—he just freezes up, until a body would think he don't even want the little one."

Now tears ran freely down her cheeks. A sob caught in her throat. "I just don't know what's wrong or what to do about it."

Ned patted her arm. "There, there, now. Don't go makin' yourself sick. Come sit down in the shade for a bit."

She sat on a rock under a spreading oak at the edge of the field. Nearby Little Piney Creek made soothing sighs as it caressed rocks and bank and then rounded the bend. Ned sank onto the ground and leaned against the tree. He stayed silent for a while.

"War changes a man—does funny things to his head. Becky said I was more than half-crazy when I came home the first time. I'd wake up in the night shaking and yelling, just like I was in the middle of a big fight." His eyes sought Elijah again. "Give him time. He'll come around."

She bit her lip. "I don't think it's the war…although I shore know what you mean. He has bad dreams, too." Finally she blurted out what was really bothering. "I think he's mad at me. But law, I don't know what I've done!" She bent her head into her hands and wept.

Ned stood and took her shoulder. "I'll talk to him. See if I can find out what's eating him."

They both turned as a rider paused on the far side of the creek. As Ned picked up the rifle propped against the tree, Cindy quickly dried her eyes. The man on the piebald horse was, she thought, as big as a mountain. He approached cautiously looking all around and then stopped.

"Howdy," he said and then began to sneeze. "Damnation," he muttered, drawing out a handkerchief.

"Sampson, don't you know better than to come near a hayfield? You always sneeze your head off."

Elijah had arrived unnoticed by Cindy. It was the first time she had seen him smile in ages. Her heart twisted. It was wonderful to see, but bittersweet with the knowledge of how seldom it occurred.

"Howdy, Lige. I like to a' never found you, hid out in these hills. And yer neighbors is mighty close-mouthed."

"Well, step down and give old Baldy a breather. Pa, this is Sampson. I told you about him."

Ned gave a friendly nod. "Glad to make your acquaintance."

"I calculated you was Elijah's pa. He's got the looks of ya." Sampson swept off his hat. "And I'll bet yo're Miss Cindy."

Cindy wondered if she was just imagining or if Elijah's voice grew cold.

"Yes, this is Cindy."

"Well, I declare, I always thought Lige was bragging when he spoke of you, but dang if you ain't ever' bit as pretty as he said." Sampson's face beamed.

As Sampson started to alight, Ned interrupted, "Let's go up to the house. Becky will have dinner on the table about now."

Sampson smiled. "Now that's right neighborly of you, sir."

Elijah looked glum as he turned and strode toward the cabin hidden from view by the pines on the far side of the field. Cindy hung back, pretending to gather the bucket and dipper. When she turned from wiping tears from her cheeks onto her apron, Ned had waited. He took the bucket and walked alongside.

"It'll all come right," he reassured.

She nodded, but her heart felt heaver than the weight of the child slowing her tread. "I'll be along soon," she said. "I need to rest a bit." When he hesitated, she insisted. "No, I'll be fine. I just want to be alone for a minute."

He nodded and went on reluctantly, glancing back before the trees hid him from view.

Cindy bit a trembling lip, crossed arms over her chest, and looked at the sky. It was cloudless and blue, holding promise of the soon-coming autumn. She had so looked forward to the coming fall and winter and the birth of the baby. Now her joy seemed ashes. Elijah might talk to his pa—tell him what was wrong. But she doubted it. He seemed shut tighter than a bear trap. She glanced toward the cabin where cook fire smoke traced the sky. Then she drew a ragged breath and started forward. If she didn't hurry, they would be waiting dinner on her.

When she crossed the pasture and drew near the side of the cabin, the big man and Elijah stood under the pines, deep in conversation.

"Lookie here, Lige, Troy has been down-right generous with ya. He ought to have come after you weeks ago—ya stayed out way past yer leave."

Cindy drew back into the shadows and listened.

"We need every man we got. The Yankees came swarming back so Colonel Brooks ordered guerrilla action."

"I've done it before but I despise it," commented Elijah. "Always seems like a skulking dog slipping up behind a body to bite. I'd rather meet a man face to face on the battlefield."

Sampson nodded. "Me, too. There's skirmishes most every day. We had a big dust-up just last week at Potts' stage stop on the yon side of Russellville. Charlie Taylor and Ken Henley is both so busted up they're out of the fight fer good." He stopped to sneeze and wipe his nose. "There's a big force marching agin' us from Little Rock. Price was at Dover a few days back; I've no idea where he is now, 'er if we can count on help from him. We're headquartered at Clarksville—which is where I reckon we'll make a stand. Least ways Hill and Stirman and Brooks is all there now. Anyway Troy said for you to come."

The big man looked at Elijah beseechingly. Elijah stared at the cabin, chewed his jaw a minute, and then nodded. "All right, Sampson. I'll come."

Cindy barely stifled a sob.

Sampson let out a deep breath. "I'm right glad to hear you say so. I wasn't lookin' forward to trying to make you."

Elijah slapped him on the back. "Come on inside. Ma will feed us good before we leave."

"I got to get on back this afternoon," said Sampson, "but you can say yer good-byes and come on down tomorrow."

In spite of Samson's jovial conversation, dinner was a subdued meal. Elijah ate little, and Cindy none at all.

Elijah looked up when Ned entered the barn. "Son, before you go, I'd like to talk to you."

Elijah's jaw squared. He figured he knew what Pa wanted to discuss. But this was his own private hell.

Ned picked up a leather punch, took a piece of worn harness from a peg, and then sat down on the lid of the empty salt barrel. Elijah had a surreal feeling he had lived this moment before.

"Me and your ma can't help but notice there's something wrong between you and Cindy. Do you want to talk about it?"

Elijah's jaw grew harder. His trouble with Cindy was a shameful, private thing and a matter he would discuss with no one, not even Pa.

"Nope," he said, jerking the saddle from the stanchion wall. He slung it atop the blanket already on the sorrel's back. The horse shifted a bit and then stood still as he tightened the cinch.

Ned sat with the leather in his hands untouched.

"I recollect sitting here once a long time ago, talking to a boy about controlling hisself—"

Elijah interrupted, "I've not flown off the handle in a long time."

"No, you've not," Ned agreed. He slowly drew the leather strap though his hands. "But I reckon there's a lot more to it than just not throwing fits—there's coming to grips with a thing, facing it head on, and then doing the right thing to fix it."

Elijah stayed stiff and silent.

"Well," Ned finally said, "yo're a man, now. And the time is long past for me to tell you how to run yer life. But a man ain't never too old to listen to good advice." He paused. When Elijah said nothing, he went on. "I recollect a verse yer granny is partial to—something about how a woman can tear her house down with her own hands. I don't reckon that applies only to females. A man can ruin things, too." He stood. "I've no need to tell you that war is nasty business. You might not come back alive. You got a good woman who loves you. Don't leave her with a heart that's broke worse than necessary."

Elijah watched Ned's back as he stepped from the dimness of the barn into bright sun. For just a moment, he leaned his head against the sorrel. He didn't much care if he did get killed. The past weeks had been hell—ever since the day Cindy had muttered in her sleep. As bad as he hated to admit it, ever since then he had known. Their marriage was over.

Now he straightened.

He'd be damned if he'd be like Uncle Caleb—letting a woman fool him for years on end!

He had said his goodbyes in the morning sun, hugged Ma, shook Pa's hand, and because they were looking on, he had given stiff, red-eyed Cindy an obligatory peck on the cheek. Now he led the sorrel from the barn, mounted, and without a backward glance, rode away.

Sampson was right. Clarksville, warm with afternoon sun, was full of troops. Elijah crossed the covered bridge and road slowly around the barricades and on down the street crowded with cavalrymen, horses, and foot soldiers. Ragged tents lined Spadra Creek. He hunted until he found his own company near the outskirts of town.

Hankins, seated on a camp chair near an open tent, cocked his good eye over the rim of a steaming cup. "Glad to see you back, Loring. Even saved you a cup of this wonderful brew." He curled his lips and threw the brown liquid in his cup onto the ground. "I'll swear if I don't think the Yankees invented this nasty stuff. Cornbran coffee takes the heart right out of a man." He looked Elijah up and down. "Well, you've got a long face. Can't say as I blame you having to leave that pretty little wife—"

A soldier rode up and skidded to a stop, sending dust flying. "Captain, sir, Major Kirby wants you right away. He said on the double quick, sir."

Hankins frowned. "All right. Tell him I'll be right there. Sergeant, bring my horse." He faced Elijah. "I suppose Sampson told you we're expecting trouble. There's a big Federal force moving this way. Brooks decided we'd make our stand here. I wonder if he's suddenly changed his mind." He sat the cup down, mounted, and hurried away.

He returned shortly to bark curt orders. "Sergeant, tell everyone to fall in, quick. Damned Yankees are a day earlier than we expected. Our pickets have already tangled with them. They'll be here in about an hour."

Elijah fell into line with thirty other men and listened while Hankins related a plan of action. It suited him fine to be going into action…at least his mind would have something to dwell on besides bitterness. Shouldering a rifle, he took position in a line of men filing forward toward barricades made of cotton bales, barrels, timbers, old doors, and a hodge-podge of anything that would conceivably stop a bullet. He hunkered behind a likely spot and checked the load in both rifle and pistol. With a polite shake of head, he declined the offer of a chew from an older unkempt man kneeling nearby with jaws full of tobacco. Elijah wasn't sure which smelled worse, the man or the horse droppings near his boots. The man eyed a buzzing greenfly. He waited until it lit on the horse dung and then sent a stream of spittle flying. With a triumphant grin he faced Elijah.

"Bet you never seed spittin' like that afore."

"Pretty good," Elijah admitted. "Never saw better—except for my granny. She can hit a housefly on the wing three yards away." The deflated man, as Elijah had hoped, thereafter kept silent.

Now he could hear musket fire in the distance. It drew closer. Soon the shots came from just over the bridge.

"Hold your fire, men. Let our pickets through. Here they come!"

On the heels of the shout, horses thundered across the bridge and veered aside. A few jumped the barricades. Elijah tensed. Then his breast tightened with hate. Billy, atop a tall buckskin, veered aside and headed up the creek. He made a perfect target. If Elijah took the shot, no one would ever know it was not an accident. Men were killed just so every day.

Strangely his mind jumped to childhood and one of Granny's Bible stories, the one about King David purposefully sending Uriah the Hittite to his death. Always before that sinful deed had seemed to Elijah a far greater sin than wife stealing. Now his teeth ground as he decided that wife stealing was at least equal to murder.

He held the rifle steady on the top of a cotton bale and kept the site aimed at the covered bridge opening. First came Union cavalry. As blue uniforms on horseback poured across the bridge, Elijah fired, reloaded, and fired again. A wagon loaded with firing men exited the bridge, careened away from the barricades and onto a side street while return fire bit into the canvas top.

"Fall back! Fall back!"

Men scattered, firing and running. The man alongside Elijah flung out his arms as he fell. Near his sightless eyes, tobacco spittle and blood mingled in the dirt.

A wedge of Yankee horsemen knocked aside the barricade. Elijah squeezed off a shot and then ducked behind the closest red brick building. Without missing a detail of the action in view, he reloaded with rapid, smooth motions. When he heard hooves pounding, he knew the Union cavalry was circling behind. He drew the pistol, turned, and hugging the building, hurried down the alley towards the rear. When a window shattered, a young woman bolted from the back door. The child in her arms clung to her fiercely and another ran alongside, looking back with huge terrified eyes as she dragged him forward by the hand toward the woods.

Suddenly Elijah tensed. Directly across the alley, Billy hunkered behind the next building, firing into the Yankee hoard.

Elijah's eyes narrowed. He could let the Yankee who was slipping up the alley shoot Billy—he deserved killing the same as had his philandering pa. Now Elijah swore bitterly and shot the Yankee instead. Crimson spread across the blue-coated breast.

Billy jerked and then looked over and grinned. "Thanks, cousin. Glad to see you've not gotten rusty. Watch out!" Billy fired at an oncoming horseman just as shot exploded alongside Elijah's head.

"We don't seem to be making much headway," called Billy as he reloaded. He stuck his head around the corner to look down the street. "They just keep coming, and we're losing men fast."

In spite of heavy resistance, Elijah could see that the Yankees did keep coming, pouring into town like water over a rapids. When the order to fall back came again, he joined Billy and ran to the horses tethered near the woods. Along with other rebel troopers, they mounted and rode away, occasionally firing back while dodging return fire.

After a brisk ride, they halted in thick timber. Sporadic gunfire sounded faintly in the distance and then quit. Billy took a canteen from the saddle horn, drank deeply, and offered it to Elijah.

He shook his head, his face a mask of displeasure.

"Aw, we'll whip them next time," admonished Billy. Then he eyed Elijah closely. "Whathahell's the matter with you?" he asked. "You're a lucky man. You never even got a scratch. If your luck holds, you'll make it home to Cindy a whole man."

Just then Sampson rode up. He pulled his horse to a stop. "Lige, you seen Troy?"

Elijah barely shook his head.

Sampson looked back. "What a gol-durn mess. Don't know why we didn't pull out sooner. At least they ain't followin.'" He chewed his lip. "If you see Troy, tell him I'm lookin' for him." He nudged the horse and rode on.

Elijah looked around, but Billy was gone. It was just as well. He turned the horse and headed deeper into the woods. He had not gone far, however, before pulling rein again. Ahead in a small clearing stood a knot of dismounted soldiers staring at something. Elijah's mouth went dry. Hankins' mount, bearing an empty blood-soaked saddle, shied away from the man trying to grab the trailing reins.

Sampson rode up. He dismounted, and men parted to let him through. He knelt down. Tears streamed his big face. Gently, he picked up Hankins' riddled body and carried it a few paces. Without a word, he laid it over the back of the nervous horse. He climbed on Baldy and then took the black's reins.

"I'm taking him back to Danville to bury him next to his mama. Tell the major I ain't coming back."

While everyone else remounted and rode away, Elijah stayed. His eyes traced the clearing. Grasshoppers rose from tall wheat-colored grass heavy with seedpods. One bloody patch still held the imprint of Hankins' body. He would miss Hankins—in his own salty way he had been a good man. Elijah wondered how many more friends he would lose in this war.

Pa was right. Life was uncertain.

His gaze lifted to the wooded slopes beyond. Leaves on the hickories were barely tinted with gold and sweet gums had a hint of coral. He and Cindy had been married almost a year. He had been gone too much of it. Suddenly he wanted to live. And he wanted it badly. He had a fresh revelation of how much he loved her. Even if she had made a mistake, he still loved her. She had once loved him. He would win her back. At least he would try.

He turned the horse north. The major would find out soon enough that he was leaving.

Just then a rider thundered up. He sawed a lathered horse to a stop. "Major Kirby sent me to find you. He needs you right away."

"Any idea what he wants?"

The soldier shook his head. "All I know is he was grumbling over losing his best scout."

Elijah looked north and then reluctantly turned the horse around.

Chapter 13

Dread knotted Elijah's stomach. The cabin was dark. No one was home. Something was wrong; it wasn't normal for everyone to be gone after sundown. He should have ignored the major's summons and returned home a month ago. Someone else could have acted as scout to see where else the Yankees had regained control. Now, apprehensive, he remounted the bay and headed for Granny's.

Little Piney Creek was a low murmur where katydids rasped in the darkness. As he crossed the creek and topped the ridge, the moon emerged from a cloud to shine silver on a skunk in the trail ahead. It ambled from the path, not even bothering to cast a look in the bay's direction.

Every inch of the trail held memories. While trying to stave off a sense of foreboding, Elijah recalled moments from the past. There was the spot where he had first held Cindy's hand. And just beyond was the old hickory where his little pup Belle had treed her first squirrel. He rode on and then stopped for a moment to look deeply into the woods. Only a few rods away was the brutal scene where Lew Willis had butchered Bo Morrision and where Lew had almost killed him.

This trail, he thought, *is like a ribbon all strung with doodads, some bitter and some sweet.*

He kneed the bay and rode on.

Near the barnyard, he spied the outline of a wagon and the unhitched mules lying in the pen. A dim light shone from the cabin windows. Before his boots had touched the ground, he froze. An agonized scream rent the night.

In two strides, he crossed the yard and bounded up the steps. He threw open the door without knocking. Viola sat in a chair near the table, gray hair loosed from the customary knot and her eyes empty and staring like a person without good sanity.

The familiar room was suddenly eerie. Shadowy figures hovered around the four-posted bed in the far corner. Even before he saw the face—pale as death on the pillow in candlelight—he knew it was Cindy. Her eyes closed, she writhed in pain and screamed again.

"There, there," shushed Granny. "Hit'll soon be over, child, and you'll have a babe to love and cherish." She looked up. "Oh, praise the Lord! Look here, Cindy. Hit's Elijah!" She motioned him forward. "Come here and take her hand. She's a pushin' awful hard, but she's about give out. You a' being here will give her new strength."

As Becky stepped back and let go of her hand, Cindy's eyes flickered open.

"*Elijah?*" She croaked through swollen cracked lips. Her hair was loose and wet with sweat.

He grasped her hand. It was limp. Her eyes squeezed shut.

"It's way too early for the baby! How long has she been like this?" he whispered.

Granny and Becky exchanged looks. "Since early this morning."

He groaned and his knees almost buckled. Someone pushed a chair under him, and he dropped into it. Then Cindy gripped his hand. It started as a moan. The pitch rose and swelled into a hoarse, pitiful cry. It was the most intense torture Elijah had ever known.

Then Cindy breathed hard and fast, gulping for air. Her eyes fluttered open. "Lige," she rasped, "yo're squeezing my hand off."

Immediately he loosened his grip. "Oh, Cindy…" He tried to speak, but nothing got past the lump in his throat.

"I prayed you'd come," she whispered.

He bent to gather her into his arms. "I'm here. I'm here. I'll never leave again," he vowed. Before he could say more she was lost in a swirl of pain. He held her and willed strength into the tired, tortured body.

And he prayed. He didn't care what she had done. He could forgive anything…anything except her leaving him alone. In the hours that followed, he promised God everything he could think of and then he started all over again. If only God would spare her.

As the night drew on, her cries weakened. He despaired. Surely no one could endure such agony.

"Granny, am I gonna die?" she asked. She moaned and reached for him. "Elijah," she gasped out through hot dry lips, "if I die, don't you go off again. You stay here and take care of our baby. You hear me?"

Cindy was dying. And he would never be able to make right the last months of hurt between them. "I promise," he managed to utter.

"Hit's just the pain a'talking," reassured Granny.

Over and over again, Becky bathed Cindy's face. Then with sorrow-filled, sympathetic eyes she squeezed his arm. Ma and Granny both looked exhausted. Granny was hobbling worse than ever.

"Where's Pa?" he suddenly asked.

Becky motioned him away from the bed and then lowered her voice. "Polly is pretty bad off. Your pa and Deborah are sitting up with her while Simon gets some rest. I didn't want Deborah here anyway. Cindy and I were making dye with Granny when the pains took hold."

He walked to the window to look out. Dawn painted the east pink. He felt—just like the patriarch Jacob—he had wrestled with God all night, begging for a blessing. No longer did he feel the urge to beg for her life. He wanted her suffering to cease. Even if it meant losing her.

The broken cry was long and loud.

"There now," said Granny. "That was a good one. Hit won't be long. Another one like that and hit'll be here." She glanced around. "You, Elijah, get over here," she called, "Hold on to her—give her somethin' to push agin.' Yep, here it comes."

The tiny whimper did not penetrate Elijah's agony.

"Oh!" cried Granny, "A dandy boy."

Elijah did not glance at the child. His eyes were filled with Cindy slumped deathlike on the pillow. He took her limp hand and pressed it to his lips. Breath died in his chest and stabbing pain ripped his heart. No one could survive with such a great loss of blood. Bowed, he closed his eyes and drowned in a wave of despair. She would never know how much he had loved her. Grief, raw and terrible, racked his body. He didn't want to live without her…

No, God, he silently cried, *I can't stand this!*

But he must. He set his teeth.

And now there was the boy. Billy's child that was taking her life. Resentment flooded his breast. Then a new thought pushed it aside. The child was Cindy's, too. Its flesh and blood were a part of her. Her last wish had been for the child, and he had promised.

Yes, he'd do as Caleb had done—he'd claim the child…raise him. It was the right thing to do. Cindy would want that. It flickered through his mind to wonder if perhaps Caleb too had known the truth about Billy.

"So…hit's a boy."

At the weak voice, Elijah jerked.

"Yep, honey," declared Granny with a tired smile. "He's tiny, tiny but he's jest fine. Good thing he warn't no bigger since you had sech a hard time. I allow he weighs less than five pounds. Ain't no wonder. He come sa early and we ain't none had overly much to eat in a good while."

Elijah sat bolt upright.

Cindy looked more dead than alive, skin pasty and eyes deep set and bloodshot in their sockets. His eyes flew to Granny. "Is she all right?" he choked out.

Granny scoffed. "Course she is."

"But she's lost so much blood—"

"Not no more than usual," said Granny.

Cindy would live. He felt life flow back into him.

Her eyes briefly closed. "Lige, what are we gonna name him?"

Granny interrupted, "Now, get away and let her rest. She's got a big job to do. When we get him cleaned up a mite, she's got to feed this youngun of yores." She wiped the squirming body on one side and then turned him over. "And lookie here, Becky," she said "hit's the Tanner birthmark, big as life—big red blotch shaped jest like a strawberry on the back of his little head halfway up in the hair...jest like Ned and Elijah and ever' babe with ery a drop of Tanner blood." She cut her eyes toward Viola and glowered. Then she dropped tiredly into a chair. "I'm plum tuckered out. This here is the third generation of my own I've helped to birth—Ned, Elijah, and now this 'un; but I'm gettin' too old fer it. Here, Becky you take him."

Becky took the baby and laid him on a blanket. "He looks like you, Elijah, but his hair is fair like the twins." She picked him up, held him close, and touched his chin. "Ever since my babies died, my arms have felt empty." She smiled through tears. "Until now." She looked at Elijah. "Your pa is going to be so proud."

In a daze, Elijah blinked and looked around.

Cindy's eyes opened. "What was yer babies named?"

Becky looked at the baby in her arms. "Benjamin and Samuel—their names were Benjamin and Samuel," she finished with a sad smile.

"Benjamin Samuel Loring," said Cindy. "I reckon that's a right fine name." As her bloodshot eyes met Elijah's, he nodded. "Let me see him," said Cindy. While Becky held the baby near, Cindy reached to touch the child. Her hand fell weakly back to her side. "Well, hello, little Benjamin Samuel Loring." Her voice was a raw whisper, but her eyes were joyful. "Oh, he's just the prettiest little thang."

Elijah came to himself enough to glance at the child. So this was his child. Then he drew in a sharp breath.

How could they think that pitiful thing was pretty? He stifled a groan. The way its head was misshapen, he doubted it would have good sense. Maybe it was God's judgment for his jealousy, for how he had misjudged Cindy.

Granny chuckled and Becky outright laughed.

"I never seed a man yet," said Granny, "didn't draw up like he was gut kicked at the first sight of one. Never you fear, Elijah Loring. He had a hard time gettin' here, so he looks a mite beat up; but he's a fine boy. And that-there head will shape up fine and dandy in a day or two."

Thankful and greatly relieved, Elijah let out his breath. Cindy weakly patted his hand.

"Pa always said birthing was harder on him than on Ma," she said. "But I'll swan I doubt that's true."

A weak smile crossed Elijah's face. Silently he agreed with Simon.

Cindy sat in the rocking chair and snuggled the tiny form close. She touched his tiny nose as he suckled. Granny was right. His head was beautiful now. He was perfect in every way.

It is the strangest thang, she thought, *how quick a body loves with all their heart and soul. Why, I'd die for the little mite right this minute.*

Then her brows quirked. She very nearly had. She reckoned—just like Jesus said—the actual pain was already overshadowed by the joy of having a son; but the shadow of the memory remained. She had always wanted a big family, a least a dozen younguns. She bit her lip. It would take a tad more forgetting before she was ready to face that again!

She smiled stiffly when Elijah leaned to kiss her forehead. Then he kissed the baby. On the surface things had been cordial between them, but underneath roiled a thunderstorm of suppressed emotions. She didn't know what had come over him. In the past two weeks he had barely left her side except to cut firewood and do a few chores for Granny around the place.

Her eyes traced the room. Everything was neat and cozy. The small fire blazing in the fireplace was homey, but it wasn't how she had envisioned things—living with Elijah's granny. However, it was better than crowding up with his folks now that Ned was home. Besides Granny needed help—especially with Caleb and Billy gone.

She was surprised when Viola asked, "Kin I hold him?"

These days Viola usually sat in her room, her eyes empty and staring. In spite of everything that had happened, Viola had stayed. As

Granny said, "She ain't got no place else to go. She's lived here since she was seventeen year old. I've put up with her fer years. I don't reckon a few more will kill me."

Cindy reluctantly placed Benjamin into her scrawny arms. After a few minutes, she took him back and put him into the crib. Viola went into her room and shut the door.

Cindy turned. "Granny, you been inside all day. Go on outside and gather that stuff you was talking about, the nut hulls for your dye and the herbs. I'll do the dishes."

Today was the first day she had felt up to doing chores. Even so Elijah insisted on helping.

After Granny had shuffled outside, Cindy held the dishrag still for a moment.

"Lige, I can't get it out of my mind—how you acted all them weeks. And then when you just up and rode off with hardly a by-yer-leave. More nights than not I've cried myself to sleep. Don't you think you owe me a explanation?"

The dishtowel stilled in his hand. His look said he had dreaded this moment. "I told you I was sorry," he hedged.

"And I'm telling you I want to know what was wrong. I got a right to know."

He let out a deep breath. "Yes, I reckon you do. I want no lies or secrets between us." He paused for a long moment, hunting for words. "Remember the day we went to Dover—the day we saw Billy?"

She nodded.

"Your face lit up like a candle when you saw him. And he looked at you like...like a man ought not look at another man's wife. And the first thing his eyes went to was your middle..." His voice faded. "Your face turned beet red every time I said a thing about him." His voice hardened. "And that night you called his name in your sleep."

Her mouth dropped.

He became defensive. "You were alone with him for days on end. I know now I was dead wrong, but at the time I thought—"

"*You thought!*" she sputtered, "Oh, of course the first minute I'm alone with a man, I just naturally turn into a hussy like Lizzy Tate. That's what you thought." She threw down the dishrag, and then she picked up a bowl and flung it at him.

It caught him in the chest. He stood still as it crashed to the floor. "I know you're mad, and you've got every right to be. I was wrong to ever think such a thing. And I'm asking you to forgive me."

When she picked up a plate and drew back her arm, he turned. As he walked outside, it crashed against the doorframe.

Granny hobbled across the front yard.

Cindy overheard when she said, "I was wonderin' when you two would get this hashed out. You best go on back inside and take yer medicine," she said and picked up the bucket. "I'll jest go gather some more nuts."

"You come in that door," Cindy called, "I go out it." Her tone was hard and clipped. And she meant every word. It would feel shameful to run home to Pa and Ma, but she would prefer that to spending another night under the same roof with him! She clenched and unclenched her fists. *How could he believe such a thing?*

She paced back and forth. Tiny whimpers came from the crib. She, however, paid no attention until they became insistent cries. She picked up the baby. Always before she had smiled while watching him wave his arms or hungrily suck his fists. Today the scowl remained as she sat down. There was something Elijah had said…just now it eluded her. But it had stung like a nettle.

Then she stared at the baby and sucked in a breath. He had said Billy stared at her middle. *Why, he must have thought the baby…surely not!* And yet she knew he had. Fresh outrage swept her, sending blood pounding in her ears.

She jumped up. How dare he! She wished he'd poke his head back inside so she could throw something else! Then she huffed an angry breath. So this was the thanks she got for being a good wife, for fretting over him, for almost making herself sick from worry.

Somehow she endured the long afternoon, vacillating between anger that he could have had such an outlandish notion and amazement that in all the weeks of stony silence he had never once tried to talk to her, to give her a chance to defend herself—although she ought not have to defend herself from such slander. Why, she'd walk across hot coals before she'd play the harlot.

Finally, tucking Benjamin in alongside, she went to bed to stare at the smoky rafters. Granny's soft snores penetrated the thin bedroom door. Although known for being outspoken, the old woman had left her to herself today. Right now Cindy wanted nothing more than to be left alone. Tears fell on the baby's head as she leaned to kiss him. *Poor little tike.* She prayed he never learned of the hurtful notion his pa had.

Slowly anger ebbed away to be replaced by a sharp hurt. The unjust accusation wounded deep, leaving her as bruised and bloodied as if Elijah had struck her. He had attacked who she was. He ought to know how much she valued virtue; Pa and Ma had raised her to shun even the hint of indecency. It seemed impossible that Elijah—who should know her better than anyone—knew her not at all.

Elijah glanced back at the cabin door. Cindy was mad now, and she had every right to be. It was the anger talking, but he suspected she was more hurt than angry. He regretted hurting her, and yet he still thought truth was best.

He'd just go on to Pa's and spend a night or two. Then hopefully they would work things out and be happy again. He bemoaned the weeks of misery that his jealous fit had wrought.

He missed their happy times. He also missed their times alone. Not that he wasn't thankful for a roof overhead, but he dreamed of the time they'd be on their own again. Of course, now that the children had started coming, it would be years before he and Cindy would live alone, but a man liked having his young ones around his own hearth.

Just before the trail dropped below the brow of the hill, he looked back again. He really hated being away from Cindy and the baby, even for a day. It surprised him how much the little fellow had already wormed his way into his heart. He already found himself daydreaming about how things would be when the boy grew older. He anticipated taking him hunting, fishing, teaching him the things Pa had taught him about the woods and ways of wildlife. And of course he'd teach him how to be a good farmer, how to get the most from the rich bottomland along Little Piney that would one day be his.

Likely there would be more children, but he suspected there was something special between a man and his firstborn son.

He stopped to brush away a spider web sticking to his arm and then glanced into the woods. The leaves were coloring, the black gums oxblood, the dogwood and sassafras tinged with pink. The underbrush had thinned. He could see all the way to the bottom of the hill where a squirrel scurried up the side of an oak. Frost was late in coming, and mast had been good this year. The critter appeared fat and ready for winter.

A slight frown creased his brow. He broke off a sassafras twig and began chewing. Although he'd sworn never to own another dog after his own beloved Belle had died, he imagined Benjamin would want a dog. A boy needed a dog—even if it broke his heart to lose it.

That decision made, Elijah started forward. He'd start looking right away. Maybe some of the Matthers clan were yet in the country and still had a pup from Old Scrapper. The old redbone raised the best treeing hounds around. He'd ask Tom Sorrells. Tom made it his business to know everything that went on in the hills.

As he turned from the main trail onto a dim path, he shook his head. Nature had almost reclaimed the route his bare feet had etched into the mountainside. It was only natural, since no one but him had ever used the shortcut. Then he grinned, imagining how Benjamin would wear the path smooth again. Abruptly the grin died.

Uncle Caleb is gone. And Granny is so old now, it's not likely she'll live much longer. More than likely Benjamin won't be running back and forth to her house like I always did.

He drew a ragged breath at the sad, sobering thought. It was the way of things. The new came on. The old died. Since Adam and Eve it had been so. But that did not ease the pang in his breast. He shook his head again and stared onward, down into the hollow toward the rushing swish of Little Piney. He could hardly wait for tomorrow to get things settled with Cindy.

The next day Cindy refused to see him. All the time he held the baby, she stayed in the bedroom with the door shut tight. After a bit, he left. She had a right to be miffed. Granny was right, he supposed. He'd just have to wait a while and take his medicine, however, when a week had passed and she still refused to talk, he strode into the bedroom. She sat in the rocking chair drawn near the window.

"Cindy, don't you reckon this foolishness has gone on long enough?" he blurted out.

Lips stiff and white, she stared. "Foolishness!" she cried. "Foolishness…after what you done, you call this foolishness?" Her eye shot fire. "Elijah Loring, get out of my sight!"

His mouth opened and closed. Then he turned on his heels and left. In exasperation he rubbed his chin. He stared at the closed door. In retrospect he admitted he had not handled that very well. But he'd already asked her forgiveness, tried to explain—what more did she want?

After Elijah moved back in with Ned and Becky, Granny urged Cindy to stay on. Cindy cooked and cleaned and tended the baby. She breathed in and out and pretended to live, but apart from an aching heart, she felt wooden and lifeless. For two weeks she had mulled over the problem. She was no closer to a solution. Divorce was a disgraceful, almost unheard of thing, and yet she could not live with a man who thought so little of her. *And yet can I go on without him?* It was a thought she could not face.

Today she sat on the porch soaking up a warm patch of sunshine. The cabin wall provided shelter from a sharp wind rattling the brown oak leaves. She thought of her wedding day and the happy times and wondered if Elijah now felt as miserable as she did. Granny said he was eating his heart out. For a fact, he had looked hollow-eyed and drawn the last time he came.

Again and again, images came—Elijah toting countless buckets of water for her, his eyes soft and full of love, the feel of his strong arms as, after setting down the bucket, he gathered her close. The way he sniffed the air with appreciation when she called him inside to dinner. The way his dark hair plastered to his head as he washed up at the washstand, and after taking the towel she offered, he kissed her lips.

Her chin trembled. Those short months of happiness were a mockery. She and Elijah had never been one…not if he knew her so little.

While fresh tears rolled down her cheeks, she looked across Granny's hay meadow and watched a flock of wild turkey hens and their nearly grown young feeding in the ankle-deep course grass. The drab brown birds darted back and forth, necks extended, to snatch fat grasshoppers and gobble them in one jerky motion. Suddenly a hen raised its head. The flock abruptly melted away. Cindy quickly wiped the tears. Ned walked down the trail, crossed the yard, and climbed the steps. With a soft smile, he removed a battered hat, sat down, and propped it on his knee.

"Nice here in the sunshine," he said, "but that wind is sharp as scissors."

She did not welcome company and only weakly returned the smile.

He drew a deep breath. "Ever since that pneumonia, seems I can't get enough air into my lungs. I'm gaining though. A while back I couldn't walk a mile—even on flat ground. I pulled that hill today and hardly slowed down."

"I'm mighty glad," she said and meant it.

He chewed his jaw a bit.

"Elijah don't know I'm here. And I reckon I'm butting my nose into yer business. I hope you'll hear me out and then think on what I say."

She stared across the pasture at a distant blue ridge and waited.

"Elijah and I had a long talk. He told me what happened. He says every time he comes here you won't even see him. I know you're riled—and you got every right to be. He was wrong. Dead wrong. He knows that. But now you got two choices: forgive him or don't forgive him."

As hurt roiled, she shot out, "Hit ain't that simple."

"Yes, it is." He was gentle but firm.

She drew up stiffly.

"I ain't no preacher like yer pa," he said, "but I know there ain't no grudge on earth the good Lord gives us permission to hang on to."

Her jaws set stubbornly. *I reckon he thinks I should just forget it,* she thought, *and then everything will be just fine and dandy. He doesn't even care how much Elijah wronged me!*

Ned looked down and worried the hat brim. "That prison camp was a breeding ground for hate. And I have to admit it took a while to work my way through to forgivin' some that wronged me. But as soon as I did—even though I was still locked up tight in that hell hole—I was a free man." He looked out across the meadow and his forehead creased. "A soldier sees a powerful lot of human nature at its worst. I ain't trying to make excuses for Elijah. But many a man who was true blue at home gets to thinking he ain't gonna live long so he grabs onto pleasure any way he can. And I don't doubt that some women has them same feelings, too. I reckon you could say Elijah knowed you and Billy was just flesh and blood, and his mind got carried away with the knowing of how it can be with a man and a woman left a long time alone together."

She drew up straight and opened her mouth to protest, but Ned went on, "You might try to imagine how he felt all them weeks. Wrong as he was, his heart was broke. Much as he loves you, I reckon he suffered the tortures of the damned. Whether you think it or not, it almost killed him. Just think on it, daughter. It'll come to you—the right thing to do." He stood. "Can I see the boy before I go?"

Back rigid, she opened the door and led him inside.

Viola was bent over the crib. "Hush, little Billy," she said. "Mama's here."

A chill traced Cindy's spine. It was not the first time she had caught Viola hanging over the crib; it was the first time Viola had mistaken the baby for her own child. She was getting downright crazy.

While Ned kindly led Viola to a chair, Cindy grabbed up Benjamin and held him close.

That night, as gentle rain drummed the shakes, Cindy tossed and turned. Ned's words rang in her head. Although she knew he was right, every time she envisioned forgiving Elijah, the injustice of the thing boiled over inside like an overfull kettle on a hot fire. He needed to suffer, she concluded. Lord knows she had. In frustration, she throttled the pillow and then tried to lie still for Benjamin's sake.

Now, for the first time, she pondered Elijah's view of things. While in the army, he had, no doubt, seen plenty of evil. Even Pa said folks these days could make Sodom and Gomorrah blush. But Elijah ought to know she wasn't stitched from that bolt of cloth!

Then she recalled the unguarded longing on Billy's face the day he had seen her with her hair down. Her cheeks grew warm thinking of it. That day in Dover Elijah must have seen just such a look. She reckoned that was enough to make a husband jealous. Cindy admitted to herself if she ever saw Lizzy Tate looking at Elijah like that, she'd want to scratch her eyes out.

She chewed her lip. Elijah was right—her face had reddened when he spoke of Billy. No wonder the subject made her touchy. She well remembered Elijah's fiery temper and how he had almost beaten Dillon to a pulp because he was jealous. And Billy really loved her—or thought he did. To be perfectly honest, on the long trip she had grown fond of

Billy—oh, not in any unseemly way. She admired Billy. He was brave, honorable, and kind. And, for an unmarried woman, plenty desirable.

Then her jaw squared, and she shook her head. Elijah ought to know her vows were sacred. And he certainly ought to know she loved him with all her heart and soul.

I would never misjudge him so—

Cindy sat bolt upright. The memory knocked breath from her. Why, she had misjudged Elijah, misjudged him terribly—when he had first come home from the army, the day she'd come upon him about to hang Doc Lucas. That day she had thought he had turned into an evil bushwhacker. To this day she could see the hurt and disbelief in his eyes as she had accused him.

She sank back onto the pillow. "Being thought a bushwhacker ain't as scandalous as being thought a harlot," she rationalized in a whisper. The words rang hollow in her own ears.

When daylight shown yellow through swirls of fog, she still had not slept. She fed the baby and got up. The floorboards were chill on bare feet as she dressed and then went into the main room and tucked him with woolen blankets into the crib drawn near the fireplace. She caressed the shiny wood. Pa had done a beautiful job. She hoped Ma felt like coming to see the baby this week. When Pa brought the crib yesterday, he had said she was better.

The cold morning made Cindy dread winter. She had known too many babies who did not survive their first winter. After stoking the banked fire to life, she added a few more hickory logs, then, stifling a yawn, she glanced at the sleeping child. It was early yet. Granny had not arisen. Cindy abruptly decided to lie down for a bit.

Sun was streaming full in her face when she awoke. She never remembered sleeping so late. From the angle of the sun she decided it was almost noon. Chagrined, she rubbed heavy eyelids and stared outside. Except for a few wispy patches near the spring, the fog had vanished. Bright sun bathed the catalpa tree near the window and glistened droplets of water still clinging to the leaves.

Hurriedly she sprang up. It was surprising the baby had not wakened. His feeding was long overdue.

"I was wonderin' if you was dead," teased Granny. The loom made a comfortable sound as she tamped down the thread with a beater.

"I never closed an eye last night," apologized Cindy. "But I never meant to sleep the day away," she said while twisting up her hair. "I'm surprised the baby slept so long— "

"Granny!" she whirled. "Where's Benjamin?"

Granny batted her eyes and then stared into the empty crib. "Why, I reckoned he was sleepin' with you."

"No!" Cindy paled. "I tucked him into the crib about daylight. Where's Viola?" she asked with her heart in her throat.

Granny shook her head. "I've not seen her this morning."

Cindy had already thrown open Viola's bedroom door. Clutching the doorframe, she turned back. "She's gone."

"She can't have gone far," avowed Granny.

Cindy ran through the house and out the door. A quick search of the yard and outbuildings proved futile. Now her palms grew sweaty.

Granny limped up behind her. "Did ya look in the cellar?'

"I've looked everywhere. Granny, where could she be?"

"Likely she ain't gone far, just fer a walk."

Cindy's heart pounded. She called and called. When she stopped to listen, a drumming woodpecker was the only sound echoing from the hills. Without hesitation she flew down the trail. Elijah would find Viola and the baby.

"What's wrong?" Elijah jumped up from the table to catch her as she almost collapsed inside the doorway. His own pulse raced as he imagined the worst. *Bushwhackers…something wrong with the baby…with Granny.*

Cindy gulped in air. She clutched his arm. "Viola's run off with the baby. She's been gone for hours. You got to find 'em!"

By the time Becky had helped her into a chair, Elijah had already grabbed a rifle and headed through the door. Ned took down a shotgun hanging over the door and followed.

"We'll start at Granny's and see if we can cut her trail. Likely she hasn't gone far," said Elijah. They both set off at a quick pace; however, Ned soon fell behind.

"Go on ahead," he called. "I'll catch up."

Elijah nodded and began to run. Surely Viola had not gone far. More than likely she was already back home at Granny's with Benjamin safely tucked into the new crib. Nonetheless his heart pumped with anxiety. Viola was crazy, and Benjamin was so tiny and helpless…

Granny met him in the yard and shook her head before he even asked.

"I couldn't go fur," she lamented, "but I seed her footprints near the spring."

He raced across the pasture, scattering grazing sheep, and then vaulted the rail fence and headed into the woods at a lope. Granny was right. Alongside the spring several sharp-toed boot prints pressed deep into soft mud. The tracks soon vanished, erased by plush moss and deep pine needles. He circled wide and finally found another track in an old deer trail that headed off the mountain. With eyes strained from looking, he saw no further sign. After hours of futile searching, he had covered miles and shouted until his voice grew hoarse. Now stopping to tilt his head to listen, as before, he heard only his own ragged breaths. Then an owl hooted on the far ridge.

He'd known fear on the battlefield and torment when he thought Cindy lay dying, but nothing had ever squeezed his heart with more dread than it now squeezed for Benjamin. Viola was crazy. If he became cumbersome, apt as not she might just lay him down and go on. There were bears and cats aplenty in the woods…and even wolves.

Elijah wiped sweat from his brow and bowed his head. It was the first time he'd actually stopped to pray—although in his heart he'd been crying out all along. He sure hoped Granny was right about special guardian angels. Tiny Benjamin sure needed one.

His mind jumped to Cindy. She must be half-crazy herself just now. He wished he could be with her to give comfort. Then he recalled that she did not want him around. It was a harsh and painful thought that she might never want him again. She had certainly hardened her heart towards him. In the past weeks he had slept little, tossing and turning over the agony of the thing.

He threw up his head. A shot, faint and far away, reverberated in the stillness.

"I got to—," began Cindy.

"You sit right here and catch your breath," insisted Becky, "and then we'll both go. Even though Viola's mind isn't quite right, I know she won't hurt the baby. I'm sure of it. Here, take a drink of water."

Cindy drained the dipper. She hoped Becky was right. And yet fear ate at the corners of her heart.

Becky drew on a shawl. "No, Deborah, honey, you stay here. Wash up the dishes and keep the door locked."

Deborah's face fell. She loved the new baby beyond measure.

By mid-afternoon the neighbors had heard the report and joined in the search. Cindy, arms and face scratched and bleeding from tearing through the brush, was almost out of her mind. She sank onto a rock, and with a hand to her breast, she groaned. By her own pain she could imagine how hungry the baby must be! *Was the Lord punishing her… punishing her for not forgiving Elijah?*

Twilight shadowed the hollow and turned the hills dusky blue; still there was no hint of the agreed signal, no shot announcing the child had been found. When Becky finally convinced Cindy to return to Granny's cabin the yard was filled with horses, old men, women, and children. Even frail Polly stood alongside tall, slim Simon, her face a mask of worry.

Hushed voices in sympathetic murmurs greeted Cindy as she collapsed onto the porch steps. Her head bowed low at the news. In spite of circling the cabin for miles in every direction, except for a few footprints near the spring, there was no trace.

"I even put my hound on the trail," said fat Tom Sorrels, woefully. "O' course he ain't no blood hound. I give him a sniff of that blanket, but he never done nothing but flush out a few turkeys and jump a couple of deer."

"Elijah?" asked Cindy.

"He's not come back," answered Simon. "Him ner Ned neither. Daughter, I had just suggested we all have a word of prayer—"

"Look! Lookie there!" Tom pointed down the trail. "Hit's Lizzy Tate, and she a' carryin' something. Yep, shore as yer born, hit's the babe!"

Cindy flew down the road. Heart hammering, she grabbed for the baby. He was still. It was a long terrifying moment before she saw that he was breathing. His face was pinched and red from bug bites, but his eyes were open now and he gave a tiny whimper as she clutched him to her chest.

"Oh, dear God, thank you," she breathed and then focused on Lizzy. "Oh, thank you so much!"

Lizzy's face was scratched and bleeding, one cheek badly clawed.

"Lizzy, what in the world happened to ya?" asked May Sorrells.

"Viola fought me like a wild cat, but I wasn't in no way gonna let her take that baby." She looked at Cindy. "I knowed he must be yours and that she ought not have him out in the woods. I'd already heared she was tetched and queer acting lately. When she said she was going to see Jared Rawlings, I knowed she was crazy. Why, everybody in the hills knows he's dead as a doornail."

As people gathered around, Lizzy began answering questions.

"I was going to see…well, never mind where I was a' goin,'" she said with a nervous laugh. "Cutting through the woods on that old trail that goes off by Bear Branch, I heared a pitiful sound and thought to myself,

Why, that sounds like a youngun crying. Then I stopped and waited for a bit and sure enough, here come Viola down the trail a carryin' a baby. Since I knowed she was tetched, I tried talking to her all soothing and gentle-like to coax her along home. She started running. I chased her down. She fought something fierce, but I got the baby." As they walked toward the house, she rubbed dried blood from her cheek. "Granny, you got some ointment for these scratches? They're stinging like prickly pears."

"'Course I do. Come on inside," said Granny while looking at the baby in Cindy's arms. "Except fer a few bug bites, he don't seem none the worse fer wear," she said with a relieved smile. "Where's Viola?" she asked.

Lizzy shook her head. "I reckon she's still back there at the creek—last I seen her anyway."

Everyone jumped when Tom Sorrels abruptly fired a shotgun. More shots echoed as various searchers sent the signal onward.

Tom flushed when Simon reminded, "We ain't found Viola yet."

"Pret' nigh too dark to look tonight," Tom pointed out. "Besides, Lige and Ned need the good news."

Elijah knocked softly and then opened the bedroom door. His legs almost buckled. There was Cindy and the baby in the rocking chair, and Benjamin looked just fine. Granny and Ma both vowed the baby was all right, but he had to see for himself. Cindy, snuggling Benjamin close, looked up as he entered. He quickly fell to his knees alongside the chair to touch the baby's face. The tiny eyes were closed, but he breathed regular and even.

Relief strong in his heart, he looked at Cindy. "You all right?"

She nodded. Her hand trembled as it smoothed Benjamin's fair hair. "I've never been more scared in all my life," she whispered.

"Me neither," he said. "He seems fine though."

"Yes, thank the good Lord," she agreed.

He started to speak and then closed his mouth. There wasn't time to say what he wanted to say, so he left the words unspoken. Then he rose and started for the door.

She quickly asked, "Where you goin'?"

"Pa and I are heading out to search for Viola. It'll soon be dark, but there's a bit of daylight left. I hate to think of her being in the woods all night. Maybe we can find her before it gets too dark."

Cindy's eyes widened. Her grip tightened on Benjamin. "We can't ever trust her near the baby."

He let out a deep breath. "I know. But we've got to find her."

It was three days before they found Viola. Elijah—who had camped each night during the search—came home, carrying her. She was nearly dead, reeling in the saddle and covered with bug bites, scratches, and scrapes. After ravenously wolfing down a bowl of stew, she slumped in a chair. But when Granny tried to doctor the scrapes, she straightened, narrowed her eyes, and hissed, "You old witch! You always did hate me. But I'll tell Jared. When he comes to get me and Billy, he'll fix you good."

Distraught, Cindy faced Elijah. "I'll not rest easy as long as she's under the same roof."

His face was tight. "Me either." He looked at Viola. "Granny doesn't need this, not at her age. I'm sending word to Billy to come tend to Viola. After all, whether he likes it or not, she is his ma."

Cindy cringed at the harsh tone. She reckoned he would always feel hard towards Billy. She had intended to have a long talk with Elijah, apologize for not forgiving him. Now she drew up tight on the inside and fought back tears. *How had things gone so wrong between them? Would they ever be right?*

"Would you step outside with me a minute?" he asked.

She wrapped a shawl around Benjamin. Not for a second was she leaving him alone again.

Elijah, face pensive, leaned stiffly against the porch post. He waited until she had shut the door and joined him.

"For the last three days, I've been thinking on what to do. You're right—you and the baby can't stay here with Viola. The best I can figure, you ought to go to Pa and Ma, and I'll move in with Granny. I doubt that will be to your liking," he hurried to add, "but your ma is too sick to have a young one around and I can't think of any other thing to do just now. I'll start this week on building you and the baby a cabin." He went on, "When Billy comes back to help Granny, I'll move in with Pa and Ma."

She turned away and looked at the sky. He sounded so matter-of-fact, so unconcerned, when he spoke of dissolving their family. Of course she was the one who had pushed him away when more than once he had tried to reconcile. Maybe he was fed up with her sulks and wanted shed of her, but she had to try.

"No, that ain't to my liking a'tall," she said and then turned and looked at him.

He stood up straight. "Be that as it may, it's the best plan—"

She cut him off. "No, hit ain't." Her eyes dropped to the baby. "The best plan is for us to be together—wherever that has to be—at your ma's or in our own place. I want us to be a family again, Lige."

As his eyes lit with hope, she went on, "I still think what you done was awful wrong—but the way I acted was wrong, too. You been asking and asking me to forgive you and now I'm asking the same. All that day the baby was missing, I was thinking how the Lord must be chastisin' me for how I been acting. I promised if I got the baby back I'd ask you to forgive me. I ought not to a' hardened my heart when you said you was sorry."

He took her face in his hand and kissed her. "Don't apologize," he said. "I had it coming—every bit of it. I was a fool. I just hope now you really will forgive me."

"I already did days ago." Then she broached a painful subject. "There's one more thing I'll be asking you."

He nodded encouragement.

"I want you to truly forgive Billy. I promise you faithful that he never once stepped out of line."

"I believe you," he said and pulled her and the baby close. "I've done a fair amount of pondering on that, too. It came to me how he could hardly help loving you. I still don't like the idea, and yet I really can't blame him." Then he gave a wry grin. "He'll just have to find himself another woman…maybe Lizzy?" he teased.

She spoke against his chest. "Lige, I never was so grateful to anyone as I am to Lizzy Tate. And to think how I always despised her."

He tilted her face and drew a finger slowly down her cheek and smiled. "Like Pa says, there's good and bad in all of us. I reckon it's a good thing we humans aren't the final judge of folks."

Comfortably seated in Becky's front room with Benjamin draped with a shawl and held to her breast, Cindy looked up from the rocking chair. Elijah smelled of cold air and autumn sunshine. Then her nose flared.

"Oh, I smell muscadines!"

He laughed, reached into his jacket pocket and popped a large purple grape into her mouth. She chewed, relishing the tangy juice that spurted in her mouth.

"I thought you'd like that," he said with a smile and kissed her again. "When you get through feeding him you ought to come outside. Wrap up good. It's chilly but the woods are a sight to behold. I never saw prettier colors. Sort of looks like some of Granny's dye spilled all over the hills."

"You go along with him," encouraged Becky. "I'll tend the little one. We'll all too soon be housebound from the cold."

Cindy pulled her dress shut, placed Benjamin in the crib, and then gathered the shawl tight. She stooped to kiss Benjamin once more and started for the door. Her eyes smiled at Elijah for holding the door for her. Yes, everything in her world was good. And it had been a long time since she had felt that way.

"You feel like walking?" he asked.

She nodded and fell into step. "Where we goin'?"

"You'll see." He took her hand and shortened his stride to match hers.

Leaving the main road, in drifting leaves, they followed a faint trail up the hill and along the lip of the ridge. Her eyes feasted on gold, orange, coral, and red, on hills and hollows spread with the brilliance of Granny's best coverlets.

"Tom Sorrels saw Billy and Michael yesterday at Spadra Bluff," said Elijah. "Billy says he'll come as quick as he can. Looks like the war is about over. Can't last more than a couple more months. We control the valley now, but no doubt the Union will win. We're almost out of supplies, manpower, everything it takes to win a war. Even Michael admitted it. Brooks is still patrolling the river, but it's just a matter of time before they drive him away."

"How was Michael?" she asked quickly.

He chuckled "Fine I reckon. He told Tom to tell Lizzy he'd be seeing her first chance."

This time, rather than scowling, Cindy laughed. She still did not approve of Lizzy's manner of living, but she could no longer look on her harshly. She was content to let God be the judge. As Elijah said, humans weren't too good at that.

Finally Elijah stopped and hunkered down. He patted the ground alongside him. She sat down on a grassy spot and let the stillness and beauty sink into her. Below, Little Piney Creek was a sun-kissed blue ribbon, weaving back and forth, in the hollow beneath cupped hills that overlapped in the distance.

"When I was a shirttail kid, this was my shortcut up the ridge to Granny's. Always stopped here to look. It was one of my favorite spots. Still is," he said.

"I see why," she breathed. "It's a fair place."

He took her hand. "Pa and I have enough timber cut. Tomorrow we'll start building our cabin right down the road from Pa's. Some of the best farm land in the country." He toyed with her long slim fingers and then kissed them. "Cindy, we've had some rough times. We've still got a long way to go before times are really good. But I promise you, from now on things will be better."

She snuggled close. "Laws-a-mercy, if they get much better I don't know as I can stand hit…it," she corrected herself and smiled.